Steamboat Gothic

Novels by
FRANCES PARKINSON KEYES

FRANCES PARKINSON KEYES

Steamboat Gothic

1952
EYRE & SPOTTISWOODE
LONDON

*This book, first published in 1952, is printed
in Great Britain for Eyre & Spottiswoode
(Publishers) Limited, 15 Bedford Street,
London, W.C. 2, by Billing and Sons Ltd.,
Guildford and Esher*

G4780

Contents

Steamboat Gothic

PROLOGUE

PURCHASE PRICE
1869

PROLOGUE

THE day was warm for March, and the stranger, who had been walking for nearly half an hour along the river road, took a fine embroidered handkerchief from the tail pocket of his burgundy-coloured frock coat and mopped his face with it. Then he flicked the handkerchief lightly over his tight-fitting mouse-grey trousers and his shining congress boots. He had no mind to reach his destination dripping with sweat or powdered with dust.

He had been reasonably well pleased with his appearance when he had surveyed this, before starting out, in the blurred mirror of his room at the dirty little hostelry with the pretentious name of Grand Hôtel Pierre Chanet. To be sure, he had fiddled for some moments with the long bow of his black silk tie before it suited him; but there had been no doubt whatsoever that his plain gold studs gave the finishing touch of refinement to the starched shirt bosom which the large — and undeniably flawed — diamonds, worn for so long, had failed to impart. Lucy had never made any comment on those flawed diamonds, or on the still larger — and still more imperfect — one which had formerly adorned the third finger of his left hand. But he had caught her glancing at them several times, and he had noticed the change in her expression when he substituted the gold studs, and the heavy gold ring whose seal duplicated the one on the charm which dangled from the chain spanning the figured white waistcoat.

Well, it had taken him time to learn how to dress like a gentleman, but by slow degrees he had done it; and he could be thankful — and was — that he possessed the natural attributes of a fine person to set off his good clothes. If his stomach had not still been as flat as a sixteen-year-old boy's, he could have ill afforded to call attention to it by that gold chain. The mouse-grey trousers could be worn to good advantage only if they fitted closely over narrow hips and the burgundy broadcloth would have lost its effect if it had not been cut to fit wide shoulders. Moreover, there was satisfaction in the knowledge that, in addition to the advantages which his figure gave him, his fresh colour belied the belief that a man must live an active outdoor life in order to have an appearance of ruddy health, and that no amount of care would have given his reddish-blond hair its burnished look if it had not been abundant and glossy to start with.

He had run a small ivory comb along its low side parting and the wavy locks above his temples before the final adjustment of a shining grey beaver 'stovepipe' and, the last thing before leaving his hotel room, had passed his hand over his cheek and chin below his side-burns. It was less than an hour since he had shaved with a fine Swedish razor, but still he wanted to be sure. . . . And, though the surface was smooth enough to suit him, he had frowned a little at the sight of his hand, as he saw this reflected in the mirror before which he was still standing. It was blunt fingered, and the back of it was haired with down, the same colour as the locks he had just combed with such care. But it was softer and whiter than the hand of a vigorous man ought to be. It detracted from the fresh ruddiness of his face. He must do something about his hands. Perhaps riding about a plantation would help, getting out into the sun, handling the reins. . . . Well, the thing to do now was to reach his destination as soon as possible and find out what the prospects were. He had already told the slatternly little Negress, who brought early morning coffee and a noon breakfast to his untidy room, that he wanted her to send up one of the boys from the livery stable attached to the Grand Hôtel Pierre Chanet. The awaited knock came while he was adjusting the beaver hat.

'Get the best rig you can turn out for me, and straight off, you hear?' he had directed the grinning darky who answered his summons. 'I've been waiting for you the better part of the morning already. So slope right along now.'

'Ah sho' is too sorry, Cap'n, me, but us got no rig for you dis day, suh, no,' the boy replied, chuckling as though this were a jest of rare proportions. 'All both of us buggies is took out, suh, dey is and dat's for true. Ki-yi-yi-yah!'

The boy had suddenly burst into high-pitched cackling laughter, as if the humour of the situation had now completely overcome him.

The stranger made a gesture of impatience. 'Try another livery stable then,' he ordered. 'Surely someone in this pocky——' He caught himself up short. If all went well, he would be part and parcel of the local scene himself in the not too distant future. Best to get off on the right foot. In a milder tone, he continued, 'Surely someone hereabouts still has a horse and buggy for cash hire!'

'Ah tells you frankly, me, Cap'n-suh, it ain' ere other rig, no,' the little darky chuckled. 'Anyways, us rigs is too pitiful, Ah specks, me, for a quality gennelmun to drive.'

'Well then, as I cipher it, I'll have to ride shank's mare. As for you, I've told you once already not to stand there grinning at me. Now cut stick!'

The small stableboy scuttled away, without waiting for a second bidding, and the disgruntled guest, shrugging his broad shoulders, selected a cigar from a yellow leather case and lighted it with a sulphur match. Then, with a final glance of distaste at the rumpled bed and the dingy mosquito bar hanging limp and awry from its tester, he left the room, went quickly down the rickety stairs, through the open space which served as a lobby and across the unpainted gallery of the hotel. In front of this, a weedy, crescent-shaped driveway, bordered along its outer arc by a hitch rack, curved away from a sawed butt of cypress which, apparently, served as a carriage block. Also within the range of vision were a general store whose canopied front extended over a loading platform, a small weather-beaten church with a squat spire, and a long brick shed which was obviously a warehouse of sorts. Beyond lay the open road, fringed on one side by the levee and on the other by open fields spreading back toward swamp forests.

'Of course I never expected any of it would look the same from the land as it did from the river,' the stranger muttered to himself. 'But I didn't expect it would be so *damned* different, either!'

No one spoke to him as he went through the lobby and crossed the gallery. The night before, when he stepped off the gangplank, there had been only three white men at the steamboat landing—obviously a storekeeper and his assistants. They had glanced up from the bales and crates whose tally they were checking, and even in the smoky, fitful glare of ironwork torch baskets, the stranger had been able to recognize as a sneer the glance directed at his gaily patterned carpetbag. Then, almost immediately, the three men had turned their backs on him with elaborate and calculated ostentation. Now the wispy little clerk at the hotel and the drab loungers on the front gallery, after one equally eloquent glance, looked away just as pointedly. Well, this was by no means the first time the newcomer had been treated like a pariah, and it probably would not be the last. If he had not instantly been appraised as a carpetbagger. . . . But what did it matter, as long as Lucy, far from misprizing him, had trusted him from the beginning, and had finally given complete proof of this by confiding her future into his safekeeping?

The thought of Lucy, of her trustfulness and her steadfastness, was what he needed to restore his self-confidence. At the bottom of the gallery steps, he paused before the demilune of patchy turf enclosed by the arc of the driveway, to which a cluster of azaleas in full bloom gave the only touch of beauty in sight. Aware that the eyes of the loungers were still on him, even though they seemed averted, he broke off a spray, fastened it into the buttonhole of his burgundy-coloured coat and, humming the tune of 'Green Grow the Rushes, Oh', set off down the river road.

However, he did not continue to hum after he was beyond earshot of the loungers. No matter how much he tried to pretend, no matter how often he told himself that Lucy's love was all that counted, he wanted the goodwill of men, too—wanted it and needed it, if he were to live as he hoped and expected in the future. The obvious lack of it rankled; and now there was also that disturbing consciousness of change.

'Different — all so damned different,' he repeated, half-aloud this time. The river looked different, seen from the land; and the land itself was unrecognizable as the same he had so often regarded with absorbed attention from the texas of a passing steamboat. Even in seasons of high water, when the boats were elevated far above their normal level, so that spires and belvederes were plainly discernible above an arched screen of live oaks, magnolias and pecans, the countryside had not looked like this from the river.

For one thing, as a voyager, he had always been conscious of continuing motion, and not merely of the vessel's throbbing drive, or of the tormented current whose ageless sweep was carrying a continent, grain by grain, into the sea. The river banks seemed to be in motion, too, passing sedately, without haste yet without halt, in and out of sight, or approaching and receding with every landing, whether this were at a plantation, a village, a wood yard or the wharves of a city. Here on shore, however, the prevailing impression was one of stillness. Metallic beyond the batture, the river itself seemed bereft of movement. Even time had become static. Dust motes, inertly suspended above the shimmering road, had apparently been left there by the creaking passage of yesterday's carts. Was it possible that a steamboat had brought him to this place of immobility only the night before . . .?

His train of thought was interrupted by the appearance of a wizened Negress, hobbling toward him up the river road along which he had now been trudging for more than half an hour. She wore a shapeless calico garment and three wide-brimmed hats, one perched atop the other and all made of coarsely plaited palmetto strips. He remembered now that he had seen her from the upper gallery, earlier in the day, hitching along across the path of two men who were proceeding at a leisurely pace toward the warehouse, engrossed in conversation. As her course intersected theirs, she had snatched off the top two hats, extending one, upturned, to each of the men with the single wheedling word, 'Mishay!' and each had dropped a small coin into the hat nearest him. The third hat had remained on her head, shading her woolly pate from the burning sun. She was now approaching the wayfarer in much the same manner, except that she removed only one hat. He felt in his pocket, extracted three silver dollars and tossed them to her.

'Here's a coin for every one of your hats, Auntie!' he said. 'Wish me luck!'

'Praise de Great I-am, mishay!' the Negress exclaimed. 'Praise de holy angels in he'm what bring Moppy to dis day o' glory. Wish you luck, mishay? Shur, you don' need no mo' luck dan you already is got. Moppy tellin' you what Gawd love, mishay, you gwy' git yo' wish dis day, same as you taken keer o' me. Hallelujah! Bless you to de bones an' de heart an' de soul, mishay. Moppy gwy' cast her spell fo' you fo' true. Go git yo' wish, mishay. Go git it now.'

She hobbled off and, almost immediately, he saw, beyond an abrupt bend in the road, the house toward which he had so persistently been heading. In fact, it came into view so suddenly as to give him the triumphant feeling that, leaving aside all question of 'spells', luck was with him at last; for here before him, gloriously unaltered in the midst of the prevailing change, was the object of his heart's desire.

He stood back to look at it, in the glowing light of the afternoon sun. Yes, this was as he remembered it; only, now that he was closer to the mansion of his covetous recollection, it was even more impressive, even more splendid and desirable than he had been able to discern from afar. It was not long and low and rambling, like so many of the early examples of Louisiana architecture; its Corinthian columns surrounded a massive structure which stood foursquare and which rose to the soaring height of three full stories, without even counting the belvedere which surmounted these. Neither did it have the much vaunted simplicity—which, to his way of thinking, was mere severity—of the neoclassic ante-bellum mansions; the columns, superb as these were in themselves, formed only one feature of adornment. Their iron entablature was studded with stars and wreathed with acanthus leaves; and the railings of both galleries—a lesser located above a greater—were elaborately wrought. But it was not only this variety of embellishment that made the house before which he stood a marvel in his eyes; it was likewise the almost uncanny resemblance which it bore to the most magnificent of those floating palaces where he had founded his fortunes. The broad galleries were like spacious double decks; the twin stairways, widely separated on the ground, met, high above it, at the front door, exactly as similar stairways approached the grand entrance to the main saloon on a luxurious river steamer; even the belvedere, with its glitter of glass, suggested a pilothouse. This, too, was a palace, all the more to his taste because it stood on solid ground instead of moving over the water. His wander years, or so he hoped, were behind him. He wanted a place where he could strike roots. Since this palace could not float, neither would it glide away from him, leaving him stranded.

He was still standing, his eyes fixed in fascination on the sight before him, when the front door opened slowly and a lady came out on the gallery. He felt quite sure that she must be aware of his presence; however, she did not immediately glance in his direction, but turned a little to the right and, leaning lightly on the railing, looked down toward a nearby fountain in the garden as if there were something about it which required her attention or arrested her interest. He had almost completely overlooked the grounds, because of his absorption in the house; after all, gardens did not loom large in the consciousness of a man whose best years had been spent on river steamers. But he was glad of the opportunity afforded by the lady's apparent abstraction to observe her carefully while still not seeming to stare at her.

She was wearing black and her dress was distinctly outmoded; it had all the amplitude of the pre-war days, instead of the more restrained fullness currently in vogue. Nevertheless, she wore it well, even with a certain dash. Her face was oval and properly pale, bespeaking care not to risk her complexion to the sun; since she had half turned away, he could not see her eyes and quickly regretted this; on the other hand, her position gave him an advantageous view of her profile, which was piquant rather than pure, and further stimulated the admiration aroused by her sloping shoulders, swelling bosom and small waist. Her hair was as black as her gown and had far more sheen; there were quantities of it and it was elaborately arranged in a profusion of ringlets and plaits, ending in a 'waterfall'. Shrewdly, he guessed that she lacked the wherewithal to buy new clothes and either the skill or the incentive to remodel old ones, but that she took pleasure in following the fashions of hairdressing as displayed in *Godey's Ladies' Book*. The large locket which hung from a velvet ribbon at her throat, the still larger brooch which clasped without confining the laces at her breast, and the wide bracelets which encircled her wrists were evidently all parts of a ponderous parure that had no great intrinsic value. But somehow they seemed peculiarly suited to her apparel; they became her and she wore them with an air, just as she did the overfull, rusty black dress. All in all, her appearance was intriguing. He was conscious of no disloyalty to his treasured Lucy in appreciating its charm, and its harmony with the house of which this more provocative lady was obviously the châtelaine.

She turned away from the fountain, slowly, as she had emerged from the portal, and allowed her gaze to linger on a flowerbed, before glancing in his direction. Then she drew back hastily, with a slight, smothered cry, while grasping the railing with one ringed hand and raising the other, in fluttering fashion, to her lace-veiled bosom. She so plainly wished to give the impression of having been startled that he tactfully forestalled a confused greeting. He was already bareheaded, but, holding his hat in his hand, he made a low, sweeping bow and then looked up toward the gallery with an ingratiating smile.

'Good evening,' he said, without stepping forward and speaking in a way which was somehow both respectful and flattering. 'I must ask you to forgive this intrusion, which was really involuntary. In passing along the road, I was so struck by the beauty of your house that I could not help coming closer to it and pausing to admire it. . . . And the longer I lingered,' he continued, the flattery now slightly outweighing the respect, 'the more I found to admire.'

He bowed again, less deeply, and again looked up toward the gallery, with a still more ingratiating smile. The lady found it increasingly difficult to assume a displeasure she did not feel.

'I confess that you did frighten me, monsieur, for a moment,' she said. She spoke with a decided accent, but like everything else about her, this accent was exceptionally attractive. 'I live such an isolated life that I have ceased to expect visitors.'

'If your life is isolated, madame, it must be through your own choice. And it must leave many unfortunate persons—perhaps you will permit me to say many unfortunate men—quite disconsolate.'

The lady extracted a handkerchief with a wide black border from the hollow between her breasts and raised it to her eyes. However, she did not conceal her face with it very long.

'I am the disconsolate person, monsieur,' she said. 'My dear husband—the best, the kindest, the most adorable creature who ever lived—died eight years ago—before this house, which you have been good enough to admire, and in which we expected to have many years of happiness together, was entirely completed. Since then, I have lived here alone—all through the terrible war—all through the desolation which has followed. There is no visiting back and forth any more, as there used to be among the old river families; most of them are in mourning, as I am. They lack the spirit for society; in fact, they are utterly crushed. As for strangers, why should they seek us out? There is nothing left to bring them to the great plantation houses now.'

'I am in no position to judge about the old river families. But you can see for yourself that one stranger, at least, has been irresistibly drawn to a great plantation house.'

She did not answer immediately; instead she stood toying with the black-bordered handkerchief. Again he came to her rescue, this time by asking for the invitation which he knew she was longing, but not quite daring, to extend.

'And he is lingering, madame, with the hope that you will not think him overbold if he says that he most earnestly desires to see more of it. In short, with the hope that you will permit him to enter it, not only in order that he may study its marvels, but in order that he may be in a more advantageous position than his present one, while offering his homage to its charming mistress.'

The lady met his eyes at last and he saw, as he had expected, that hers were almost as dark as her hair, and lighted with a sparkle which more than matched its sheen. However, she still hesitated to speak, although it was obvious by this time that the words of welcome were fairly trembling on her lips.

'Perhaps I should have identified myself more promptly,' her visitor went on, with increasing suavity. 'My name is Clyde Batchelor. Yes, I realize that would mean nothing to you. But, unless I am much mistaken, I had the privilege of a slight acquaintance with your late lamented husband. Was he not a frequent traveller on the great river boats? And am I not addressing Madame Labouisse, the widow of Marchand Labouisse, who was known to everyone as a great planter and an even greater gentleman?'

'Yes!' she said quickly. 'Yes, monsieur, you are right! And to think that I have kept you standing outside all this time, like some intruder — a friend of my dear dead husband!' Again the handkerchief came into play, but even more briefly this time. 'I beseech you to ascend,' she went on. 'Why, I have probably met you before myself — how could I have forgotten it? Most of my husband's trips were taken before our marriage — after it, he was preoccupied with the building of our home. But now and then he was still obliged to travel, and on these occasions I accompanied him, for he never consented to any separation from me, however brief.'

While she was speaking, she had moved from the railing to the top of the stairway and stood, her hand already extended in welcome, while Clyde obeyed her injunction to 'ascend'. When he came close to her, he took her extended hand and raised it to his lips, the gesture, like his earlier speech, one in which respect merged gradually into a less impersonal form of tribute. He gave no direct answer to her statement that probably they had met before; instead he made a remark which was even more pleasing to her.

'I can well understand the reluctance of Monsieur Labouisse to be separated from his wife for a single day,' he said. 'Or a single . . .' He did not actually pronounce the word 'night'. But it hovered on his lips, as her invitation had hovered on hers a few minutes before, and she knew, as surely as he had, that it was there, and that only regard for the conventions kept it unuttered — conventions which did not affect his thoughts, or hers, however much these might curb their speech. She withdrew her hand, not abruptly, but in such a way as to imply a slight reproof.

'You confuse me, monsieur, with your compliments,' she said. 'Come, let me lead the way into the drawing-room. Then I will leave you and order some light refreshment. I am afraid it will be most inadequate. When my dear husband was alive, we dined royally every day. But since his untimely death, I have had no reason to keep the larder stocked. As I told you, I now lead a very solitary life, and I have no appetite, myself. . . . Enter, monsieur, I beg of you.'

She threw open the great portal under the spreading fanlight. Inside, a hall, which failed to appear wide only because of its still greater length, bisected the entire house. In this respect, it followed the general plan of plantation houses in the Deep South; but the double drawing-room, into which Madame Labouisse next ushered her guest, was far from doing so. Like the hall, it ran the length of the house; to be sure, an arcade of pillars separated the front parlour from the back parlour; but this added, rather than detracted from the whole effect of spaciousness. Nothing in the shape or size of this drawing-room was suggestive of the usual square style and its type of decoration was even more extraordinary. Walls and ceiling were alike lavishly covered with frescoes; and though the light in the room was dim, because the shutters were closed against the brightness of the afternoon sun, Clyde could follow, in a general way, the design of these paintings: on the walls, a high trellis entwined with flowers and overhung with vines and, above the trellis, birds of bright plumage darting back and forth against a brilliant sky; on the ceiling, a correlative trellis, enclosing the twin cherubs who appeared to support the crystal chandeliers.

'I see that you appreciate beautiful frescoes,' Madame Labouisse said softly. She had not failed to notice the searching glances which her guest cast about him, or to hear his exclamation of delight at what he saw. 'I will leave you to study them while I give orders for such poor entertainment as I can offer you. They are the work of Dominique Canova, the famous artist who also painted the dome of St. Louis Hotel. I am sure you are familiar with that?'

'Of course. I have frequently made it my headquarters when I went to New Orleans; and I have always thought the rotunda a work of art. But, to my way of thinking, madame, it cannot compare with this drawing-room.'

'It was our idea that the whole house should be a bower of beauty. Alas, for all our dreams of happiness! However, if it interests you, in its present sad state, I shall be glad to show you more of it after you have had some coffee. Meanwhile, perhaps you will find the étagères amusing if you tire of looking at the paintings. My poor husband's collection of Parian figurines was considered very fine by some authorities, even though he had hardly begun it when he died. And, needless to say, I have never had the heart to add to it.'

She left the room with gliding grace, her immense skirt billowing about her; evidently the vogue of the 'Grecian Bend' had not reached the river road. Clyde's eyes were no longer turned on her unfashionably large hoops; instead they were fixed on her almost unbelievably small waist. The ideal of feminine beauty, in this respect, was still traditionally one which could be encircled by a man's hands; but he had seldom seen a waist which could actually meet this test. Lucy's could not, he remembered rather ruefully. He had been so sure it could that, one day, when she was in a rather melting mood, instead of putting his arm casually around her, he had deliberately pressed both outstretched palms against her middle, with his fingers meeting in the back. But his thumbs failed to meet in front, as he had so confidently expected, for he had always considered Lucy's figure faultless. And Lucy had drawn away from him, flushing, whether with chagrin — since she had of course divined his expectation — or offended modesty, he could not tell. Lucy was extremely sensitive, when it came to love making. In spite of the fact that she had borne two children, it was hard, sometimes, to realize that she was a young widow and not a young virgin. . . .

Well, this woman had been married, too, and she certainly did not require a widow's weeds to reveal that she had been acquainted with matrimony. Her behaviour was wholly correct, but there was nothing virginal in her looks or bearing. Clyde found himself wondering how she would react if he tried to span her waist. Of course he had no idea of making the attempt — just then. But if he should happen to do so on the occasion of some future meeting. . . . Somehow, he felt that there might be future meetings and that possibly, just possibly, on one of these he might be tempted to find out. . . . Naturally, she would begin by repulsing him with indignation; she might even try to slap his face. But, when he had succeeded in doing what he wanted to do, she would certainly feel no chagrin. On the contrary, she would be filled with joy, because she had met the test when so many women — including Lucy — could not do so. If she flushed, it would be with pride. And her pride might very well contribute to a mood more melting than any in which he had so far found Lucy. Not that he had lost his desire for Lucy, who was so sweet and so lovely and so completely representative of everything that a Southern gentlewoman should be. But, after all, Lucy was in Virginia and he was in Louisiana; and this hostess of his, this charmer with the small waist, was not, he believed, a Southern gentlewoman in the generally accepted sense of the word. According to rumour, Marchand Labouisse, in the course of his European travels, had met a French girl, Dorothée Somebody-or-Other, with whom he had fallen violently in love, almost at first sight. Well, Clyde could understand that, now that he had seen this girl, or rather the *grande amoureuse* of her later development. For there was no doubt in his mind, by this time, that she was a *grande amoureuse*, or at least that she had the makings of one. The miracle was that she had remained a widow all this time. . . .

He tried to stop thinking about Dorothée Labouisse and her small waist and to fix his attention on the Parians which, being snow-white themselves and set out on black lacquered whatnots, were easier to see in the dim light than the multi-coloured paintings. He picked up several of the figurines and examined them closely; but they seemed cold to him, figuratively as well as literally. For the most part, they were reproductions, in miniature, of famous statues. A few of them were nude, or near nude; but the majority were discreetly draped or were modelled to show only a head and shoulders. They were remarkable only for their number; Clyde had never seen so many of them gathered together in one place; and since, according to his hostess, they represented only the beginning of an interrupted collection, he idly wondered to what dimensions this would have run, if death had not put a stop to it. Nothing else in the room interested him much, either, except the frescoes; and he was considering whether he would be inexcusably presumptuous if he opened the shutters a little, in order to see the design more clearly, when Madame Labouisse re-entered the room. She was now followed by a massive and rather untidy Negress, bearing a handsomely set silver tray.

'Put that down here, Belle,' Madame Labouisse ordered, indicating a small carved table in front of a brocaded sofa. 'You needn't stay.' And, when the Negress had taken her apparently reluctant departure, after staring for a moment, with frank curiosity, at the unexpected visitor, the lady of the house went on, in a low voice, 'These modern Negroes know nothing about civilized service and it's impossible to teach them anything they don't want to learn. I don't know whether it's because they're too stupid or too lazy. Now, when we still had slaves . . .'

She left the sentence unfinished and shrugged her shoulders prettily. Then she began pouring from a delicate Sèvres pot into an equally delicate cup. Yes, she was the sort of woman who would have enjoyed having slaves, Clyde reflected, as he stirred sugar into the coffee she handed him; but she was also the sort of woman who enjoyed a tete-a-tete and was not above fabricating an excuse for one. However, he suspected that Belle might be eavesdropping from the hall and guessed that Madame Labouisse shared his suspicions, for she invited no further compliments, but kept up an agreeably impersonal flow of chit-chat, while he drank three cups of coffee, which he found excellent, and ate two of the small sweet cakes, which were served with it, and which were very much less to his liking. She did not ask him what had brought him to the plantation, or even how he happened to approach it on foot, though both would have been natural questions. But eventually she asked a rather surprising one.

'Would you care for a cigar? My dear husband always liked to smoke one after finishing his coffee.'

'I should like one very much. But I've always thought ladies found it most distasteful to have men smoke in their presence — indeed, that they did not consider any man who would do so really a gentleman.'

'I appreciate your delicacy, monsieur. But in this locality most ladies are somewhat more lenient.'

'You say *in this locality*. What is there about it that causes this agreeable leniency?'

'You betray the fact that you are not a Louisianian. Did you never hear of perique tobacco?'

For the second time he made no reply to an indirect question which called for one. But he answered the direct question instantly and eagerly.

'Now that you speak of it, it seems to me that I have. But I know very little about it. Is this where it is grown? On your plantation?'

'Yes, and on those directly to the north of it. And strangely enough, nowhere else in the world. Perique has never flourished except in a small triangular area in this immediate vicinity.'

'Perique. . . . That seems an odd name for a type of tobacco. Wouldn't you say so?'

'It is a nickname for Pierre. The first settler who grew it was a certain Pierre Chanet. When he and other Acadians came here from Nova Scotia, they found the Indians raising this so special tobacco. Pierre Chanet showed them how to make it better, so they named it after him. It made him rich, too. Some of his descendants still carry on its cultivation – the Vincents, for instance, who live on Victoria, the plantation just above here. . . . But I should not be boring you with all this ancient history, especially as you are not smoking while you listen. I rather took it for granted that you would have cigars with you. I hope I was not mistaken, for I have none to offer you.'

'Not even some made from tobacco grown on your own plantation?'

'No. I sell the cane crop, standing, to the Vincents, and the tobacco to Auguste Roussel, as many others do. And, in any case, I doubt whether you would care for perique; it is very strong in its natural form. Generally, it is mixed with milder types.'

She had begun to speak a trifle impatiently. Obviously, she did not consider the subject one of sufficient interest to discuss at greater length. Clyde again drew a cigar from the case he carried in the pocket of his maroon coat, removed the red band which bore its trademark and started to light it. Then, with a match already in his hand, he paused.

'I appreciate your graciousness in permitting me to indulge my bad habits,' he said. 'But I still hesitate to do so in this elegant drawing-room. Perhaps you have forgotten how the odour of smoke – even the smoke from a mild cigar – clings to draperies and upholstery, especially in a place where the windows are closed. Possibly we could go somewhere else?'

'You are most considerate. If you like, I could take you to the gaming-room.'

'The gaming-room!'

'Yes. It is directly across the hall, in front of the dining-room. Probably you expected to find a library there. I think myself that it would have been much more appropriate – that was the one point on which my dear husband and I differed. I insisted that the gaming-room might equally well be placed on the ground floor, along with the wine cellar, the store closets and the rooms for business visitors. The location is, of course, unsuitable for books, because of the occasional dampness. And it is my opinion that every house should have a library – it imparts an air of culture which is otherwise lacking. All the other plantations of any importance have their libraries. Perhaps that was one reason why my husband stood out so stubbornly against one. He was determined that this house should be different, in every way, from the others. He said he did not wish it to have an air of culture; he wished it to have an air of gaiety. He intended it to be a centre of enjoyment, even of revelry, not only for us but for all our friends. Above all, he wished it to be a constant reminder of past delights which he had experienced – the delights of the great river steamers – in its atmosphere as well as its architecture. That is why he insisted on giving a place of such promin-ence to the gaming-room.'

She stopped, a little breathlessly. Then she rose and looked at Clyde, as if awaiting some comment from him before he followed her into the gaming-room. This comment was not instantly forthcoming. Clyde had lighted his cigar, after all, but his countenance had now lost its eager and alert expression; as far as it had any at all, this was one of patient politeness. But it did not have very much; it was curiously blank. Fleetingly, Madame Labouisse recalled that she had heard such blankness described as 'poker faced'. But the expression had never meant much to her. Americans had many strange ways of saying things, and most of these had no meaning to her, even now. She had never tried to understand them. They bored her even more than they puzzled her. . . .

She did not guess that Clyde's mind had been much less blank than his face while she had been talking to him. In fact, his thoughts had raced ahead so fast, that only his exceptional mental quickness had enabled him to keep abreast of them. First, about that missing library. . . . Of course Lucy would consider any house ill-equipped which did not have a library; in this respect, if in no other, she and Dorothée Labouisse would have been in one accord. Her grandfather's library had been famous throughout Virginia, where there were many fine libraries; and fortunately, nothing had happened to it during the war, though afterward Lucy had been on the point of regretfully sell-ing some of the rarer books, when he, Clyde, had succeeded in dis-suading her, by convincing her that the need for such sacrifices was past. . . . But that idea of demoting the gaming-room from the main floor to the ground level was a good one, and there was still no reason why it could not be carried into effect. Possibly, it would be best to make this change without consulting Lucy beforehand, though of course he would explain to her that, in this part of Louisiana, there were no basements, as the term was understood in Virginia, and that the dining-room and drawing-room were on the 'main floor' and not on the ground floor of the house which was to be theirs. But there were all kinds of advantages to the latter location for a gaming-room – quiet, privacy, an opportunity for detachment and freedom. Besides, chips and cards and felt-covered tables would not suffer, like books, from dampness. . . . Probably it would also be possible to provide for a small office, which would connect with the gaming-room. It would be more convenient than one in a separate building, such as most planters used. But, if so placed, it would not affect the general tone of the establishment. Personally, though Clyde knew Lucy would agree with Dorothée about the library, he himself agreed with the late Marchand Labouisse about the atmosphere that the house should have; most of all, about the memories it should evoke of the great river steamers in all their pleasurable and exciting aspects. . . .

'If you are not interested in the gaming-room, we could go outdoors. We could walk in the garden while you smoke your cigar,' Madame Labouisse suggested. Although she did not bother her head about the way Americans expressed themselves, when they called blankness poker faced, it bothered her very much if any man, whatever his nationality, appeared to lose interest in what she was saying to him. And, up to the very moment when she had mentioned the gaming-room, this engaging stranger had been all attention. She desired to have this attention continue and, if possible, intensify.

'Of course, it never became what we planned and hoped,' she went on. 'It was our idea that it should be, in miniature, something like the garden at St. Cloud. It was there that my dear husband and I met. . . . Possibly you have already guessed that. You would have easily divined that I am French, with your delicate perceptions, monsieur, even if no one had told you so. And then, the name of this plantation——'

'But it is called Cindy Lou, is it not?'

'Yes. But of course that is a corruption, like perique.' She was patient and polite now; after all, two could play at such a game. 'We named it St. Cloud after – after our first trysting-place in my own beloved country; and then we went through more trouble than you can believe, because almost everyone who saw it written insisted on calling it Saint Clowd instead of San Cloo. You would think in a locality where there are so many persons who, if not French, are at least of French extraction or who claim it . . .' Again, she shrugged her shoulders prettily, leaving a sentence unfinished. 'Of course, I suspect there were few Parisians among them. I believe they were provincial before they ever left France, and their sojourns in such places as Nova Scotia and Santo Domingo certainly did nothing to improve their culture. But let that

24

pass. . . . We finally convinced our neighbours and my husband's business associates that they must say San Cloo; and then, as usual, the slaves promptly corrupted the name. It became Cindy Lou to them and presently everyone was calling it that — a sad ending to a proud title. But this is a place of sad endings.'

He was smiling persuasively again. He still cared nothing about seeing the garden. Among other reports that had reached him concerning the house was one to the effect that the entire third floor was designed to be a great ballroom, that its ceiling was formed from panes of multi-coloured glass which had been set in lattices beneath the raised floor of the belvedere. Through the use of a complicated arrangement of powerful carbide lights and raised reflectors, the multi-coloured glass was intended to give a kaleidoscopic effect to the dress of the dancers, as they swung and swayed to the lilting sound of music — or so it was rumoured; and Clyde would have vastly preferred to gauge the possibilities of this ballroom for himself, rather than to wander along the unkempt path of a garden which had failed of fulfilment. But he decided this was not the time to express a preference; to reach the ballroom, it would be necessary to go through the upper hall, where the doors doubtless stood open into the bedchambers; so if he said, on his own initiative, that he would like to do this now, he might seem lacking in that delicacy on which his hostess had just complimented him. Moreover, though he himself knew nothing about gardens and cared less, Lucy knew a good deal about them and cared for them greatly, like most Virginians. In her interests, he could not afford to miss the opportunity offered.

'By all means, let us wander in the garden,' he continued, with this in mind. 'And while we do, tell me more about the plans you made for it. Unfortunately, I never saw the original St. Cloud.' He was careful to give it the proper pronunciation. 'But I cannot believe that it is half so beautiful as its namesake.'

'As its namesake might have been, you mean,' Madame Labouisse corrected. But though she managed to tinge her tone with sadness, she did not speak severely; she was already mollified. Again she glided from the room, and again Clyde, following in her wake, was aware of her waist's tempting smallness and not of her skirt's unfashionable fullness. He thought he saw the immense, untidy Negress lurking in a corner of the dim hall, and realized that if he were not mistaken, she had been eavesdropping, as he had expected she would. But the suspicion neither angered nor disturbed him; instead it gave him a fleeting sensation of amusement, mingled with scorn. How speedily and effectively Lucy would have dealt with such a creature! Inside of a week, the Negress would have been neat in person, respectful in manner, and capable in service — or she would have been turned out of

25

the house. And Lucy would have accomplished the transformation – or, if necessary, brought about the dismissal – without once raising her voice or losing her air of detached serenity.

His admiration for Lucy increased every time he appraised her attributes; but this did not keep him from making other appraisals. He hardly took his eyes off the revealing black bodice as he and Dorothée Labouisse went out on the gallery and down the branching staircase. Once on the ground, however, it was clearly indicated that he must walk beside and not behind her. Regretfully, he fell into step with her and paced slowly along, smoking his cigar, while she talked to him about the garden.

'You see we have only one fountain. We had planned for a series of these, on terraces going straight to the river. I am sure you know that most plantation houses in Louisiana are approached directly through an allée of live oaks. But at Ashland, for instance, a terraced garden goes straight to the river, and a beautiful grove of trees is located at the side.'

'Yes. I have observed all that many times from the river, and admired it.'

'My husband and I observed it at close range, when we were invited to Ashland,' Madame Labouisse replied. She was not adverse to letting this outsider know that she had formerly enjoyed an entrée at the home of Duncan Kenner, who had been Jefferson Davis's Minister to Europe during the days of the Confederacy; it was the war and its aftermath which had isolated her, not lack of social standing. Perhaps she should drive this point home. 'As I told you, my dear husband did not wish this house to be like any other; he wished it to be unique——'

'As indeed it is!' Clyde interrupted her.

'But he felt differently about the grounds – after all, he could not re-create steamboat days in those! Rich and resourceful as he was, he could find no way of imitating waves and currents in flowerbeds!'

She tossed back her head and, for the first time, permitted herself a little laugh. The tinkle of her ear-rings mingled with the tinkle of this laugh and the sound was very pleasant. Her quick movement had slightly disarranged some of her glossy ringlets, and she raised both jewelled hands to pat them back into place; the gesture was close to coquettish.

'So it was his decision and mine that we should adapt the models that pleased us both to our own uses,' she went on. 'We wished to remind ourselves of our happy days in France, to have our own St. Cloud here on the Mississippi; and, at the same time, we did not mean to copy the original garden slavishly. We were also guided by successful local patterns like Ashland's. But we intended to surpass these. We meant to have a maze. We meant to have every rare tree which will thrive in this region, and such a variety and profusion of exotic flowers that they would be almost bewildering. We meant to have peacocks strutting pridefully from terrace to terrace!'

At last she had spoken of something which he could visualize. He had never been to France, as he had confessed, and he had never seen Ashland from the viewpoint of a privileged guest, as she had inferred. He knew nothing of landscaping, of mazes and terraces and fountains, of rare trees and exotic flowers. To be sure, he knew nothing about peacocks, either. But he could see that they belonged. In fact, their iridescent feathers would seem a fitting complement to the multi-coloured frescoes and the kaleidoscopic lights. He looked out over the neglected expanse of grass before him, gilded by the setting sun, and suddenly it came alive with regal birds, strutting for the delight of Lucy's children, who were so soon to be his.

'Are you never homesick for France?' he asked abruptly.

'Am I never homesick for France! Monsieur, how can you ask such a question? You must know there are days — and nights — when I think I shall die of longing for it!'

Here at last was a cry straight from the soul. She was no longer posturing and pretending, she was no longer seeking to impress him with her broken heart and her undiminished charms. She was confessing, without elaboration or artifice, her desolation amidst the alien corn.

'Then why not go back there?' he asked, still more abruptly.

'Why not go back there? Again, I demand why you ask such a question? Do you suppose, if I could have found a purchaser for this place, that I would not have gone long ago? I lied to you when I told you I loved it. I loathe it! But I cannot abandon it. It is not a rich plantation any more — you have been deceived, monsieur, if you thought it was. But it provides me with a livelihood, such as it is. And I have no other. I — I was not a wealthy girl. My family could do nothing for me. I did not even have a proper dowry. My husband took me without one — for love. The home that he provided is all the shelter I have left. And sometimes, I have been so hard pressed for ready cash that I have tried to think of some way I could retrieve the gold pieces which were buried in the cornerstone when the house was started, in accordance with local custom.'

'Well, in that case——' Clyde began. Then he started over again. 'If you want to stay here, out of sentiment, that's your affair. But if you don't, if you really meant what you said about loathing the plantation and longing for France, there's no reason why you shouldn't take the next boat.'

'I — I do not quite follow you, monsieur.'

'I'm telling you that you've got a purchaser for the place and everything on it. I'll buy it from you, today, with all its equipment, if you'll sell it to me.'

27

She had continued to toy with her curls while she talked of peacocks, but she had swiftly lowered her arms when he asked his first question about France. Now, she raised her hands to her face and looked at him wide-eyed above the fingers digging into her cheeks.

'You're joking,' she faltered. 'You're making fun of me, monsieur. The jest is unworthy of you.'

'I'm not joking. I'm not making fun of you. What do you consider the place worth? I mean land, livestock, buildings, equipment, furniture, everything. Thirty thousand dollars? Fifty thousand? I'll pay you for them, in cash, as soon as we can pass papers. If you like, I'll give you five thousand to bind the bargain here and now.'

She screamed, without smothering the sound this time, and swayed toward him. He caught her around the shoulders to steady her. Then, still holding her firmly, his hands slid down over her arms to the elbows. After that, it seemed so inevitable they should encircle her waist that he did not even stop to consider whether the great cistern which towered above the garden walk would conceal them from the road, or whether some servant might not observe them from a rear window.

He planted his fingers in the small of her back and curved his outstretched palms around her. His thumbs not only met in front; they overlapped. He could feel the whalebone with which her corset was mercilessly stiffened; but though its lacings were tightly drawn, there was a tiny space where the two sides of the corset did not quite meet. Here the lacings merely formed a lattice-work over the thin cambric chemise beneath them, and under the cambric was warm, yielding flesh. As Clyde became increasingly aware of this hidden softness, his grip tightened and he drew Dorothée closer to him.

He had been only partly right in his guess. She did not repulse him with indignation, she did not try to slap his face. To be sure, she did flush; but he knew this was with triumph even more than with pride. Her joy was so great that it swallowed up all semblance of resistance. He had hoped only for a melting mood and he had got, or could get, everything from her that he could possibly desire.

He did not deceive himself. He knew that, though she had been attracted to him, as he had to her, she would not have found him irresistible as a man if he had not been able to free her from the plantation and send her back to France. Indeed, it was quite possible that she considered her acquiescence a part of the purchase price. Well, he had not thought of it that way, but what difference did it make, since she had? He had never been one to lose sight of an unexpected advantage and he thought none the less of Dorothée Labouisse because she was prepared to give him one.

Of course, it would have been entirely different in the case of Lucy.

BOOK ONE

POSSESSION

1894

Chapter One

AS usual, dinner at Cindy Lou had been a rich repast, conducive to pleasant somnolence. It had begun with a dish of butter beans and fresh river shrimp — actually a stew rather than a soup — in the concoction of which Belle eclipsed every cook within a day's journey. Next had come a *grillade* — thin, tender slices of veal, browned in a rich sauce; and with this, flaky rice, crowder peas and corn on the cob were served. A cheese platter had accompanied the green salad; and finally, one of Lucy's famous Spanish Creams had been proudly brought into the dining-room. This was unlike all ordinary Spanish Creams, partly because the blending of its ingredients was timed in such a way as to leave half of the main mould clear and half opaque, giving it a striped effect; and partly because this main mould was surrounded by a galaxy of small ones, made of jewel-coloured sherry jelly which, in turn, were ornamented with whipped cream and candied fruits. Like many Virginians of her time and class, Lucy always made the daily desserts for her family, unless she were ill; if there were sickness among their friends in the neighbourhood, or among the servants, she made a double quantity of sherry jelly, so that there would be plenty for general distribution; and she also made broths, gruels and shrubs which were highly prized as gifts. But the Spanish Cream was her *chef d'œuvre*.

Clyde had done full justice to this and, indeed, to the entire dinner; but, after rising, with a sigh of satisfied repletion, and kissing his wife as they reached the threshold of the dining-room, he had gone direct to his favourite wicker armchair, under the great oak between the house and the first fountain. He had not meant to make a practice of taking a daily nap, any more than he had meant to permit himself a preference for any certain chair; both the practice and the preference were telltale signs of advancing years and, as such, distasteful to him. But the chair was so comfortable, the drowsiness so agreeable! Why forgo the one and fight off the other?

No reason at all, he told himself, sinking back luxuriously and closing his eyes. After all, advancing years were different from declining ones. Indeed, advance of any kind usually carried with it the connotation of progress. And the man he now was — the happy husband, the fond foster father, the landed proprietor, the substantial citizen — had progressed a long way from the street arab who was better at crapshooting than any of his lawless cronies — not to mention the card sharper who had made his way from the lowest dives of St. Louis to the shanty-boats, swarming with pedlars, medicine men, prostitutes and lottery operators, and thence to the gaming-rooms of the great river steamers; the professional gambler who had turned purveyor to sutlers when the river steamers made way for gunboats; and the speculator in tobacco and cotton whose first southern associates had been hoarders and profiteers eager to welcome the outsider possessed of ready gold.

It often seemed to Clyde Batchelor that the third step had marked his greatest stride forward; and this was less because he had so materially furthered his fortunes by following a victorious Union Army into the stricken South, than because he had found an even richer reward in another way. It was in Virginia that he had met Lucy Page and persuaded her to marry him; and that was no mean achievement for a man whom she could not possibly classify as a gentleman and whom she did logically classify as an enemy. When he thought of the loathing which the feminine members of Richmond's first families almost universally felt for the invaders, the scorn these ladies did not hesitate to show even high-ranking officers of impeccable conduct, he realized that his wooing and winning of Lucy was the supreme triumph of his life, and the one which had called for the greatest patience, adroitness and suavity.

He had heard her speak before he saw her, and it amused him to tell her — after he knew her well enough to risk a mild jest in her presence — that he fell in love with a voice and not with a woman. Since the voice was characteristic of the woman, the statement was not as extravagant as it might otherwise have been. He was passing along Franklin Street when he was arrested by the sound of sobbing beyond a garden wall and of soothing words spoken in comfort.

'Don't cry, honey. There'll be something to eat tomorrow.'

'You told me that yesterday.'

'I know, and there was, wasn't there? Not much, but something. And I'm almost sure there'll be more tomorrow.'

'But I'm hungry *now*.'

'If you'll come to bed, like a good boy, you'll forget that you're hungry. I'll read to you out of *Susie's Six Birthdays* until you get sleepy.'

'That's a *girl's* book! A *Yankee* book! Father said so. I don't want you to read to me out of that book. Father doesn't want you to, either!'

'I'm sorry, honey. Then I'll read to you out of *Dick and His Cat*.'

'But I'm h-u-n-g-r-y!'

Clyde could stand it no longer. He went up to the garden gate and rapped boldly on it. When it was not instantly opened, he rapped again, harder and more loudly.

The second time, his knock produced results. The sound of sobbing ceased abruptly, to be followed by the sound of soft, swift steps, accompanied by small, pattering feet; then by that of a drawn bolt and a turned key. The gate opened to disclose a fair-haired girl, framed against a background of brilliant box and cascading wisteria, with a pale, peevish-looking little boy dragging at her mauve muslin skirts.

Clyde's spontaneous sympathy for the little boy subsided almost as quickly as it had been aroused. This was the sort of child who would whine whether he were really hungry or not. Clyde had seen dozens of disagreeable, pampered children in the course of his travels up and down the Mississippi; he recognized – and despised – the type at a glance. But the feelings awakened by the girl were vastly different. Everything about her was as lovely as her voice – her fair hair, her grey eyes, her clear skin, the expression of her face, her general bearing. Yet this loveliness in no way suggested a lack of staunchness. This girl would never whimper because she was hungry; she was made of the stuff which faced privation with serene and smiling fortitude.

'Good evening,' she said pleasantly, and without the slightest indication that she was surprised by the presence of a stranger at her door.

'Good evening,' Clyde responded mechanically. Then he suddenly found that it was hard to say anything further. The girl stood, with no visible sign of impatience, waiting for him to do so. But the disagreeable child tugged again at her delicately tinted skirt and whined, 'What does the man want? What has he come here for?'

'Hush, Bushrod. The gentleman will tell us in a minute,' the girl said softly, stroking the little boy's tumbled hair.

'Is he a Yankee?'

'Of course not, honey. The Yankees all wear uniforms – blue uniforms.'

Her artlessness was disarming; in the face of it, Clyde decided there was nothing to do but plunge straight into the truth. 'I am afraid I must undeceive you,' he said. 'I'm from St. Louis and I'm at present – er – connected with the Union Army, though not in a military capacity. So I suppose you would call me a Yankee. But I happened to overhear this little boy crying and I thought he said he was hungry. It so happens that I have – well, access to plentiful provisions. So I hope that, perhaps——'

'He *is* a Yankee!' the child said shrilly. It was evident that the words 'access' and 'plentiful provisions' were beyond the range of his comprehension. 'Why don't you send him away? Father'll be very angry.'

'The suggestion wasn't meant to be presumptuous,' Clyde hastened to say. To his annoyance, he feared that he was flushing. 'It was just that——'

'I am sure it was not,' the girl said quietly. 'You are very kind. I shall be thankful to accept anything you can conveniently spare. My little boy *is* hungry. And my husband is very ill. He has been wounded four times, each time more severely than before, but each time he has returned to the battle line. Now he has been brought home to – to rest.'

Her husband! Well, Clyde might have known! Any man would be tempted to do some swift cradle-snatching, if he found someone like this, and what was more, any man should be forgiven if he yielded to the temptation, provided he could get away with it. But the girl in mauve did not look a day over eighteen, in spite of the telltale signs of fatigue in her face; and if that horrid little boy was her son, instead of her brother, as Clyde had at first supposed, she must be at least five years older than that. But after all, this was beyond the point and he did not see why he wasted a moment's thought on it. The point was that, if her child was hungry, she was undoubtedly a good deal hungrier, since she would certainly have gone without herself in order to feed him; and when she said her husband had been brought home to rest, that meant, of course, that he had been brought home to die. Why, if he did, this girl would be a widow, a charming young widow – hang it all, that was not the point, either!

'I know this is Franklin Street,' he said hurriedly. 'But I did not happen to notice the number of your house. And the name is . . .?'

'The number is twenty-one. Twenty-one West. And the name is Page. I am Lucy Page and this is my little son, Bushrod. My husband, Forrest Page, is a colonel on Lee's staff – that is, he was.'

Clyde took a small notebook, to which a tiny pencil was attached, from his waistcoat pocket and wrote rapidly. 'Thank you, Mrs. Page,' he said, replacing the memorandum. 'I will send you a few – ah – delicacies immediately. I hope they will serve to tempt an invalid's appetite.'

'They will probably save his life,' Lucy said, speaking more quietly than ever. (How typical that had been! Never to lose her serenity, but never to dissemble, either!) 'You reveal your own delicacy, sir, in so referring to nourishment that is more sorely needed than you can know.'

An unaccountable feeling of happiness permeated Clyde's senses as he listened to her. He had performed many similar kindnesses before, especially to children, for he had never forgotten what it had meant to be hungry as a child; but none had ever given him this sensation of warmth and well-being. It was as though he were receiving a benison, rather than bestowing a favour. He would have loved to linger, to enter that walled garden filled with the fresh fragrance of box and shaded with purple wisteria. So many doors had been closed to him that the half-opened gate seemed to offer a glimpse of Paradise. And its guardian angel was this girl, whose hair and eyes and manner of speech were all the acme of loveliness.

'I will return tomorrow, if you will permit me, to make sure my

34

little offering has arrived safely and to inquire for the colonel's health,' Clyde said. After all, this was no time to linger. The provisions were badly needed, there was not the slightest doubt of that; it would be no indication of 'delicacy' to retard their delivery. But to make sure they had arrived and that they filled a cruel want — why, that would be only taking a proper precaution, only showing common courtesy!

'Thank you. I shall expect you,' Lucy replied. She did not shut the garden gate, but stood still, holding it open, as long as he could see her — as long, or so he believed, as she could hear his rapidly retreating footsteps. She had given him no sense of dismissal. Quite the contrary — so much the contrary that, had the idea not been fantastic, it would have seemed as if she were watching him until he was out of sight and hearing because she wanted to prolong the time when she was conscious of his presence, as a woman will do only when a man means much to her. . . .

So that was the way it had begun, soon after the Fall of Richmond. Later, Clyde Batchelor, perforce, frequently went north, in connection with his manipulations; but meanwhile the big grey house on West Franklin Street lacked nothing that he could send it; and, every few days, when he was in town, he called there 'to make sure his offering had arrived safely and to inquire after the colonel's health'. He never saw the colonel, who, though reported as 'miraculously improved', was still reputedly unable to stand the strain of receiving visitors; but Clyde did meet Lucy's mother, Mrs. Virginius Cary, who had lost her husband and all four of her sons in the war. Their plantation home had been burned during Dahlgren's Raid, and she lived with her only surviving child, Lucy, and Lucy's husband, Forrest Page, at their Richmond residence. Clyde guessed that the colonel resented the largesse he was receiving, that he would have declined to accept it had it not been for his little son, and that Mrs. Cary was hardly less resentful. Doubtless she consented to see the Yankee interloper only because, otherwise, Lucy would have seen him alone, except for Bushrod who, now that he had enough to eat, rushed noisily around, banging doors and bursting in on orderly conversations. Mrs. Cary probably thought that such interruptions did not contribute enough of a safeguard, that at any advantageous moment the obnoxious creature who had added to the insult of his mere presence in Richmond by making them his debtors, might 'attempt liberties'. She need not have worried, and Clyde would have liked to tell her so, angrily; he would no more have made improper advances to Lucy than he would have desecrated a shrine.

As time went on, his profitable business ventures required longer and longer absences from Richmond; and, after one that was unusually protracted, he saw, as he hastened along Franklin Street from the Exchange and Ballard House, that workmen were swarming over the big grey mansion which now meant so much to him, painting it in gaudy colours, and that other workmen were passing in and out of the garden gate, which stood wide open. He quickened his pace and went rapidly up the front steps.

Beyond the gaping entrance, leading to the denuded hall which had once afforded so seemly and gracious an approach to the double parlours in the rear, a burly and begrimed individual, evidently a foreman of sorts, confronted him with a belligerent stare.

'Well, what's your business here?' this hostile artisan inquired abruptly.

'I am calling on Mrs. Cary and Mrs. Page,' Clyde informed him coldly. The coldness was meant to be cutting, but it was uncomfortably akin to the chill of foreboding which was creeping through his being. The foreman laughed, disagreeably.

'Then you're in the wrong pew. This place is the property of Ross Judson.'

'Ross Judson!'

In his horror, Clyde had echoed the name before he could stop himself. Unscrupulous as he had been himself, he had never stooped to the level of this wily and notorious trafficker with the enemy of his own people. The foreman's stare became increasingly belligerent.

'That's what I said. And now you know the Cary tribe ain't here any more, maybe you'll shove along and let me get on with my work. This old ark was just about falling to pieces when Mr. Judson took it over. I aim to put it in good shape for him.'

Clyde went down the front steps as rapidly as he had mounted them. He was not only seething with rage; he was consumed with anxiety. Almost the only acquaintances he had in Richmond were his business associates and he shrank from questioning them about Lucy. The boon companions with whom he had formerly spent such convivial evenings at Johnny Worsham's elegant gambling parlours were now scattered to the four winds; and, even if this were not the case, he would have been still more loath to mention Lucy in their hearing. However, he overcame his reluctance sufficiently to make discreet inquiries at the Exchange and Ballard House and there, information was readily forthcoming: Colonel Forrest Page had died, leaving his widow almost penniless. The mortgage on their house had been foreclosed, and it had been sold at auction. Mrs. Page and her mother had gone back to the plantation. The Carys had always been country people; it was the Pages who were city folk. So perhaps, in a way, the ladies were not taking the loss of the Franklin Street house as hard as they might have. But how could they live in the country, Clyde wanted to know?

36

The plantation home had been burned, hadn't it? Yes, the Cary plantation home, Amalfi. But Mrs. Cary, before her marriage, had been Sophia Peyton and the Peyton plantation home, Sorrento, located on the next 'curl' of the James to Amalfi, was still habitable — that is, more or less. It had run down after the death of Alexander Peyton, who took more pride in his library than he did in his crops; and it had been damaged, though not destroyed during the war. Rumour had it that, when Dahlgren's Raiders went there, old Mrs. Peyton — that is, Mrs. Cary's mother, who had afterward died as a result of the shock — had stood her ground with great bravado when the invaders came. She had actually invited the Union officers to help themselves to the contents of her fine cellar. Sometimes, when the Union officers drank too much, they became doubly destructive; then again, sometimes it worked just the other way. It did that time. So, Sorrento was spared and that was where Mrs. Cary and Mrs. Page were living now. It would be hard for two lone ladies. There was a lot of land, now that Amalfi and Sorrento were thrown together. And there were no slaves left to work it. Besides, it would be bitter cold down there, with winter coming on and no house servants, or hardly any, to tend the fires. . . .

Clyde hired a horse and buggy and set off down the rough road where the thick red mud was already freezing in deep ruts. He started early in the morning, but though the distance from Richmond to Sorrento was allegedly only ten miles or so, it was well past noon before he turned in at the driveway which answered to the rather vague description that had been given him of the one leading to the plantation house. There were no signposts left anywhere and he met almost no one as he jogged and hitched along. The stray Negroes whom he saw, at lengthy intervals, for the most part merely stared at him stupidly when he questioned them; and those who answered did so in a disjointed and contradictory fashion. After he had turned in at the driveway, he still went on and on, through fields that must once have been fabulously fertile, but which were now bleak and barren; then through shadowy woods, where the branches of the trees, to which only the bronzed and brittle oak leaves still clung, seemed to close in upon him, shutting off both progress and escape; and still he saw no sign of a house or anything that suggested the approach to one. Then, when he had almost decided that he must be hopelessly lost, the branches parted and he beheld a great unkempt lawn, edged in by shaggy bushes, and beyond it, the noble façade of a mansion that was still stately and symmetrical, despite the state of decadence into which it had sunk.

He hitched his tired horse and went up the broad grassy path leading to the front door. The bell pull hung loosely against the wide panelling, but it worked; he could hear it pealing sharply and then echoing, as if its sound had travelled a long distance. But there was no response until he had rung three times. Then he heard doors opening and shutting and shuffling footsteps, approaching slowly and uncertainly. At last a bolt was drawn back, to the accompaniment of much muttering and mumbling, and the door opened to disclose a very shabby, very aged, very decrepit Negro.

'Are Mrs. Cary and Mrs. Page at home?' Clyde inquired. The Negro cupped his ear with his hand.

"Scuse me, suh, Ah don' heah so good no mo'.'

'Are Mrs. Cary and Mrs. Page at home?' Clyde repeated, shouting now.

'Oh, yessuh, yessuh. Would you kindly step into the parlour? Ah knows Ah ought to reckernize you, but Ah don' see so good no mo', neithuh. Who shall Ah tell Miss Sophie done come to see her?'

'Tell her Mr. Clyde Batchelor.'

'Mistuh Hyde, yessuh, yessuh. Miss Sophie sure will be mighty pleased to see you.'

Of course, she was not. She was perfectly polite — her code would have permitted nothing else. But she acknowledged his expressions of sympathy on the death of her son-in-law as briefly as was consistent with courtesy. Yes, it was all very sad. The colonel had seemed so much better — in fact, so much like his old self — that they had been greatly encouraged. But an old wound had broken open and infection had set in. It was just six months now.... She and her daughter had retired to the plantation for the period of their mourning.

As Clyde had never yet seen Mrs. Cary when she was not swathed in crêpe, he feared that Lucy must now be practically smothered by it. He remembered how fresh she had always looked, in her cool greys and lavenders, and hated to think of her as loaded down with widow's weeds. She had once explained to him, almost apologetically, that her husband found it depressing to be surrounded by black on his sickbed, and that therefore she had not worn it, as long as was customary, for her father and brothers. Clyde could almost hear the colonel telling her, in one of his more irritable moments, that there would be time enough for that after he was dead. Clyde knew that very possibly he was unjust; but since Bushrod in no way resembled his mother, it was not too illogical to assume that the obnoxious child might be a second edition of his father. Well, inevitably, Lucy would be wearing deep mourning now, but Clyde's distaste at the thought of this was mitigated by the realization of its underlying meaning: Lucy was no longer another man's wife and he himself could make her an honourable proposal of marriage at last, after wanting her ever since he had first heard her voice beyond a garden wall....

'I do not wish you to feel that I am intruding on your solitude or

38

hers,' he eventually told Mrs. Cary. 'But, before I leave, I should like to pay my respects to Mrs. Page, also.'

'I am very sorry. My daughter is not able to see anyone at present.'

'She is ill?' Clyde asked in alarm.

'No, not exactly. But she is of course completely crushed by sorrow and——'

Clyde interrupted her. 'I shall be very careful not to say anything which could possibly add to her grief,' he said hurriedly.

'I had not quite finished, Mr. Batchelor. My daughter is completely crushed by sorrow *and* in addition to this, she has been called upon to undergo the greatest ordeal of womanhood. Less than a fortnight ago, after prolonged travail—lengthened no doubt by the strain she had already suffered in her husband's death—she gave birth to a little girl. She is still prostrated, as I said.'

Clyde's first reaction to this statement was one of rage that he could hardly conceal. So this hero of a hundred battles, despite his weakness and his wounds, had still been able to beget a child! Lucy would never have failed in her wifely duty, he felt certain of that; but the fact that she fulfilled it unflinchingly could not have meant that she had accepted willingly, much less gladly, the embraces of a moribund man! It was sickening to feel sure that a child conceived as a result of such sub-mission would be even more obnoxious than the one who was pre-sumably the offspring of bridal rapture.

Clyde was almost instantly ashamed of the resentment which caused his anger and which, he ruefully admitted to himself, was not untinged with jealousy. Momentarily, he had forgotten that Lucy, now more than ever, should be the object of his deepest sympathy. She was bereft, and certainly she must once have loved her husband, or she would not have married the man in the first place; now that he was dead, and dead of wounds suffered for the Lost Cause, his every pleasing attribute and daring deed would have taken on new glamour and glory in her eyes. There was no doubt that her sorrow was not only sincere, but profound. And she had given birth to her child 'after prolonged travail' on this lonely plantation, probably with only some ignorant coloured midwife in attendance; unquestionably, Mrs. Cary had not exaggerated in saying that her daughter was still 'completely prostrated'. Moreover, there were no signs of circumstances less straitened than those with which the family had been obliged to cope in Richmond. The frayed furniture in the cold drawing-room was bursting at the seams, and Mrs. Cary had not offered her visitor any refreshment; this would never have happened, he knew, no matter how unwelcome he had been, if there were anything available to eat and drink and anyone on hand to serve it. In fact, everything about the once proud plantation bespoke bitter poverty. This time, he did not dare suggest help; but he had brought a basket of wine with him, as a courtesy gift, thinking that he could present it on the grounds that such imports were still not coming freely across the Atlantic and that he had happened on some good vintages by a fortunate chance. Mrs. Cary did not decline the gift and, after a barely perceptible pause, she even asked Clyde if he would not open one of the bottles so that they might share the savour of its vintage. He declined, saying that it was getting late and that he would rather not attempt the trip back to Richmond, over unfamiliar roads, after dark. Since he could not see Lucy, much less propose to her, since he could not even immediately help her, his visit had failed of its purpose.

But he had never been one to accept defeat for long. He felt certain that Mrs. Cary would not stoop to intercept, or read, her daughter's mail; and the next day he wrote to Lucy, expressing his disappointment at not having seen her and his hope that her health would permit her to receive him the next time he came to Richmond. Her answer was delayed in reaching him, because several forwardings were required before it could do so; but when it came, it brought him back, post-haste, to Sorrento. She had been very sorry to miss him, Lucy wrote. Indeed, if she had known he was calling, she would have insisted on seeing him, so that she could show him her beautiful baby. She had named the baby Cary, since there was no one else, in the direct line, to carry on the family name. Mr. Batchelor probably knew that this was not at all an unusual custom in Virginia. Lucy was disappointed because Bushrod did not seem to be much interested in Cary; however, that was not surprising; very often boys were not interested in their little sisters. But everyone else adored Cary. Lucy was sure Mr. Batchelor would find her enchanting and hoped that he would not postpone his next visit until she had outgrown her sweet baby ways. Besides, Lucy herself would be extremely glad to see him, to thank him in person for the wonderful wine, which had proved such a valuable tonic during her convalescence, and to take him around the plantation, which was still worth seeing, though not, of course, comparable to what it had been before the war. And she was, very sincerely and gratefully his friend, Lucy Page.

The final lines of the letter were the ones which had brought Clyde post-haste back to Sorrento. He was not at all interested in the baby girl; in fact, he was inclined to believe that her charms, like those of every other infant, existed largely in the imagination of her doting mother. But when he was ushered into the drawing-room, he found Cary in her cradle, beside her mother's chair. She had a pillow behind her, but she sat up sturdily enough without it, and she swayed slightly back and forth, singing to herself. Her shapely little head was covered with soft ringlets, bright as spun gold, and her blue eyes danced, as if with some secret infantile joy. The child whom he had expected to find detestable was adorable instead. When she caught sight of Clyde, she laughed, and held out her chubby little arms for him to take her. From that moment, he was her willing slave. . . .

He proposed to Lucy the same day. It was too soon, he knew, by all conventional standards, and he also knew, that by some of them, his suit would smack of presumption at any time. But she had not thought him presumptuous when he offered her food; there was just a chance that she would not do so when he offered her lifelong security for herself and her children, and with it lifelong devotion.

She heard him through, gravely, according him the same courtesy and consideration that she would have shown had he been pleading some other cause. Cary had been in the room with them all the time and, when she began to show signs of restlessness, Lucy had picked her up and quieted her. Then the baby had been put back in her cradle, where she had drowsily nestled down, and the young mother had looked at her suitor across the cradle of her sleeping child.

'I thought you would ask me to marry you,' she said in that serene voice which was music to his ears. 'I am very much honoured by your proposal.'

'Very much *honoured*!'

'Yes, of course. Any woman is honoured when a decent man asks her to become his wife, to become the mistress of his house, to take his name and——'

She stopped, flushing for the first time.

'You don't know that I'm a decent man,' he said impetuously. 'And I haven't a name like Cary or Page to offer you. I haven't told you much about myself yet. I ought to. You have a right to know.'

'I will have if we both decide, later on, that it is best for us to be married,' she said. 'But you interrupted me – or rather, I interrupted myself. I was about to say, any woman is honoured when a decent man asks her to become his wife and the mistress of his house, to bear his name and—to be the mother of his children. Then I stopped, because there is something I ought to add to that and it is not an easy thing to say. I do not mean merely because it brings up a subject which is not usually discussed between men and women, unless they are intimately connected. I would not want you to think I was immodest——'

'As if I could ever think that!'

'Thank you. But it is also hard for a young woman to confess that she may never be able to have any more children and, in justice to you, I must do that. I – I had miscarried twice before Cary was born and I did not have much care either time. It seems nothing short of a miracle that I was able to carry her to full term. I think it must have been partly because I wanted her so much that I was determined not to

41

lose her. But there was no one here with me when she was born except my mother and an old, old Negress who is half blind like her brother, Simeon, whom you have seen. She did the best she could for me, but — a good many things went wrong. Since then, I have managed to consult a doctor and he has told me what I have told you. You will want children of your own, like any normal man. And I probably could not give them to you.'

'Lucy, darling, it's you I want.'

'You feel that way now because you're in love.'

She was speaking with exceptional candour for a woman of her kind and her class, and every word she said seemed to endear her to him the more. In his eagerness, he leaned forward and took her hand.

'Why should I care whether I could have any children of my own if I could have Cary? She's never seen her own father — she'd always think of me as one. Why, we're friends already! You saw how she held out her arms to me the minute I came into the room! I'd adopt her legally, I'd make her my heir. I'd ask you to let me give her my name, too, only, as I've tried to tell you, it's a name that doesn't stand for anything great or even good. I can't rob her of her father's, when that stands for so much.'

'Would you adopt Bushrod? Would you make him your heir, too?'

Momentarily, Clyde hesitated. He had never overcome his first dislike for Bushrod; instead, it seemed to grow greater with time. But he knew that if his answer were no, he would lose all chance of getting Lucy; she would not, indeed she should not, permit discrimination between her children.

'Of course,' he said, speaking hastily, as if to make up for his first hesitation. 'Of course I'd do everything I could for the boy. And I can afford to give him a good education, a good start in whatever profession he chooses. I want to.'

'Thank you,' Lucy said again. Then she rose. 'I think perhaps we'd better not talk about this any more today,' she went on. 'You will not consider me unreasonable, will you, if I ask for a little more time to think it over? Perhaps you ought to think it over, too. It would represent a very important step for both of us, you know.'

'I don't need to think it over any longer. It's a step I want to take just as soon as I possibly can. But of course I won't try to hurry you against your will.'

'Thank you,' she said the third time. 'I will try to answer you more definitely in the course of your next visit — if you do not come too soon. . . . Would you care to take the walk around the plantation which I suggested in my letter? If you would, I will ask my mother to sit with Cary while we are out.'

He gave her six months, meanwhile writing her restrained but affec-

42

tionate letters, which she answered in a friendly way, without making any reference to the few lover-like passages which they contained. He also sent her such conventional gifts as sheet music, classical novels in cloth bindings and bon-bons in hand-painted satin boxes. These she accepted without demur; but when he slipped a brooch in among the bon-bons, she returned it to him, without any word of explanation, obviously considering that he should need none. However, he brought the brooch with him on his return and boldly handed it to her, though without much hope that she would accept it. The reason she gave for doing so surprised him as much as the fact itself.

'I wasn't pleased when I found it hidden in the candy, as if it were shameful for you to offer it to me or for me to accept it,' she said. 'But now that you've brought it openly, that's different.'

'May I put it on for you? I'm afraid the fastening is a little complicated.'

'I'm not ready to wear it yet. When I am, I'll be glad to have you put it on. Not because of the fastening though. I think I could manage that.'

'You said *when*! Does that really mean . . . ?'

'May I ask you a few more questions?'

He had an instant of panic. *Now I've got to tell her everything*, he thought. *I suppose I'd have to tell her sometime. But if I could only wait until after we were married.* 'Of course,' was all he said aloud; and the questions proved undisturbing, after all.

'Where would we live after we were married?' she asked. 'You haven't told me much about your business interests – naturally, there's no reason why you should have. But a good many of them seem to be in Virginia. There are reasons why I'd rather live somewhere else, if we could. You see, I'm afraid there's bound to be a good deal of opposition to our marriage, from the Carys and the Pages both. I hope it doesn't hurt your feelings to have me say that. But I think we'd have a better chance of happiness if we went somewhere else. Of course, that would leave my mother very much alone, unless I could find some relative who would be willing to come here and live with her, someone who would be congenial to her. A good many of our kinfolk have died or moved away, but still I think . . . And if I could, that might be a solution.'

'I hope it would. Because you haven't hurt my feelings and I agree with you that it would be better for us to live elsewhere. I do have business interests in Virginia, but there's no reason why they shouldn't be very quickly liquidated. How would you like to live in Louisiana?'

'Why – I don't know! I've never thought of doing so. How did you happen to think of it?'

'I've thought of it for years. I've wanted to do it for years. Not just

43

in Louisiana, either. On a certain plantation, beside the Mississippi River. In a certain house.'

'I've heard about those houses, along the river road. I've been told they're just as beautiful as any we have in Virginia, that they're truly classic in style. Why, some kinfolk of ours, named Conrad, live in one of them! They're connected with us, distantly, through the Washingtons. Did you know that the earlier Conrads are the only persons, besides the Washingtons, who are buried at Mount Vernon?'

'I didn't know about the burial at Mount Vernon, but I do know the house you mean. It's called The Cottage, because it has only twenty rooms in it.' For a moment his eyes twinkled and his lips curved in a rather mocking smile. 'The house I want isn't classical in style. It looks like a river steamer.''

'*Like a river steamer!*'

'Yes. Some of the men who'd travelled up and down the Mississippi, in the golden days of steamboating, thought there was nothing to equal those floating palaces, as they were called. So these men built houses that would resemble them as much as possible. The type isn't called ante-bellum, like one you've been talking about. It's called Steamboat Gothic.'

'*Steamboat Gothic!*'

'Yes. I think that's rather intriguing, don't you?'

'Yes, it is intriguing,' she said slowly. If she felt any disappointment, if his first words about a mansion on the Mississippi had conjured up a vision which was now dispelled, she did not say so. 'Who built these houses? Retired captains?'

'Sometimes; and sometimes, steamboat owners. As a matter of fact, the captain and the owner were very often one and the same man. Captains frequently drew the plans and supervised the construction of the boats they commanded, and were already aboard when these slid down the ways for the first time. But the Steamboat Gothic houses were generally built by wealthy planters whose business took them up and down the river. The one I want was built by a planter named Labouisse. But I've heard he never lived there. I believe he died before it was finished.'

'Then it's unoccupied? It's for sale?'

'I don't know. But I can easily find out. It wouldn't take long to run down to Louisiana. Besides, I'd enjoy doing so. I told you I've always wanted to live there.'

'You've spent a good deal of time there already?'

'I've spent a good deal of time on the river steamers – most of my time, before the war. I've been past the house I'm talking about over and over again. I saw it when it was being built. In fact, I noticed the preparations for the building before they actually started. The location's unusually fine – there's more of a rise to the ground sloping back from the river right there than there is on most of the land so far south. That makes it outstanding.' He checked himself suddenly. The fact that the place he coveted was so pleasantly situated, geographically speaking, was not the only reason it had arrested his attention. It was just below a meander in the Mississippi which the rivermen had nick-named Aces and Eights Bend, to commemorate the bloody killings of an epochal poker game aboard the *Winged Victory* – a game in which he had played a rather conspicuous part. It had been on the tip of his tongue to mention this meander and its nickname would certainly have roused Lucy's attention. 'I saw the thick, bristly willow scrub cleared away from the site,' he went on hurriedly. 'Then I saw some-thing that looked like a magnified molehill on the clearing – and another and another. Those were the kilns where the bricks for the walls were fired. Presently, I saw slaves digging pits among the molehills and I knew the lime putty for the mortar and the plaster was being slaked. After that, the walls began to rise and I saw them getting higher and higher.'

The haste with which he spoke gave the impression of excitement so enthusiastic that it was contagious. Lucy leaned forward, catching her breath a little and fresh colour came into her pale cheeks.

'You make me see it all, too, Clyde, while you're telling me about it,' she said, speaking excitedly in her turn.

'Can I really? Can I make you see the roustabouts unloading the trappings for the house that were sent over from France – the porcelain bathtub, the marble mantels? Can I make you hear them singing at the landing while they do it? Songs that go something like this:

> *"They ain't but a thousand mo' –*
> *My knee bones is achin',*
> *My shoulder is so' –*
> *When I make this trip*
> *Ain't gonna make no mo'.*
> *Coonjine, nigger, coonjine."* '

'Why, Clyde, you never told me you could sing! You've got a good tenor voice! We could sing duets together!'

'I'm afraid you wouldn't care to join in the only kind of songs I know.'

'You could learn others, couldn't you? And anyway, I enjoyed that one. Do you know more like it?'

'Of course. I know any number of rivermen's songs. And a few Negro spirituals. The slaves who built the garden terraces, shovelful by shovelful, at this place I've been telling you about, sang songs like this:

"Oh Je-sus nev-uh come in the morn-in',
Nei-ther in the heat uv the day, But come in the cool
uv the eve-nin', An' wash my sins a-way."'

'That sounds almost like a jungle chant.'

'You're right, it does, almost. No wonder. That's what it is, almost. . . . Well, when this house I've been talking about was finally finished, it was the most magnificent mansion I ever saw.'

'And that's the house you'd like for yours? That's where you'd like to take me as a bride?'

'What I'd *like*! What would mean more to me than anything else in the world!'

For the first time, he tried to take her in his arms. She slipped from his embrace, shaking her head.

'Not yet, please, Clyde. Give me another six months.'

'Good Lord, Lucy! I've waited for years already.'

'Then couldn't you wait a little longer?'

'I suppose I could. But I certainly don't want to.'

'It's so important for me to be certain. I'm afraid if you can't wait the answer will have to be no.'

'Well, of course, in that case . . .'

In some ways, the next six months were easier than those that had just passed. Despite Mrs. Cary's tacit disapproval, Clyde came to Sorrento as an acknowledged if not an accepted suitor. When Lucy played for him, at dusk, on the old square piano, he turned the sheet music he had given her. When she bent over her embroidery frame, by lamplight, he read aloud to her from the classical novels he had sent her, skipping lightly over the passages which he thought might offend her. And, on the 'pretty days', as she called them, of early spring, they wandered down to the riverbank, and sat on the sandy beach, talking or keeping silent, as suited their mood. While this left him unsatisfied, he found it extremely pleasant. Besides, he realized that it was a privilege for a man like him to be received as a guest at such a plantation, even though this hospitality brought with it no special perquisites; he understood now how logically he might have thought himself lost, the first day he came there, even if the way he took had not been so strange and forbidding. The plantation drive, which traversed the once fertile fields and the still shadowy woods, extended five miles from the gateposts to the high cliff overlooking the James, where the house and gardens were located; even without the addition of Amalfi, the domain was one of princely proportions. The great brick house had been built from plans drawn by Thomas Jefferson shortly after his return from France; its central portion was connected by covered passages to the wide-spreading wings on either side; the whole effect was one of dignity and grandeur; and the extensive gardens, where every flower bed was outlined in dwarf box and every walk shaded by ancient elms and yews, enhanced the general effect of spaciousness and elegance, none of which was lost on the visitor. Moreover, he marvelled at the wonders Lucy had already wrought. Somehow, she had found and gathered together a few scattered and bewildered Negroes and brought them 'home'. That was the way she referred to it; they did, too. Ploughing and planting had begun, grass had been cut, flower beds weeded, brick walls repaired. Indoors, the change was equally great. The house had been swept and garnished and, in the process, it had lost much of its air of shabbiness and gloom, though, as far as Clyde could see, its furnishings remained much the same, except that the worn places in the draperies and upholstery had been neatly darned and broken chairs and tables skilfully mended. He missed no important feature of equipment or adornment in any room, and would probably not have done so, had it not been for overhearing a conversation between Lucy and her mother, one morning as he was coming down the stairs, when they supposed him to be still asleep.

'You had no right to sell that highboy, Lucy. It was an heirloom.'

'In Cousin Tom Carter's family. But Cousin Tom gave it to *me* when he joined Stuart's Cavalry and told me to do whatever I wanted with it.'

'He meant, of course, that you could keep it at Sorrento or at Richmond, whichever you preferred. He never dreamed that you would dispose of it.'

'I've acted on what he *said*, believing that was what he meant. And I intend to sell other things, if necessary. Even Forrest's things. It's better to keep some in decent order than to let them all go to rack and ruin. And it's infinitely better to make this plantation productive again than it is to have a child go hungry again. In fact, I don't want to go hungry again myself. I don't intend to.'

'I should never have believed that you would show so little sentiment, Lucy.'

'Or so much sense? I'm sorry, Mother, that you don't approve. I hate to hurt your feelings. But it shows more delicacy, doesn't it, to sell a highboy, or even several highboys, than to make a mercenary marriage?'

'I think you will have other chances to marry, Lucy, if you'll wait a little. In fact, I have certain knowledge that you will. Only a man lacking in fine feeling would have addressed you so early in your widowhood. A man of your own class would have shown proper respect for the dead.'

Clyde did not hear Lucy's answer, for he turned on the stairway and went, as quietly as possible, back to his room. He was not especially ashamed of his involuntary eavesdropping. But he knew he ran the risk of discovery where he was, and that Lucy would be deeply chagrined and her mother furiously angry, if they found out he had overheard. On the whole, however, he was pleased that he had. He did not like to think of Lucy selling her furniture, or anything else she possessed, and he wished he had the authority to put an instant stop to such sacrifices. On the other hand, he knew now that if Lucy did accept him, it would not be on account of his money; it would be because she cared for him—not as much as he wished she could, but that was too much to hope; at least enough to prefer him to those laggard suitors who had still not had the gumption to approach her. He sat down by the open window of his bedroom and looked out toward the fields, where two Negroes were singing as they sowed, and toward the woods beyond, where the redbud was just bursting into bloom beyond the fringe of feathery weeping willows, and suddenly he felt at peace with the world. And when he started down to breakfast the second time, Cary, who was walking quite steadily by herself now, came toddling out to meet him with cries of joy. And in the dining-room he found a bright fire burning behind the polished andirons—for the early morning air was still crisp—and Lucy waiting for him at a table set with shining silver service. He lifted Cary into her highchair and helped her spoon oatmeal from her porringer, while he and Lucy drank their coffee and ate home-made sausage and eggs which had been gathered that morning and hot biscuits dripping with freshly churned butter and preserves made from the figs for which Sorrento had been famous before the war.

The day marked a turning point. In the state of contentment and well-being which it engendered, he could afford to overlook even Bushrod's behaviour, which had hitherto been a thorn in Clyde's flesh. The boy was less noisy and obstreperous than when he was younger; but he had turned sullen and would hardly speak to the visitor. This attitude, like his grandmother's, created a strain in the atmosphere. However, Clyde managed to ignore this now and Lucy's detachment troubled him less and less; though she continued to be elusive, Clyde knew this was not from coquetry, but from caution. She was trying hard to be fair to everyone—to her mother and her dead husband's family and her children; most of all to Clyde himself. She was honest in her claim that he could offer more than she could give in return. And at last she capitulated: she would marry him, she said, the following autumn. If he wished, he might go to Louisiana at any time convenient for him and find out whether the house he wanted was for sale. If it was, she would go there with him to live. . . .

He returned from his trip, flushed with triumph, and handed her the deed to Cindy Lou Plantation. She laid it down on the table beside them, as if it were of minor importance and, for the first time, on her own initiative, threw her arms around his neck.

'Oh, I'm so glad you're back!' she exclaimed. 'I've missed you terribly!' and raised her face to his.

He never knew how long they remained, locked in that fond embrace. But it was he who finally released her, not she who sought release.

'Lucy,' he said, wondering why his voice sounded so strange to him. 'Lucy—I haven't asked you this before, but . . . I know you're fond of me in a way, I've known it for a long time. I know you have confidence in me, too. You're sure I'll always be a good husband to you and a good father to your children. You're not marrying me just for my money. I wouldn't insult you by such a suggestion. And not out of gratitude because of the little I've done for you, either. That would be hard for me to take, too. I know you've got—well, it's a queer thing for me to say, but I believe you actually have a certain amount of respect for me, though Lord knows I don't deserve it. But I've never dreamed that you loved me—at least, that you were in love with me, the way I am with you—never that is, until just now.'

'Why, of course I am!' Lucy exclaimed; and put her arms around his neck again.

It was a great moment, the greatest in his life. But it might have been so much greater if it had only come before he went to Louisiana.

Chapter Two

IT was years now since that regret had risen from the past to trouble him. Lucy did not suggest a further postponement of their marriage, as he had half feared she might; on the contrary, she consented willingly when he asked to have the date slightly advanced. The thought crossed his mind that she felt the first embrace she had so spontaneously given him was more appropriate for a wife than for a sweetheart, and that since she had inadvertently revealed she was capable of passion, she should not risk further betrayals of her feelings until she had crossed the threshold of the conjugal chamber. He was faintly amused by this suspicion, but at the same time it raised his admiration of Lucy to still greater heights. What a lady she was!

What a lovely, refined, cultured lady! In his highest hopes for success, he had not dreamed that anyone like Lucy would become a part of it. He would never quite believe in his good fortune until they were actually married.

The wedding took place in the parlour at Sorrento in the presence of a mere handful of guests. Lucy had asked Clyde if he had relatives or intimate friends whom he would like to invite; and when he told her he had not, she murmured sympathetically that she was only beginning to realize how lonely his life had been and that she hoped it would be very different in the future. Apparently it did not occur to her that a waif might not even be certain of his parentage, or that it was the calibre and not the lack of later associates which made him loath to introduce them to her presence. As far as her relatives were concerned, most of the Peyton and Cary kinfolk and all the Pages disapproved of the match and found pretexts for absence; Clyde was not deceived by this, but neither did it disturb him, and he made himself so agreeable to the few who did come that they went home to spread the tidings that Cousin Sophia Cary must have been mistaken in her estimate of Mr. Batchelor or that they must have misunderstood her : he was entirely presentable, indeed very good looking, his manners quite polished, his conversation that of a cultivated gentleman. After all, it was not quite fair to condemn him as a Yankee, because he came from St. Louis. Everyone knew, or should know, by this time, that Missouri, like Maryland, had been largely southern in its sympathies, even if the baser elements in its borders had kept it in the Union. And it was sad to think that his family had been completely decimated, exactly like so many in Virginia. . . .

Among the relatives who voiced this opinion most persistently was Mrs. Cary's elderly cousin, Miss Mildred Caskie, who had needed very little persuasion to attend the wedding and to stay on at Sorrento indefinitely. Her brother, Edmond Caskie, had been one of the small but notable group of ex-Confederate officers who had emigrated to Mexico, rather than take the oath of allegiance to the United States Government; and since he and she were the only members of the immediate family left, Mildred had loyally accompanied him. Now Edmond, like his revered leader, Kirby-Smith, had married a Mexican and settled down to comfortable and contented domesticity. But no suitor had mitigated Mildred's exile; and though her brother and his young bride had been kind to her, and assured her that their home would always be hers, she had known she was not needed there, and that, sooner or later, her presence would seem superfluous, if not actually irksome. She had welcomed the pretext of returning to her native heath so providentially indicated by Lucy's marriage and Cousin's Sophia's consequent need of companionship. The least she could do was to express approbation of the bridegroom who had put an end to her banishment; and, as a matter of fact, she found to her relief that she could do this without perjuring herself.

Clyde was conscious of the good impression he had made on the relatives present at his marriage, especially Cousin Mildred, just as he was conscious of the reasons which had kept the others away; but he was no more gratified by one attitude than he was upset by the other, for all his thoughts were centred on Lucy. She was beautiful as a bride, in a gown of rich garnet-coloured silk and garnet jewelry. The dress was not new, she told him blushingly, when he complimented her on her appearance; it was her mother's second-day dress, which had been carefully kept in a trunk under the eaves, and she had made it over herself. Clyde had never heard of a second-day dress before, so Lucy was obliged to explain to him, blushing more deeply, that a second-day dress was always included in the trousseau of every well-equipped Virginia bride; that is, every bride who was a — every bride who was marrying for the first time. Such a bride wore a white dress, of course, for her wedding, and a veil; but she was also supplied with an equally handsome coloured dress to wear after — well, the next day. Of course, Mrs. Cary's wedding dress was in that attic trunk, too; it was very beautiful, as everything in her trousseau had been, because at the time she was married, in the Thirties, there had been plenty of money in the family. Perhaps little Cary would wear that bridal dress some day. Lucy hoped so. But she herself could not wear it because . . . She stopped, entirely suffused with blushes. Candid as she was in all other respects, there was one subject on which she could not touch without self-consciousness.

'Well, I think the garnet silk is superb,' Clyde assured her. 'In fact, I believe it's more becoming to you than the white outfit would have been.' He did not say he really preferred seeing her in garnet; it was impossible to lie to Lucy, and of course, like any other man, he would have preferred to have his bride a virgin, rather than a widow. But, as he had often observed before, many of Lucy's attributes were singularly virginal. Among these were her inability to speak naturally of anything connected with sex, her conviction that ardent caresses and the feelings which inspired them should be restrained — attributes in which Dorothée Labouisse had been so singularly lacking. Sometimes Clyde had moments of fearing that even after marriage Lucy might feel joy in self-abandonment was slightly shameful on the part of a gentlewoman, though she would expect a man to demand and desire complete submission. She would never forget it was ordained by Scriptures that a woman's husband should rule over her and she would conduct herself accordingly; but compliance would not be enough for Clyde — Lucy had shown that to her first husband. He wanted her to

51

stop thinking about love as a sentiment and recognize it as a vital force which could not attain its full power and majesty unless passion were reciprocal. And then he would reproach himself for this yearning and remind himself again how overwhelmingly fortunate he was to have her at all.

The wedding ceremony was deeply impressive. The parlour where it took place, decorated with autumn foliage, gave a far greater effect of spaciousness than it would have if it had been overcrowded with disapproving relatives. The coloured servants gathered around the doorway, their black faces beaming. They had favoured Clyde's suit from the beginning, and not merely because of the generous tips he gave them, either; now they were delighted that he had won through and they showed it. The elderly clergyman who performed the marriage service was a benign figure, his still abundant hair as snowy as his robes. Cary was a bewitching flower girl and even Bushrod's sullenness was in abeyance : he acted the part of a page boy to perfection. Mrs. Cary gave the bride away, since there was no close male relative still living, and this gave an added touch of solemnity to the occasion; and after the benign clergyman had pronounced Lucy and Clyde man and wife, he kissed her gravely on the brow and told her he hoped she would be very happy with her husband in her new home. Then Clyde kissed her himself, rather gravely too, because he was greatly moved; and after that her mother and her children and her other relatives came up to kiss her and a few of the kinfolk kissed Clyde, too, telling him he was now one of the family and that this was a cousin's privilege. Gradually, the solemnity gave way to festivity. Everyone went out into the dining-room to drink the champagne which Clyde had insisted on providing and to cluster around the bride while she cut the cake she had made herself. Finally, someone suggested that there should be dancing in the hall, and a pickaninny was sent running to fetch old Blind Simeon's fiddle, and he played for reels and lancers and waltzes until everyone sank back breathlessly, admitting that it was impossible to dance any more and that, perhaps it was time to permit the bride and groom to slip away.

Clyde had suggested a Grand Tour in Europe for a wedding trip, but Lucy objected that Cary was too young to leave for so long or to take on such a journey; it would be better to wait for the Grand Tour until she was a little older. However, Lucy made no objections to leaving both children, temporarily, at Sorrento, with their grandmother and their Cousin Mildred, with the understanding that Cousin Mildred should bring them to Louisiana later on; and she also agreed to Clyde's second suggestion in favour of New York for their honeymoon. The journey was a tedious one, since it involved a jolting carriage ride from Sorrento to Richmond; a trip from Richmond to Aquia on a train with only antiquated equipment; a second train from Washington to Jersey City; and finally, a ferry crossing to New York. Lucy slept a little on the way to Richmond, supported by Clyde's arm around her waist and resting her head against his shoulder, as the carriage went jerking along in the darkness of the November night after the wedding dance; and she had a really good nap in one of the little cabins on the side-wheeler. But she had vetoed Clyde's recommendation that they should break their journey by a stop-over in Richmond, and he had not insisted, rightly divining that the memories of her later years there were still so painful that she did not wish to associate that scene, in any way, with her honeymoon. The idea of a stop-over in Washington was equally distasteful to her; she still visualized this only as the place where the downfall of the South had been plotted and been brought about and Clyde could understand that viewpoint, too. But the unbroken trip taxed her strength to the utmost and despite her efforts to conceal her weariness, Clyde realized that Lucy was very tired by the time they reached the Fifth Avenue Hotel; before they escaped from the reception hall, her exhaustion was still more obvious. The marble-tiled, brightly frescoed foyer was filled to overflowing with fashionably dressed people; the air heavy with cigar smoke, the confusion of sounds bewildering. The office bell, ringing incessantly, sent servants scurrying in a dozen different directions at once, to execute peremptory orders; and porters, bearing huge trunks on their shoulders, pushed their way through the crowds with shouts of warning. One vociferous group was discussing a burning political issue; another, almost equally excited, the latest developments of the stock market; and above the babel of voices came the clink of glasses and the echo of laughter from the bar-room beyond. Lucy clung to Clyde and the look she turned on him was one of mute and involuntarily appeal. He guided her expertly toward the marble counter enclosing the offices at the rear and wrote their names in the visitors' register, where other newcomers had already filled several pages that day. The reception clerk glanced at the signature and inclined his head respectfully.

'Good evening, sir. Good evening, madam. I hope that you will be pleased with the suite that has been reserved for you. We have tried to follow all your instructions meticulously, Mr. Batchelor.'

'What instructions did you give them?' Lucy whispered, as the clerk reached for a big key and rang for a bellboy.

'I said I'd expect them to make us comfortable and I think you'll find they have. This way, dear. No, you don't have to climb up that mammoth staircase. There's an elevator right here on our left.'

'I — I don't think I know just what you mean.'

'An elevator is a sort of enclosed cage that's hoisted by pulleys from one story to another — the Fifth Avenue Hotel installed the first one in this country. Don't be afraid. It's perfectly safe and a great saving of time and effort. I know you're tired to death. But we'll be out of this hubbub in a moment now and then you can rest.'

He realized that she was experiencing fresh qualms as they entered 'the cage', but she suppressed her fears as she had suppressed her weariness. They had now been joined by an elegant functionary of the hotel who introduced himself as Mr. Puthammer, one of the managers, who had taken charge of their key, informing them that he was giving himself the pleasure of seeing them to their suite; he wanted to make sure, for himself, that everything was satisfactory. He continued to give directions to the laden bellboys as he and his charges alighted from the elevator, and steered them down a long hall, flooded with brilliant gaslight, and so deeply carpeted that their feet sank noiselessly into the rich pile. Then he paused, glancing at the number on a panel of black walnut and, having inserted the key in its ornamented lock, threw open a double door and stood back, bowing, to permit the entrance of the bridal pair.

Beyond the vestibule, a second door opened into a large parlour, furnished with the utmost opulence and decorated with a profusion of flowers. A fire burned brightly under its marble mantel; its centre table was already set for dinner with spotless linen and sparkling silver and nearby, the gold-wrapped neck of a champagne bottle emerged from the shining ice bucket in which it was immersed. On either side of the parlour, still other doors opened out, revealing glimpses of a chamber dominated by a huge black walnut bed and a dressing-room with a tall mirrored shaving stand. Clyde went rapidly from one to the other, assuring himself that there were fires and flowers everywhere, and that there was a private bath beyond the dressing-room. But Lucy stood as if transfixed, just beyond the threshold and when Clyde rejoined her, she reached suddenly for his hand, with an exclamation so expressive of amazement and delight that he knew her weariness and her qualms were all forgotten.

'Why, Clyde, it's – it's like a vision of fairyland!' she exclaimed. 'Are you sure it's real? Are you sure *we* are?' Clyde returned the pressure of her hand and glanced at Mr. Puthammer.

'The suite is entirely satisfactory,' Clyde informed him. 'We will ring when we desire service. I wish you good night.'

'That dummy cheated me out of lifting you over the threshold,' Clyde told her when he released her from the embrace in which he had enfolded her as soon as the door closed behind the obsequious manager and the grinning bellboys. 'Never mind, I'll do it at Cindy Lou. After all, that's going to be our real home – this is just a way station.'

'I tell you, I believe it's fairyland,' Lucy insisted. She went readily enough now, under Clyde's guidance, from one part to another, still giving little unsmothered cries of delighted amazement. However, when he suggested ringing for a maid to unpack their bags, she shook her head.

'It won't take me any time at all to do that.'

'But you're tired. And, of course, I can't let you unpack my things.'

'But of course you can. I'm your wife now.'

'Yes, you're my wife now. And that means you're never going to lift your finger again, unless you feel like it.'

'But I *do* feel like it. I suppose we'll have to let a waiter bring us our dinner. But don't you think, except for that, it would be pleasanter not to have any — any intruders?'

He was obliged to admit that it would be; and eventually, they agreed that he should unpack his bag in the dressing-room while she unpacked hers in the bedroom and that, when she had changed her travelling costume for a *robe d'interieur*, they should meet again in the parlour and that Clyde should ring for dinner. She pronounced all the dishes which were brought to them delicious and praised the service highly, both in the hearing of the deft waiter and after he had withdrawn. But Clyde noticed that she was eating very little of the rich viands which he consumed with lusty relish and merely sipping the champagne which he was quaffing in deep draughts. The pinched look of fatigue was coming back into her lovely face, too; it was not rapturous any longer; and suddenly Clyde realized that returning exhaustion was not alone responsible for her expression. When the waiter had noiselessly withdrawn for the last time, Clyde rose and held out his arms.

He could not honestly have said that Lucy was slow in rising to her feet or that she came to him with any sign of hesitation. She was sweet, she was smiling, she was utterly compliant; but the spontaneity which had meant so much to him on the rare occasions when she had shown it was lacking.

'Lucy,' he said tenderly, 'Lucy, darling! A little while ago you reminded me that you're my wife now — as if I needed any reminder! As if this hadn't been the greatest day of my life! But you said it as if it meant that I would expect you to wait on me. I tried to tell you that I don't, that I not only don't expect it, I don't want it, I won't allow it. I think I ought to tell you something else. I don't want a "dutiful" wife, much less a "submissive" one. I think the word "obey" ought to come out of the marriage service. You're terribly tired. You've had a hard journey on top of all the strain of getting ready for the wedding and of the wedding itself. If it would be a relief to you to go into the bedroom and shut the door, and lie down to sleep, knowing you wouldn't be disturbed, that's what I want you to do. I'd never reproach you for it in my mind and I'd never refer to it again.'

'But——' Lucy began falteringly.

'Please let me finish, darling. I'm terribly serious about this and I'm trying to be completely sincere, too. That *is* what I want you to do if it would be a relief to you. But I'm not sure that it would. I'm afraid you wouldn't go quietly to sleep. I'm afraid you'd be disquieted, not just by the feeling that you'd been unfair to me, either – I've told you to stop thinking about that, once and for all – but by the vague consciousness that you weren't fulfilling your own destiny as a woman. Because you wouldn't be. You won't be until – well, until I've helped you to do it. It's just as instinctive for a woman – a woman like you, I mean – to resist physical union as it is for a man to seek it. At least, that's the primary instinct. Once it's overcome – once you've given me a chance to overcome it – you'll want it as much as I will.'

'But——' Lucy said again.

'I haven't quite finished even yet, darling. There's something else I want to make clear to you, if I can. In fact, it's even more important for me to tell you what I do want than it was to tell you what I don't want. I want you to get over the idea that it's shameful for a woman – and again, I mean a woman like you – to feel passion and to show that she does. It's normal for men and women to share the full experience of love, and they can't do it, if the desire for it is one-sided. *It's got to be mutual.* And it will be for us, if you'll just believe me, if you'll just trust yourself to me.'

'I do believe you, I do trust myself to you. Oh, Clyde, I'm so – so grateful to you for talking to me like this! No one ever did before. No one ever explained – no one ever revealed. . . . I'm not tired any more, truly I'm not. I'm not afraid, I'm not ashamed. I want you to come to me and stay with me, I want you to overcome that instinctive resistance. I want our desire to be mutual and I know it is going to be. *It is already.*'

So the opulent bridal suite had become the scene of repeated raptures, for, as Clyde had promised Lucy, their marriage quickly became one of shared desires and shared delights; but he was also insistent on her need for repose and refreshment and, because of his loving solicitude, the fatigue of travel was quickly overcome and Lucy swiftly embarked on a round of shopping and sight-seeing and theatre-going which Clyde mapped out for them. The garnet silk dress was beautiful, Clyde told her again. (She had brought it with her, for it was the best one she had.) But there were to be no more made-over dresses in her life. They would find out immediately who were considered the very best dressmakers, and then Lucy must order a complete outfit of new clothes, including a quilted skirt, to wear over her hoops, and a full-length sealskin coat; also a tippet and muff of chinchilla which, Clyde had been told, should be worn with a velvet casque. And of course she must get several evening gowns — she would find that everyone in the hotel dining-room was in full dress, the ladies' toilettes magnificent; he wanted her to outshine all the others. The garnet jewellery became her and he knew she valued it as an heirloom; but she must also have diamonds and sparkling gems, which he and she would select together at the great silver and jewellery house of Tiffany, Young and Ellis. And she must not neglect to get household linens and all such supplies for Cindy Lou; he knew she had not felt free to draw on the depleted stock at Sorrento, and that it was still impossible to buy such things in any quantity or of any quality at the Richmond stores. Nonsense, what was she talking about? It was the bride's place to supply such things as linen? Well, that was just what he was asking her to do! Why, of course she was spending her own money! Didn't she understand, even yet, that the money he had settled on her *was* her own, that he had no further claim on it and would never consent to an accounting of it!

The shopping excursions alone would have left Lucy breathless with delight. She could well understand why the establishment of Lord and Taylor, at the corner of Grand and Chrystie Streets, should be called 'one of the architectural wonders of Manhattan'. It had a large central rotunda, surmounted by a dome, and the windows were as handsome as those at St. Patrick's Cathedral. Lucy was prejudiced against Lord and Taylors at first, because it made so much of the fact that Mrs. Abraham Lincoln had been one of its most prodigal customers; she said she would prefer to purchase from Arnold Constable, which had a really exclusive clientele and did not need to publicize this or seek to enlarge it — indeed, its window displays consisted of nothing more elaborate than a half-dozen umbrellas, arranged fan-shaped, or a few lengths of dress goods. But she was drawn back to Lord and Taylor's in spite of herself and she also went to Stewarts' and McCreery's and Hearns', finding at each some special attraction which would have satisfied her completely if she had seen nothing else.

However, Clyde insisted that the magnificent stores were only one of New York's great sights; they could not see them all, and they must not try to see so many that Lucy would be tired and not feel like going to a play in the evening. How could she get tired, she asked, when everything was made so easy for her? She was getting disgracefully lazy, breakfasting in bed, bathing and dressing at her leisure, sitting down to perfect meals without a thought as to their preparation, their service or their cost, and then getting into a carriage every time she and Clyde covered more than a few blocks. The only exercise she had was in walking around their suite. To be sure, that was enormous — almost as large as the second story at Sorrento. But in the Fifth Avenue Hotel she did not even walk up and down stairs — not that it would have been any effort to do so, but she had become fascinated by that strange contraption called an elevator and readily consented to Clyde's insistence that she should always take it. She really wondered that he would permit her to walk as far as the Fifth Avenue Theatre, though that was directly back of their hotel!

They joked about this, and Clyde offered to carry her; he might even have made a show of doing this, if he had not known that Lucy hated to be made conspicuous. But he could not refrain from pressing close to her as she took his arm to cross the street, or from holding her hand when the lights had been dimmed in the rose-walled, mirror-lined parquet; and through the performances of *She Would and She Would Not* and *Much Ado About Nothing*, he was far more conscious of her intoxicating nearness than he was of Fanny Davenport's fascination as Viletta and Mary Scott-Siddons' charm as Beatrice. Lucy, divining this, chided him gently, reminding him that Fanny Davenport was the most photographed young actress of the day, and Mary Scott-Siddons a direct descendant of the greatest actress of all time. But Clyde only retorted that the reason Fanny had such a clear field was because far more beautiful women declined to be photographed, and that all the critics were saying Mary was 'no real successor' to 'the Magnificent Sarah', her great-grandmother.

How could those critics tell, Lucy inquired, with mock haughtiness, disregarding the comment on photography, which, she knew, was aimed at herself. Had any of them seen the Magnificent Sarah in the flesh? Of course not! Well then! As far as she was concerned, she thought the current Beatrice could not have been better and she wanted to see Mary's Viola, too, if Clyde did not think they were spending too much time — and too much money — on the theatre. Why, they had all the time there was, and all the money, too, Clyde answered. Besides, he added, studying his programme, *As You Like It* was a matinée, a special performance at special prices; they could go to that in the afternoon without spending much money and still get to another play in the evening — perhaps something a little lighter than Shakespeare. What would Lucy think of *Little Nell and the Marchioness* at Niblo's Garden?

The Fifth Avenue Theatre, like the Fifth Avenue Hotel, laid great stress on refined elegance; but Niblo's Garden was even more glamorous, and proclaimed its presence at the rear of the Metropolitan Hotel by a great, illuminated sign, composed of gas jets in red, white and blue glass cups, strung on an iron pipe. Clyde gathered that Lucy did not admire this sign quite as much as he did, and that she preferred Scott-Siddons' interpretation of Viola to Lotta's performance of *Little Nell*. But it was not because of anything she said or did to dampen his enjoyment, only because he was more and more sensitive to her tastes, her moods, her feelings, more and more eager that nothing should mar her pleasure or offend her delicacy.

Following the theatre, there was always a midnight supper, at the Metropolitan or the St. Nicholas or Delmonico's. Lucy gasped and remonstrated when she caught sight of a check setting forth a charge of ten dollars a plate for breast of chicken; and after that, Clyde systematically hid the checks from her, teasing her again and saying he had no idea he had married a miser. He would not tell her, either, how much he spent on carriage hire when they drove through Central Park at the smart clip of six miles an hour, or went as far afield as Claremont for a day's outing; so presently, she ceased to ask even casual questions about money. He realized then that she was sensitive to his feelings, too, that she knew he did not want to talk about it, only to spend it; and he tried to tell himself that his prodigality would atone for the devious ways in which he had won his wealth, and that when Lucy found out what these had been, as sooner or later she must do, he would succeed in making her feel that way about it, too.

Finally, they went to grand opera at the Academy of Music – a superb performance of *William Tell*, in which Madame Biol sang Mathilde and the great Le Franc Arnoldo. This was an occasion when Lucy must wear her most striking dress, Clyde told her, and all her most dazzling new jewels. He was ready to agree with her, by this time, that, generally speaking, simplicity became her more than showiness and pearls better than sparkling gems. But there were exceptions to every rule and this time he wanted her to be resplendent. So she put on her parure of rubies and diamonds and a satin dress, striped in shades of magenta and cream, and trimmed with black velvet and rosepoint lace. It had just been delivered from Sophia Diedens and was made in the latest syle, with hardly a suggestion of a hoop, but with a hint of a bustle – a dress that accentuated her charms and revealed her figure to a far greater degree than anything she had ever worn, except in private. She tried to draw her great circular cape of white swansdown more closely around her; but it kept parting and when she took her seat in the central box of the grand tier, opera glasses were turned upon her from every part of the house and an audible murmur of admiration rippled through it. Lucy blushed so deeply that Clyde realized she did not wholly share his undiluted pride in this tribute to her beauty; and, as they sat at supper, after the spectacle, she asked him a question which revealed afresh her instinctive aversion to attracting public attention, tactfully as she worded her suggestion.

'I'm sure nothing could surpass the splendour of that opera. Don't you think perhaps it would be a mistake if we tried to find something that would?'

'Just what do you mean, honey?'

'Well, I've been wondering – just wondering, of course – if we shouldn't begin to think of leaving New York. You said you wanted to celebrate Christmas at Cindy Lou. I'd like that, too.'

'All right, we'll consider that settled. Even so, we don't need to hurry. It isn't as if there'd be a lot for you to do after we got there. The house was left in perfect order when it was vacated.'

'You mean by Madame Labouisse?'

'Yes, of course. She was the former owner. You knew that.' He realized he had spoken abruptly, almost reprovingly, but he could not help it; and suddenly he feared that his discomfiture might have betrayed him, that he might have grown red in the face, instead of assuming that blank expression which, hitherto, he had always been able to command at will. 'She saw that it was thoroughly cleaned,' he went on hurriedly. 'In fact, I imagine she did a good deal of the cleaning herself – she had only one house servant left, a Negress named Belle, who, incidentally, has great potentialities as a cook.' He paused and took a sip of wine. 'However, you'll find the house completely staffed now. When Belle got wind of what was happening, she began calling in all her kith and kin and they're pretty numerous. I couldn't stay around long enough to find out whether they were any good or not and Doro – Madame Labouisse was eager to be on her way to France as soon as the sale went through, but——'

'Of course she was,' Lucy interrupted sympathetically. Apparently she had not noticed his slip. 'Of course it would have been painful to stay in or near her old home after it belonged to someone else. Remember how I felt about Richmond!'

'Yes,' Clyde answered, swallowing hard. 'Well, she left – immediately, as I've said. But I spoke about my problem – about wanting to be sure you had suitable house servants, I mean – to Monsieur Gilbert Ledoux, the notary who handled the sale, and he introduced me to a Mrs. Surget, the widow of a very eminent physician who used to practise in that locality. I'm sure you'll like her very much, Lucy – in fact, I believe you and she will become great friends, though she's considerably older than you are. I could tell, at a glance, that she's your kind. She lives all alone now, in rather reduced circumstances, and her house isn't large or pretentious – indeed, except for a rather remarkable collection of some odd little bedside lamps she calls *veilleuses*, there's nothing especially valuable in it. I'm afraid she's had to sell a good many of her other treasures, to keep body and soul together.'

'The poor woman!' Lucy exclaimed, still more understandingly than she had spoken before. 'I never heard of a *veilleuse* before. Can you describe one to me?'

'Yes, I can, because Mrs. Surget showed me the whole collection,' Clyde answered, glad of the diversion. 'A *veilleur* is a watchman, isn't he? I don't know much French, of course, but I believe that's what Mrs. Surget said and that *veilleuse* would be the feminine form of the noun. Well, anyway, the kind of *veilleuse* she has is a small vessel something like a teapot which fits on a stand large enough to contain a short candle or a little lamp, just big enough to float a wick in oil. I understand that the wick of the lamp now serves a dual purpose: it gives enough light to prevent a room from being completely dark and it keeps the contents of the vessel warm. Mrs. Surget says *veilleuses* are not used, currently, quite as much as they used to be, but that, in provincial France and rural Louisiana, they still serve to keep a baby's milk or an invalid's *tisane* warm through the night. You'd be surprised to see all the shapes the little pots are made in. Elephants carrying howdahs, castles, loving couples, madonnas complete with angels, jolly friars with baskets of bottles. There was even one shaped like a nun with a little cup in her hand as if she had been preparing a drink for an invalid herself. Mrs. Surget's enormously proud of her collection and it's one prize possession she's kept intact. I think though, from something she said, she plans to give you a choice item from it for a wedding present.'

'That would be very, very kind of her,' Lucy said warmly. 'But I wouldn't like to feel I was taking anything from her that she really valued, when she's lost so much already.'

'I think she'd really like to give you a *veilleuse*—that is, if she takes to you, and of course she will. I just told you, she and you are the same kind. And, even if she has had to dispose of some things she valued, everything about her house revealed good taste and good management,' Clyde went on, 'and she herself struck me as being not only a lady of great culture and refinement, but one of considerable efficiency. I asked her if she would be willing to take charge of training a corps of house servants and otherwise preparing Cindy Lou for your reception and she said she'd be delighted. Naturally, I put the transaction on—well, on a practical basis. I didn't ask her to do it as a favour.'

'And I'm sure you did it very tactfully, just as you offered to bring "delicacies" to the house for me and my family when we were starving,' Lucy said with a glance of grateful affection. 'Very likely you kept her from going hungry, too. You're always doing kind things for people, aren't you, Clyde?'

'Not by any means. But I certainly intend, as I've told you before, that you shan't ever lift a finger again, unless you feel like it. You won't need to do anything, when you get to Cindy Lou, but walk into your new house and enjoy it. Someone else will have done all the hard work. We could be ready to celebrate Christmas the day after we arrived, if we wanted to, which means we could stay in New York at least a week longer and still have time enough.'

'But we have to begin to plan for the trip a little while beforehand, don't we?'

'Yes, we can begin right now, if you like. I thought perhaps you'd enjoy an ocean voyage. We can take a steamer direct from New York to New Orleans. It's the quickest and easiest way – the pleasantest, too, I believe. The boats are very good now and we'd have no changes to make, none of the confusion you find so tiring. Why, it wouldn't begin to be as exhausting as the trip from Sorrento to New York!'

'You mean we couldn't travel on the Mississippi *at all*?'

It was the first time she had ever voiced disappointment at any suggestion he made. He felt sure it was the first time she had ever felt any.

'Well, we'd go from New Orleans to Cindy Lou by boat.'

'But Clyde, I've been looking forward so much to going down the river all the way from St. Louis! One of our cousins, Stanard Daingerfield, who lives in Louisville, has written me about a new floating palace that's named the *Richmond*. He travelled on it last year, and he said he'd never seen anything to equal it, even in the so-called "Golden Days" of steamboating – that it really would beggar description! I admit I didn't want to stop over in the real Richmond, and perhaps you thought on that account . . . But this would be different. It would bring back all the happy associations and none of the sad ones. I'd taken it for granted that we'd go to Louisiana by the river, because you've spent so much time on it and love it so much. And I've been meaning to ask you whether we couldn't take the *Richmond*, because that would mean so much to me and because——'

She broke off, looking at him with an expression in which bewilderment was mingled with appeal. He could not wonder at this: so far, he had forestalled her every wish before she could express it; now she had voiced a wholly reasonable desire and he did not know how to answer her, much less how to grant the favour she asked. She still had no inkling, obviously, of the way he had spent his time on the Mississippi; she would have to know some day, he fully meant to tell her himself – some day. But not yet. Not until he had proven himself worthy of her lasting love. So far, as she said herself, he had given her a glimpse of fairyland; he had taken her from scenes of tragedy and ruin, from associations with defeat and death, from a life of privation and toil, to a gorgeous and triumphant metropolis where she was lapped in luxury and laden with gifts. To be sure, he had done more than that: while treating her with the utmost tenderness, he had given her buoyant companionship and initiated her into secret delights. But he could have done all this, even if he had not changed the pattern of his former life; indeed, almost any man, who was rich and vigorous, and whose intelligence and kindliness had not been engulfed by his wealth and his virility could have done that much. And, in the long run, Lucy would instinctively feel that her husband had failed her if he offered her only prodigality and passion. She would not only want, but need to respect and admire the man she had married, to value his opinions, to defer to his judgment, and to find quiet communion, as well as overpowering rapture in the intimate hours which they shared.

'Besides,' she went on, while Clyde was still groping for the words in which to answer her, 'I've been hoping you'd show me St. Louis You've been to Sorrento, you've been to what's left of Amalfi. You've told me it interested you to see where I grew up, to learn more about the life I led as a girl—a very happy life until I . . . That is, until we knew there was going to be a war. It would interest me just as much to see how you grew up.'

Clyde knew she had almost said, 'It was a very happy life until I was persuaded to marry a man I didn't love.' Ordinarily, a reminder of the compulsion which had been put upon her would have roused him to such indignation that he could not have thought of anything else until his wrath subsided. As it was, his resentment was swallowed up in consternation. While he had been trying to frame an answer to her first suggestion, his thoughts had been racing toward a compromise: he really needed to go to Pittsburgh, to see how the new ventures on which he was embarking were getting on; if they made the first part of their journey by train, and then took one of the smaller packets as far as Cairo, or even as far as Memphis, the danger of discovery would be greatly lessened; it was on the real floating palaces that he had operated. Besides, he had never had either a 'capper' or a permanent partner; only at rare intervals had he joined forces with another member of the outlaw fraternity to bring off some special project. Moreover, he had been wonderfully successful in the matter of masquerading. During the course of his career, he had, at various times, impersonated a lumberjack, a government agent and a wealthy planter, and had played the rôle of each so convincingly that detection had been infrequent. Even when it had occurred, he had seldom run into real trouble, for he had never deliberately invited it. He had been proud of the dexterity which was partly inherent and partly the result of long practice; he had always preferred his winnings dependent on skilful, rather than fraudulent manipulation, and had derived far more satisfaction from a game in which he could match his wits against those of a reasonably adroit antagonist than from one in which he had a miserable 'sucker' for his opponent. Not that he had ever allowed another professional to victimize him; he was not above resorting to shady practices himself when confronted with a crooked gamester bent on winning by foul means, if he could not win by fair ones; but he could still flatter himself that he had been primarily an expert card player. Surely, if he were aboard the *Richmond* only a few days, he could manage somehow; indeed, once they were aboard a more modest steamboat, Lucy could even be persuaded that it would be senseless to go to all the trouble of transferring to a larger one. . . . Yes, he would be almost sure that some such plan could be carried through without disaster. . . . And here she was saying she wanted to see St. Louis because that was where he had grown up!

Abruptly, he motioned to their waiter to bring the bill and rose, with equal abruptness, before he remembered that, of course, he should have waited for Lucy to give the signal that they were to leave the table. He hardly spoke on their way back to the hotel and, once they had reached their suite, he went straight to his dressing-room. Lucy was already in bed when he rejoined her. She had lowered the lights, but she had not extinguished them, and she had not composed herself for slumber, by lying relaxed on her side, with one arm under her, but was sitting up, with two pillows behind her. Even in the semi-darkness Clyde could see that her expression was troubled. She held out her arms to him.

'Darling,' she said softly. 'I've offended you in some way, haven't I? You must know I didn't mean to. But please forgive me, anyway. I'd rather die than hurt your feelings.'

'You sweet angel, you haven't hurt my feelings,' he answered quickly; and, as he spoke, he knelt down beside her. At the moment, he felt that, only on his knees, could he accept her embrace. 'But . . . Do you remember a long while ago, even before we were engaged, I offered to tell you something about myself, and you stopped me? You said there would be time enough for that when you consented to marry me – that is, if you did consent. Then, after you did, the right moment never seemed to come. But I haven't wilfully tried to deceive you, dearest, I know you'll believe that.'

'Of course, I believe that. I believe everything you say to me. And I don't want you to tell me anything until you feel the right moment has arrived.'

'Are you sure you mean that?'

'As sure as I am that I love you with all my heart and soul.'

He swallowed hard. 'All right. Then I won't try to tell you much tonight. But I will tell you this much : there isn't anything in St. Louis that you'd be interested to see, or happy to see, because it's connected with me. The first home I can remember – in fact, my only childhood home — was an orphanage and a very bleak, barren one at that. I think I know who my mother was, but I don't even know that much about my father. The woman I believe was my mother stopped coming to see me when I was around ten years old. I asked questions about her and no one at the orphanage would answer them. I waited and waited for her to come back and finally I ran away. I hoped I'd find her, but I never did and after a while, I stopped looking. I could take care of myself all right by that time anyway.'

'Oh, Clyde, you mustn't tell me any more tonight! I couldn't bear it! And of course we mustn't go to St. Louis — ever — ever — ever!'

She was weeping, weeping with grief because of his childhood misery and his childhood loneliness. Her tears moistened his face as she pressed her own against it. She was not shocked by the disclosure of his dubious background, she found nothing shameful in his doubtful paternity; her only feeling was one of infinite compassion, infinite loving-kindness. . . .

Finally, when she had grown calmer, she disengaged herself and moved away a little, slipping one hand under her pillow.

'I haven't any handkerchief,' she whispered almost whimsically. 'A woman never does have one, does she, when she really needs it? Would you get me one, Clyde? I keep them in the top drawer of the dresser. . . . Oh, thank you, darling.'

She was smiling up at him now and the smile was an invitation. He knew that her grief had spent itself, that she was ready to show her love for him in other ways, that she did not want him to kneel beside her any more, but to take her in his arms. The rapture with which she received him, when he did so, disclosed not only the ecstatic response on which he had come to count; it also revealed a passionate determination that he should find, in his joy with his wife, compensation for every sorrow that all others had given him. The revelation was one of a new heaven and a new earth. Never had she seemed so completely his as in the time that followed.

Chapter Three

THE question of going to St. Louis was not raised again; but a day or two later, Clyde told Lucy that he had tentatively reserved seats for the following Monday on one of the 'Silver Palace' cars, which ran via the Pennsylvania Central Railroad between New York and Pittsburgh. He believed she would find the journey very different from their first hard train trip, between Richmond and Aquia and between Washington and Jersey City. The Silver Palace cars were said to be almost as comfortable as anything the most luxurious steamboats had to offer: a certain multimillionaire by the name of Stoddard was pouring out untold wealth in railroad expansion and was most insistent on this phase of its development. Moreover, she would not be confined to the cars throughout the fifteen hour journey; schedules had been conveniently arranged so that travellers should be able to stretch their legs a little when they got out at Harrisburg for dinner and at Altoona for supper. On the other hand, if she would prefer the experience of travelling by night, in one of the new Pullman sleeping cars, they could leave New York at seven in the evening on the Pacific Express and get to Pittsburgh around ten in the morning. The mechanism which provided for both upper and lower berths was really very ingenious, and sheets were now supplied, which was a great innovation – 'Old Number Nine', the first Pullman sleeper, built ten years earlier, had been equipped with mattresses and blankets, but no bed linen and sometimes – well, he would not go into details. Lucy would not mind the change of climate, for this new car was heated with a hot air furnace under the floor – another great innovation and an immense improvement on the small wood-burning stoves, one at either end of Number Nine. The Pullman sleeper he was suggesting also had black walnut woodwork, handsomely inlaid, French plush upholstery, and a Brussels carpet, not to mention a spacious washroom. What did she think?

He could see that it was difficult for her to decide; and he teased her a little because her ultimate decision was in favour of the day trip. He was not sure, he told her, whether this was really because she wanted to see the countryside; he thought it was partly because she did not like the idea of dressing and undressing on a train. Well, of course, she replied, with one of the blushes he found so entrancing, she would not really disrobe; she would just change from her travelling costume to a dark dressing gown and loosen her corset. But, inevitably, there

66

would be a little awkwardness, the next morning . . . He laughed and said there was no more reason why she should not go to bed comfortably, in a nightgown, on a Pullman sleeper than at the Fifth Avenue Hotel; but he could see she did not feel that way about it and he did not urge her. After all, he could not assure her that he would have a separate dressing-room on a train; they would have to share a compartment; and though they had now been married several weeks, they had never seen one another unclad. He realized that Lucy had been brought up to believe that no woman of refinement revealed any more of her body than she could help, even to her husband and her physician. Some day, he hoped, she would feel different about that, just as she already felt different about the marriage relationship. But he knew the time had not yet come for this. If he tried to hasten its coming, he might lose everything he had gained; he could not even talk to her about it yet, as he had talked to her about the consummation of their union. He did not want to. He wanted the next revelation of his bride to be on the same plane as those which had preceded it. . . .

So the tentative reservation for the Silver Palace car was confirmed and the following Monday they left New York at nine in the morning. The trees were already shorn of their foliage and the level countryside, bereft of autumnal brightness, was one of almost unrelieved monotony until they had been on their way for several hours; but Lucy was fascinated by the elaborate accoutrements of the car and delighted with the novel experience of eating dinner in a railroad station.

'There's a lot more style to the one in Pittsburgh,' Clyde told her. 'It's really about the toniest place to eat there — patronized by the local aristocrats quite as much as by the travelling public. Colonel Unger, who runs it, is a very genial gentleman, though at first glance you wouldn't think so — he's tall and erect, rather military-looking, in fact. His wife's just the opposite, short and fat and dumpy and always running through the corridors around the dining-room with a parrot cage clutched in her hand.'

'Why on earth does she do that?' Lucy inquired.

'I haven't the first idea. Neither has anyone else that I've ever talked to. But in spite of Mrs. Unger's little oddities, that second-story dining-room at the Union Depot is quite a place. I'll take you there and you'll see for yourself."

'I hope I'll see Mrs. Unger and her parrot. If I do, I'll ask her about it.'

'You know you'll do no such thing.'

Very probably not, Lucy finally admitted; but meanwhile they had found the Ungers and the dining-room at the Union Depot an absorbing topic of conversation for some time after they had finished their dinner at Harrisburg and gone back to their Silver Palace car. The early dusk prevented them from seeing much of the mountain scenery, and the train, swaying jerkily over its tortuous road-bed, jolted them more and more. Lucy could not go to sleep with her head on Clyde's shoulder, as she had in the carriage which had taken them from Sorrento to Richmond; their elegant plush seats could be turned so that these faced each other, but there was no way in which tired travellers could sit closely side by side. Clyde was sure that Lucy would be completely exhausted when they reached their destination, well after midnight; and though she insisted that the passage over the mountains had been a new experience and that like all other new experiences she had found it thrilling, he was not reassured. His anxiety increased as they fought their way through the depot crowds in the wake of a Monongahela House runner who had met the train, and who vociferously directed them toward a waiting bus, with an occasional triumphant and inelegant aside to some rival, as the latter sought to divert his patrons by raucously voicing the claims of the Lincoln Hotel, the Union Hotel, the Mansion House and the Washington House.

'We'll be there presently now,' Clyde told Lucy, as they clambered up the steps of the bus and squeezed into places on one of the narrow seats which ran lengthwise on either side. She nodded and smiled, but he realized she had not heard him, because he had whispered instead of shouting. Despite the lateness of the hour, newsboys were calling out headlines, drunken revellers were brawling in doorways, streetcar conductors were clanging their bells, and draymen were swearing at the heavy, slow-moving horses that clattered over the cobblestones. The tumult seemed all the more confusing because the smutted atmosphere made it doubly difficult to distinguish the source of one sound from another. Cindery soot pattered like raindrops against the windows of the bus; and even when a section of the crowded thoroughfare became visible through the obscured panes, the street lamps shielded by glass bells, gave forth such a feeble flame that the darkness was dispelled for only a short distance.

Clyde did not try to speak again, but he worried increasingly. It was bitterly cold and he was afraid Lucy would be chilled through and through, besides being shaken to pieces. The cobblestone streets were terribly rough, and the jolting and jarring they had undergone on the train had been mild to what was happening to them now. He had forgotten there were so many saloons in downtown Pittsburgh, and he began to be glad that the pattering soot prevented Lucy from seeing them and the sights connected with them more clearly. He had also forgotten that there were so many livery stables; the stench of these permeated the icy closeness of the bus, making it more and more obnoxious. . . .

A loud 'Whoa!' from the driver, reining in his horses, heralded the end of their painful progress. The entrance to the Monongahela House was flanked with cigar stores; a long interior passageway, lined with plush-covered sofas, led to the lobby at the rear, where horsehair supplanted the plush. Only a few loiterers remained in the chairs companionably grouped around the spittoons; these were apparently drummers, still relaxing after their day's work. Some of them had been celebrating, and the mellowness of their mood was reflected in their uninhibited comments on the new arrivals. Clyde tried to hurry through the process of registration and of disentangling baggage.

'I'm sorry there's no elevator here,' he said, as he and Lucy turned toward the long stairs. 'And we're on the top floor. No private bathrooms, either, though if there's a city where baths are more needed, I don't know what it is. I have got us a suite though, by going high up — that is, I've got us two rooms, and one of them will serve, after a fashion, for a parlour. But I'm afraid you'll find the Monongahela House a good deal of a come-down, after the Fifth Avenue Hotel.'

'Yes, but that was fairyland,' Lucy answered, her hand on the stair railing. 'We didn't expect to live in fairyland all the time — at least, I didn't. And I'm so glad — it wouldn't seem half so wonderful if we did.' She spoke with such buoyancy that Clyde could not doubt the sincerity of her words. 'Do you know, lots of people in Virginia think Pittsburgh is still full of Indians?' she added when they were halfway up the second flight. 'I thought so myself and I watched for them on the way up here from the depot. I saw a lot of them, too.'

'You saw a lot of *Indians*!' Clyde exclaimed, stopping short in astonishment.

'Yes, darling. I tried to count them, but I had to give up, because there were so many. I can't wait to write home about them. But they were all *wooden* Indians, outside of cigar shops!'

Her laugh rang out, fresh and gay. She had not noticed the saloons, because she had been busy counting wooden Indians. And she had not minded the soot or the noise. She had told the truth; she did not need to live in fairyland all the time, she did not even want to. When they finally reached their makeshift suite, breathless from their climb, she looked at Clyde and laughed again.

'It's *all* a new experience,' she said. 'And it's all thrilling, just as I told you before — most of all being married to you!'

Because she said all this, because she so obviously meant every word of it, she unconsciously freed him from the fear which had gradually been taking form during their passage across the mountains: in New York, his whole concern had been for her comfort and her pleasure; he felt sure that everything he had said to her revealed this, that everything they did bore out the promise of the spoken word and the loving thought behind it. Here in Pittsburgh, for the first time, he had other matters on his mind, and he had dreaded to break this to her, lest she should resent it. Now he was confident she would not. Perhaps later in the day, he told her at breakfast, the morning after their arrival, she would like to go down to the Point. The Point? Lucy repeated, questioningly. Yes, Clyde answered, the meeting place of the Monongahela and Allegheny Rivers, which merged there and formed the Ohio. Pittsburghers were very proud of the Point — they called it their Golden Triangle. She must not expect to find it beautiful, in spite of the wooded hillsides beyond the trivet harbour, for even the mellow sunshine of an Indian Summer day could not prevail against the spreading smudges of furnace and forge. But, such as it was, it was one of the sights of Pittsburgh and he would find time to take her there. First, however, he must go down to the foundry and from there on to the boatyards — it was necessary for him to make connections immediately with various ironmasters, boat builders, shippers and other industrialists. . . .

It did not occur to him that she would care to go with him and she did not suggest it. When he returned to the hotel, late in the evening, he begged her pardon for not rejoining her at dinner time or even sending her a note — some business acquaintances had invited him to join them at Newell's. One topic of conversation had led to another and it was three o'clock before he knew it. Then he realized she would have long since have gone to the dining-room without him. She had not minded at all, she assured him, without making any direct answer about the dining-room; in fact, she had been glad of a chance to ease her conscience by writing a long letter to her mother, whom she had shamefully neglected while in New York. Now she had described everything — the luxurious hotel, the wonderful shops, the theatres and restaurants, all the great sights. Had she told her mother about the wooden Indians, too, Clyde inquired with a grin. Yes indeed, Lucy answered, smiling back at him. Well, this letter had taken her practically all day to write, there had been so much to relate. And when she had posted it, she had sat by the window, looking out at the sunset, which had been very beautiful, and after that, at the flames leaping up from the great furnaces, which gave out a light more beautiful still. She had been entranced, watching it — another new experience. And another thrill, Clyde inquired, still grinning. Yes indeed, she had never imagined anything as gorgeous as that fiery rose colour. Probably he had seen it a dozen times already, so it did not matter much that he had missed it this evening. But she hoped he was not too tired after such a long-wearing day. . . .

He was not tired at all, he assured her. But after remarking that of course it was now too late for visiting the Point, he did not suggest that they should do anything else instead; and, as soon as they had eaten their supper, he sat down at the desk she had used during the day and began to cover sheets of paper with scribbled notes and columns of figures. For a time, Lucy sat quietly beside him, doing some kind of needlework, he did not notice just what; and when he finally raised his head, after prolonged concentration on the sheets before him, he saw that he was alone and realized that he had not looked up, or even known when she left. That was a great way for a bridegroom to behave, he told himself, and hastened to rejoin her. Lucy's response to his sudden need of her seemed as spontaneous and proved as satisfying as ever; neither then nor later did he have any reason to wonder whether in her heart of hearts she had welcomed him as warmly as if he had not left her alone all day and then spent the evening figuring.

The following day was so dark that they could not believe it was already morning when they first woke. In fact, Clyde did not bother to look at his watch until after he had drowsed comfortably for nearly half an hour, he was so certain that it could not possibly be time to get up; then he had to rush off, because otherwise he would have been late for an important appointment. By noon, a steady rain had set in, and by evening, this had become a downpour. Clyde did not forget, again, to send Lucy a message; but this was only to say that he might be even later than the day before in getting back to the hotel. He assumed she would occupy herself with more letters; however, he doubted whether she would care to fill pages and pages, in writing to anyone except her mother, and he wondered, for the first time, whether she kept a diary. Most women did, he believed; and he rather hoped she followed the current custom, for, if she did, she could while away a good many hours in setting down her thoughts, as well as her 'experiences'. He realized that there would be no sunset for her to watch this time and that she would hardly be able to see the flames from the furnaces, either; and, intermittently, he was troubled by the thought of the tedium she was enduring. When, drenched to the skin, he finally rejoined her, he brought her a damp newspaper and pointed to an inconspicuous item, illustrated by the miniscule woodcut of a boat and appearing under the heading, *River Packets*.

'For Memphis and New Orleans——' she read, following his guiding finger, 'the Steamer *Messenger*, Captain Jesse Dean, will leave for the above and intermediate ports on the rise.

'Chriest & Swaney,
'Flack & Collingwood, Agents.'

'Is the *Messenger* the boat we're taking?' she asked.
'Yes, I hope so. If it doesn't leave too soon.'
'But this notice doesn't say when it's going. It only says, "on the rise". I don't understand.'

'You wouldn't, of course. The packets on the Ohio don't have any set schedule, like ocean liners. They go and come as the condition of the river permits. If this rain keeps up, the *Messenger* can get away fairly soon. That means I've got to keep on putting in long days at the foundries and yards, in order to finish up my business here before she pushes off. It also means that if this rain hadn't come, just when it did, we might have missed our connection with the *Richmond*. So maybe you'd better regard the downpour as a blessing in disguise, even if it does keep you cooped up.'

He left her studying the notice and went into the bedroom to shed his wet clothes and take a quick rubdown. She was still reading the paper, with a rather puzzled expression, when he came back, his face glowing, his hair sleek, his linen and broadcloth immaculate.

'Come on down to supper. I need a good hearty meal and I'm sure you do, too. I'll explain to you about the rise – the raise a lot of the older captains call it – while we eat.' Then, when they were pleasantly seated in the big dining-room and had ordered oyster stew and roast beef, he went on, 'Rains hereabouts are seasonal and they have a very important effect on river traffic. Old-timers can tell, by the amount of rainfall, just about how high the river will go. So many inches of rain mean so many feet, correspondingly, in the rise of the river.'

'And they keep official records of just how many inches have fallen?'

'Well, not as accurately or as scientifically as you've told me your grandfather's friend, Thomas Jefferson, used to do it. But there's an old stone gauge at the end of Market Street, marked to show the depth of water, in feet, over the nearest sandbar. Just as soon as it indicates a rise, the waterfront starts to hum. All the commodities that have been stored in warehouses are hurried down there in drays and the loading begins. It was in full swing when I was coming back to the hotel tonight.'

The oyster stew had arrived, rich and creamy, and Clyde went on talking about the busy waterfront while they ate it. When the waiter took away their soup plates and set great slabs of rare roast beef before them, he made a suggestion.

'Perhaps you'd like to try some of our special horse-radish sauce, sir? I don't know whether the lady would care for it, too – it's biting, of course. But it's getting quite a reputation for excellence.'

'I'd like very much to try it. My father always liked horse-radish with his roast beef, and I used to fix it for him myself, because no one else could do it to suit him,' Lucy said. 'Of course I was terribly proud, but I can't pretend that I enjoyed grating the roots – I shed more tears in the process than I ever did peeling onions!' Then, as she helped herself to the relish the waiter presented and tasted it tentatively, she added,

'It *is* good. Much better than mine ever was. I don't wonder you use a lot of it. But I hope your cook gets extra pay for preparing it.'

'The cook gets paid plenty and I'll tell him you like the sauce. But he don't shed no tears over it.' The waiter, who was conversationally inclined, welcomed Lucy's tacit invitation to explain and went rambling on. 'If there's any crying done over this horse-radish, it's way out in Sharpsburg, by a young fellow named Heinz. His people have got a big kitchen garden, same as most of the folks there, and this youngster's been marketing their produce to the grocers, here in town, since quite a while back – gets up at three in the morning, so's he'll be sure to have his stuff here fresh and it can be used the same day he brings it. Well, sir, this kid hit on the idea of grating the horse-radish himself and bottling it; it's all ready to use when he fetches it in, along with his fresh vegetables.'

Lucy was intensely interested. She would like to see those kitchen gardens herself, she said. Perhaps she could even see this wonderful sauce in the process of preparation. If that Heinz boy could drive back and forth every day, Sharpsburg must be near enough for her to visit, easily, in the course of a carriage ride. Certainly it should be, Clyde agreed; as soon as they had finished supper, he would make inquiries about the availability of a suitable vehicle for her. If there were one, and the weather cleared, she could have a pleasant side trip; he was only sorry that he could not go with her, but he would have to be in Shousetown all day.

'Shousetown?'

'Yes, sixteen miles down the Ohio River. There's a big boatyard there where steamboat hulls are built and the framing. Afterward, they're towed to Pittsburgh for their boilers and machinery and the cabin finishing.'

Inquiries at the office resulted in a favourable reply; there was no reason why a suitable carriage and a fine pair of horses with a reliable driver should not be available for Mrs. Batchelor at any time. The clerk did not think there was much to see, especially so late in the season, though he supposed some harvesting was still going on; but if the lady wanted to go to Sharpsburg, it was perfectly feasible – that is, if the rain stopped. If it did not, he would hardly advise the undertaking; the roads would be terribly muddy, the horses might flounder, the carriage might get stuck. . . .

The next morning Lucy confessed to Clyde that, every time she wakened during the night, she had raised her head and listened, and that she had been a little disappointed because she had continued to hear the steady beat of rain, mingled with all the other sounds. 'Of course that Heinz boy must go back and forth every day, no matter what the weather is,' she added rather wistfully. 'I could, too,

73

if I knew the road the way he does, or if a city coachman and his horses——'

'But you don't and they don't,' Clyde said firmly. 'I'd worry about you all day.'

'Why, Clyde, I'm used to country roads! I've ridden over them all my life.'

'On horseback. Over familiar roads. That's different. I'm sorry for your disappointment, darling. I know you must dread another long monotonous day. On the other hand, the harder it rains, the fewer you'll have of them. I'll go and talk with Danny MacAleer while I'm out and see what he thinks our prospects are.'

'Who's Danny MacAleer?'

'Pittsburgh's unofficial weather prophet. My own guess is that there have been even harder rains above here, and that the river has risen already enough for a light-water boat. But the *Messenger*'ll need more than that.'

'How much?'

'I don't know exactly, but Danny does by this time. I'll tell you when I get home.'

'Four feet and a half,' he informed her that evening, adding triumphantly that Danny had confirmed his own guess about the amount of the previous rise. Even if there were no more rain—and it did seem to be clearing at last—the *Messenger* would be able to leave early on Saturday—the announcement was in the evening paper. Saturday would suit him to a T; he would have just time enough to wind up his own affairs. Lucy surprised him by responding that, before they left, she would like very much to see a foundry and boatyard herself; could he manage to take her the next day, if that would be their last one in Pittsburgh? Why yes, he supposed he could, as far as time went, Clyde said hesitantly; but she would find a foundry terribly dirty. Her feet would sink down into the deep black sand which covered the stone floors; she would not be able to keep her hoops clear of it and she would ruin her white stockings; besides, she would be stumbling over crude castings with every step she took; she might very well hurt herself. She was very sure-footed, Lucy replied with spirit; moreover, she was not afraid of showing her ankles in a good cause and she had plenty of stockings. And wouldn't she see anything at all that would make up for the dirt? Why yes, Clyde said again, still more hesitatingly, she might find the wooden patterns interesting; and when the pouring began, the molten metal, flowing from the great ladle into the moulds, was really a gorgeous sight. Well then! Lucy persisted. But Clyde was persistent, too. It was not customary for ladies to go into foundries, he told her. The workmen went about half-clad, or rather less than that; her presence would be a source of embarrassment, both to them and to her; and anyway, he was sure the grime would make more of an impression on her than anything else. He would admit that they might live to see iron make men richer than all the gold in California. However, that was far in the future. . . .

In the end she yielded, but he sensed her disappointment and blamed himself for it. Everything he had told her was true and yet, as had happened before about more important matters, he had not told her the whole truth. He could have given warning of her coming so that the men might be prepared; he could have arranged to have her arrive at the foundry just when the pouring, which always occurred at a fixed time, was about to begin; and he could have placed her advantageously, in order that she could see the 'really gorgeous sight' without walking so far that she would ruin her stockings or expose her ankles. Then, as soon as the pouring was over, he could have told her there was nothing more to see and taken her away. But he was afraid that some chance remark which she might overhear, or which might even be addressed to her, would give away his precious secret, no matter how careful he was to caution everyone beforehand. So many of his secrets were disgraceful that he hugged all the more closely to his heart this one whose disclosure would be a source of pride and not a source of shame. They would be coming to Pittsburgh again, she could go to a foundry some other time. Decidedly, it was better that she should not do so now.

He tried to convince himself that this reasoning was sound; but he did not succeed very well; and the next morning he said there was hardly time to go to a foundry now anyway, as he must return to Shousetown and this was practically an all-day trip — it involved taking the Pittsburgh and Fort Wayne Railway from Alleghany City after crossing over the Federal Street bridge, riding sixteen miles on the train, getting out at Shousetown Lane and then crossing the river again by ferry. However, if she really wanted to see a boatyard, here was her chance.

She fell in readily with his suggestion, making no further reference to the foundry, but chatting merrily about various inconsequential things. Once arrived at the boatyard, Clyde placed a chair for her in the shelter of a tool shed, spreading his fine linen handkerchief over the period seat. She sat there for a long time, sniffing the pungent odour of chips and shavings: oakum and tar, and watching him while he clambered agilely into a skeletal structure of hewn yellow timbers, which looked like a mammoth rib cage. Men with adzes were skilfully flaking away bright chips of oak from this and its heavy beams rang to the stroke of metal. Eventually he returned to her, accompanied by a rather foppish-looking young man, whom he presented as Mr. Cyrus

Thatcher, one of the establishment's office staff. Mr. Thatcher had sleek mouse-coloured hair, which merged from his temples into side-burns and from these into a moustache, forming a single unbroken curve across his countenance, and not a lock of this curve was out of place. His coat sleeves were carefully protected by black bombazine sleevelets and he wore a stiff collar so high that when he turned his head he, perforce, turned his body as well. He bowed formally to Mrs. Batchelor and, after a few stereotyped remarks about the weather and the wonderful progress of Pittsburgh, produced a small leather-bound notebook from his pocket and jotted down entries in it, while Clyde talked to him about matters which were quite unintelligible to Lucy. For the most part, Mr. Thatcher nodded in agreement, but once or twice he embarked on a long involved argument. This went on for some minutes; then Mr. Thatcher bowed again, even more formally than the first time, and begged Mrs. Batchelor to excuse him : he was needed at the office and – if he might be pardoned the suggestion – it would perhaps be well if Mr. Batchelor accompanied him. But first, they would conduct her to the home of Mr. Porter, he added, indicating the owner's large white frame house on the hill behind the boatyard. Mr. and Mrs. Porter would be delighted to receive Mrs. Batchelor – in fact, they were expecting her. He was sure she would take pleasure in meeting them, too. . . .

When Clyde came to fetch her, some time later, he found her seated at a table lavishly spread for tea, in the company of her genial hosts. Her enjoyment was so obvious that he reproached himself for his neglect of her. He had never taken her to the tony dining-room at the Union Depot, as he had promised to do, or even to Mrs. Morgan's Place, beside the Sixth Street bridge, for ice cream; and though several of the ironmasters and shippers with whom he had spent his days had suggested that he should bring Mrs. Batchelor to their homes for supper, saying that their wives would be glad to meet her, he had de-clined all these invitations. Probably that had been a mistake. Pittsburgh was noted for its hearty hospitality and the huge houses of its solid citizens were well suited to dispense this. Besides, a good many im-portant business transactions could be satisfactorily consummated when the gentlemen 'repaired to the library' after the evening meal, leaving the ladies to chat in a more refined and less significant manner amidst the cluttering elegances of the draped and festooned parlour. But he had wanted to spend his evenings figuring, he had seen enough of the solid citizens during the course of the day and had preferred to be alone with Lucy, and he had been obsessed with anxiety lest she should be told something he did not want her to hear. Even now, the Porters had difficulty in persuading him to join them at the tea table. This time, however, he saw the impossibility of refusing and, to his great

76

relief, his secret was still safe when he and Lucy bade the hospitable couple good night and went down the hill again.

It was dark now and the night shift had already begun its work by torchlight. This yard — and in fact most of those in the Pittsburgh area — was operating at full capacity, Clyde told Lucy on their way to the ferry, and still none of these could keep up with their orders; the men she saw at work now were getting double wages because of the hours they kept. The yard could well afford to pay them. Of course there were plenty of people who went around predicting that the great days of steamboating were over, that the war had precipitated the ruin which the railroads had already begun. He thought that even the brief glimpse she had had of the activities that evening would convince her such gloomy prophets were mistaken. To be sure, the gunboats had temporarily driven the floating palaces of ante-bellum days off the Mississippi. But bigger and better boats were being built now than ever before and business was booming again. She would see. . . .

He had to admit that she could not be expected to visualize this resurgence of past glories when they went aboard the *Messenger* early the next morning. The waterfront was actually more drab and dirty than the rest of the city and it rang with a greater confusion of sounds than the streets around the Union Depot. He was obliged to help her dodge among the drays, laden with glassware and ironware, bales of paper and cases of whisky; and when they finally reached the gangplank, they were harried by a disreputable gang of water rats who lounged nearby to watch the passengers embark and to make ribald remarks about them. Lucy had said, two days earlier, that she did not mind showing her ankles in a good cause and Clyde knew she had meant it then; now, as she lifted her long skirt to clear its hem of the befouled planking, he realized that she was shuddering inwardly, less because of the filth which surrounded her than because of the coarse jests and rude oglings which her passage provoked.

He had hoped that matters would improve once they were aboard the *Messenger*; but he saw, almost immediately, that this was not the sort of packet which he would have chosen for Lucy's first river trip. A three piece 'orchestra' was assailing a tune which might once have been 'Robin Adair', but which retained little resemblance to it; a singularly unattractive crowd of passengers jostled them as they made their way up the grand staircase to the boiler deck; and the clerk in the little office at the left of the uncarpeted entrance regarded them nonchalantly and tossed them a key to the stateroom he said had been assigned to them, without adding that he hoped they would be comfortable and that their trip would be a pleasant one. As they walked past the pot-bellied stove and down the long saloon, where the tables were already set for dinner, Clyde's doubts about the merits of the *Messenger* increased; and when he opened the door of the stateroom, 'Maine', and saw the two narrow bunks, the built-in shelf equipped with bowl and pitcher and the three-legged stools which cramped the inadequate space beside these bunks, his disappointment deepened into acute displeasure.

'There's some terrible mistake, darling. Of course I engaged the bridal suite. It won't be luxurious, on this boat, but it ought to be a lot better than a hole like this. Just wait here for a few minutes, will you? If the porters arrive with our baggage before I come back, tell them to leave it outside in the saloon—here's some money to tip them with. A steward can look after our things later.'

He hurried off, leaving Lucy seated on the straight chair, and made his way back to the office. The clerk, who had been merely nonchalant before, now became close to insolent, in Clyde's prejudiced opinion. Yes, he knew that Mr. Batchelor had specified the bridal suite; but it so happened that a cousin of the captain's was on her wedding journey, too. She and her husband—the son of Captain Dean's minister—were already installed in the quarters Mr. Batchelor wanted—in fact, they had come on board late the night before and were not even up yet, the clerk added with a slight leer. Of course Mr. Batchelor would be entitled to a rebate on his fare; the clerk would give the matter his attention when he was not so busy. At the moment he was fully occupied with other arrivals.

Unless he created a scene, which he had excellent reasons for not wanting to do, Clyde was powerless. With an inward vow that the clerk, the captain and the usurping couple should all have reason to regret what they had done, he returned to Lucy. Their baggage had all been neatly stowed away and she was standing by the door to the deck, looking out of the small, four-paned window. She came forward at once and handed him most of the money he had given her.

'The porters didn't expect so much,' she said. 'I didn't know what was fair, of course, so I asked them, and they told me. You're much too generous with everyone, Clyde—it's your one fault. They objected to putting the baggage down on the carpet of the saloon—said it would get them into trouble—so I thought I'd better let them bring it in, after all. This *is* our room, isn't it? Well, I think the arrangement of those bunks is very amusing. It would have been something like this, wouldn't it, on that night train we didn't take? Do you remember how you laughed at me because you thought I wouldn't like dressing and undressing on a sleeper? Now you'll have a chance to laugh a lot more, because I'll have to do it on this boat! But I don't care how many jokes you crack at my expense, because I think we're *both* going to have fun! And anyway, we don't have to spend all our time in our stateroom. Of course you'll want to be in the bar, with other men, part of each day, and I'll want to meet some of the ladies on board.

I'm sure there must be at least a few I'd find very congenial, even if we haven't seen any who looked as if they might be. Right now, I want to see what's happening outside and I can't, very well, from here. Why don't we stay on deck until dinner's ready?'

He could not tell her that he had counted on the bridal suite not only for comfort, but for seclusion. In the spacious quarters which he had envisioned, they could have spent practically all their time; but it was unthinkable that they should do so in this miserable little state-room. They would have to go out on deck, there was no help for it; and, for a short time, Lucy's naïve pleasure in the various sights around them diverted his thoughts from their unwelcome trend. She was much intrigued by the gilded sphere, surmounting a high pole, which was the *Messenger's* most extraordinary adornment; and she listened, with eager interest, to Clyde's explanation that nearly all the river packets carried some ornament characteristic of their captain's taste—usually anchors, globes or stars set in rings, but in one instance a mammoth white hat, modelled on the strange headpiece which the master him-self wore. She was greatly fascinated by the various bell strokes, sig-nalling—as Clyde also explained—that the boat was about to take her departure. Then, once they were underway, the changing pattern of the brown water, laced with creamy foam, as this was swept back from the bow, held her rapt attention. However, the *Messenger* had hardly started downstream when they were subjected to exactly the sort of an ordeal which Clyde had been dreading.

They were standing side by side, with their elbows resting on the white rail of the forward guard, when someone behind them said, in a smooth voice, 'Your pardon, sir. Your pardon, madam.' Lucy, slightly startled, whirled about with a little cry of astonishment. Clyde, turning more deliberately, saw a slim, fashionably dressed man standing before them, his beaver hat held at the level of his waist as he bowed.

'Colonel Ballou?' the interloper began, with a slight rising inflection.

'No, sir. Batchelor is the name,' Clyde answered—with extraordinary coolness, considering that, inwardly, he was far more perturbed than Lucy.

'And mine is Fanchon, Major André Fanchon of New Orleans.' The stranger waited a moment, evidently hoping that Clyde would present him to Lucy, and then bowed again. 'I apologize if I have made a mistake. But I could have sworn that we were fellow passengers on the *Eclipse* in Fifty-nine or Sixty. I realize that is quite a while back, but still——'

'I assure you that you have made a mistake in thinking that I am— who was it? Oh, yes—a certain Colonel Ballou. As I said, the name is Batchelor, Clyde Batchelor.'

'Then the resemblance to the gentleman whom I had the honour of knowing is most amazing. Possibly you have a half-brother or an own cousin——'

'I regret that I am not fortunate to have either. And now, if you will excuse me . . .'

He offered his arm to Lucy. She slipped her hand through it and turned compliantly away, but not before saying, 'Good morning, Major Fanchon.' For the first time, the indestructible quality of her courtesy was annoying to Clyde. He had certainly made it plain enough that he wished to have nothing to do with the man who had approached them, both by his failure to include his wife in the conversation and by his own curtness—and still she had spoken as pleasantly to the blackguard as if he were a long lost friend! Clyde guided her toward their stateroom in much the same manner that he had betrayed when she innocently suggested the trip to St. Louis at their festive dinner. But before they reached it, he realized that, for the second time, he was completely unjust. Of course there had been mutual recognition between Fanchon and himself. He had indeed travelled on the *Eclipse* in Sixty—in the guise of a colonel from Alabama by the name of Melvin Ballou; it had been one of his most successful rôles. Clyde and Fanchon, who was posing as a cotton factor, had, between them, made a very considerable killing. He even remembered the bumptious young Creole, eager to prove himself a mettlesome man of the world, who had been their principal victim, and with whom they had dealt so adroitly that he blamed himself and not them when he disembarked with a heavy heart and a light purse. He must follow Fanchon at once and have it out with him.

'If you'll excuse me, my dear,' Clyde said abruptly, as they reached the threshold of their stateroom. Then, realizing that he must say something more, he added, 'I've a notion you're right, as usual. I ought to spend a little time in the bar, now and then. This seems a good moment. You look rather tired. I'm sure a short rest would do you good.'

He kissed Lucy hurriedly, and left her, inwardly cursing his inadequacy. Then he hastened off toward the doorway through which Major Fanchon had just passed, conscious of Lucy's troubled and bewildered glance. He passed rapidly through the main saloon, by the ladies who were already gathered about the stove, to the masculine bailiwick, flanked on one side by the office of the clerk, who had dealt with him in so summary a fashion, and on the other by the alcove, bridged by a counter and backed by a mirror, which served as the bar. Here a brass rail, sadly in need of polish, was raised above the floor on iron supports; and four or five passengers were using this as a foot rest, while they tossed off the drams which the bartender drew from a whisky keg.

Clyde saw, with relief, that the man he sought was not only among these early customers, but that he was standing near the end of the counter, where he could most easily be approached.

'I'd like a word with you, in private, at your earliest convenience,' Clyde said abruptly.

The ready response to this demand was accompanied by a wave of the hand toward the counter. 'No time or place like the present,' the man replied cordially. 'Perhaps you'd join me in a dram – the bottled whisky, of course. I've been hoping you'd see your way to——'

'I said a word *in private*,' Clyde repeated. 'I suggest the guard, forward. It appears to be deserted at the moment.'

'Small wonder. It's the chilliest spot aboard. But as you wish. Pray lead the way. I'll follow.'

Clyde stalked away from the bar, drawing his coat more closely about him by its flared lapels when he reached the open deck. Then he wheeled around and faced the interloper who had presented himself to the bridal couple as Major Fanchon.

'I've called you out here to tell you that you made a great mistake in speaking to me at all and a second one, even greater, in addressing me as Ballou, which is not my name,' Clyde said coldly. 'There must be no repetition of these mistakes. You will therefore oblige me, Pettigrew, by not approaching or addressing me again, whether I am alone or in company.'

'Fanchon's the name, now. Major Fanchon, from New Orleans. And I'm a thinkin' that if there's a mistake, I'm not the one that's making it. Hear me, now. There's a soap-lock from Ohio aboard, milk-fed, pump and prime for plucking. Naturally, we'd have to keep our eyes peeled for Dean, because he's the kind of captain who acts like steamboatin' and Sunday-schoolin' are one and the same. But the bartender's our cove. I tell you, it's a rich thing for true. There'd be enough for a tall poke of sparklers for the lady who——'

'I earnestly urge you not to make a third mistake, Pettigrew!'

'Fanchon, I said. And if I should not choose to accommodate my druthers to this psalm-singing play of yours?'

'That would be unfortunate. I might let the authorities at Helena know some interesting facts about the killing of a deputy marshal there in Sixty. I think it was Sixty – anyway, it was at the time of that trip on the *Eclipse* to which you referred. . . . Or I might find ways of irritating you into attacking me before witnesses, so that I could kill you – in self-defence. I think there is no need to remind you, Pettigrew, that I am a man of my word.'

'*Fanchon*, dammit to hell! I suppose you realize I could rig the same description of saw on you, since I've got your notions. That makes us even – Steven.'

'Not quite. I've never killed anyone — yet.'

For a moment they looked steadily at each other. Then Fanchon's eyes shifted before Clyde's steely stare. He managed to shrug his shoulders, but the sneering reply he meant to make died on his lips. Instead, he spoke almost civilly.

'I see no profit for either one of us in further talk. I bid you good day, Mr. Batchelor.'

'Good day to you — Major Fanchon.'

Well, that had been that, and there had been no further trouble on board the *Messenger* with Fanchon or anyone else of his stripe. But Clyde had had no assurance of this, and the uncertainty kept him on edge, and made him an easy prey for general dissatisfaction. He had travelled the Ohio before, and had thought it deserving of its Indian name for beautiful river; but that had been at a season when its well-wooded banks were green, not when the stark branches of the trees were leafless against a grey sky and the grass beneath them was dun coloured. A cold east wind blew persistently and, from time to time, there were little flurries of snow; it was far too chilly to sit on deck, or even to walk there, for long periods. Indoors, conditions were not much better. The early dinner was bountiful, but it was unimaginative and sloppily served. The food was heavy and greasy and most of it was lukewarm when it was set before them; though Lucy made no comment, Clyde was conscious of her surprise at its mediocrity and at the multiplicity of the small oval dishes set down around her.

'This is the foundering meal you're getting — and of course served steamboat style,' he whispered to her. 'Dean's one of the captains that gives orders he doesn't want an inch of tablecloth showing on the first dinner aboard. The more shells, the finer the feast; the more indigestion afterward, the less interest in future meals. At least, that's his idea.'

'Foundering? Shells?'

'Yes. The passengers are supposed to be so full after dinner that they can be compared to a foundering ship and these bird baths with potatoes in one and beets in another and peas in another and corn in another are called shells.'

'They must make a lot of extra dish-washing for somebody.'

'He doesn't worry about that.'

'Then I don't understand——'

She did not finish the sentence; but he saw her hesitate when the man on her other side passed her the butter dish and she realized there was no butter knife on it, that she was expected to cut into the pat with her own, as everyone else at the table was doing. Her bewilderment was natural, of course; one butter knife, more or less, could not possibly have mattered to the members of the cabin crew who were washing hundreds of shells. But Captain Dean's pride was centred on dishes rather than cutlery and, as a matter of fact, Clyde did not believe that anyone at the table, except Lucy and himself, had minded, or even noticed, the omission which had offended his bride's sense of suitability. In spite of the hopes Lucy had expressed, their fellow passengers seemed to be a rather sorry lot and their table companions among the sorriest of these: two New England cotton buyers, evidently brothers, whose prominent Adam's apples bulged above their celluloid collars and whose chapped hands had the look of being perpetually blue with cold; a tow-headed young man – less ministerial than bucolic in aspect, in spite of his black clothes – accompanied by a pale, flat-chested young woman and a sullen, pasty-faced child; a massive matron whose 'waterfall' was matched by a rippling cascade of chins and who was corseted like an ironclad; and a faded, silly lady of fashion, with unnaturally bright patches of colour on her wrinkled cheeks and too many rings, each of little value, on her bony, veined hands. The black-clad young man betrayed his clerical calling by asking a detailed and sonorous grace, while the stewards waited with laden arms and in obvious impatience for the 'Amen!' which would permit them to unburden themselves. The child squirmed in his seat and refused to eat anything put before him; and the pale, flat-chested young woman pleaded in vain with him and looked appealingly toward her husband for help, also to no avail. The cotton buyers bolted their food with hardly a word to each other and none to anyone else; then pushed back their chairs and disappeared in the direction of the bar. On the other hand, the massive matron and the faded lady of fashion chatted incessantly. Before the *Messenger* had been under way many hours, they had already sized up one of their fellow passengers to her distinct disadvantage.

'That Madame Pourrien and her three nieces!' the massive matron said gloatingly. 'You'd think, to hear her brag about their "refinement", that butter'd be too brash to melt for them. Nieces, indeed! Baggages, every one of them. She's got them herded into their staterooms and has ordered all their vittles sent there. There's nothing green in my eye and I give you gracious leave to tell her I say so. Nieces!'

'Shameless!' agreed the gentlewoman. 'But that is what one must put up with in these times, yes. Ah, I tell you fr-r-r-ankly, me, you should see them on the Esplanade in the evening, driving by in so shining carriages, with an audacity you would not believe, no. I must explain you it is for *réclame*, so that *tout le monde* can observe how new nieces, them, have make arrival at the house of Tante Frou-Frou. I tell my husband, him, we must to move from the Esplanade, we have young girls in the family who should not see such things, no, never, them. But he does not wish to move to where *les Américains* live. I say that is fine biffo the war, yes, but with the *bêtes* of carpet-baggers taking over everything, even the St. Louis Hotel, them, better we should live among *les Américains* who are not Yankees, no.'

She glanced in the direction of Lucy, as if to put her in that hated category. Lucy returned the look smilingly, but steadily, and turned to Clyde.

'What did you tell me your friend Madame Surget's maiden name was, dear?' she inquired. 'Oh yes, Randolph. I didn't realize before there were any Randolphs in Louisiana. So few members of the Cavalier families have married among the Creoles. And, of course, next to the Lees——'

Again she left the sentence unfinished. But, as she rose, she bowed pleasantly to the two women who were regarding her speechlessly.

'We shall look forward to seeing you again at supper,' she said, taking Clyde's arm. 'And at the concert afterward. There is a concert, isn't there?'

With some slight confusion, they assured her that there would be a concert and that they were also looking forward to the evening. Then there was a moment of comparative silence as they watched the un-hurried departure of the bridal couple before they began their whispering again.

'Of course they're talking about us now,' Lucy said unconcernedly, when Clyde and she were out of earshot. 'I gave myself away by not knowing about the shells, so they realized right off I'd never been on a river boat before. And I'm afraid you and I don't act or look like people who've been married a long time. But do you care? I don't! I think half the fun of being a bride is having women like that jealous.'

'Why, Lucy! I wouldn't have believed it of you! But then I wouldn't have believed you'd put "women like that" in their places with one quite casual remark, either. I had no idea——'

'That I had a sense of humour? Or that I could be malicious about anything? Or that you'd have a good time with me? I mean, even when we weren't in fairyland, even when we weren't making love? Why, Clyde, that was terribly short-sighted of you! If we couldn't have a good time together, whatever happened, it wouldn't have been worthwhile getting married.'

'Well, I'm ready to take oath it was worthwhile,' he assured her, with conviction.

He had done nothing to relieve the monotony of her days in Pittsburgh, but somehow she beguiled the tedium of the afternoon and the

84

banality of the evening for him. She was not very good at games, he knew that already, she reminded him; but sometimes, in bad weather, she had played chess with her father, who always won and who enjoyed it. Perhaps Clyde would enjoy it, too? The chess game, which he did win, but with enough effort to make it interesting, lasted until early evening, and afterward, Lucy said she would like to see the pilot-house and have some of its mysteries explained to her; when Clyde took her there, she seemed to grasp its functions without difficulty. At supper, she dealt gently but efficiently with the sullen child, whose parents still seemed cowed by him, and entered easily, both as a listener and a talker, into the conversation, which had become more general than at dinner time. The tow-headed young man identified himself as the Reverend Thaddeus Willswood, only recently ordained and on his way to Arkansas, where he had been called to ride a circuit of churches out of Marked Tree. His wife, Maria, had formerly taught at the district school in the village near his father's farm. The cotton buyers were less autobiographical, but divulged the hope, which came as a surprise from such a quarter, that they might be able to organize a quartette. The massive matron and the faded gentlewoman continued their comments on their fellow-passengers, though less acidly than before; evidently Lucy's comment on the Randolphs had not been without its effect. Clyde was still glowing with secret pride as he accompanied her to the inevitable concert and sat beside her during four-handed pianoforte versions of 'The Battle of Prague' and 'The Last Link is Broken', followed by an elocutionary proclamation, with appropriate gestures, to the effect that 'It was the schooner Hesperus that sailed the wintry sea'. When the concert was over, Lucy said that, in view of the early hour they had been up that morning, she thought they should consider it was now bedtime; and, after an exchange of half-serious, half-jesting remarks about their 'separation', Clyde clambered into the upper berth and settled down for the night more philosophically than he would have believed possible.

He was wakened from his first deep sleep by the consciousness that the boat was no longer moving. There were none of the sounds which presaged the normal approach to some regular landing, and his long acquaintaince with every form of possible disaster on inland waterways made him immediately alert. He did not want to alarm Lucy needlessly and, at the same time, he felt he would be unforgivably careless if he did not investigate the cause of the boat's interrupted progress. The stateroom was provided with no light except that which came in through the transom; but his eyes were accustomed to such dimness and, after focusing his gaze carefully on his watch, he was able to make out the time. It was just after midnight. Of course it was possible that the engineer had decided to strengthen the strap iron to one of the pitmans, before proceeding farther, but this was unlikely at such an hour, unless the *Messenger* were actually in danger of 'running through herself'. Perhaps a valve on the 'doctor' that fed water to the boilers might have jammed, or a bearing might be running hot. In fact, any one of a dozen minor mishaps might have occurred, which could be remedied on the spot, without dockyard facilities. However, he would not feel easy until he knew exactly what had happened. Moving as quietly as he could, in the hope that he would not disturb Lucy, he slid to the floor. But she was already awake.

'Is something the matter, Clyde?'

'I don't think so. But I'm going to find out. Don't worry. I'll be right back, whatever it is.'

He had slipped into his trousers and slipped a coat over his night-shirt while he was speaking. The saloon was empty and quiet when he entered it; there were no signs of excitement or sounds of confusion anywhere. He had almost reached the bar before he even saw anyone; then he encountered a solitary member of the cabin crew, sweeping up some broken bottles.

'What's happened?' he inquired curtly.

The man stared at him blankly for a moment and then gave a cackling laugh. 'Ain' nuthin' happened,' he croaked ' 'ceptin' that Cap'n William alluz wants we should choke a stump on Sundays, him, and Captain Jesse, being his brother, humours him. Likely you ain' never travelled with him before. Come midnight Saturday, he just pull up to de bank, wherever us is, and stay dere till de nextes' midnight. Yassuh. Has services in de saloon, too. Just like us was ashore in a sho' nuff church. Hymns and preachin' and all de rest. *Yassuh!*'

'. . . And we're not even to Wheeling yet,' Clyde told Lucy disgustedly, slamming the stateroom door after him. 'At this rate, we'll spend the rest of our lives on the Ohio River.'

'Hush, dear! You'll wake up everyone. . . . Does this mean we'll miss our connection with the *Richmond*?'

'It could, very well. But we did have a couple of days to spare, if I reckoned right.'

'And you said I wouldn't like the wait in Cairo anyway.'

'Kay-ro, darling. You're not in Egypt or even in a Select Southern Seminary for Young Ladies. You're in the Middle West, where people don't see any reason why you shouldn't pronounce "ai" the same way in the name of a town that you pronounce it in rain and pain.'

'All right, I'll try to be logical. But however you pronounce the name of this town, you said it was a horrid little hole with mud even on the walls of the houses.'

'Well, yes. Cairo's pretty mucky — two big rivers overflow it every spring. The first people who tried to settle there gave it up as a bad job and so did a second set of pioneers. But it looks as if the third lot were going to hang on. I think they deserve some credit.'

'Of course they do. And I don't suppose that Jamestown, or even Richmond looked like much when they weren't any older than Cairo. But since that isn't very attractive – yet – aren't we just as well off on the *Messenger* as we would be there? And if we've got two days to spare, and the captain's only stopping for one, why shouldn't we still make our connection?'

'Lucy, you're altogether too logical now.'

'I'm sorry.'

'And altogether too lovely.'

'I'm glad.'

Sunday was not as bad as he had expected, after all. Captain Dean read from the Scriptures with the ease of long familiarity and the young Methodist clergyman preached a simple, but rather moving sermon. Although plenty of the passengers had been ready with sentimental songs, it appeared that not many knew the good old hymns; and when volunteers were called for, Lucy hesitantly said she would try to play them, if there were really no one else, and Clyde derived the same pleasure from seeing her at the piano on the *Messenger* that he had when he saw her, similarly engaged, at Sorrento. Under the influence of her persuasive touch, the saloon was presently ringing to the sound of 'Onward, Christian Soldiers' and 'All Hail the Power of Jesu's Name', with everyone joining in the chorus. Thus encouraged, she consented to play again later in the day, a different kind of hymn – 'Abide with Me' and 'Lead, Kindly Light' and everyone joined in those, too, with the happy result that, the first tensions having thus been eased, the passengers seemed on better terms all around. They began to pace the decks with each other and to call each other's attention to points of interest along the river bank; and by Monday they had begun to coalesce into various intimate groups. Games of every sort were in progress; the New England cotton buyers had organized a male quartette; and an informal sewing circle, whose members cheerily exchanged patterns and gossip, met in the ladies' parlour every morning. Though Clyde's obvious reluctance to have Lucy leave him prevented her from joining this regularly, she did so occasionally, overriding his objections by insisting that she wanted to be friends with everyone and renewing her suggestion that he should spend more time with other men.

'I don't want to spend more time with other men. All most of them do is to lounge around on the main deck and shoot their guns at anything they feel like trying to hit, from driftwood to ducks. The exception's a man who lies in his berth all day, playing a fiddle. His

room-mate's nearly crazy, and some of the passengers have bribed the
stewards to keep closing his door. You don't suppose I'd enjoy being
with him, do you?'

'No, but——'

'I want to spend all my time with you. I'm sorry you don't feel the
same way about spending all yours with me,' he said, almost accus-
ingly. Then, as she protested, half-playfully, half-seriously, that he
was not being fair, he added, 'Never mind me, darling. I seem to be
getting up on the wrong side of the bed these days—not that there's
more than one side I can get out, from that horrible little bunk. And
then you're not in it, which makes matters all the worse. Of course
I want you to be friendly, but you can be friendly for both of us, since
I'm such an unsociable cuss. And you can't make me believe that most
of those old cats are really congenial to you. What about that war-
horse at our table? Mrs. Goldthwaite, is that her name? And her
Creole side-kick, Madame LeFevre? Judging from the remarks they
make at meals, they never heard that charity's a virtue.'

'W-e-ll, I admit those two do gossip a good deal. But most of the
others——'

'Never mind about the others. What do those two gossip about?'

He caught the look of surprise on her face. He should not have shot
the question at her like that. No wonder she was astonished. She must
be asking herself why on earth he should be interested in the malicious
chit-chat of the sewing circle. But it was too late now to bite back these
words.

'W-e-ll,' she said again. 'That young Methodist clergyman, for instance—the one who sits at our table and preached such a nice sermon.
They claim he isn't an ordained minister of the Gospel at all.'

'Any more than Madame Pourrien's young charges are really her
nieces?' Clyde answered, his reply a half-question. 'I rather like him,
though I don't care much for the way he says grace. Somehow he
sounds as if he were asking the Almighty's blessing on just our group
and leaving all the others to their fate. However, they apparently don't
realize their peril; they always begin eating without waiting for him
to finish and what with the clattering dishes, I doubt if they even hear
him.'

'Clyde! You shouldn't joke about a thing like that!'

'You're right, I shouldn't. . . . Well, at that, it's quite possible he's
an impostor. . . . What else?' Now that he had made the mistake of
beginning, it would be better to have the thing out.

'They talked a good deal about a young man from Dayton, Percival
Fremont, I think his name is. Not in a very complimentary way, either.
They describe his as being "all scent and soaplocks", whatever that
means. It seems his father's the owner of a big stove foundry, that

he's taking a lavish cargo of castings down to New Orleans and that he has "a pocketful of rocks in his jeans". However, Mrs. Goldthwaite seems to think he won't have the "rocks" much longer, because he's been playing cards or dicing every day and far into the night and because——'

'Yes?'

'Because most of the time Major Fanchon's playing or dicing with him. The — the gentleman who spoke to you just after we left Pittsburgh. I haven't seen him since, except at a distance. Perhaps you wouldn't remember.'

'Yes, I remember. What about him?'

'He's another person the gossips insist isn't who he's pretending to be. They say he claims to be a New Orleans sugar factor and that he's really nothing but a professional gambler with a very bad record for — well, for cheating. And — and fighting, too. They say they wouldn't be a bit surprised if Captain Dean put him off the boat.'

For the first time, Clyde made no immediate answer. Lucy, whose look of surprise had gradually faded, went on of her own accord, after a moment's pause.

'I thought you were rather cool to him, Clyde, that morning. To tell the truth, I felt you were almost uncivil. But of course I realized there must be some good reason. Now I think I know what it is.'

He swallowed hard. Perhaps the moment for which he had waited, the moment for full confession, had come already, sooner than he expected. He had known for a long while now that Lucy had married him for love and not for money; but neither had she married him for his past. Their marriage would survive that knowledge; he knew this, too. But he was still uncertain whether her love could do so. And that love, a kind which he had never dreamed would be his portion, was the one thing he did not dare to hazard on any chance. Not yet. Unless someone else had betrayed him, he would continue to keep his shameful secret. But it was quite possible that such betrayal had occurred already. He attempted a laugh, not very successfully.

'And in the midst of all this scandal, you haven't heard anything slanderous — about us, have you? Overheard, rather — naturally, those old harpies wouldn't say anything to your face.'

'Oh, but they have! Not slanderous things, nice things! Of course they spotted us right away as a honeymoon couple; but that was my fault, showing how bewildered I was by a dinner served steamboat style. If I hadn't done that, perhaps it wouldn't have occurred to them it was strange you didn't spend most of your time playing cards and telling stories in the bar. But I roused their suspicions. As Mrs. Goldthwaite put it, "Any man who would stay by his wife, like he was a sick kitten and she was a hot brick, even when one of those scrawny

Canterbury sisters is clawing the keys out of that poor old piano, is either a honeymooner or a saint. And I'm telling you Colonel Batchelor is a sight too good looking for a saint".'

Lucy's mimicry of the old gossip ended in a laugh, as carefree as Clyde's had been forced. He had realized, from the beginning, that her disposition was unusually even and pleasant, but he had thought of it as grave rather than gay; since their marriage, its sunniness had seemed to increase from day to day and it had remained entirely unaffected by his recent irritability, of which, indeed, she seemed quite unconscious. Apparently, she derived pleasure from even the most commonplace sight: a snow-mantled river bank, a sky streaked with turquoise and crimson at sunset, a flight of wild geese in V-shaped formation, a stop at some landing where tides of arriving and departing passengers met and eddied and freight was carried ashore by shuffling roustabouts. The *Messenger* had been rounding out from Cincinnati while they were talking, and she had stood watching the scene as intently as if the docks at Pittsburgh and Wheeling and Marietta had not already acquainted her with its basic pattern. The night was dark and such light as there was came from the torch baskets, which had been thrust into the river bank, near the gangplank, by means of the long rods to which they were attached. The fire in these baskets had been kindled with pine knots to which resin was added; and now the flames leaped high about the iron holders. In their fitful glow, the shawled figures of the roustabouts were now vivid, now obscure. There was something eerie about the sight; and the mournful chant which accompanied the 'coon-jining' made it all the more uncanny. Lucy watched it with fascination.

'Mrs. Goldthwaite kept calling you "my handsome Colonel" until I corrected her,' she said at last, speaking more soberly than she had before. 'I told her you'd been connected with the Supply Department of the army in an important civilian capacity, but that you'd never held military rank. She was perfectly satisfied with my explanation, even though I didn't tell her which army. Perhaps I should have. But somehow . . .'

Nothing had roused her suspicions about his past. Yet she had not been able to confess that it was the Union Army with which the man she loved had been connected. In spite of all her tenderness, all her passion, all her adoration, she still found this hard to accept, she was still trying her best to forget it.

'You're — you're not ashamed of me, are you, Clyde, because I didn't tell her — everything?' Lucy asked in a troubled voice.

He had tried to assure her, more earnestly and more eloquently than he had ever spoken to her before, that shame of any sort was utterly alien to the temple of love where he had enshrined her. Later, in a calmer moment, and apropos of nothing in particular, he said that almost nobody told the whole truth about anything, in fact, it was probably just as well that nobody should. He reminded her, laughing almost naturally this time, that he had never told her the whole truth about himself yet, but that no doubt Mrs. Goldthwaite would ferret it out and pass it on to her before they reached Cairo. Mrs. Goldthwaite had ceased to talk about him much, Lucy reported; she was so excited because her prediction about Major Fanchon had come true that she had spoken of almost nothing else in the sewing circle.

'It seems he'd been stirring up fights among the Negroes on the lower deck and betting on the winners. Mrs. Goldthwaite called it "a scandal to the jaybirds". Then finally, last night, he offered a demijohn of liquor as a prize to whichever one of the Negroes won in a fight where they all had their hands tied, and could only hit each other by butting.'

'Lucy, I'm not surprised that you're shocked, but you don't need to be so stricken. The Negroes really enjoy those fights. However, I suppose Captain Dean came along at the wrong moment?'

'Yes, or the right one, whichever you choose to call it. Anyway, he ordered Major Fanchon off the boat then and there. He didn't even wait to get to some dock. He just pulled up beside the river bank, the way he did Saturday night, only you didn't wake up this time.'

'No, I didn't. . . . Well, Captain Dean's action doesn't surprise me, either. It's not an infrequent occurrence for the master of a boat to take action like that.'

He spoke nonchalantly, but the nonchalance was assumed. Actually, he was hard put to it to conceal his overwhelming relief. With Fanchon gone, with Mrs. Goldthwaite's attention diverted, with the end of the trip to Cairo already in sight, he had little left to fear aboard the *Messenger*. He no longer clung to Lucy's side 'like a sick kitten leaning up against a hot brick' or remained stubbornly in the stuffy little stateroom, pretending to work at the inadequate table, but began to move more freely among his fellow passengers. If the periods he spent in the bar were brief, if he expressed a preference for chess rather than cards, that was his privilege. After all, he was admittedly a bridegroom, with a bride of whom any man might be proud. He told himself that there was probably not a single male passenger who failed to regard him with envy.

The limitations of their quarters and her own sensible attitude in regard to these had done a good deal toward lessening Lucy's self-consciousness about the lack of privacy; but Clyde realized she had not wholly overcome this, and mindful of a modesty which he respected, made a practice of taking a turn around the deck every morn-

ing and again every evening, so that she might have their tiny stateroom to herself while she dressed and undressed. At first, these promen-
ades had been more or less solitary, for his attitude discouraged friendly
advances; but as he showed himself less forbidding, some other man
had usually joined him, and they had talked about matters of mutual
interest as they walked. Clyde had come to enjoy these conversations
and to anticipate them; therefore, he was feeling vaguely disappointed,
on the eve of the *Messenger's* arrival at Cairo, because he seemed to
have the deck to himself again, when his hat was suddenly snatched
from his head. He whirled around, with a hasty exclamation, to see a
young girl standing close beside him, her back to the side of the boat
and her hands resting lightly on her hips. It was too dark for her
features to be distinguishable and her hair seemed only a part of the
surrounding obscurity; but her lips were a startling scarlet in her
white face and her skin seemed luminous in itself. A great deal of
this was visible, for her dress was extremely low cut; and the gleaming
flesh-coloured satin of which it was made enhanced the effect of nudity
and luminosity. She moved forward a little and, as she did so, Clyde
could see that her hair was very black and her waist almost unbelievably small. Suddenly something about her evoked the stabbing memory
of an episode which he had done his best to forget and which he had
hopefully believed would never be revived. He turned quickly away,
without a word. The girl caught at his arm.
   'Don't you want your hat back, m'sieu?' she asked. 'Madame might
wonder where you left it.'
   'And your "aunt" might wonder where you got it,' he said coldly,
'which would be quite all right, of course, if she sent you out here.
But I rather think you're doing this on your own. If I'm not mistaken,
you're being saved for New Orleans.'
   'What will you give me if I hand you back your hat and don't make
you any trouble with madame?'
   'I think you'd better give it to me without doing any bargaining. I
can make a good deal more trouble for you than you can for me. You'd
better believe that, because it's true.'
   The girl laughed and, releasing his arm, sprang forward and started
to toss his hat overboard. But he was quicker than she was. It had
barely skimmed the railing when he caught it. Then, with his other
hand, he seized her wrist.
   'No, I'm not going to hurt you,' he said, as he saw her jeering expression change quickly to one of fright. 'But I am going to give you a
word of advice. The next time a man plainly shows you he's through
with your kind, don't monkey with him. You might not get off so
easy again.'
   He strode away, even angrier with himself than he was with the

girl. She had upset him more than he would have been willing to admit, not because she had been successful in rousing the slightest shameful desire, for she had not; but because she had so successfully roused the memory of a past shameful desire. If he could have followed his inclination, he would have gone to the pilot-house—since he no longer felt secure on deck—and remained there until his mood was calmer. But Lucy would be wondering what had become of him—in fact, she was probably worried already, because his absence had been more protracted than usual. He still seldom left her for long, and he had noticed that, when he did, she was apt to look troubled on his return, though she did her best to conceal this. Once he had asked her, jokingly, if she thought he had fallen overboard; and though she said quickly, 'No, of course not,' she added, after a minute, 'You see I can't help imagining . . . I know it's silly, but I love you so much, the thought that anything might happen . . . I've never been happy like this before. I can't believe, even yet, it's real—that it's going to last. . . .'

Since Lucy felt like that, he had no right to give her a moment's unnecessary concern. He could not do so now. He went back to the saloon and, when he re-entered their stateroom, found that she was not already in bed, as she usually was at such times. She had on her night-gown, but she was sitting on the edge of her berth, her nightgown open at the neck, and she was engaged in brushing her hair, which was still unbraided and fell over her shoulders and arms in long golden waves. It was the first time that Clyde had seen it like this, though he had greatly longed to do so, and the loveliness of the sight far exceeded his expectations. He leaned over and placing his hands on either side of the white part, let them slide slowly down, bringing her closer and closer to him while he did so. Then, drawing her to her feet, he enfolded her in a fond embrace.

Suddenly, he was conscious of some change in her person, a change so slight that he could not instantly identify it. Then, with a start, he realized what it was: there was a firmness to her bosom which it had lacked when they were first married. He drew away and looked down at her searchingly. The only light in the room was that which came in through the transom; but he knew, even though he could not see, that Lucy was blushing as she had never blushed before and that the rosy colour suffused not merely her face and neck, but that beautiful transfigured bosom. Nevertheless, she did not draw away from him, and she did not instinctively try to cover herself more completely, as she would have done such a short time before. Instead, she returned his look, with adoration in her gaze.

'I—I waited up for you on purpose,' she said. 'It needn't have taken me so long to brush my hair. But I thought perhaps if you came in while I was still fixing it, you—you'd do exactly what you have done.

93

Of course, it's too soon to be sure, even though it must have happened right away—that is, if it did happen. But I hope—I believe—Oh, if God will only be good to us! I—I prayed for this! Long after you went to sleep, that—that first night, I lay awake—praying. Not just that we'd have a child, but that you'd given me one *then*, at the same time that you'd taken away my fear of fulfilment and taught me what it meant to be a woman!'

He could not answer her, he could not voice his happiness or speak his love. But this time, it was he who lay awake, exultant, long after she was sleeping peacefully. It did not matter any more if that riff-raff in the bar despised him as a quitter and a coward, a former go-getter who now let everything slip through his fingers, a hard hitter who had gone soft because a pretty woman had enslaved him. It would not even matter overwhelmingly—though he must never let Lucy know this—if she could not carry their child full term. Neither must he let her know that, deeply moved as he was by what she had told him and by the manner of its telling, the reasons for his joy were different from hers. He, too, had hoped that their first union might be fruitful. But this was less on her account than on his own. Indeed, if he had given thought to it, he would have shrunk from the prospect of her suffering in childbirth; but he had wanted immediate evidence of his virility, he had craved another proof of his power to wring from a reluctant fate everything life had to offer. In marriage, as in everything else, he had triumphed.

Chapter Four

IT was mid-morning when the *Messenger* rounded to for a landing at Cairo's levee, shouldering a place for herself among the steamboats tightly ranked along the entire length of Commercial Street. The mate had already marshalled the roustabouts, so that they would be ready to run out the gangplank after the boat had completed her turn against the current; the hoarse bellow of her whistle and the anguished squall of her orchestra had heralded her approach to shore. Now the seething babel which was apparently an essential element in all landings mounted in pitch and volume. On the levee—so low that it provided no more than a sloping approach to the flat bank—a number of young tatterdemalions were capering about in high glee, jigging and turning cartwheels; on the railroad track beyond, a small locomotive with a turnip-shaped stack was switching a string of dingy freight cars back and forth.

'Look at that waterfront!' Clyde exclaimed triumphantly. He and Lucy were again standing beside the rail of the forward guard, as they had when they left Pittsburgh, and his sweeping gesture of satisfaction included both the long line of steamboats and the chugging little train. 'Now can't you see why I don't hold with the crêpe hangers who insist that the great days of steamboating are over? That railroad over yonder's nearabouts the first one built full length in the Mississippi Valley, running the same way as the river. It comes all the way from Chicago. And did it kill the steamboats? All I ask you to do is look at that waterfront again.'

A little cry from Lucy terminated this triumphant questioning. Following her glance, Clyde saw that she was looking past the drab little town, downstream to the point where a river, mightier and muddier than the Ohio, caught and reflected the November sunlight.

'Yes!' he said, 'That's the Father of Waters. You can't see the place where the Mississippi and the Ohio come together, over there to the left, because of that packed file of steamboats. But you will see it, once we're on our way south from here. And if luck's with us, that'll be in a few hours now.'

Luck was indeed with them, for, on disembarking, they learned from the wharfmaster that the *Richmond* would arrive some time that afternoon. 'Times have certainly changed,' he conceded sociably. 'Not too long back, all we could've told you was she hadn't come till yet. But now, the telegraph brings us news from up the river at St. Louis and elsewhere 'most before it happens, seems like. Yes'r. She'll be comin' 'round the p'int d'rectly the Halliday dining-room closes after dinner, give or take an hour either way, and you nee'n' to tote your grips off the wharfboat, sir, lessen you've a special mind to. I'll jes' keep my eye on 'em for you, whilst you'n' your good lady pass a pleasant time of day strollin' 'roun'n' about our fair city . . . 'f I was to make so bold, I'd segest you walk down yon to where the levee turns. That's where Fort Defiance was, and if I was to tell you . . .'

'Thank you very much,' Clyde interrupted when he saw the stream of conversation was not likely otherwise to be shut off. 'We'll do as you say, and if you'll kindly let us leave the baggage, that will be a help. . . . Would you like to come, Lucy? I want to see what arrangements they have here for moving cargo from steam cars to steamboats, and the other 'way round, too. It'll be right on our way to the Fort.'

'Of course I'd like to come.'

There was no hesitancy about her answer; but they had gone no distance at all when Clyde realized that, from her point of view, the 'stroll' must inevitably have been a mistake. Freight laden, horse-drawn drays churned the waterfront into a sea of sticky mud; and spindle-shanked pigs fled squealing from the heavy wheels of these 'floats', hotly pursued by mangy curs. A blowzy old slattern, her underlip bulging with packed snuff, gave her deserted bird's nest of a hat a more rakish tilt, as she passed them and spat voluminously in their direction. Everything that distance had softened or hidden, when viewed from the deck of the *Messenger*, was now revealed in dismal detail.

'I expect we'd better go right to the Halliday after all,' Clyde suggested.

'Well. . . . Perhaps we had. At least, perhaps *I'd* better. I don't want you to miss seeing anything you want to. But this mud——'

'Remember I forewarned you. . . . It's a good thing, after all, that Captain Jesse always 'chokes a stump' on Sundays. I don't need to be told that you'd rather spend two hours than two days here.'

He took her by the shortest possible route to the hotel and installed her in a suite, remembering, just in time, that she would have been loath to set foot in it if he had told her it was distinguished primarily for its occupancy by General Grant during the swift campaigns which had resulted in the capture of Fort Henry and Fort Donelson. When he was assured of her comfort, he left her, to pursue his investigations as to the shipping of cargo; and when he returned, he spoke of these with the same enthusiasm that had marked his satisfied observations earlier in the day.

'It's about what I thought,' he reported. 'They'll never work out a smart way to transfer goods from the cars to a steamboat, because they can't run the tracks beside the river, because the river's not the same height two days hand-running – halfway up the houses in the spring floods, and 'way out by the sandbars in September droughts. So stuff has to be unloaded from the cars into drays, and then from the drays on to the boats, and that's just too much handling to pay. To my idea, folks will decide to ship all the way by either boat or rail, and if I've got to make a choice, I'll put my money on the steamboats to win – with maybe barge tows to give them capacity. . . . Well, I didn't mean to run on like this when you must be starving to death after all these hours of waiting. Let's go down to dinner.'

Dinner was surprisingly good and as bountiful as it was excellent. The item of 'cold jellied buffalo' at the top of the menu caused Lucy to exclaim she had not realized they were *that* far west! And she was slightly disappointed when Clyde laughingly explained that the buffalo in question was only a kind of fish! There was catfish, too, cut in steaks and beautifully browned, a choice of three roasts, and for entrées, spitted pigeons and calves' tongues. Half a dozen kinds of pie and as many varieties of cake brought the banquet to a leisurely end; and when they left the dining-room, the afternoon was already half gone. Clyde had rather expected to find, at the desk, some word about the *Richmond's* expected arrival and he was not disappointed; a look-out, keeping watch from a northern mansard window, had already sent word that the *Richmond* had passed the island and was rounding the point: this meant that there was no time to lose. Clyde paid the bill and he and Lucy hastened back to the wharfboat to reclaim their luggage.

As the *Richmond* came floating into view, her clean-cut bow swelling gracefully back toward her great wheels, she rested with such apparent lightness on the water that the effect was almost one of some ethereal craft, gliding toward the shore of a magic lake, rather than that of a powerful river boat, slowly approaching a dingy city wharf. Clyde, who was watching Lucy as intently as she was watching the boat, herd her catch her breath in a little gasp of ecstasy. She had told him in New York that he had taken her to fairyland; but he knew that the splendour with which he had surrounded her there paled, in her eyes, before the radiance she now beheld. And here, too, was the embodiment of all he himself had tried to capture forever, in choosing, as their abode, a mansion modelled after such a vision.

He could see that the spell was still unbroken, after they had gone aboard and were passing slowly through the main cabin to their state-room. All the wonders of which she had heard, but in which she had hardly believed, were now holding her enthralled. Here was the thick-piled, rich-coloured carpet, extending the entire length of the vast channel-like saloon. Here was the rosewood furniture, elaborately carved and upholstered in satin damask. Here was the concert grand piano, also of rosewood, also elaborately carved. Here was the great series of golden chandeliers, glittering with glass prisms, bright with a thousand burners. Here were the skylights of tinted glass, emblematically depicting scenes and products of the Southland — the cotton fields, the orange groves, the avenues of magnolias in full bloom. Here were the gilded mirrors and mouldings, the fretwork and marquetry, the panels depicting the city of Richmond, to which this floating palace owed her name, and the city of New Orleans, which was her home port. Lucy felt for Clyde's hand and squeezed it hard; he could see that her lips, usually so firm for all their sweetness, were trembling a little and that tears were glistening on her lashes. But she did not speak to him, and she seemed hardly aware of the other passengers moving to and fro in gay little groups, of the hurrying porters laden with baggage, of the stewards already standing respectfully at attention beside the long array of white-covered tables, and of the coloured orchestra which, this time, was not doing violence to a pleasant tune, but performing melodiously. Clyde was conscious before she was of a fine-looking man who gave them a quick look and then turned toward them with outstretched hands.

'Lucy! I've looked and looked for you! But I thought you'd be getting on at St. Louis, and when I didn't find you . . .'

Without finishing his sentence, he threw his arms around her and kissed her warmly on both cheeks. Then, releasing her, he turned to Clyde and again held out his hand.

'Mr. Batchelor—or may it be Cousin Clyde from the beginning? Stanard Daingerfield of Sapphire Downs, at your service. Lucy and I are kissing kin, as you must have gathered just now. It was a disappointment, a very great one, that I had to miss your wedding—a confounded race-track complication. But we'll make up for it! I said so to myself when I got Cousin Sophie's letter, telling me you were taking the *Richmond* on my recommendation, and I say it again to you now.'

He wrung Clyde's hand, beaming on both of them with unmistakable goodwill. 'Have you seen your stateroom yet?' he went on, scarcely giving them time to return his greeting. 'No? Well, after you get Lucy settled there, Cousin Clyde, you'll find me waiting for you at the bar. Yes, yes, I know this is a honeymoon. Even so, a man needs to get with other men once in a while, if only to make him appreciate a lovely lady more when he rejoins her. And you *have* got a lovely lady here and no mistake. Marriage must agree with her. I never saw her look as charming as she does now; and even if I'm getting to be an old man, and am a blood relation of hers besides, I can understand that you'd be loath to leave her. But I've some friends aboard I want you to meet. You'll like them and they'll like you. Shall we say in half an hour? Oh, incidentally, of course Captain Neal will be expecting you to sit at his table. No doubt he'll be paying you his respects and telling you so himself, as soon as we're under way. Meanwhile . . .'

He waved a cheerful farewell and disappeared in the direction of the bar. Lucy looked up at Clyde with a shining face.

'Stan's my favourite cousin,' she said happily. 'I thought we might find him aboard—in fact, I meant to watch for him, but I was so entranced with everything, I forgot. You're glad, too, aren't you, Clyde? You know I told you about him, I said it was he who first suggested——'

'Yes, I remember,' Clyde answered. He must not speak to her curtly again, he would not. But his mind was in a tumult. He had known, immediately, how to deal with Fanchon; for years, they had played the same game and spoken the same language; now he was confronted by a situation with which he was far less qualified to cope. Stanard Dainger-

98

field was no faker, no cheapskate, no pretender to honourable rank; this man was genuine through and through, warm-hearted and likable – the sort of man whom Clyde had never had for a friend and who, all his life, he had yearned to claim as one. But how could he accept such friendship, now that, at last, it was offered? Those other men of whom Stan Daingerfield spoke – was there not sure to be among them at least one who would recognize him, possibly one whom he had victimized? And the *Richmond's* captain, 'Stut' Neal, had been on the river for years. He had started out as a poor boy and had worked his way, by slow and painful steps, up to his present proud position as the designer, owner and commander of the finest river steamer afloat. His path and Clyde's had crossed more than once before. Now that these paths had crossed again, what would he do or say, in the light of those past meetings?

Clyde was so preoccupied by these disturbing thoughts that he forgot to look at the names on the doors of the staterooms they went by; if Lucy had not paused by the one labelled, 'Virginia', he might have passed that, too. But, fortunately, something impelled him to stop before it was too late. 'Yes, this is ours,' he said hurriedly. 'I thought perhaps it would please you to be back in the Old Dominion again, at least by inference. You know the roustabouts call this boat the "Rebel Home", so you ought to feel at ease everywhere on it; but, of course, I hoped you'd be especially so in our own quarters.' He had succeeded in keeping the curtness out of his voice, he was thankful for that. At the same time, he was all too well aware that it was toneless. And he had expected to speak with such loving lightness, as well as such pride and joy! For, on this ship of her dreams, he could once again offer Lucy a fitting habitation. This stateroom, unlike the one on the *Messenger*, was both spacious and luxurious. It was draped with damask and Brussels lace. In the foreground were some comfortable chairs, a marble-topped centre table and a mirrored wardrobe; at the rear, half-concealed by a rich hanging, was a double washstand equipped with a porcelain toilet set and, beside it, a double bed, with a spotless linen sheet folded down over a silken counterpane and big square pillows peeping out on either side of an embroidered pillow sham. Here they would sleep together again, instead of being separately confined in narrow rigid berths. Here – or so he had planned – they would eat their meals, in comfort and privacy. And here he would tell her the great news – second only in significance to the great news she had told him – which he had been hoarding for the time when he could say, 'So the *Richmond's* come up to your every expectation, has it? I'm very glad. I'll agree it's a fine boat. But wait until you see the *Lucy Batchelor*. . . .' Then, when she looked at him in rapturous amazement, he would continue, 'You must have thought I was neglecting you in Pittsburgh. Yet, all the time I was out with young Thatcher, who's a lot smarter than he looks, and those shippers and ironmasters you didn't even meet, I was going over plans – I was working out designs. I was making arrangements for the financing . . .' And she would catch her breath and throw herself into his arms, laughing and crying at the same time, because of this culminating gift – a boat which would bear her name.

Well, of course, that could still occur, just as he had visualized it; nothing in his triumphant utterance should betray his inner tumult. Of course Lucy would lie beside him again, with her head on his shoulder and his arm around her as she drifted off to sleep; no interloper could penetrate their private paradise and prevent that. And of course they could still have some of their meals at that little marble-topped table – it would not be considered a discourtesy if they breakfasted by themselves at least, especially if they invited Daingerfield and perhaps one or two of his friends to some of their other meals; the table would seat four comfortably and could, at a pinch, accommodate six. Meanwhile, the sooner the inevitable showdown was over, the better it would be for everyone.

'Well, I suppose I'd better be on my way,' he said with an attempt at levity which did not fall quite as flat as he feared. 'We were hardly aboard the *Messenger* when you insisted the bar was the place I belonged. That time, I tried to hold out, but now that your Cousin Stan has the same idea, I know I might as well give in, first as last. Not that I wouldn't a lot rather stay right where I am. But I'll be back as soon as I can and, at least, I'm not leaving you in a cell like the one on the *Messenger*.'

'Don't hurry. I know you and Cousin Stan will find lots of things to say to each other. And I want to unpack. I think the pink net dress with the black polka dots, that I wear with the little black net jacket, would be just the thing for the captain's table, don't you?'

She was singing 'Lorena' under her breath as she opened the lid of her small square trunk, obviously happy, both in her actual occupation and in the prospect of a gala evening. Clyde retraced his steps through the long cabin and entered the bar, which was no mere alcove, like the one on the *Messenger*. Contrary to current custom, the *Richmond* had two offices, one on either side of the entrance to the gentlemen's cabin, and, at the rear of the starboard office, was a third compartment of similar shape and size. Here an enormous oil painting, representing the Bacchanalia, as envisioned by a contemporary artist, surmounted a mahogany sideboard, decked with a sparkling array of glassware and rows upon rows of bottles. The multi-coloured liquors, with which these bottles were filled, caught and reflected the rays of the sun, streaming in from the cabin window; and in front of the sideboard stood Billy, the head bartender, and his two assistants, all busily engaged in filling orders. The bar was already crowded, but Daingerfield and the man with whom he was talking, were outstanding among the others. Clyde, who had always taken immense satisfaction in the fact that he had never resembled the pale-faced, sable-clad gambler of tradition, was struck by the lack of any likeness between Daingerfield and the conventional Kentucky colonel, complete with goatee, frock coat, and soft black hat. Lucy's kinsman was smooth-shaven, and the ruddiness of his complexion was accentuated by the blondness of his hair, which drifted back from his forehead in soft abundance. His portliness enhanced his air of dignity rather than detracting from it; and his hands and feet, which were slender and shapely, looked all the smaller in comparison to his substantial build. He was dressed in a heather-mixture sack, so high buttoned as almost to conceal the matching waistcoat, but setting off the bronze-coloured ascot, loosely knotted below the V of the immaculate collar. He wore no rings, but the folds of the ascot were fastened with a stickpin headed by a large black pearl; and as he thrust one of his small hands into a front trouser pocket, to extract a fine linen handkerchief, the black silk ribbon of a watch fob, adorned by a golden seal set with a large precious stone, was casually revealed. The man with whom he was talking was almost bald, and his skin seemed tightly stretched across the dome of his head. His frame was spare almost to the point of emaciation and though he looked the scholar, it was the scholar who had spent too much time indoors. Only his deep-blue eyes gleamed with the clarity of great vitality.

'I agree. There's no profit to be made at Metairie, either in purses or bets,' Daingerfield was saying to this companion. 'There's not much spare money in circulation down yonder yet—couldn't be, less than five years after the war. But I figure I can get a good price for this colt at Saratoga after he's been conditioned by a winter's racing in New Orleans. . . . Ah, Cousin Clyde! I was wondering what was detaining you—or rather, I would have been, if I hadn't known! Carteret, let me present Mr. Clyde Batchelor of Cindy Lou Plantation, Louisiana. He's recently married my cousin, Lucy Page of Sorrento—you know, Sophia's daughter. So of course that brings him right into our fold. . . . Cousin Clyde, my friend, Judge Carteret Paine of Frankfort. And when I say friend, that's no figure of speech, as you'll see for yourself when you've joined us in a drink of his Bourbon. He takes along a supply of it, ample for us and our friends, whenever we travel. What's more, he puts aside two casks from each year's run for me, and holds them for ten years before shipping them on to Sapphire Downs. Then, when they're emptied, I send them back to him, to be used over and over again. His father and mine followed the same practice. It's fifty years since some of the casks I have now were first coopered and charred of good white Kentucky oak. Billy—a julep for Mr. Batchelor. And I'm counting on you to convince him he's never really tasted one before!'

'Yes, sir! Right away, sir. A special Superior for Mr. Batchelor. Yes, *sir!*' The bartender deftly took some pieces of ice from a cedarwood tub, wrapped them in a napkin and reached for a heel-worn wooden mallet. With this in hand, he paused and looked at Clyde, one eyebrow cocked inquiringly upward. 'With or without a jigger of rum, Mr. Batchelor?'

'Are you out of your mind, Billy?' exclaimed Daingerfield in the same instant in which Judge Paine cried: 'Lord God of Hosts!'

'Without, of course,' Clyde said mildly, as soon as he could make himself heard.

'I only asked because some of the gentlemen . . .' the bartender began defensively, but Clyde interrupted.

'Some of the passengers, you mean. No gentleman would debase the Judge's superior Bourbon with . . .'

'To be sure,' agreed Billy. There might have been just a hint of suppressed mirth in his tone. 'A Special Superior for Mr. Batchelor, coming right up.' The mallet banged down upon the wrapped pieces of ice.

'Excuse me, Judge,' Clyde smiled, turning from the bar and extending his hand. 'I'm mighty proud to meet you, sir. Perhaps, one of these days, when you and Mr. Daingerfield visit us at Cindy Lou, I'll be able to return your hospitality—though not with anything as fine as your Bourbon, I'm sure.'

'Why not?' rejoined Carteret Paine. 'I'd be a low sort indeed if I couldn't send a cask to Cindy Lou as a welcome-to-your-new-home gift for Stan's cousins.'

'Your Special Superior, Mr. Batchelor,' interrupted Billy, passing a tall tumbler crowned with aromatic green across the bar. In the one brief instant which thus brought them face to face, Clyde noted that the carefully curled moustache, which had once been merely brilliantined, was now also dyed, that the greatly thinned soaplock must now be held in place by bears'-grease, that the diamond which gleamed from a scarlet cravat was larger—and more obviously flawed—than the one he himself had affected before meeting Lucy. Without a visible sign of recognition, however, he took his drink, murmured, 'Thank you!' and rejoined Daingerfield and Paine. Together the three walked to the gentlemen's lounge at the after end of the main cabin, and took seats at an unoccupied table among those where others were playing cards, or merely chatting over their drinks.

'I was just telling the judge about a colt I've got aboard,' Daingerfield went on. 'I must take you down to see him — you'll find him as fine a piece of horseflesh as you ever clapped eyes on. Sapphire Sky, I've named him. Lucy'll want to see him, too. She's a good judge of horses as well as a first-rate horsewoman — couldn't very well be otherwise, with her background. A great land lover, too, like most Virginians. She'll be out riding the crops with you. Of course, she'll have to learn about cane and perique — that's what you raise, isn't it? But it won't take her long. When I think of what she's done to bring back the soil at Sorrento . . .'

He paused, taking a long, leisurely pull at his julep. Clyde was thankful for the respite. The conversation had taken a turn very different from the one he expected, but momentarily he forgot his original reasons for concern in regard to it. *Horses!* Lucy would expect to find horses, fine saddle stock, at Cindy Lou; and fatuous fool that he was, he had made no provision for this! There were draft animals on the place, and some sort of mounts for the overseers: the stock that went with the place when he bought it; but while priding himself that he had not overlooked the smallest item which could add to Lucy's pleasure, it had never occurred to him that they should have a stable of their own. He had bought horses for the army — not many, because mostly he had bought mules; however, there had been some horses, too. And he had been to the race track at New Orleans every so often, because such visits fitted in well with his major pursuits. But travelling the river, and moving about from place to place, as he had, without any sort of roots, he had regarded horses merely as a commodity to be secured, at will or at need, from the nearest livery stable. Not that this had always been possible. Ruefully, he recalled the irritating lack of rigs available at the Grand Hôtel Pierre Chanet, and then his thoughts strayed in the even less welcome direction of his first visit to Cindy Lou — there was enough to worry about in the present, without dwelling on the past. He had a great deal still to learn before he would fit into the pattern of the country gentry. And the worst of it was, that Lucy . . .

'By the way, I happened to hear yesterday that the Duncan Kenners are giving up their stable at Ashland. Of course I've no idea what you need, Cousin Clyde — perhaps you're overstocked already. But it just occurred to me that it might be a lucky break for you.'

Daingerfield took another long, leisurely pull at his julep and saluted an acquaintance who had just entered the bar. The newcomer glanced from Daingerfield to Clyde and then, instead of coming on toward their table, entered into jovial conversation with Billy, the bartender. Clyde had seen the look and felt himself growing hot under the collar. There was no question about it; he could not let matters drift along like this, while he and Daingerfield chatted casually about old Bourbon and fine horses. But in spite of his resolution, the reference to Kenner halted him. Again he thought, involuntarily, about his first visit to Cindy Lou and Dorothée's boast of visiting at that beautiful nearby plantation called Ashland, before the owner had gone to Europe as Jefferson Davis's Minister. Later, Clyde knew, the entire property had been confiscated; and he had also heard that, though it had eventually been returned to its rightful owners, they had not been able to disassociate it with mournful memories and preferred to spend most of their time elsewhere. But he had never heard of their stables. Evidently, from what Daingerfield said, these had been fine ones. The new-found 'kinsman' was right; this was a lucky break.

'No, I'm understocked,' he said. 'I mean, for the stable. Have you — could you get in touch with Kenner right away and — buy up everything?'

Daingerfield laughed, easily. 'That would saddle you with rather a large order, wouldn't it? There, I didn't mean to make a bad pun. Of course, I can get in touch with Kenner, if you like. We're kinsmen, too, and I served under him, abroad, for a while, after Davis decided he had more use for me as a diplomat than as a soldier. It was a good deal of a blow at the time, though I'm proud to remember it now. Well, as I said, I can get in touch with him if you like. But if time's the essence, I think it would be better for me to wire my New Orleans agent, Moise Riviere, from Memphis, and tell him to pick out whatever you need. Could you give me an idea of about what that would be?'

'No. I'd be grateful for suggestions.'

It was the judge who glanced appraisingly at him now. But this time Clyde did not care and Daingerfield, apparently, saw nothing strange about the abrupt admission.

'Then I'd say perhaps . . . Two walking horses for you, a gaited saddle mare or gelding for Lucy, a pair of matched hackneys for carriage service, a Shetland pony for Bushrod — no, wait! A couple of Shetland ponies! Cary'll be in the saddle, too, before she's much older and you may as well be ready — meantime, both ponies could be used in a governess cart. Would such a selection suit you?'

'It certainly would. And if you would tell your agent to send those horses to Cindy Lou, straight off, by boat, so that they'd be there before us, that would suit me mighty well, too.'

'It's as good as done. And now, what about coming down to the main deck with me and having a look at Sapphire Sky?'

'I'd be glad to.'

'You joining us, Judge?'

'Good lord, man, don't I see enough horseflesh on shore without climbing over a steamboat to look at a colt I've seen off and on ever since he was foaled? Talk about a busman's holiday! I was just getting ready to order another julep. Sorry you and Mr. Batchelor won't join me in a second round. Nobody can fly with one wing.'

'You see a julep once in a while ashore, too, don't you, Carteret? Well, we'll let that pass—and rejoin you later for that second round.'

Daingerfield set down his empty glass and rose. Then he threaded his way, without haste, among the crowded tables, stopping every now and then to speak with still other acquaintances, to all of whom he presented Clyde as his kinsman. Instead of walking out to the guard, however, he eventually turned in the direction of the main saloon.

'Come and have a look at my stateroom, on the way,' he said. 'It isn't quite as grand as yours and Lucy's, but it's pretty comfortable, at that—all of them are on the *Richmond*. I want you to get it located, so you can look me up any time you're in the mood—I'm not afraid you'll wear out your welcome, with the counter-attraction you've got waiting for you in the Old Dominion.' Then, as he threw open the door of a stateroom which was, indeed, both spacious and pleasant, he added, 'Sit down and make yourself at home. I've got some of the judge's Bourbon here, too. I won't bother to make a julep or send for one. But a small shot's never amiss with a little talk.'

He brought a bottle and two glasses from the washstand, poured out the liquor, and sat down beside Clyde at the little table. 'As a matter of fact,' he said, savouring his drink, 'when Bourbon's as good as this, I believe I prefer it straight. What about you?'

'It's prime Bourbon, all right,' Clyde agreed. 'In fact, I don't remember ever having tasted better, Mr. Daingerfield.'

'Mr. Daingerfield? Here I've been calling you Cousin Clyde straight from the start. Isn't that all right?'

'It's more than all right. It's—it's——' He left his sentence unfinished and took another drink. 'The only thing is—well, I don't know just how to say it. But I'm still not right down certain you could really want me to call you Cousin Stanard.'

'Cousin *Stan*,' corrected Daingerfield. 'The family decided long ago Stanard was too much of a mouthful. And the family includes you now, too, of course. But I do know what's likely to be troubling you. No, hold on!' He raised his hand in a gesture of protest against interruption. 'Let me be the one to say it. I'd be a sorry specimen if I put that particular monkey on your back by way of welcoming you. You were thinking, no doubt, that I might have confused you with someone I knew by—er, reputation!—years back. I want to set you straight about that. I did my level damnedest to get to your wedding, but since I had to miss it, I want to make up for that as well as I can now. And I want to begin by saying how happy I am to meet, at long last, and for the first time, the man my Cousin Lucy married – the man who's taking his first trip down the river, with his bride.'

For a few moments, Clyde stared unseeingly at his glass. At length, with his eyes still fixed on his drink, he said slowly, 'I hope there'll never be a time when you'll change your mind about being happy to meet me. Because what you've just said means more to me than you'll ever realize.'

'I don't expect to change it. I believe I can still tell the difference between a hawk and a hacksaw. Besides, if we do have to rake up the past, my own conscience isn't too clear. None of us out here had the first notion how hard things were going with Cousin Sophie and Lucy – if we had, they'd have had all the help they needed. Of course you can say it's partly their fault for being too plagued prideful to let their own kin know how much they needed help. But it's a lot more the fault of the kin who didn't take the trouble to find out. You did.'

'I don't deserve any credit for that. I went to Sorrento because I was in love with Lucy. And of course, since I was in love with her——'

' "You can give without loving, but you can't love without giving", eh? Yes, I know the old saying. But it didn't apply in my case. A long, long time ago, I was in love with my Cousin Sophie. She never had eyes for anyone else, from the moment she met Virginius Cary. Besides, I was younger than she was, she thought of me as just a kid and a kinsman. But it was different with me. She was the most beautiful creature I ever saw, though I suppose you wouldn't guess it to see her now, after all the grief and privation she's been through. . . . Well, anyway, I never married. But still I didn't go to Virginia, after the war, to see if I could do anything for her. I got back to Sapphire Downs as fast as I could and I've never left it yet, except to further my own fortunes, selling hay at Louisville and tobacco at St. Louis!'

He set his glass down on the table with a bang. 'One look at Lucy was enough to tell me all I need to know,' he said. 'She's got roses in her cheeks and stars in her eyes. She was a lovely looking young girl, but she was a little on the solemn side, if you know what I mean – not stiff, but very serious. And she didn't have any colour; she was so slim you felt she might break in two. You've changed all this. Of course you've given her fine clothes and handsome jewels, but dammit all, Forrest Page did that much! He was a rich man, too, when the war broke out, and I saw her when she was a bride before – lord, what a difference now! She's radiant with happiness – happiness you've given her. If you'd never done anything else – or no matter what else you had done – you'd do to take along. At least that's my judgment, and I'm not often mistaken.'

'Thank you,' Clyde said again. 'I—I do think she's happy. And of course you understand that I don't want anything to happen that would make her less happy, that it's on her account . . .'

'Of course. If you were by yourself, you'd have a free hand, you wouldn't have to step carefully. As it is, you can't afford to risk having your apple cart upset. . . . Well, perhaps I'm mixing my metaphors, but I get your meaning and you've got mine. We're seeing this through together, you hear?'

Clyde was very deeply moved, so deeply that he would have been glad to leave, ending the talk on this note. But he knew that however Stan Daingerfield might feel, there were others to be reckoned with.

'You said Captain Neal had asked Lucy and me to sit at his table,' he began.

'So he has. I'm sitting there, too. And I've already put a bee in Stut Neal's big hat. When I got through explaining things to him, he agreed with me that he'd never met my Cousin Lucy's husband, either. He and I've been closer than molasses and cornpone a good many years now. With me at his table, he'd be slighting me—wouldn't he?—if he didn't invite my cousin and her new husband to sit there, too. It only stands to reason and it's all settled, fair and square and no king's-ex!'

When Clyde returned to the Old Dominion, he found that Lucy had a change of clothing laid out for him and that she was already dressed for supper in the pink net with the black polka dots. The stewardess had helped her unpack, she told him—the nicest old coloured woman she'd met since she left home. She had not worried over his absence, he could see that, as she had when he left her for any length of time on the *Messenger*; and the thought crossed his mind that she had not divulged all her reasons for her former uneasiness, that she had guessed more about his acquaintance with Fanchon than she had admitted, and that she felt very differently when he went to the bar to meet her cousin than when he had sought out his ertswhile associate. But he did not dwell on the question or permit it to depress him; with Daingerfield as his ally, he would be able to meet any immediate situation and the future would take care of itself. He still intended to tell Lucy everything, some day; meanwhile, whatever she might have divined certainly had not affected her spirits and that was all that mattered. Daingerfield was right; there were roses in her cheeks and stars in her eyes; she was radiant with happiness.

As the evening advanced, there seemed to be more and more sparkle to this radiance. Their companions at the captain's table, besides Stanard Daingerfield and the judge, were an English novelist and his wife; a celebrated Italian singer who was including Memphis and New Orleans in her concert tour; the elderly relative who acted as her duenna; and an ex-Senator from Mississippi, with his daughter, who, since the end of the war, had been living in France, but who were now returning to their home in Natchez. The service and the décor were in every way worthy of such a distinguished company. This was no 'foundering' meal, nor were any 'shells' in evidence. The superlative supper was served in restaurant, not in steamboat style; the gold-lined silverware, engraved with the letter R, was exquisite in design; and the porcelain and crystal, similarly marked, would have done credit to any perfectly appointed establishment. Moreover, conversation was easy and delightful from the moment the elaborately pleated napkins were unfolded, to the one when the captain gave the signal to clear a space for dancing. The ex-Senator immediately asked Lucy if she would honour him and Clyde, with equal promptitude, bowed before the Senator's daughter. Stately quadrilles and lancers were interspersed with lively polkas and languorous waltzes; and the programme came to an end with the spirited execution of the paw-paw patch. By that time, everyone in the grand saloon was in such good spirits as to be well disposed toward everyone else; and when the great diva consented to go to the piano, and sing some of the arias for which she was most famous, this evidence of her graciousness and talent made a fitting climax to a period of flawless pleasure.

The captain, in bidding his guests good night, had tactfully assured them that he expected to see none of the ladies and 'only the unattached gentlemen' at breakfast. So the first meal which Clyde and Lucy had together at the little marble-topped table was all he had pictured it in coziness and intimacy. Indeed it was he who finally suggested that they should take advantage of the ladies' and gentlemen's baths, located, respectively, beside the nursery and the barber-shop, and that after that they should finish dressing and go out on deck. A news-sheet, entitled the 'Richmond Headlight', had been delivered to them with their early coffee, and Lucy was still reading aloud from it, with an eagerness which amounted to fascination, long after they had finished the copious repast of chicken with gravy and biscuits, and hot cakes with sausage, which arrived later.

'Listen to this, Clyde. "Paris is to have, in January, a dry goods store with twelve hundred salesmen." That's even more than at any of the New York stores, isn't it?'

'I don't know, but I should think so.'

' "The Government has advice of the fact that several Spanish men-of-war are on their way to New York. Not doubting their friendly intentions for a moment, the Government has ordered a fleet of iron-clads to that village to render them due honours." Does "that village" mean New York?'

'I suppose it must, but that certainly is a queer way of referring to it.'

'Oh! . . . Here's almost a whole column devoted to murders! "A. F. McCury, a merchant tailor of Cardigan, Ohio, killed his son Thursday afternoon by shooting him through the head. A family difficulty is said to be the cause of the rash act." . . . "In Johnson County, Arkansas, a few days ago, a dispute arose between Mr. Johnson and three men who were packing cotton for him, concerning its weight, when they attacked him with knives, and he defended himself with one, and the result was that two of them were killed and he was cut in more than twenty places, but not fatally." What terrible people there must be in that part of the country, Clyde!'

Clyde rose and leaned over her shoulder, scanning the column from which she was reading. Then he laughed. 'Evidently, you didn't notice the first of those entries, honey,' he said teasingly. 'Listen to this: "At Fluvanna Court House, Va. on Wednesday, Captain Richard Harlan was shot and killed by Washington Shares. The parties were highly respectable. The quarrel grew out of a law suit." It sounds to me as if there must be terrible people in Virginia, too,' he went on, in the same bantering tone. 'Washington Shares may be considered highly respectable at Fluvanna Court House, but if he is, I'd say that was just a local idiosyncrasy. Now, now — you know I'm only joking! Evidently, you didn't read the last entry in the column, either: "A good wife makes the poorest and most desolate home a paradise, and moulds the most negligent and indifferent husband into a tender and thoughtful companion. The influence of woman — quiet, imperceptible and all-persuasive — is irresistible when directed by woman's instinctive tact and affection." Well, I agree with every word of that anyhow. . . . But, listen, we mustn't sit here and read that newspaper all day. You must get out and have a look at the landscape. You'll find it very different now.'

'How different?'

'Well, we're farther away from the banks, of course, because the river's so much wider, and that makes it seem as if we were moving more slowly than we did coming down the Ohio — though, as a matter of fact, the *Richmond's* going along at a pretty smart clip. And there won't be any more bustling, large city landings till we get to Memphis, and you'll find that different, too, from Louisville and Cincinnati. Meantime, there's mile after mile of bristle-brush thicket, cottonwood and willow. But somehow, the scenery isn't monotonous. At least, it's never seemed that way to me. There's a restfulness about it, if you know what I mean.'

'Yes, I know what you mean. I'll go up to the ladies' observatory and watch it from there. That'll give you a chance to meet Cousin Stan and the Senator in the bar before dinner. I heard the Senator invite you, as we were saying good night.'

The Senator had invited him to have a drink, the English novelist drew him into conversation about perique, but it was Stan Daingerfield who suggested a poker game and called on Billy for cards and chips. There would be six of them at the table, Stan said: Senator Fletcher, the returning Mississippian; the English novelist whose name Clyde seemed unable to remember; Clark – 'Captain' Clark – whom Daingerfield had saluted in the bar on the occasion of Clyde's first meeting with Cousin Stan there, but who had coolly turned to join another group; Judge Paine, Stan himself and Clyde. For one momentary flash, Billy's imperturbability was lost in the glance of involuntary inquiry he shot at Clyde. But this met no answering gleam. Clyde's expression remained as blank as rain-washed glass.

'Wake up, Billy!' snapped Captain Clark. 'Didn't you hear Mr. Daingerfield? We want two new decks and a case of chips.'

'Certainly, sir; right away!' The bartender's moment of indecision had passed and, as Clark, having received the desired supplies, handed the racked red, white and blue chips to Paine, he said, 'You pass them out, seh; since this heah's to be a frien'ly pastime, I sh'd jedge a hunnerd a piece would jes' about cut the mustard. . . . Or perhaps Mr. Batchelor would prefer to bank the game?' Clyde shook his head in denial, and watched almost absently the fashion in which Clark broke the seals on the two decks – one blue, one red – tore off the inner waxed paper wrappings, flipped out the jokers, and shuffled. Yes, they were readers. He could identify them from the backs clear across the table. But Clark was shuffling them honestly. Was it possible Billy, the barkeep, had introduced the readers for his – Clyde's – benefit, and that 'Captain' Clark was not the sharp gambler Clyde took him to be? More probably, concealed somewhere upon his person, Clark already had the cold deck, which would be substituted at a given moment for the one with which the game began. Meanwhile, Clyde considered, he could make certain, thanks to the familiarly marked cards, that he did not win, and at the same time he could keep Clark from fleecing any of the others.

The play and the talk that companioned it shifted and progressed. Senator Fletcher was saying: 'Nothing is further from the fact than our notion that the French, as a nation, are immoral. We have no more right to judge France by what visiting Americans see in Paris, than our British cousins have to judge us by what they might see on the Bowery.' Judge Paine opened a cigar case, and withdrew from it a satiny blond claro. Clark, deck in hand and ready to deal, ceremoniously produced a match, struck it, and leaned across the table to proffer the flame. In doing so, he knocked some of his chips to the floor and, after the judge's cigar had taken on an even glow, Clark shook out the match and leaned down to retrieve them. Instantly Clyde was aware that, during the fractional moment when Clark's actions were concealed as he fumbled under the table for his chips, the deck in his hand would be switched for another in which the order of cards had been prearranged — the traditional 'cold deck' of the sharper.

Reading the backs of the cards as they were dealt around the table, Clyde realized that Senator Fletcher was the one who had been selected for shearing. That would have been fairly obvious, in any case, he reflected, for Clark did not really know whether Clyde Batchelor was what he now seemed to be or what, by repute, he had been. Thus Clark would neither chance failure by trying to fleece him, nor risk reprisal by victimizing those who might be under his protection — his kinsman and his friend. That left only the novelist — Grindle, the name sounded like when the others addressed him — and Senator Fletcher. The novelist might be too unskilled to be lured by whatever inviting bait the sharper planned to use; that left the Senator in the position of chosen victim.

Clyde noted that Fletcher had been dealt a pat full house — a hand that would beat anything but four of a kind or a straight flush. Paine, Daingerfield and Grindle held merely cards, but Clyde had been dealt five miscellaneous spades, and to himself, Clark had given the four, five, six and seven of hearts. That made the line of the planned drama plain as a pikestaff. Senator Fletcher, holding an almost invincible hand from the outset, would bet heavily before the draw. So would Clyde, if he were an innocent, since his hand, likewise pat, was nearly as good as the Senator's. Moreover, if he were not an innocent, he would bet high anyway, to tempt additional Fletcher bets into the open, and would later demand a cut of the winnings. Meanwhile, Clark, pretending dismay, would mourn the ill chance which had dealt him a hand he could not afford to abandon. Reluctantly, protestingly, he would call the bets his two opponents continued to force upon one another. When the money was all in, Clyde and the Senator would stand pat; groaning, Clark would discard one of his five pasteboards; but the one he would draw in its stead would be either the trey or eight of hearts, giving him the winning straight flush.

Clyde winced as he thought of the dollars he must sacrifice, but there was solid assurance in the look he gave Cousin Stan when the latter tossed away his cards after Senator Fletcher had pushed a hundred dollars into the pot with the remark, 'Any ribbon clerks or other faint-hearted counter-jumpers had best stay out of this one. It's marked, "For Men Only" — one hundred dollars, and there's more where that came from.'

'Up to a hundred,' Clyde countered stolidly.

'Too rich for my blood,' sighed Judge Paine, flipping his hand to the centre of the table. Grindle hesitated before following suit, and Clark looked at his hand with well-feigned woe.

'Smack where the hair's shortest,' he wailed. 'I got no more business in this here pot 'n a rabbit's got at a houn' dog's kennel, an' I can't afford to drop. Go easy on a poor orphan child, gentlemen. I got to call.'

The betting swiftly reached a climax; the disordered pile of chips and banknotes at the table's centre rose swiftly in height. Finally, the last bet was in. Clark picked up the deck and turned to Senator Fletcher.

'Cards?' he asked. 'I'll play these,' the Mississippian proclaimed triumphantly, and Clark conceded, 'I was sure you would, seh.' Turning to Clyde, he inquired, 'Cards?' Instead of saying, 'Mine's pat, too,' Clyde picked up his hand, peered cautiously between the squeezed edges, and, with a sudden look of consternation, burst out, 'Good Lord! I must have overlooked my hand!' In what seemed to be a sudden fit of temper, he slammed his cards among those already in the centre of the table and snapped, 'Give me five fresh ones. I've paid for the privilege of looking at another hand, even if I haven't the ghost of a chance to do anything more.'

Clark did not actually gulp, but he looked as though he had. Clyde's demand meant, of course, that neither the trey nor eight of hearts, now unquestionably the top two cards, would find their way to Clark, whose hand, therefore would remain a 'bobtail', worth exactly nothing. What Clark had planned to do, no doubt, was to pass Fletcher the deck, with the request, 'You deal me one off the top, please, seh. I jes' naturally don't have the heart to do it to my own self.' And the Senator, having himself dealt him the top card, which would be either the trey or the eight of hearts, could therefore not be suspicious of the chance that had topped his pat full. Only now, the trey and the eight would both have to be dealt to Clyde — by Clark.

'I'm waiting — Captain,' Clyde said, his equanimity seemingly restored. 'Five off the top, if you please.'

Thoughtfully, Clark dealt the cards, one at a time, across the table, picked up his hand for a farewell glance, and then went through with the projected play by turning his four hearts face up, discarding the fifth card, a club, and passing the deck to the Senator. 'You give it to me, seh,' he said. 'The topmost one, and if it's right, I'll bet, if not . . . Easy come, easy go, like the soldier said when he spent his month's pay, the whole seven dollars, in a single night. . . . Well, well, well, another club. I was afraid so, but a gentleman can't lay down a four-card straight flush open at both ends, seh. . . .'

'I told you this was for men only,' rejoiced Fletcher, sweeping in a miscellany of cards, chips and banknotes toward him. 'Reckon I'll be able to lift a mortgage or so now, when I get back to old Oktibbeha.' He began to sort and stack his winnings. Clyde rose.

'I expect this'll have to do me for a while,' he confessed, warmed by a gleam of understanding — and admiration — in Cousin Stan's gaze. 'I could have bought Mrs. Batchelor a right pretty bauble for what the Senator's got in front of him.'

'Let's not break up the game. . . . You can't quit now,' urged Clark anxiously.

'It's like the Senator said — Captain,' Clyde responded. 'I'd better stick to the boys' games. I'm not quite up to these "for men only deals".'

'We might as well all draw the fires,' chuckled Daingerfield, rising and clapping Clyde heartily on the shoulder. 'Enough's a plenty. I'm going down to see how they're treating Sapphire Sky. Care to join me, any of you?'

Clyde did his best to hide the sense of satisfaction he felt over the outcome. Clark would never know, of course, whether Clyde's act had been calculated, or whether the cards had been so ineptly stacked as to justify what had followed. But, as Clyde turned to accompany Daingerfield, he noted that, though Billy had turned his back to the bar, the mirror revealed, under the dyed moustache, the bartender's lips parted in a wide and gleeful grin.

They reached Memphis late that same afternoon and again, the wharf scene fascinated Lucy. She had seen cotton bales occasionally in Richmond, and had once been taken through a spinnery in Gastonia while visiting one of her schoolmates there. But never could she have imagined so vast an acreage of bales, all alike, their coarsely woven covers of brown jute bulging out between iron tie straps. As far as she could see along the levee, both upstream and down, the bales formed a brown-and-white prairie, its several sections marked by snapping flags or painted standards representing various playing cards in their several suits. In the midst of this prairie, brawny roustabouts chanted mournful improvisations as they manipulated their cotton hooks with remarkable dexterity and skill; and, under the spell of this music, enormous bales actually seemed to dance up the gangplank.

'De Great I-Am say yeah, man! He done tell me his ve'y own se'f I got a bale to tote to Misto Jack o' Di'mon's. Got to tote Misto Jack o' Di'mon's bale lessen de Great I-Am say put de bale down. Po' man, oh, po' sinner, got a bale to tote to Misto Jack o' Di'mon's an' cain' put de burden down tellst de Great I-Am say go yonnuh wid all de Jack o' Di'mon bales. Oh Law-awd, tell de po' man whe' at you wants Misto Jack o' Di'mon's bale put!'

'What do you suppose some psalm-singing down East spinner would say,' chuckled Clyde, 'if he knew his cotton was all being shipped to one of the devil's picture cards?'

'I suppose he'd be very indignant,' conceded Lucy. 'Why on earth should they use playing cards instead of big numbers or letters?'

'Because the roustabouts can't read, but every one of them knows the cards, frontways, backways, and everywhichaways. Tell 'em to take a bale to Number Fourteen and like as not he'd fetch up in Arkansas. But tell him to take it to Mr. Jack of Diamonds, and he'll go there like a martin to his gourd.'

The chants rose and fell, and though the stream of incoming bales was rarely interrupted to permit other cargo to be discharged or brought inboard, the expanse of bales still seemed unbounded. 'That's one commodity the railroads or nothing else will ever take away from the rivers,' Clyde observed as he and Lucy leaned forward to look down upon the swarming activity. 'As long as cotton is ginned, it will be shipped by boats. River steamers to New Orleans. Ocean cargo vessels to Liverpool or Boston, or 'round the Horn to China and India. If you think Memphis is something, wait until you see it in New Orleans! There's a special breed of work-along-shoreman — screwmen, they're called — who load cotton in the ocean vessels. They take jack-screws and tighten those bales down into the hold of a ship till it's a caution. Why, there have even been cases when a ship's timbers were sprung and strained, so tightly were the cotton bales stowed. They get top wages, those screwmen. A silk-hat crowd of workers.'

The great singer disembarked at Memphis, to everyone's regret; she had inspired affection as a woman, besides rousing admiration as an artist; and she would soon be returning to Italy, which meant that most of her fellow-passengers would never see her any more — though, to be sure, with improving conditions, the Grand Tour would soon be a possibility again. At Natchez, Senator Fletcher and his daughter left the boat and this was likewise a matter of general regret. But after all, Natchez was not far from any given point in Louisiana; there would be visiting back and forth between plantations. For the time being, however, all that the southbound passengers saw of Natchez was a line of brick-front houses, set shoulder to shoulder, like stairsteps, on a stately ascending roadway cut into the face of an abrupt bluff. This was Natchez-under-the-Hill, Clyde told Lucy; the city proper was out of sight, beyond the top of the bluff. . . . Baton Rouge was built on a bluff, too, she discovered afterward; but there, the city's principal landmarks — among them the dilapidated pseudo-Norman castle which, before the war, had been a capitol building — were clearly visible. Lucy found the skyline an arresting one, both in itself and its contrast to the flatlands on the opposite shore, which faded back from the low levee into misty cypress swamps. She stayed on deck, chatting with Cousin Stan, while Clyde went ashore to send a wire to Convent, announcing their impending arrival at Cindy Lou. A telegram, he explained would be relayed by courier; they would find everything in readiness for them when they reached home. . . . As Clyde moved away, he heard Daingerfield say, 'That means he's arranged a royal reception for you, my dear. I'm looking forward to it myself – it ought to be quite a spectacle, seen from the *Richmond*.'

'Why not come ashore with us and have a share in it? You know you'd be more than welcome.'

Daingerfield laughed. 'Later, my dear. And I'm looking forward to it. But on your first night in your new home? Don't be absurd, Lucy. Besides, I've got to get in touch with my agent, Moise Riviere, the first thing tomorrow morning.'

Clyde could not hear the rest of the conversation. Later, he asked Lucy what she and Cousin Stan had talked about while he was gone.

'He said he was very fond of me – that, as he didn't have any daughter of his own, he'd like to put me in the place of one, as far as possible. I was touched, Clyde, because he said it as if he really meant it.'

'I'm sure he did. I'm touched, too.'

'And then, he said something else. He said, "I like your husband. I like him very much. I was prepared to welcome him into the family, of course, for your sake, from the first. Now I'm prepared to welcome him into it for his own. You've found yourself a real man, this time, Lucy. He'll never fail you, he'll never even disappoint you. It goes without saying that you'll never fail him or disappoint him." '

Clyde swallowed hard. 'And what did you say?'

'I said I knew he was right. I said I knew the failures and disappointments of my life were all behind me now. I thanked him. And he wanted to know what for.'

'And then you said——'

'Why for accepting me as a foster daughter,' she said. And looked steadily into his eyes.

It was almost midnight when the *Richmond* swung around the bend which brought the Big House at Cindy Lou suddenly into sight. There was a lamp in every window from the belvedere to the basement and little lanterns were set along the railing of the great curving staircase which led from the gallery to the garden. The terraced walk between the house and the landing was flanked with field hands, each holding aloft a flambeau; and the flames from these spread out to meet the flames rising from the torch baskets by the gangplank. When Lucy stepped from this to the shore on Captain Neal's arm, she stood for a moment, gazing at the dazzling sight with a speechlessness more expressive than any cry of rapturous wonderment could have been. Then, still without speaking and completely forgetful of her escort, she turned and looked at the lofty pattern made by the twinkling lights which outlined the pilot-house and the decks of the *Richmond* in tiny points of radiance. Clyde made no effort to shatter the magic moment by speech. But finally her brimming eyes met his, revealing the unity of their thoughts: land and river, boat and house, were all part of the same pattern, and their own loves and their own lives were part of it, too.

Chapter Five

THE *Richmond* sounded its last warning bell, Captain Neal went back to his post on the roof, the paddle wheels began to turn, and the stately white boat glided slowly away, its light duplicated by the blurred reflection in the dark water, its bow crowded by the roustabouts who had forgathered there to sing:

> 'Ah stepped across de Natchez
> Ah stepped across de Lee
> Ah stepped across de Richmond
> An' she flewed fum under me
> Ah—Annie—ah
> She flewed fum under me.'

Briefly, while listening to the music, Clyde and Lucy continued to watch the receding plume of spark-shot smoke which marked the boat's progress down the wide river. But the magic moment was over. Clyde turned and greeted the waiting Negroes.

'Good evening,' he began cheerily. 'Miss Lucy—Mrs. Batchelor—and I are happy to see all of you. But you'll get to know her a lot better in the morning. Meantime . . .' He turned to Lucy. '. . . Will you excuse me just a moment, honey, while I explain to them about the luggage?' he asked. Then, raising his voice, he called, 'Zack! Where are you, Zack?'

'Heah's me, suh,' a deep musical voice replied from the darkness.

'This way, then,' said Clyde. His words trailed off into indistinct murmurs as he took the servant back to the heap of trucks, satchels and bags which had been put ashore by the *Richmond's* porters. So he was sure Lucy did not hear his anxious whisper, 'Zack, tell me quickly — have any horses been shipped here the last day or so? Just nod your head — or shake it.' Then, as Zack gave the hoped-for signal, accompanied by a broad grin, Clyde turned back to Lucy and, drawing her hand through the crook of his arm, said tenderly, 'Come, dear. We don't stop to see the gardens or anything else now. It's late and everything will still be here tomorrow. Besides, I can't wait to claim the privilege of carrying you over the threshold.'

When he set her down, it was in the drawing-room, which was not dim, as he had first seen it, but superbly illuminated by its crystal chandeliers, so that its arcade of pillars and its frescoed walls were brilliantly revealed. Lucy looked about her with delighted appreciation and told him she was surer than ever that he meant to have her live in fairyland. But he suddenly realized that she was very tired; there had inevitably been a let-down after the excitement of their arrival, and she was really overwhelmed by the splendours revealed through their approach to their new home and their entrance within its walls. He suggested that she should not try to see the rest of the main floor that night, but let him take her straight upstairs; the next day they would make a 'tour of inspection', both inside the house and over the grounds. She agreed, almost eagerly, that this would be much the best plan. Belle drew a bath for her in the great porcelain tub of which Clyde was so inordinately proud; and soon she was settled among her pillows in the immense bed with the canopy lined with azure satin, after the most approved fashion for a *lit de ciel*.

Clyde was not sorry that Lucy's weariness had furnished a pretext for postponement. He felt that, with one exception, the results of his foresight, consultations and expenditures were pleasingly evident. But the space created for a library, when he moved the furnishings of the gaming-room to the ground floor, had presented a major problem to him; he knew little and cared less about books. So he had installed a few handsome bookcases and decided to tell Lucy that he had purposely left these only partly filled and had attempted no other furnishings, while waiting to find out what, if anything, she desired to bring from Sorrento. Therefore, he was greatly relieved, the next morning, when, after one casual glance about the great square room at the left of the front door, Lucy said there would be plenty of time to talk about all that later, when it was not so beautiful outside. Then she went back into the hall and, turning toward the gallery, closed the door after them. The view from the gallery was certainly very pleasant: the terraces had taken shape, the fountains were playing, the trees and shrubs set in their appointed places, and many of the flower beds were in bloom; although there had not been time for the grounds to make any show of luxuriance, this was already foreshadowed. From the gardens, Lucy wanted to go on to the orchards and from there to the stables; the horses which Moise Riviere had succeeded in securing and shipping, at top speed, were already in roomy stables, from which they were led out, one by one, for her enthusiastic inspection. With the only tinge of regret that she expressed about anything, she whispered to Clyde that she supposed she should not do any riding for the present. Fortunately, she could not foresee the miscarriage which, in spite of every precaution against it, occurred early in the new year, temporarily clouding her happiness and, for a much longer time, limiting her outdoor activities.

Meanwhile, it interested and occupied her to remedy the inadequacies of the library's equipment. The handsome bookcases Clyde had already installed were filled with such promptitude that he instantly recognized the necessity of supplementing these. Mrs. Cary had maintained that Lucy was entitled to take as many of her grandfather's books as she chose from Sorrento, since she had insisted that Colonel Page's library must be kept intact for Bushrod. In Mrs. Cary's opinion, this was an evidence of fine feeling which should not go unrewarded; and she knew it would mean much to her daughter if, in her new house, the bride could have around her the well-worn volumes to which, from childhood, she had been accustomed. Alexander Peyton had not been outstanding as a scholar; but he had considered a general acquaintance with the classics and with current literature a requisite in the well-ordered life of a country gentleman; and he had never regarded lightly his responsibilities as a landowner, a justice of the peace, and a church-warden. His library reflected his standards, his tastes and his sense of duty. With Shakespeare's Plays and the King James Version of the Bible as its twin cornerstones, it grew to include the complete works of Scott, Byron and the other British writers of their period. It also contained La Fontaine's *Fables* and Racine's Plays in the original French, besides numerous acceptable translations of other foreign authors; and, along with these, were ranged Mayo's *Guide to Magistrates*, Gunn's *Domestic Medicine* and Frank Van Dever's *Sermons*.

Mrs. Cary had been right in believing that it would mean much to Lucy if she could have part of her grandfather's library with her in Louisiana; and, in making her selections, the bride had included not only the classical fables, plays and novels, from which he had read aloud to her on long winter evenings, and the *Medical Companion*, with the contents of which her mother had acquainted her gradually, but Byron's Poems, which she was not supposed to have read, and some of the old law books, which she had really never read. Like Alexander Peyton, she was cultured and conscientious rather than scholarly; but she loved the sight of the beautiful tawny old volumes bound in half-calf or suede, on her well-filled shelves, whether she ever looked inside them or not. They adorned the great square room which had been voided of its gaming table, and gradually she embellished it still further with huge globes, chaste marble busts and old etchings. All of these seemed to harmonize wonderfully well, both with the books and with the rich draperies and heavy carved furniture. Clyde came to share Lucy's pride in the library and to watch for the sales which were all too often precipitated by fallen fortunes and — acting on Lucy's suggestions — to make wise purchases which filled the gaps in her own collection. But he never took the same degree of enjoyment in this room that he did in the rest of the house, which, as season succeeded season, more and more completely filled its builder's dream that — according to Dorothée — it should be a bower of beauty and a centre of enjoyment, even of revelry, not only for its owners, but for all their friends.

To be sure, during the earlier years of their marriage, the Batchelors did not have many visitors. Cousin Stan almost always stopped off for a few days when he was on his way to and from Kentucky, bringing with him an atmosphere of great good cheer and casks of Judge Carteret's Bourbon. Captain Neal and the officers of the *Lucy Batchelor* and her sister steamboats, which were built soon afterward — the *Cary Page* and the *Sophia Peyton* — also came frequently to Cindy Lou; but Mrs. Surget was the only lady living in the immediate vicinity who dropped in often and who was regarded by Lucy in the light of an intimate friend. Lucy realized that her lack of verbal fluency in French — which she read with ease and wrote with grace — and the fact that she was an Episcopalian instead of a Catholic automatically created barriers between herself and her neighbours and that the trying period of Reconstruction was not conducive to conviviality; but she would have been amused, rather than offended, that Creoles might consider themselves the social superiors of a Cary. If she missed the greater degree of intimate and informal sociability to which she had been accustomed in Virginia, she never said so, and it did not occur to Clyde that she did. She seemed to feel his company all-sufficient, his devotion completely satisfying; indeed, he had the impression that guests would have appeared to her like intruders in this fairyland of his creation, that she desired to share it with no one except those nearest and dearest to her, who, when all was said and done, were only Cary and himself. Cousin Mildred Caskie had brought both children to Louisiana, in accordance with the prenuptial agreement, as soon as the bride and groom were really settled; but, when she returned to Virginia herself, after one of the long visits typical of the period, she took Bushrod with her. As things turned out, he was comparatively little at Cindy Lou after that; it had been decided by all concerned that it was best for him to go to school in Virginia, where he could have greater educational advantages, and to come to Louisiana only for his longer holidays. But part of these vacation periods were spent in Sorrento, quite logically, since this property would some day be his and thorough acquaintance with it was highly desirable. So months at a time went by in which his mother and sister and stepfather hardly saw him.

Apparently, his mother did not resent this, for his prolonged absences were another matter on which she did not comment, and nothing could have suited Clyde better than to have Bushrod in Virginia. The boy was rapidly outgrowing his less pleasing attributes. He no longer whined or sulked; in fact, his manner was unusually suave for one of his age. The sallowness of his childhood had now changed to a clear pallor, which rather enhanced the dramatic quality of his good looks. His dark eyes were keen, his mouth mobile and his expression watchful. He was slender, but exceptionally well proportioned and, despite the air of indolence which he affected, he played an excellent game of tennis, rode horseback with the careless ease of a born equestrian and danced with almost professional perfection. Without being a brilliant scholar, he did reasonably well in his studies; and without being outstandingly popular among companions of his own sex, he was liked by most of his classmates and was a great favourite with their sisters —whose parents, for some reason they did not attempt to explain, viewed him with less enthusiasm. His grandmother adored him and his mother viewed his faults indulgently; but Cary had never accorded him the respect normally shown by small sisters to their older brothers and there was still no real harmony between him and Clyde.

Cary's relationship to her stepfather was, however, entirely different. In a sense, she was even more of a companion to him than Lucy, for the little girl tagged everywhere at his heels, while her mother was occupied with the meticulous supervision of the great house; and, as soon as Cary was old enough, she rode with him, whenever he went about the plantation or on jaunts up and down the river road. Lucy did not ride any more. She had stopped, immediately, when there was first a prospect of another child, hoping against hope that the doctor she had previously consulted might have been mistaken, that she could, after all, give Clyde a son of his own. Her hopes had been vain, not only then but later; nevertheless, she clung to them for a long time; her repeated disappointments were the sole cloud on her happiness and she could not bear to admit the permanency of its shadow. Eventually, her physician suggested that she would be wise to forgo riding, in any case. Her general health was good and remained so, if she was spared fatigue. But she easily became exhausted, and the handling of a spirited horse, or even a gentle one, was too much for her limited strength when this was constantly overtaxed in many other ways.

So it was Cary who went everywhere with Clyde, and to whom he talked about local happenings and the management of Cindy Lou and the lore of the countryside as they 'rode the crops' along the headlands which separated the various fields and, later on, along the experimental levees erected in an effort to stay the might of the spring floods. Apparently, the beloved child, like the man who adored her, never wearied of ranging the countryside, of gazing at the shifting panorama which the landscape provided, of learning its secrets, of exploring its splendours. Together, they always found something wonderful to do, something wonderful to see, something wonderful to discuss. . . .

For months on end, of course, the sugar crop received their absorbed attention—the first tender shoots, 'the fine stand of cane', the rows of tall stalks falling to the ground under the gleaming knives. Then, in mid-December, when grinding was drawing toward its close, perique came into its own, and the progress of this, from seed-time to harvest, seemed even more thrilling to Cary than anything the cane fields and the sugar mills could offer.

First the tiny sandlike granules were mixed, in equal parts, with wood ashes. This, Clyde explained to Cary, was in order that the seeds might be more widely separated in the sowing. She nodded her understanding and watched, with the same intensity that he did, while the mixture was carefully scattered over long narrow beds and covered with palmetto leaves. Then she waited for the bright days when the leaves would be lifted to admit the warm winter sunshine and asked her stepfather anxiously, on chilly nights, whether they had not better go and make sure the covers had been replaced. Clyde always assured her that the palmetto leaves were back exactly where they belonged; but sometimes he took her to look at them, just the same. He knew she would sleep better if she saw for herself that the little plants, which had sprung from the tiny seeds, were all right.

Next, Cary waited with impatience for April to come, for then the seedlings would be taken from their long narrow beds and planted in the fields, which were already prepared to receive them. By that time, the bright stalks of cane would already be springing up from the old rows of stubble, so that the growth of the two crops could be watched simultaneously for many weeks. But by late June, near the Feast of St. John the Baptist, the perique crop was ready to harvest, while the cane would remain in the fields until near the Feast of *Toussaint*, which fell on the first of November.

Cary would have liked to dismount and get out among the children who were shown how to break the suckers carefully from each stalk of perique, so that not more than twelve leaves would remain on any one; Clyde had explained to her that this was done in order to ensure the size and strength of the plants and she wanted to help, for she took immense pride in their vigorous growth. But he also told her that, while it was right and proper for some children to work in the fields, others must learn 'to plant from the saddle' and that she was one of those who belonged to the latter group. When she said she did not see why, he told her that she would some day, and that, meanwhile, he hoped she would take his word for it. When he put it that way, she said of course she would. She would take his word for anything.

Perique, like cane, was cut with wide, cleaver-shaped knives. This was done when the sun was high, so that the leaves would be wilted by the time the cut stalks were taken to the drying sheds; on the other hand, after the dried leaves had been stripped from the stalks, they were cleansed and gathered into 'twists' very early in the morning, while they were still pliable from the dew. So, with the coming of summer, Clyde and Cary were up even earlier than usual, first to watch the harvesting and then to follow the carts in which the leaves were hauled to the drying sheds and unloaded beneath canopies which protected them from the sun. Women were waiting to drive nails into the butts of the stalks and suspend these on wires, where they remained for about two weeks. Next, men came and took the dried stalks from the wires and beat them on logs to remove the dust which had collected on them. After that, they stripped the leaves from the stalks and moistened them under a very fine spray before turning them back to the women, who sat at long tables and, by deft flicks of the wrist, removed the centre veins—a process which Cary watched with endless fascination. Even after this work was completed, she loved to linger in the curing sheds while the twists of tobacco were placed in strong wooden boxes, with oaken blocks on top of the bundled leaves. Long poles were laid over these blocks and weighted down with heavy stones, so that the tobacco would be pressed in its own aromatic juices. Then, every so often, these stones were removed, to release the pressure on the leaves. The brawny men who lifted off the weights let Cary 'help' them and, afterward, they showed her how the packed leaves, once the pressure was lifted, would suck back part of their own moisture and soak it up again. She came to understand that it was this process of alternate pressure and release which finally gave the tobacco the rich flavour which was so highly prized; and she thought it was very wonderful that anything that looked so simple should be so important.

Her interest did not end with the curing. She found endless excuses for visiting and revisiting the warehouse, to watch the packaging of the perique, after it had been properly pressed, into the five-pound bundles, tightly bound with ropes and canvas, which were called 'carrots' and in which it was eventually marketed. 'Please, papa!' she would say coaxingly. Once in a while, Clyde demurred, reminding her that they had been to the warehouse only the day before, that nothing was happening there which she had not seen many times already and that it was more important for him to inspect the cane carts which were under repair, or the powerful 'sugar mules' which had just been shipped in from Missouri. Then, still more engagingly, she would prattle about the 'nice funny sweetness' of the scent which permeated the warehouse and which he knew she loved to sniff, or remind him that, the last time they went there, she had not 'helped' weight down a single lever; and she would end by creeping into his lap and snuggling close to him while she whispered, *Pretty* please!' between the kisses with which she showered him. So he would forget about the carts and the mules and remember only that Cary was the darling of his heart and that he could deny her nothing.

The wild creatures which belonged to the land, as well as the crops which grew on it, were a source of never-ending joy and wonder to the little girl. Clyde had not long been familiar with these birds and beasts himself, since he had not been raised as a countryman; but he took pains to learn about them as rapidly as he could, from Lucy, from the neighbours and from the Negroes, and then proudly passed on his new-found knowledge to Cary as fast as he acquired it himself. One day, as they were skirting the angle of underbrush, along two inter-secting ditch banks, a little brown quail apparently tumbled out of the thicket on to the turf at the very feet of their horses.

'Oh, the poor little thing!' Cary exclaimed. 'It's been hurt.'

'No, she hasn't,' Clyde chuckled. 'But she's got a nestful of babies somewhere near here and is pretending to be helpless, so that we'll follow her instead of finding them. Come on, honey. Let's let her have the fun of feeling she's fooled us. Slowly, now.'

Fluttering in seeming panic along the ground, the little quail man-aged to remain just beyond reach until she had led them far from the precious brood; then suddenly, she rose with a drumming of wings, which startled the horses, and flew away across a broad drainage canal.

'Isn't that smart though?' Cary cried delightedly. 'Do all quails know how to do that, papa?'

'Most mothers know just how to shelter their babies,' Clyde told her. 'One of these days you'll be keeping a youngster from trying out bright new ways to get himself killed. Then you'll realize how that mother quail felt when we came riding up to her nursery.'

Even more fascinating to Cary than the wild creatures which belonged to the land, were the human beings who belonged to it also, and who were not afraid that she might do them harm, like the mother quail, but who returned her friendliness. There was Moppy, the wizened Negress who always wore a shapeless calico garment and three hats, one perched on top of another. Whenever she met Clyde and Cary on the river road, Moppy snatched off two of her hats, extending one, upturned, to Clyde, and the other, also upturned, to Cary, with the single wheedling word, 'Mishay!' Clyde always dropped a silver dollar into the hat nearest him and handed another dollar to Cary, so that she could give Moppy one, too. Then the wizened Negress mumbled blessings on their heads and told them she had cast her spell on them 'for true'. The first time this happened, Cary was very much astonished, both at the size of her stepfather's largesse and at the deference he showed the weird woman. But he explained that he had met Moppy the first day he had gone down the river road, seeking his fortune, and that he had had all the good luck she had wished him; so he had been grateful to her and generous toward her ever since, and he intended to go on showing his gratitude by generosity as long as Moppy lived. After that, Cary understood and herself treasured Moppy's good wishes, feeling sure these would bring her luck, too.

Besides hobbling Moppy with her three hats, there was Milly Sue, as mountainous as Moppy was wizened, who did not beg and who always carried a small white blossom in one huge black hand. Milly Sue was remarkable in that she could walk among her many hives without getting stung and she never referred to her bees except as 'my little folkses'. Clyde and Cary did not meet her by chance on the river road, as they met Moppy, who never revealed her abiding place. They went to Milly Sue's cabin on purpose to inquire whether she was getting palmetto honey from her bees, because, if she were, they would ask Belle to make hush puppies for breakfast; there was nothing in the whole world better for breakfast than hush puppies with honey.

'Sho 'nuff,' Milly Sue would say, raising the fragile flower in her hand toward her broad blob of a nose and sniffing at it as she chuckled a greeting. 'My little folkses done be making plenty honey, them, for most three weeks now. Ah specks Ah'd better clean one 'em beehives after you-all gone away, cose dey's fractious today by the long dry spell. Soon as ever a shower of rain fix it so dey don' have to work too, too hard, dem, dey be's feeling more better.'

Then there was Aunt Vicey, who was an herb woman, and whom they saw both on the river road, where she went to gather sassafras leaves, and at her cabin, where she pounded them after drying them in the shade. She also went into the swamps, to look for bay leaves and other plants, from which she brewed herb teas that were highly regarded. Clyde and Cary did not often see her when engaged in such a search, partly because they themselves spent less time in the swampland than on the river road and in the quarters, and partly because Aunt Vicey preferred to do her searching, like her brewing, in secrecy and they respected her feeling about this; they knew it was different from Milly Sue's pride in her skill with bees, which she was only too glad to proclaim, and from Moppy's begging, in which she felt no shame. On the rare occasions when Cary, who was a very healthy little girl, had one of her infrequent illnesses, Aunt Vicey always came at once to Cindy Lou with some of her brews, and Lucy did not hesitate to give these to the child. They never did her any harm and sometimes, surprisingly, they seemed to do her good. Cary herself believed quite as implicitly in Vicey's herbs as she did in Moppy's blessings.

Lucy had never tried to keep Cary away from the noisy tumultuous life of the quarters and Clyde was glad of this. The little girl was at ease among the women who sat stuffing black moss into ticking for mattresses, or bent over their open hearths as they prepared their food and heated their sadirons, and even more at ease with their children. She loved the piccaninnies who tumbled about the dust-packed yard and was loved by them in return. The arrival of each new pinkish brown baby was a source of rapture to her, even when she was puzzled because their mothers did not seem to be much pleased about it – like the time when Ginny Lou's fourteen-year-old daughter, Ma'y Lou, who delighted in making sugar tits for all the babies in the quarters, suddenly appeared with a bouncing little boy of her own, and Ginny Lou grumbled that Ma'y Lou never had no business finding no woods baby; but then all girls was sinners nowadays.

'Moppy must have wished Ma'y Lou luck, too,' Cary told Clyde enviously. 'More luck than she did me. I want a little brother the worst way. And I've looked and looked all through our woods, over and over again, and I've never found a baby. Next time I see Moppy——'

'All right, the next time you see Moppy, you can complain to her, if you want to,' Clyde told her. 'But we haven't time to worry about that now. Did you hear that favourite whistle of yours? We've got to hurry if we're going to get down to the landing before the *Cleon* gets in.'

He knew there was no surer way than this to make Cary forget about the woods baby. The *Cleon* was the mail boat and Cary always wanted to be waiting to see it appear around the bend. She wanted to see the roustabouts lolling among the cotton bales and the hogsheads of sugar. She wanted to see the men whose occupations were more important moving about in the pilot-house and the texas; most of all she wanted to see Captain Mossop and his daughter, Marianna.

Captain Mossop was the owner of the *Cleon* as well as its master, and Cary considered Marianna one of the luckiest children on earth, because she could ride on her father's boat every day, if she wished, and very frequently she did. She was always very much dressed up, much more dressed up than Cary, for Lucy believed that children's clothes should be kept simple. Apparently, Mrs. Mossop, who was never in evidence, had different ideas, for Marianna was invariably clad in a white dress with a great deal of trimming, including fluttering blue ribbons; she also wore a large, floppy hat. She was older than Cary and Cary considered her very beautiful. Marianna spent most of her time reclining in a deck chair and drinking lemonade. The lemonade was served in a tall glass and plump, red cherries floated on top of it. Whenever Cary came on board the *Cleon*, Marianna summoned a steward to bring a second tall glass of lemonade, and Cary sat down beside her hostess and tried to sip and drink slowly, as Marianna did. But the lemonade was so delicious that this was very hard for her to do. She wanted to drink it down in great gulps; she was sure it was the best lemonade in the world.

Sometimes Clyde teased her a little about the *Cleon* and Captain Mossop and Marianna and said she was a greedy little girl; she proved it by liking the *Cleon* better than any of the many other boats that stopped at the Cindy Lou landing, delivering plantation supplies or picking up carrots of perique, instead of merely bringing mail. He told her he could not see why she liked it better even than the *Morning Star*, whose pilot, Dick Blair, had made up a special rhythm of whistle blasts as a welcome to Cary, telling her that it was their very own 'rooty toot' and that no one else up or down any of the rivers was permitted to use that signal. Cary was proud because Dick had selected her for such an unusual honour, but she still thought the *Cleon's* whistle was deeper and mellower; it was never sharp, like the whistle of the *Morning Star* and those on many of the other boats. And though she liked Dick very much, it was true that she did not regard him with the envious awe which Marianna inspired in her breast. It was not until she was quite a big girl that she changed her mind about Marianna, and realized that her idol was silly and vain and condescending, and that Dick was merry and kind and capable. She confessed this to Clyde and he told her he had known all along that sometime she would feel differently, and not just about Dick, but about nice young men in general.

Unlike Clyde, Cary loved the land and its crops and its creatures more than she did the river. He could have taught her to love that, too, he told himself, if he had dared to talk about it more freely, or to take her on enough trips to familiarize her with its beauties and its wonders. But he was afraid that some story, harmless enough in itself, might prove to possess dangerous ramifications; and he had come so close to betrayal, on his wedding journey, that he was loath to risk further encounters and further disclosures which might rouse Cary's suspicions. Even after all these years, Lucy had never voiced any; but he knew hers must have been roused, and he was thankful to feel that Cary's trust in him had never been put to a similar test. She had been less than three years old at the time of the *Lucy Batchelor's* maiden voyage — too young for participation in any of the attendant festivities. To be sure, she had been taken aboard eighteen months later, when the *Cary Page*, its flags proudly flying, its approach heralded by a booming cannon, had made its first dramatic stop at the Cindy Lou landing. She had been given a sip of the champagne cup in which the captain toasted her and everyone had made much of her. But she confessed, several years later, that all she could really remember about the party was the confusion of sounds, caused by the great jangling of bells as the vessel came to a halt, mingling with the cheers of the passengers and the crew, and her own tiredness after she had been led from one boat to the other, amidst continual exclamations of admiration in which she did not especially share. Then, when the *Sophia Peyton* had been launched, two years later still, it was her grandmother and not herself who had been the centre of attention. Most of the guests, in Cary's opinion, were very dull elderly people, who could not be expected to act as if they were having fun, though she supposed that, in their own queer way, they must be. . . .

Secretly, Clyde was pleased when he found that Cary felt like this; and afterward, there were no more gala landings and pompous launchings, for his interest shifted from floating palaces to towboats and barges, and these did not call for the same kind of réclame. It had always been his way to better himself by changing conditions and, once he had designed, owned and operated the three finest steamboats that had ever graced and glorified the Mississippi, and made money on them, despite the encroachments of the railroads and the gloomy prophecies of his would-be competitors, he was ready to turn his attention to another form of river transportation. So he organized an inland navigation company, calling it the C & L; invested in a new fleet of steamers which flew its house flag; and opened an impressive office in New Orleans, near the Bienville Street levee, staffing it with a port captain, a port steward, a book-keeper and a host of clerical workers. The navigators, pilots, mates, roustabouts, barkeepers and other functionaries who manned the C & L vessels were hired from this command post. Here also, freight was accepted and billed: purchases of supplies that ran the gamut from fuel contracts along the river's length to liquor for the bar, valve parts for the steam engines, provisions for the galley, lime rods for the calcium searchlights and cup grease for the bearings of the titanic twin pitmans.

The profits of this venture, like those of all his previous ventures, were both speedy and substantial. When it came to large commodity shipments, such as grain from the Missouri River Basin, iron and coal from Pittsburgh, and cotton from the South, he could still underbid the best offers the railroads could make and continue to show an impressive percentage gain. The card of the C & L Navigation Company first appeared in the *Picayune* amidst a host of similar notices, giving the schedules of other river boats, ocean liners, sailing vessels and barks: these occupied a full page and he spread the sheet out before Lucy with a thrill of pardonable pride: as against this lordly display, only two railroads besought public patronage in a few inches of typed space, tucked away in an obscure corner of the financial page!

Although his presence was, of course, periodically required in New Orleans, Clyde directed the affairs of the new company almost entirely from Cindy Lou. The office which adjoined the gaming-room was large enough for all practical purposes and he equipped it for efficiency with a roll-top desk, a good-sized safe and a number of tavern chairs. Moreover, the ground floor, besides the premises which he had appropriated for his special needs and the laundry, wine cellar and store closets, contained four bedrooms, a bathroom and a dining-room suitable for the use of business visitors. He could summon members of his staff to Cindy Lou whenever he chose, with the knowledge that they would be comfortably housed and still not infringe upon Lucy's privacy. No arrangement could possibly have suited him better. He was satisfied and stimulated beyond measure by his latest success; at the same time, he was increasingly reluctant to leave his home and family; and the less Cary saw of barges and towboats and their personnel, the better he was pleased.

As the years went on, he was more and more sure his reticence and his hesitation had been wise. It had, perhaps, been less wise, to express his doubts as to the practicability of the new levees. But one spring day he spontaneously voiced his anxiety. He had always encouraged Cary to talk freely with him; it seemed natural for him to talk freely with her in return.

'These levees may be fine things,' he said, shaking his head and then looking out toward the clover-covered enbankment. 'But I'm afraid they'll have their drawbacks, too. Now, when the river spreads, it does so gradually and the overflows are never very deep. But the trend is toward a higher and higher levee. If there were a crevasse – and there's bound to be sooner or later – it would do a great deal of damage.'

'What's a crevasse?'

'A breach in a levee – that is, a big gap where turbulent waters come boiling through and rush all over the countryside. There's never been one, in this vicinity, since we've lived here. I hope there never will be. But I wish I felt surer of it.'

'What does tur-bu-lent mean, papa?'

'Rushing and riotous. The way the waters become at the bottom of a cataract. That may happen because there's been so much melting ice, way up north, after a long, cold winter, that the river was swollen to unnatural size.'

'You'd never think the river would be tur-bu-lent, would you? It looks so smooth and slide-y.'

'Yes, it does, right now. But it's given trouble, ever since its banks were settled. There have been lots of wrecks on it, too — it's full of snags, it's often completely engulfed by fog. And sometimes, in the old days, bands of river pirates swarmed on to the beautiful steamboats from their skiffs and seized the strong boxes in the pursers' offices and robbed the passengers of their gold and jewellery.'

'Oh, papa, how exciting!' Cary looked away from the levee, which she could not visualize as a menace, no matter how carefully Clyde explained about crevasses, and gazed at him with rapture. 'You mean to say there really were river pirates? They weren't just in stories, like fairies? Belle's talked to me about pirates, too, but I thought it was all make-believe.'

'I don't know what Belle's told you about them, but they were real, all right. They were a reckless, evil lot and it was mighty hard to rid the river of them. They holed out in deep swamps and on small islands. They could hide for a long while that way. But, eventually, steamboat captains began mounting small cannon on their forecastles and that precaution marked the decline of piracy. In due time, all the miscreants were scattered, if they weren't caught and killed.'

'Belle says it was the pirates who killed people. She says they gutted their victims, so the poor people would sink to the bottom of the river. She says there was a pirate named Murrell who boasted no one he robbed had ever floated up to tes-ti-fy.'

'Belle shouldn't tell you things like that. Your mother wouldn't like it.'

'Well, I like it. Belle says Murrell stirred up the slaves, too. He planned to make them rebel against their cruel masters. She says he meant to found a black empire and rule over it. She says——'

'I'll have a word with Belle about the stories she's telling you.'

'Oh, papa, please don't! *Pretty* please!'

'Cary, I——'

'Well, you just said yourself that the pirates were real. Didn't you ever hear about Mr. Murrell?'

'Yes, I've heard of him.'

'All right, you tell me about him.'

'He had a very sad end, which he richly deserved,' Clyde said, trying to speak severely. 'He was a boastful man and he tried to impress a young recruit to his band by telling all kinds of lurid tales about his past. The recruit was really a spy in disguise; he betrayed his leader and exposed the plan of an uprising. Murrell was convicted of stealing slaves and clapped into prison. He coughed away his life there and died while he was still a young man.'

'Yes, but before that, didn't he have a very exciting time? Didn't he travel up and down the river in all sorts of disguises? Didn't he even have a trip to Mexico?'

'I believe so. But eventually, as I said——'

'He stole gold and jewelry, too, didn't he? Not just slaves. Belle says he had a wonderful time with his money. She said he had so much he couldn't begin to use it all, no matter how much he spent. She says he hid part of it. She says there's buried treasure right here on Cindy Lou!'

Cary was still looking at her stepfather with sparkling eyes, still speaking with a joyous excitement quite untinged by fear or horror. Clyde, cursing himself for having given colour to Belle's story by introducing the subject of pirates himself, tried to shrug the matter away. It was just as he had thought. A seemingly harmless tale might have all kinds of ramifications.

'Well, of course there are always legends about what pirates have done with their loot. And the Negroes love to embroider them. But I wouldn't put much stock in this buried treasure if I were you, Cary.'

'But you've heard about that, too, haven't you?'

'Yes, I've heard about it. I've even heard where it's supposed to be located – out in the rear areas of the plantation, where there's a big gravel bed, so that the land can never be productive.'

'Couldn't we go there and dig?'

'We could, but we'd have nothing except exercise for our pains. We'd have to get rid of an enormous deposit of gravel before we'd even get down to rock bottom.'

'Well, if you don't want to dig there, can't I go and dig by myself?'

'Certainly not. You know you and I always go everywhere together. But I tell you what: some day when I'm not too busy with the sugar crop, and you don't coax me into taking you to the perique warehouse, we'll go out to that gravel bed and I'll sit and smoke while you dig. If you dig far enough, all by yourself, to get below ground, and find the buried treasure, you may keep every bit of it. How's that for a bargain?'

'Oh, papa, it's *wonderful*. I can't wait to start!'

Within a week, she had cajoled him into taking her out to the gravel bed. But, after an hour's digging, she was ready to admit that she was pretty tired and that she would like to go home for tea. Of course, they could come again, some other day. And they actually did do so, two or three times, quite close together. After that, these special outings were spaced farther and farther apart and, eventually, when Bushrod had ridiculed them on one of his rare visits, Cary ceased to suggest them. She and Clyde sometimes referred to the treasure again, in a semi-serious way. But she had become more vitally interested in matters closer at hand and she was also indirectly responsible for the emergence of her mother and stepfather from the seclusion which they had found so satisfying.

It was never suggested that she should go to school in Virginia; neither Clyde nor Lucy could have tolerated such a separation. But when she was ten years old, she began to attend the Academy of the Sacred Heart at Convent, a short distance up the river. With the same swiftness that she had won Clyde's heart, she endeared herself to her teachers and her schoolmates. Soon she was chattering in French with almost the same ease that she spoke English and was visiting at all the nearby plantations and at some of those more distant; for the 'First Families', who had sent their daughters to the Academy from the time of its foundation, had never lost the habit of doing so. It was natural that these visits should be returned; and though some of the more conservative Creoles hesitated to accept the hospitality of 'outsiders', the girls and boys who went to Cindy Lou brought back such glowing accounts of it, that all those who had not helped to make up the party were frankly jealous and complained long and bitterly to their parents, as Clyde and Lucy learned gradually, in course of time.

Everyone had such a good time at Cary's house! There was actually a tennis court; no one was expected to be satisfied with croquet or with battledore and shuttlecock. And, after a match, there was tea, not coffee. Mrs. Batchelor served tea every day, not just when she had company — on the terrace if the weather were pleasant, in the drawing-room if it were not. And she did not have just little petit-fours with it, either. There was always a big loaf of home-made *pain de mie*, set out on a round board with a carved rim, and Mrs. Batchelor buttered the bread as she sliced it. There were likewise several kinds of jam to go with the bread and, in season, big bowls of sugared berries or peeled fresh figs with cream to spread on top of them, so thick that you had to spoon it out of the pitcher. There were scones and cookies and big frosted layer cakes. And while you were eating, you could watch the peacocks. They didn't just strut around the terraces, screaming. Every once in a while, they flew right up in the air, with their great tails floating out behind them. Sometimes, you could see as many as eight or ten of them, all ranged along in a row, on top of the cistern, and, at night, they roosted in the trees. It gave you a sort of queer feeling to see the white ones up there, when it was getting dark, because they did look like little ghosts — at least, what the Negroes said little ghosts looked like. Just the same, it was all nonsense to say peacocks were unlucky. Mrs. Batchelor made fans out of the feathers they dropped and also kept great clusters of feathers in vases, on the drawing-room mantel, and she wouldn't have done that if they could have brought bad luck to Cindy Lou. She was a lovely lady, always pleasant to everybody, and so pretty, too. And would you believe it? She went to New York to buy all her dresses, but they came from Paris in the first place and so did Cary's. Mr. Batchelor got his clothes from London. He was fun, too. In rainy weather, when the crowd could not have tennis matches or ride horseback or do anything else outdoors, he took them to the gaming-room and played Casino and dominoes with them and showed them card tricks. He knew any number of card tricks and was terribly good at them. Later on, there was a huge supper, with oyster patties and chicken salad and beaten biscuit and Sally Lunn and all kinds of blancmanges and creams, even ice cream as a matter of course, and at least three kinds of cake. There were ten house servants at Cindy Lou and they never seemed to mind how much work they did or how late they were kept up. Mrs. Batchelor and Cary both had their own personal maids and Mr. Batchelor had a valet. The guests had special maids and valets assigned to them, too, who were at their beck and call, no matter what time they went to bed. Usually this was pretty late, because they danced to all hours in that big ballroom with the coloured lights and, of course, that was the greatest fun of all. Cary was a wonderful dancer. . . .

Clyde could picture the badgered parents listening with compressed lips, if they were the stern, silent type or, if they were not, permitting themselves a few scathing remarks : about the kind of people who had money nowadays and the questionable sources from which it came; about the lack of good taste exemplified by a huge house built in Steamboat Gothic style, and a fountain dominated by the cast-iron figure of a little girl, dressed in the current fashion and holding an umbrella over her head; about the absurdity of having peacocks strutting around on a series of terraces and a maze — a 'puzzle garden' as the youngsters called it — for an outstanding feature of the grounds. It gave him no little satisfaction to realize that, all the time, these die-hards knew they would have to give in sooner or later and let their sons and daughters go to Cindy Lou, if they were to have any peace in life; and still more satisfaction when he found out that, while they continued to hesitate, their hands were unexpectedly forced.

In 1884, the daughters of General Lee came to New Orleans to be present at the unveiling of their father's statue and to attend the Carnival celebrations. In the course of a conversation with a distinguished escort, during a lull in the preliminary proceedings, one of them unwittingly asked an embarrassing question.

'I had been rather expecting to meet a Miss Cary Page. You know her, of course.'

'I am afraid I do not. But I am sure I should. What is her father's Christian name?'

'Her father is dead. But he was Colonel Forrest Page, a very distinguished member of my father's staff. Indeed, he gave his life for the Lost Cause. That is to say, he was not killed in battle, though he was wounded four times. He died later as a result of these wounds.'

'I am distressed to learn that the daughter of such a gallant officer should not have been included among those invited to meet you before the unveiling and to be present at the ceremony. I do not understand how she could possibly have been overlooked, how we could have failed to know that this young lady was now living in New Orleans. If you will give me her address, I will see that the omission is rectified immediately. Cards for all subsequent festivities will be sent to her by special messenger.'

'I believe she does not live in New Orleans, but on a plantation at a short distance from here. However, the river families usually come to New Orleans for Carnival, do they not? Mrs. Page, who was a Miss Lucy Cary, the daughter of General Virginius Cary, remarried, several years after the colonel's death. If I am not mistaken, her second husband's name is Clyde Batchelor and their plantation is called Cindy Lou. But the children of the first marriage have, of course, kept their own father's illustrious name. The son, Bushrod, is now a student at the University of Virginia. I have met him several times – indeed, I am distantly connected with him and his sister through the Washingtons. But I have never met Colonel Page's daughter, who is quite a little younger. I should like immensely to do so.'

Miss Lee's escort put his memorandum pad back in his pocket, smothering a sigh of relief. 'I begin to understand the – the omission,' he said, adding quickly, 'the difference in name, you see. We had no reason to suppose that Miss Page would have any special interest in the unveiling. I believe it is generally taken for granted that the young lady is Mr. Batchelor's own daughter. Mr. and Mrs. Batchelor have lived – rather in seclusion. Also, from what you say, Miss Cary Page must still be – ah – quite young. It is not our custom to ask girls under sixteen to Carnival balls.'

'She must be just about that now. In fact, I am certain she is at least that old, if not a little older. I know she is expected at the University for Easter Week.'

'I assure you, Miss Lee, that the invitation will still go by special messenger, even though this means sending it halfway to Baton Rouge and not down the next street.'

All this, of course, Clyde did not learn at the same time or from the same person; but he was gradually able to piece the various scraps of information from various sources together, and derived both amusement and satisfaction in doing so. From then on, Cary's name had never failed to be included on a Carnival invitation list, and she had been a Maid in several of the most exclusive courts. Her first appearance as such had been the year that her classmate and dearest friend, Armande Vincent, whose family owned Victoria Plantation, just above Cindy Lou on the river, had reigned as Queen of Carnival. That same year, it became common knowledge that Armande's brother, Savoie, was deeply in love with Cary Page.

Both families, of course, had been aware of his condition for some time and neither had been altogether happy about it. Lamartine Vincent, the father of Savoie and Armande, had necessarily seen a good deal of Clyde Batchelor because of their joint interest in perique; and the Vincents, as a family, had always been civil to the Batchelors. But there had been no visiting back and forth between the two plantations until the youngsters began it; and though Lamartine and his wife had fallen under Cary's spell, as everyone else did, they had done so reluctantly; the girl did not represent the sort of alliance to which they had aspired for their only son. Clyde and Lucy, on the other hand, while admitting Savoie's attractions and finding no fault with either his intellect or his character, were appalled at the idea of having their adored daughter become a member of any family in which she was not fully appreciated. Therefore, the Vincents and the Batchelors were equally pleased because, year after year, Cary declined to lend a willing ear to the pleadings of Savoie.

She had plenty of other suitors, some of them better qualified than he to win her, in the opinion of her mother and stepfather. On Bushrod's rare visits to Louisiana, he had nearly always brought fellow students home with him, and most of these youths promptly fell in love with Cary. After her first Easter Week, the number of these swains doubled and redoubled; and each succeeding spring, when she returned from her gala trip to the University, more young Virginians seemed to find a sojourn to Louisiana imperative for one reason or another. When Bushrod began the practise of law in Richmond, where any number of openings had awaited him, his acquaintance increased still further, in both size and stability; so did the number of his sister's suitors. Even in a state where Lee was regarded as a great general largely because Beauregard had spoken well of him, the historic names of these young men carried considerable weight and their presence at Cindy Lou greatly enhanced its prestige. Young Creoles who had hitherto hesitated to pay their addresses, either because they were cautious by nature or – more frequently – because they were restrained by their parents, now flocked around Cary; and in most cases their parents were more than willing to have them do so. Occasionally, Clyde, with the girl's best interests at heart, would ask her if she did not find Valois Dupré or Nial Stuart or Andres Santana a likeable sort of fellow. Sometimes she consented to discuss the qualifications of these aspirants to the extent of saying that Valois was a city slicker and she was a country mouse; that Nial was puffed up with pride because of alleged descent from Bonnie Prince Charlie and she preferred married ancestors; and that Andres overlooked the fact that buccaneering days were past and that sensible girls liked their suitors to have mild manners however much their morals might be on the shady side. Usually, however, her only response on such occasions was to sit down on her stepfather's knee and ruffle back his hair, meanwhile looking smilingly into his eyes.

'You're not trying to get rid of me, are you, Father?' she would say. And then they would laugh together, as if she had made a very original and very amusing remark. 'Why should I marry anyone when I'm so gloriously happy at home? How could I care for any other man as much as I care for you?'

'You might care for him in a different way, honey.'

'Well – when I do, I'll let you know. I'll tell you before I tell anyone else – even the man in question. It'll be our secret for a while, yours and mine. Now I'll tell you another secret.' At this point, she would cuddle closer to him and whisper in his ear. 'You've spoiled me for every other man because you're so wonderful. I've tried to find someone who could stand comparison with you and I can't. I'm afraid the mould's broken.'

How many years was it now since Cary had first said that to him? Rousing himself from his pleasant torpor, Clyde tried to think. Five? No, it must be more than that. Ten? Why yes, at the very least. Cary had been a toddler when he bought Cindy Lou and married her mother. And that was in Sixty-nine. And this was Ninety-four. Twenty-five years – a quarter of a century! And what good years they had been, pleasant and profitable in almost every way! Not perfect of course: there had been the repeated disappointments about a child of his own. There had been the lack of harmony between himself and Bushrod. There had been the aloofness of their Creole neighbours. And there had been some material causes for discouragement: a few crop failures, a few steamboat disasters, a few unprofitable investments. But the urge to gamble was still strong within him; and though the media and methods he used had changed, the thrill he derived from taking big risks on the chance of making big profits had never lessened, and he did not expect to hit the jackpot every time – all he asked was the traditional six out of ten. Besides, of what consequences were these grievances and losses compared to all the happiness he had enjoyed with Lucy and Cary, all the pride he had taken in their home, all the satisfaction he had derived from his growing importance in the community, all the success he had achieved in nearly every field of endeavour which he had entered? Nothing, he told himself, and meant it. Absolutely nothing. . . .

And now this was Ninety-four. Savoie had been in love with Cary ever since she was sixteen and here she was twenty-six. It was impossible, but it was true. Clyde lay back in his easy chair, thinking fondly about Cary and wishing she would come and chat with him now that he had taken his nap. It was very pleasant under the big tree at this time of day. The heat of noon had passed, and a little breeze had sprung up from the river. Presently he would go into the house and see what Lucy – dear, dear Lucy – was doing; but not quite yet. She was probably still resting; it seemed necessary for her to rest longer and longer all the time. She had not been quite as well as usual lately and that troubled him. But he must remember she was not a young woman any more. It was hard for him to do this, because she was so much younger than he was. He was now a man of advancing years. He had admitted as much to himself before he fell asleep. . . .

'Did I wake you, Father? Or were you just day-dreaming?'

He looked up, with a slight start. There was Cary, for whom he had been longing, standing close beside him; and up to that moment, he had not even been aware of her presence. He gazed at her, filled with a great sense of contentment for, though he knew he looked at her with eyes of love, still it seemed to him that she was more beautiful than ever before. Her hair was fair, like her mother's, but there was more gold in it. She wore it parted in the middle, and cut to form a brief, ringleted bang above her forehead. The ringlets still reminded him of those which had framed her face and covered her head when she was a baby, for they had never lost their fine, silky texture, though now she had so much hair that, in the back, it was gathered into a great knot, above the nape of her neck. Her eyes were not grey, like Lucy's, but a deep, bright blue, and when she was especially happy or excited, there was a sparkle in them, such as he had never seen in other blue eyes. She must be especially happy or excited at the moment, for they were sparkling now. Her cheeks were always rosy, but the colour in them seemed to have deepened, too, and somehow there seemed to be new grace in her figure. She always carried herself well, but modern clothes did not give the feminine form the glamour in which hoops had invested it. However, Cary did not need clothes to give her glamour;

she had it anyway. She was wearing white this afternoon, as she frequently did: a high-necked dress with a gored skirt and enormous puffed sleeves, in the very latest fashion. The belt to it was fastened with a fancy buckle; and though it encircled a neat waist, this was not a small one by earlier standards, and Cary did not seem to mind at all. There were several little holes in the belt which would have permitted it to be pulled more closely, and Cary never took advantage of them. She had told her stepfather herself that her waist was twenty-two inches around. . . .

Well, she was a beautiful girl just the same, more beautiful in some ways than her mother had been at the same age. There was more sparkle to her, not just to her eyes, but to everything about her; more spontaneity, more vitality. But then of course Cary had never pinched pennies or nursed a peevish invalid; she had never gone hungry or borne children after prolonged travail. She had never lost other children because her strength had been sapped away from her. What was more, she had been brought up by a man who had never tried to make her feel that it was not quite ladylike to talk with him about anything candidly and without affectation. . . .

'I've come to tell you a secret, Father,' Cary said joyfully.

She sat down on his knee and smiled into his eyes. Then she put her face close to his and whispered into his ear.

'I've decided to marry Savoie Vincent,' she told him.

BOOK TWO

ACCOUNT RENDERED

Summer, 1894—January, 1895

Chapter Six

MOMENTARILY, Clyde was so stunned that he could not answer. For years, he had expected her to tell him that she had fallen in love; for years, he had told himself that it was high time she married and, since she had only to choose among any number of suitable applicants for her hand, that she should not indefinitely delay doing so. But her heart had remained untouched for such a long time that he had really begun to think no man would ever win her, that he himself would never lose her. Now that he suddenly learned he was mistaken, the news came as a shock.

Cary seemed to sense this, for she made no tactless attempt to hasten his response. Instead, she nestled more closely to him and waited for it, without visible impatience. Presently, he kissed her and, after another slight pause, managed to speak, though he found it was an effort, and not an altogether successful one, to keep his voice steady and make it sound natural.

'Why, that's — that's great!' he said. 'I'm sure you'll be very happy. Savoie's a fine boy — I should say a fine man. You couldn't have made a better choice. Doesn't your mother feel that way about it, too?'

'I haven't told her yet. She's still resting. Besides, don't you remember, Father, I've promised you over and over again that I'd tell you first? But of course Mother knows — that is, I'm sure she's guessed. Women are better about guessing such things than men are — just as men are better about lots of other things!' She ruffled his hair. 'Savoie knows too, by this time — or he will, pretty soon. I sent Zack up to Victoria with a note right after lunch.'

'And you told Savoie, in this note, that you'd made up your mind to marry him at last?'

'No, I just asked him if he wouldn't like to come to supper this evening. But he'll guess, too, even if he is a man. I've kept telling him he came to supper too often. He'll know, now that I've actually invited him, there must be a special reason for it; and there couldn't be but one reason special *enough*! Just the same, I thought he'd rather hear what it is than read it. Don't you agree with me?'

'Yes, honey, I do. After you've once told him you love him, the same words will look mighty good to Savoie in a letter. But you're right; he'd rather hear them than read them, the first time.'

'I'm glad you think I didn't make a mistake — about that or about deciding to accept him, either. It means a lot to me, Father, for you to think I've done the right thing.'

She kissed him again and, slipping lightly from his arms, drew another chair close to his and seated herself, taking his hand.

'As soon as Mother comes downstairs and Savoie gets here from Victoria, we'll hold a formal family council,' she said. 'But, meanwhile, you and I might start making plans, don't you think so?'

'If you're asking me whether I'd like to have you sit here beside me and chat with me, the answer is yes, I'd enjoy it very much. But unless I'm greatly mistaken, you've got everything pretty well planned already. What you want to do is to tell me about these plans, so that I'll be prepared to agree with you when your mother and your beau get here. Especially in case they shouldn't agree.'

Cary laughed, and Clyde realized, with a pang, that Cary's laugh affected him in much the same way as her mother's voice. He loved the very sound of it.

'You're a pretty good guesser, after all,' Cary said. 'Well, this is what I thought: I thought we'd be married around Christmastime or maybe New Year's. Of course, we've got to have a home wedding, because Savoie's a Catholic and I'm not. But the drawing-room would be a beautiful place for a wedding, don't you think so?'

'I certainly do. And I have a preference for home weddings anyhow, because that's what your mother and I had. No argument so far.'

'Well, naturally the Vincents would have liked it better if Savoie and I could have been married in church, just as they'd have liked it better if I'd been a Creole,' Cary went on, with characteristic candour. 'But we'll make the wedding so beautiful, they'll forget about their little disappointments. Of course, you'll give me away and——'

'You're sure you wouldn't rather have Bushrod do that, darling? After all, he's your own brother and I'm just——'

'Don't you dare say it! You're my *real* father, the only one I've ever known or ever wanted. There's not a girl I know whose father's meant as much to her as you've meant to me. But I know any number of girls whose brothers are more important to them than Bushrod is to me – Armande, for instance. Of course, I hope Bushrod will come to the wedding. I think Savoie will ask him to be a groomsman. But it wouldn't break my heart, if he sent word, at the last moment, that he couldn't manage it. I think he's got a sweetheart of his own, at last. If she didn't want to come to Louisiana, perhaps he wouldn't want to leave her.'

Privately, Clyde was of the opinion that Bushrod had already had several sweethearts, if such they could be called. Lately, rumours had reached Cindy Lou that Bushrod was courting an enormously rich New Yorker, and Clyde had been slightly uneasy about these rumours.

From the little he had learned about the girl, whose name was Mabel Stoddard, and whose father, George Stoddard, was a railroad magnate, Clyde did not feel she was the type that would really appeal to Bushrod's somewhat flamboyant taste, or that would fit especially well into the social pattern of Richmond. But there was no sound reason for this uneasiness, and it was not difficult for him to put disturbing thoughts from his mind. He had done so in this case.

'But why shouldn't she want to come to the wedding, honey?' he asked now. 'I should think she'd be tickled to death at the chance to meet Bushrod's family under such festive conditions.'

'We-e-ll, let's talk about that later. As I was saying, when we got sidetracked, of course you'll give me away. And whether Bushrod appears or not, I'm almost sure Grandmother will come to Cindy Lou at last. She's always promised me she would, when I got married. Grandmother'll make a great impression on the Vincents and everyone else. Mother's so gentle, she's never tried, and anyway, she's never cared. She's been too happy with you, just as I have. But Grandmother'll let everyone realize that she was born a Peyton and that her husband was General Cary and that we're kin to the Washingtons and the Lees on both sides of the family. She'll take it as a matter of course that she'll go to visit the Conrads, too, while she's in Louisiana and when she does, that'll make another impression.'

'I didn't know you set such store by impressions, Cary.'

'I don't, personally. But I know it'll mean a lot to Savoie and I think Grandmother's a wonderful old lady — I'll be glad to see her appreciated. Incidentally, I'm going to wear her wedding dress — that is, if I can get into it. I don't suppose I can, without letting it out. But there must be enough satin in the skirt to make the bodice bigger!'

Cary laughed again and again Clyde thought, with a pang, how silent Cindy Lou would seem when that laugh no longer rang through it.

'If I'm married at New Year's, I can wear a crown of white camellias,' she said. 'They'll be beautiful with Grandmother's rose point lace. We'll have a cluster of them on the bertha and we'll scatter them around the bottom of the veil, wherever we tack it to the train. I'll have my bouquet made of them, too. Of course, Armande will be my maid of honour and she'll carry a bouquet of pink camellias; her headdress will be made of them and the ruffles of her skirt will be caught up with them. She'll be in pale blue. And the bridesmaids will wear a deeper shade of blue and carry deeper-pink camellias. Can't you see how we'll all look, Father?'

'I certainly can — more beautiful than ever and that's saying a good deal. All your friends are lovely looking girls, Cary. But none of them can hold a candle to you.'

'You say that because you love me.'

'I sure do love you. But that's not the reason I say it. I say it because it's true.'

'Well . . . Speaking of candles, of course we'll have candlelight everywhere. And a wonderful supper, with magnums of champagne. And dancing with fancy figures and all kinds of favours. Naturally, I'll give Armande and my bridesmaids nice presents, but these favours will be extra.'

Just then one of the great peacocks strutted across the terrace and came to a stop in front of them, spreading his tail to its full size. 'Look at the old dandy!' Cary exclaimed. 'No wonder people talk about being "proud as a peacock"! If he isn't showing off, I never saw anyone do it. And he's given me an idea — why not have peacock-feather fans for favours? I don't see why I never thought of it before. Don't you think they'd be very striking?'

'Very. But you know, honey, some people think peacock feathers are unlucky.'

'And some people think the same thing about opals! Don't you remember telling me, Father, when I was just a little girl, that nearly everyone is superstitious about something, but that it isn't always the same thing? We'll have to hope that none of the girls who come to the wedding is superstitious about peacock feathers, because I intend to have those fans. I can see them, too, as they'll look in the ballroom — perhaps used in a special minuet, with the dancers wearing rainbow-coloured dresses! And, in the middle of the ball, Savoie and I will make a dash for the door and drive away in a carriage that's literally covered with ribbons and flowers.'

'Yes — yes, of course you will.'

'Savoie's always said he wanted to take me to Europe on our honeymoon. And I want to go. You wanted to take Mother, didn't you, Father? And she wouldn't, because I was an impediment.'

'You were never an impediment, honey. You've always been the light of our lives.'

'Well, of course you'd say that. But the fact remains that Mother never did get to Europe. You're such an old stay-at-home, you won't leave Cindy Lou if you can possibly help it! And of course Mother never leaves you! So, before Savoie gets to be a stay-at-home, too, and before I have any impediments of my own, I think we'd better make the Grand Tour. I think we'd better take our time about it, and do some visiting in France and Italy besides doing a lot of regular sight-seeing. Savoie keeps telling me about all the invitations we've had, from relatives and friends of the family. One of them is from the Marquise de Chanet. She wants us to come and stay at her château.'

'The Marquise de Chanet?'

'Yes, you know who I mean! The lady who sold you our house, when she was Madame Labouisse. You must have heard that she remarried after she went back to France! I suppose it isn't strange that she didn't keep in touch with you – after all, she never met you except that once. And she never met Mother. But she's always kept in touch with the Vincents – of course, she was their neighbour for a long time and her present husband's a distant relative of theirs, too. She's urged them again and again to come and see her. Savoie thinks we ought to. He thinks it would be fun to visit a French marquise at her chateau. I think so, too. Don't you, Father? What's the matter? You look as if you didn't like the idea.'

'Nothing's the matter,' Clyde answered, rather abruptly. 'Except that I should think you'd want to know a little more about – about this marquise before you decided to stay at her house. After all, it's a long time since the Vincents have seen her.'

'Yes, but she's sent them pictures – of herself and her husband and her son. She's beautiful, Father! Didn't you think so when you saw her?'

'As I recall it, I thought she was attractive. I don't believe I would have called her beautiful.'

"Well, probably you didn't notice particularly. Because you were very much in love with Mother then, weren't you? And you weren't thinking of Madame Labouisse except in terms of someone who had a house to sell that you wanted. . . . Well, I think her pictures are beautiful anyway, and I like the looks of her husband and her son, too!'

'How old is this son? Won't Savoie regard him as a menace if he's so good-looking?'

'Don't be absurd, Father! I don't know how old Pierre de Chanet is – vaguely, I'd say about my age – no, of course he's a little younger! And Savoie knows that, now I've finally made up my mind, I won't change it. Besides, I won't see this young marquis until after I'm married. So that takes care of that! . . . And I promise you we'll go and have a good look at the chateau and all its titled occupants, before we decide to stay there. But I'm equally sure that, in the end, we'll want to. And naturally, visits like that will prolong our trip, so we'll be gone quite a while. I thought that, perhaps, in the meantime, you'd build us a house.'

'You wouldn't be happy to live at home, Cary, after you were married?'

He did not speak abruptly any more, but his voice still sounded a little strange. Cary was afraid that, perhaps, she had hurt his feelings.

'It isn't that, exactly. But, if we lived at Cindy Lou, the Vincents wouldn't like it, and if we lived at Victoria, you and Mother wouldn't like it. Either way, Savoie and I would be conscious of that dissatisfaction and we'd feel a little guilty about it, though it really wouldn't be our fault. And anyway. . . . Yes, I think we'd be happier in a home of our own, where we could do exactly as we pleased. Of course, if there's any reason why you don't want to build one for us——'

'And of course there isn't. Of course I want to do everything I can, Cary, that you think would contribute to your happiness. . . . You didn't want this house to be far away, did you?'

'Why no! I want it right here on our land. It would have to be, wouldn't it? That is, it would have to be on our land or the Vincents'. Savoie's never wanted to be anything but a planter and I don't want him to be. After all, he's a planter's son and I'm a planter's daughter and we've both lived on plantations all our lives. They've been very happy lives. It's natural we should want to go right along in our fathers' footsteps.'

'Lamartine Vincent is a man of considerably more importance than I am, Cary. I don't know that he'd feel flattered to have you speak about us in the same breath, that way.'

'Well, of course, Victoria's a larger plantation than Cindy Lou. I know it raises more sugar and more perique. But the grounds don't compare with ours, or the house. Why, they don't even have a camellia garden! And don't forget about our buried treasure!'

'Perhaps there's been a mistake about the location of the buried treasure, Cary. Perhaps it's on the Vincents' land and not on ours.'

'Oh, it couldn't be! How can you say such a thing, Father? You've always believed it was ours, just as I have. You've always said that some day we'd find it, not far from where we're sitting at this moment!'

'I haven't said that in a long while, Cary. After all, we've lived at Cindy Lou nearly twenty-five years now, and we haven't found a sign of buried treasure yet.'

'That was because you wouldn't dig for it with me, and I got tired of digging for it alone! But that doesn't mean you've stopped believing in it, does it, Father? Why, every time anyone's made fun of us . . .'

It was evident that she still clung to her childlike belief, which he had been the first to encourage. Well, after all, her unquestioning faith in the buried treasure had as much foundation as her unquestioning faith in him. Since he would have gone to any lengths to prevent shaking the one, why should he shake the other?

'I know, honey. Well, we'll go on hoping and I'll go and watch you dig again, any time you say the word. Perhaps Savoie would help you now. You'll have to admit that you can't expect manual labour from a poor, feeble old gentleman like me.'

'What do you mean, a poor, feeble old gentleman? You're getting lazy, that's all! You could dig every afternoon, instead of sleeping for hours and hours!'

'I suppose I could. But I'm not going to—not even if you say, "Pretty please!" You're an awful tease, Cary, do you know that?'

'Well, you'll soon be rid of my teasing. I'll be saying "Pretty please!" to Savoie instead of to you.'

He sighed. 'I suppose you will. And I might as well confess I'll miss the teasing—like everything else about you. But I haven't got to worry over that for six months yet, from what you tell me. Meanwhile, what about this house I'm to build for you? It's to be on our land, I understand that now. I suppose you've picked out the exact location. So no doubt you've also decided precisely what type of a house you want.'

'Right again. I want a house something like this one, but smaller and simpler. Savoie and I wouldn't need a ballroom, because we could always use the one here. So that would take off a whole story—and a corresponding amount of gallery and railing. I think I'd like it all white, too, instead of different colours, like this one—white and glistening. And I'd like a summerhouse in the garden—what they call a gazebo in Virginia—like the one at Sorrento. Oh, I know everything will be perfect if you do the building for me!'

She leaned forward, pressing both his hands in hers. He returned the affectionate pressure and then, shaking his head, rose with a deprecatory smile.

'It won't be perfect, but I'll do the best I can for you, honey, you know I will. And of course I'll have your mother's help while you're gone—that'll make a world of difference. I think maybe we'd better go and find her now, don't you? She'll want to have a word with you herself, before Savoie gets here.'

When they entered the hall, they saw Lucy coming toward them from the dining-room and Clyde's gaze rested on her with the proud admiration which had remained undiminished through the years. As in the case of many fair women, the white showed very little in her still abundant hair; it simply altered its general effect, making her appear more truly a *blonde cendrée* than when she was younger. Her skin was as smooth as ever; none of the telltale little wrinkles which result from anxiety or overwork or suffering, more often than from age, had appeared around her eyes and mouth, for Clyde had seen to it that she was spared all that; and the tapering slenderness of her white fingers was intensified by the beautiful rings he had given her. But she was most fortunate in the natural grace of her slim, straight figure. Perhaps because Cary's remarks about her grandmother's wedding dress were still fresh in his mind, Clyde thought of the garnet-coloured silk Lucy had worn when she married him and wondered whether she had kept it. He rather hoped she had, and that she would wear it again for the splendid ceremony that was to take place in the frescoed drawing-room. There would need to be no letting out in the case of this dress; and, in a very special way, the bride's mother would be able to bear comparison with the bride, in presenting a picture which not only recalled, but revived the charm of bygone elegance. He would certainly ask Lucy about the garnet silk, as soon as they were alone; she might tease him a little, reminding him he had said, when they were on their honeymoon, that she was not to wear made-over dresses any more. And he would reply, also jestingly, that this one would not count, because she had made it over before they were married, and she would never need to make it over again, with a waist like hers! The prospect of such a bantering exchange was very pleasing to him until a second memory, evoked by Cary and obscuring the first, flashed through his mind: lovely as Lucy's figure was and always had been, it was not the one which had met the supreme test of a standard for the feminine figure which, though now outmoded and forgotten, had once possessed the power to make him lose his head completely. His passion for Dorothée had been as brief as it was violent; he had not even given her a passing thought for years. Now, reluctant as he was to do so, he could not help dwelling on her irresistible fascination.

Lucy's approach put an end to this unwelcome train of thought. She had been on the point of joining them on the terrace for tea, she said. But it was beginning to look like rain. Perhaps they had better go into the library, rather than risk having a shower come up, just after they had got comfortably settled.

The fact that she suggested the library was significant. Her husband and her daughter both realized this, for it was still the room they used least, and, as such, most suited for special occasions. She composed herself in a large armchair and listened, without interruption and almost without comment, while Cary talked excitedly, pouring out her plans. It was only when the girl paused, asking the same breathless question that she had put to her stepfather—'Can't you just see it all?'—that Lucy smiled, and that Clyde missed something in the smile, just as he had been conscious of the fact that, until then, though Lucy had been gravely attentive, she had not smiled at all.

'Yes, I can see it all, Cary,' Lucy said, in her quiet way. 'And of course your father and I will try to see that everything is exactly as you wish.' She had always spoken to Cary of Clyde as 'your father', never as 'your stepfather'; and of all the ways in which she had shown her appreciation of his devotion to her daughter, this was perhaps the one which pleased and touched him most. 'But I cannot help thinking——'

'Mother, you don't mean to say you're not delighted! Why, you've told me again and again how much you liked Savoie!'

'I do like Savoie—in fact, I'm extremely fond of him. And I am sure you are fond of him, too. But you have had a great many suitors and sometimes, under these circumstances, though a girl naturally feels very much flattered, she also becomes confused and fails to make a wise choice. I cannot help thinking that, if you were deeply in love with Savoie, it wouldn't have taken you ten years to find this out.'

'But you kept Father waiting a long time, too!'

'Not ten years. And not because it took me a long time to find out whether I loved him. I found that out inside of ten minutes.'

Never, in all her years of married life, had she said this before. Clyde's heart bounded with triumphant joy as he listened to her, and a tingling sensation, of which he had not been aware for a long time, permeated his entire being. Had he thought of himself, a few hours earlier, as a man of advancing years? Why, that was absurd! He was a man in the prime of life, and Lucy was his dearly beloved. . . .

'However, there were many other considerations, which fortunately do not exist in your case, Cary—chief among them the fact that, at the time, I was married to someone else, as you know,' Lucy went on. 'I believe I will not be guilty of disloyalty to—to the dead, if I admit to you now that I never loved my first husband as I loved—as I still love my second one.'

Again Clyde's heart leaped in his breast. The disturbing visions which had risen to trouble his spirit when Cary talked about Bushrod and Dorothée had faded from his consciousness. Indeed, he had almost forgotten that the present conference had started for the purpose of discussing Cary's impending marriage to Savoie Vincent; he had begun to feel that the real reason for it was the revelation of Lucy's love for himself.

'I was—very young when I married Forrest Page,' she was saying. 'He was a kinsman of mine—what we call a "kissing cousin" in Virginia. And he volunteered for service in the Confederate Army immediately after the fall of Fort Sumter. Well, you know all that, too. But you do not know how much pressure was brought upon me to marry him before he went away, not only by him, but by—by others. I was told that, if I did not consent to an immediate wedding, he might never know the fulfilment that comes to a man only through possessing a wife and having her bear his child.'

So there had never been spontaneity in Lucy's feeling for Forrest Page, her marriage to him never a sacrament in any true sense of the word! She was admitting herself what he had always suspected: that she had been coerced into wedlock, and the child conceived on her bridal bed was no more the product of joyous union than the one begotten by a man determined to prove his authority over a wife until he lay dead beside her! Clyde's feeling of revulsion against Forrest Page had long been submerged by his love for Cary and his complete happiness with Lucy. Now, it suddenly surged through him again, filling him with fresh rage toward Bushrod's father and renewed resentment of Bushrod himself.

'I'm terribly sorry pressure was put upon you, Mother, and I'm sorrier still if my father caused you any unhappiness.' Clyde was quick to notice her choice of words. Cary had referred to Forrest Page as her father; and she had not done it because she wanted, or intended, to hurt her stepfather's feelings, but because her own feelings were hurt. 'I honestly don't see though that there's any connection between what you've just told me and my decision to marry Savoie. Certainly, no one's forcing me to do that.'

'No, not in the way I was forced. But except for Armande, all your friends of your own age are married already.' Armande's betrothed had died of yellow fever, on the very eve of their intended wedding; although five years had now passed since this tragedy and she had received nearly as many proposals as Cary in the meanwhile, she had never even considered accepting any one of them and it was taken for granted that her heart was buried in the grave. Lucy paused for a moment, as if in respect for Armande's faithful grief, and then went on.

'These friends have begun to tease you about being always a bridesmaid and never a bride. They've contrived to make you wonder whether you really are on the verge of becoming an old maid. It's absurd for you to feel that way, but it isn't unnatural. And Savoie's gone on pleading and pleading. He's very attractive and very persuasive—in fact, I'm surprised you haven't weakened before this. But that doesn't make me any more certain that you're really in love with him. Only that you're ready for love, like any normal girl of your age, and that you're fonder of Savoie than anyone you've seen yet or anyone you believe you're likely to see. You've become impatient for fulfilment, too.'

Lucy did not flush as she made this outspoken observation, more amazing, coming from a woman of her natural reserve, than all the extraordinary remarks she had already made. But Cary was flushing, more with annoyance, Clyde rightly guessed, than with embarrassment. His own feelings had undergone so many rapid changes, in the course of the afternoon, that he had now reached a state of mental confusion, which was very rare for him. He was not certain whether he was more desirous of soothing Cary, or of reassuring Lucy, or of trying to prevent a sudden rift between the mother and daughter who had always been so close to each other and to him.

'If you really feel that Cary should wait a little longer, Lucy, before

150

coming to a final decision——' he began hesitatingly. But, at that moment, the door of the library was flung open, unceremoniously, and Savoie Vincent burst into the room. He did not even seem to be aware that Cary's parents were present. He rushed up to her and threw his arms around her.

'Darling!' he cried rapturously. 'Oh, Cary, I'm the happiest man on earth!' Then he said nothing more, because he was kissing her and she was returning his kisses and words had no further meaning for him.

Lucy did not say much more, either, after Clyde led her from the library, closing the door behind them. If she were really troubled, he suggested, trying to guide her toward the stairs, perhaps he and she had better talk all this over by themselves, in the privacy of their own room. Or perhaps, she had better lie down again; she still looked very tired. No, Lucy replied, she had nothing more to say; she feared she had said too much already. She could see that Cary's mind was made up. . . . And they must not forget that they had to be fair to Savoie, too. Cary had given him her promise now, so preparations must be made for a festive supper. Would Clyde go to the wine closet and get out a bottle of their best champagne, so that it could be properly chilled? Or maybe two bottles would be better, because someone might drop in unexpectedly. Indeed, it would be quite in order if Mr. and Mrs. Vincent should call later in the evening. And no, she was not at all tired. Surely Clyde did not think she was so decrepit that she needed to spend half her life on the chaise longue, even if she did have a son more than thirty years old!

He did not think she was decrepit at all, he told her. In fact, she still looked young enough to be Cary's sister instead of her mother; what was more, young enough to make her husband forget that he was an old man. He would give her convincing proof of his forgetfulness, right then, if she would let him. She shook her head, but she did not do so reprovingly, so he went on talking in the same vein, but even more boldly; and presently, they were laughing together at the idea that an elderly couple should be so much in love. . . .

Supper was very festive, as Lucy had said it should be. There were no inopportune visitors, but Mr. and Mrs. Vincent did call, to express their pleasure at the good news which their son had hastened to share with them, before he left for Cindy Lou. They were easily persuaded to remain for the evening meal; so, though only six sat down at table, it was spread with fine lace and set with Sèvres porcelain; and its splendour of adornment, together with the quality and quantity of the dishes which made up the repast, gave it the atmosphere of a banquet. Cary outlined all her plans again, and everyone agreed that they were delightful, except that Savoie thought they should have the wedding a little sooner. But Cary retorted that she did not intend to let him cheat her out of the fun of being engaged, and asked him how could Father get their house built, if they gave him only a moment's notice? For that matter, how could she get a trousseau ready? It took time to assemble a dozen dozens of everything, though of course a mere man could not be expected to know that! In this, Mrs. Vincent backed her up and the three ladies eventually withdrew, to make up lists of wedding guests and bridal linen and attend to other items dear to the feminine heart in connection with a wedding. Meanwhile, the three men went down to the gaming-room and talked about politics and crops and shipping over their cigars and their brandy. They had already drunk port at table, after the ladies had left them, but the gaming-room, which Clyde had equipped and arranged to suit himself, was his favourite setting for postprandial conversations, just as the office which adjoined it was his preferred place for transacting business. He had insisted that the floors in both should be made of the old, rose-coloured brick, which he had found where Marchand Labouisse had set up his kilns; and in the centre of the gaming-room he had placed a huge round table, made of figured gum from the sawmill at Gramercy, which Brunswick of Cincinnati – the same cabinetmaker who had turned out his billiard table – had made for him from his own design. The walls were lined with Currier and Ives prints of river scenes – *Midnight Race on the Mississippi, Bombardment of Island No. 10, 'Low Water' on the Mississippi, 'High Water' on the Mississippi, Maiden Rock* – and over the mantel hung an oil painting of the *Lucy Batchelor* – a work of art which Clyde viewed with special favour. But his greatest source of pride was the rosewood cellarette – a converted *armoire* which contained an impressive array of decanters, whisky bottles, brandy flasks and square faces of Holland gin, ranged above a second set of shelves where wine bottles were cradled on their sides with the necks pointing slightly downward, and still another section filled with goblets, tumblers and stemware of every sort and description. He opened this cellarette and turned to his companions.

'Your pleasure, gentlemen?' he asked. 'Or may I suggest that, in view of today's happy event, we toast the future in the finest available? I still have a few – a very few – bottles of Napoleon brandy. How could there possibly be a more suitable occasion for opening one of those?'

'There couldn't!' Mr. Vincent exclaimed. 'But tell me, my friend – do you mean *genuine* Napoleon? I didn't realize, Clyde, that even you——'

'Now, now, don't put me under oath!' Clyde retorted. He smiled as he spoke, but his expression became more grave while he extracted one of the dusty bottles from its place and, opening it, began to pour the precious liquor into large sniffer goblets. 'But I bought this brandy from Antoine Alciatore before my marriage and it's been in my possession ever since,' he went on, lowering the great bronze lamp which hung from the ceiling on gleaming chains, and lifting the nearest glass, so that the mellow light might further kindle the brandy's golden radiance. 'Antoine was no dealer, as you'll recall. He let me have this brandy as a special favour. And he told me he'd imported it from one of his most trusted shippers, shortly after he opened his restaurant on St. Louis Street. That's more than fifty years ago. This shipper, according to Antoine, boasted that he still possessed enough "genuine" Napoleon brandy to float the ship in which plans had been made to smuggle the ex-emperor out of St. Helena and over the seas to New Orleans.'

'That's all the guarantee I need,' Vincent declared. He cupped his hands about the ball of his glass, warming it before he began to savour its contents with obvious delight. 'Not many a man is toasted in such liquor as this, on the occasion of his betrothal,' he told his son, raising his glass. 'It's a privilege to propose one to you and your beautiful bride-to-be.'

'Couldn't you make it just to Cary, *mon père,* so that I could drink the toast, too?'

'Or why not make it simply to the future?' Clyde suggested. 'A bright and happy future to all those we love and all those who love us?'

'By all means,' Vincent agreed, a trifle testily. He was not accustomed to correction by his son or by his associates – especially those associates whom he regarded with slight condescension, as he did Clyde Batchelor. But Savoie flushed.

'Thank you, sir,' he said, looking toward his future father-in-law. 'I – I don't know just how to answer, but I appreciate what you did – what you said, very much.'

Clyde was not sure whether the flush came from embarrassment or pleasure, or a combination of the two, but in any case, it was becoming. He had always taken secret pride in the fact that he himself had never in the least resembled the popular conception of a 'typical gambler' who was very generally visualized as slim, dark and sallow-faced, invariably clad in black broadcloth and frilled linen and seldom disposed to remove his tall silk hat. On the other hand, he took an equal amount of satisfaction in the fact that Savoie so perfectly looked the part of the 'typical Creole'. His features were finely chiselled, his eyes dark under black brows which had a slight upward turn toward the temples, his equally black hair, worn rather long, curly at the ends. Normally, he did not have much colour, but his pallor was clear and healthy. He wore his faultlessly cut clothing with ease and grace, yet nothing about him remotely suggested the popinjay or the tailor's dummy. Unquestionably, this was an aristocrat, 'to the manner born'; but he was more than that. There was a sort of inner light which illumined his person, bespeaking the thoroughbred in thought and deed, as well as in appearance. Lucy might be justified in her doubts about Cary's choice, but only because the girl had taken so long to make up her mind. There was nothing in Savoie himself which the most captious parent could have wished to have altered. Clyde raised his goblet.

'Well, here we go then — a bright and happy future to all those we love and all those who love us,' he said ceremoniously.

The three men sat for some time, discussing the topics of the day and the part which Savoie was to play in the management of both Victoria and Cindy Lou, after his marriage. But eventually, he showed signs of impatience and, asking his father and his future father-in-law to excuse him, he went upstairs, and found Cary in the hall. She had begun to wonder what had become of him, she told him, and had missed him so much that she had almost decided to go down to the gaming-room, since, evidently, he had no idea of coming to the drawing-room. But it was a beautiful night; why couldn't they leave their parents to talk on and on, while they themselves strolled in the garden? A fresh breeze was blowing from the river, so there would be no mosquitoes.

Savoie commended the idea very highly, and the stroll was the first of many similar idylls. The period of their engagement was an extremly happy one, for both of them, but especially for Cary. Savoie remained restive, because of its length, and occasionally this restiveness took the form of moody silence, or of pleading for less delay, or of an attempt at more ardent love-making than Cary approved. But she was always able to charm away his black moods, and to put a tactful end to his pleading and to keep his love-making within bounds; and, as for herself, she was enjoying everything about her betrothal : the raillery of her friends, the teacups they sent her for presents, and the luncheon parties they gave for her; the big Tiffany solitaire which Savoie placed, with great ceremony, on the third finger of her left hand; the shopping tours for sheets and towels and table linens; the fine stitching on drawers and corset covers, ruffled petticoats and long-sleeved nightgowns, most of which were convent-made, but a few of which she and Lucy made themselves; the special attention to the lace-trimmed, hand-tucked 'wedding set' of finest batiste. She watched, with excitement, while the ground was broken for her house, and with still greater excitement as the house itself began to rise, spacious and symmetrical, in conformity with her wishes. And, when the wedding invitations were actually out, and gifts of every description began to pour in, she insisted on opening each package herself, on arranging every scrap of silver, down to the last bon-bon spoon and pickle fork, exactly as she wanted it.

In all this time, there had been only one real cloud on her happiness, and Clyde had dispelled that for her. She had written promptly to Bushrod, telling him of her engagement, and his answer had been anything but satisfactory. Of course, he sent her all sorts of good wishes; but he told her not to count on his presence at her wedding. Things were not going particularly well for him in Richmond; he had hesitated to let their mother know, because he did not want to worry her, and he had not told Clyde, either, because he did not want his stepfather to think he was asking for help. (He had never called Clyde Father, as Cary did; for a long time he had used 'Sir' as a form of address, and had always managed to make it sound mocking instead of respectful. In writing or speaking, he had referred to 'my stepfather'. Eventually, Clyde himself had suggested that, since Bushrod was now grown up, he might as well say Clyde.) But, to tell the truth, he was devilish short of money; if he could scrape enough together, he thought he might move to New York, and see if he could not do better there than in Richmond, which was really a petty, provincial place. But such a move would take every cent he could beg, borrow or steal.

Cary showed this letter to Clyde, who read it through with an expressionless face and then handed it back to her, still looking completely blank. He would like to think over its contents a little, he said; meanwhile, he hoped she would not divulge these to her mother. Shortly thereafter, he announced that it would be necessary for him to take a brief business trip north; it would have to be very hurried and, therefore, he thought it would be better if he went alone this time; later on, if Cary could tear herself away from Savoie, they would all go to New York together and make the final selections for her trousseau. It was by no means unusual for Clyde to absent himself on short trips, in connection with his shipping interests, and neither Cary nor Lucy showed, or indeed felt, any suspicion of an ulterior motive on his part this time. But, the evening after his return, he took occasion to talk confidentially to Cary, when they had been over to inspect the progress of the new house and were walking home together. Except for them, the river road seemed deserted; therefore, they were safe in assuming that no one else was within earshot.

'I found I had to go to Richmond while I was north, so I dropped in on Bushrod,' he said, speaking quite casually.

'Why, Father, I'm awfully glad! Did you find out exactly what was the trouble there?'

'Yes, I did, and I'll tell you about it if you'll let it be one of our secrets.'

'Of course I will. . . . But do you mean a secret even from Mother?'

'Most emphatically. Do you promise?'

'Yes, I promise.'

'Bushrod was badly in debt. I've paid off his debts, but I agree with him that it would be just as well if he left Richmond.'

'Why, Father?'

'Because he doesn't enjoy a very good reputation there.'

'He doesn't . . . I don't understand, Father. Merely his name . . . And he had any number of offers when he graduated from the University.'

'I know. But a name isn't enough in itself any more, if it ever was. I've always thought there had to be something to back it up, in the long run. And he couldn't get as much as one offer now to save his skin. In fact, he was asked to resign from the firm of Curtis and Dabney. And he'd already been asked to resign from the Westmoreland Club.'

'But *why*, Father?'

'Because . . . Why, Moppy! I didn't hear you, coming up behind us! And I haven't run into you on the road for a year or more. Where've you been all this time? And how've you been?'

'Ah've been po'ly with de mis'ry, mishay. Ah don' get around like Ah'd make out to do, not no more, no.'

Characteristically, she did not answer his first question; they had still never discovered where Moppy lived, and the thought crossed Clyde's mind that probably they never would now, and that there might be some sad reason for her secretiveness. Her voice quavered as she spoke. Obviously, she was very feeble; the 'misery' to which she referred was not merely a favourite fable, as it was with so many of the Negroes when they did not feel like working. She leaned heavily on a stick as she fumbled for the two hats which she extended, in turn, to Clyde and Cary. She must have approached them very slowly and painfully; it was not strange that they had failed to hear the soft shuffle of her feet on the dusty road.

'Well, here are three dollars today, one for each hat, instead of two, one for me and one for Miss Cary,' Clyde told her, feeling in his pocket and extracting the clinking coins, 'like what I gave you before I had Miss Cary here with me, remember? Why, Moppy, that was nearly thirty years ago and you looked to me like an old woman then! How old are you now, as close as you can reckon?'

'Ah'se too, too old, mishay,' Moppy quavered, peering up at him from under her wide hat brims, 'but thankee and may the Big Hand bring you the bestest luck.'

'Let's hope it will. And, anyway, you've got a claim on me, seeing as how you brought me such wonderful luck that first time I saw you. Listen good now, Moppy. I don't want you just to take a chance of meeting me on the road any more. I want you to come to the big house at Cindy Lou every Friday. You'll be expected and you'll get a week's rations and three silver dollars. If you can't come, send some-one I'll know is there in your place. But you've got to do something for me, too. You've got to bring Miss Cary as much luck as you brought me. She's going to have a house of her own pretty soon, right here on the river road, and a fine handsome husband and nice young-sters, we hope. You'll make a charm for them, won't you?'

Moppy had continued to peer up at him while he talked to her, but there was increasing blankness in her gaze, as if she had not under-stood very well. She mumbled, 'Sho'ly, missy, sho'ly, sho'ly! The very goodest luck!' Then she turned and shuffled off again, still noise-lessly and still mumbling. Cary seized Clyde's arm.

'What was it you started to tell me about Bushrod, Father, when that senile old hag came sneaking up behind us?' she asked im-patiently.

'Now, now! Moppy didn't mean to sneak. She couldn't know we were talking secrets.'

'Well, I asked you why Bushrod had been made to resign from his firm and his club and you only got as far as "Because" when . . . I believe you were really glad to be interrupted! Aren't you going to finish what you started to say?'

'You're right, I don't want to, but I'm afraid I'd better, honey. He was asked to resign because he'd been gambling.'

'But lots of men gamble, Father. Most of the men we know play cards for stakes or bet at the races, or something. And quite a few of them go into debt.'

'I know, Cary. But the men you're talking about don't cheat.'

'You don't mean to say *Bushrod cheated at cards*!'

'Yes, that's just what I mean.'

She was looking at him in horror. He tried, not altogether success-fully, to smile at her reassuringly.

'I'm sorry I had to spell it right out for you, honey. I wouldn't have, if I could have helped it.'

She continued to stare at him, her expression still horror-stricken. Her face showed all too plainly her conviction that her brother had committed an unforgivable sin. If he had told her that Bushrod was drinking too heavily, or that he had become entangled with a girl who was not his social equal and whom he had no intention of marrying, Cary would have understood and been lenient. She had been brought up to recognize and admit that, unfortunate as it was, gentlemen sometimes did do such things, and the ladies of the family forgave them. But no gentleman ever cheated at cards. What was more, no matter what the state of his finances, no gentleman left a 'debt of honour' unpaid.

'I'm afraid it had been going on for some time,' Clyde continued, speaking as gently as he could. 'But it wasn't found out immediately — in fact, not until just before Bushrod wrote you. So it's been possible to clear up — and hush up — everything fairly quickly. I hope Bushrod's learned his lesson. I think perhaps he has. Of course he's terribly ashamed — terribly humiliated.'

'Do you mean because of what he's done or because he was found out?'

'Well — both, I believe. But he's making a new start now. This girl we'd heard rumours about — Mabel Stoddard. That may be a very good thing for him, you know. Because her father's the rock-gibbed, righteous type. He wouldn't stand for any nonsense in his daughter's husband. And I think Bushrod wants to marry Mabel, very much.'

'But he'd have to tell her beforehand what he'd done! He'd have to tell her father, too!'

'Well——' Clyde said again. 'Well, perhaps he should. And then again, perhaps he shouldn't. It wouldn't do any real good. And it might do a great deal of harm.'

'You mean it might hurt his prospects?' Cary asked scornfully.

'Yes, but not only that. If he's really turned over a new leaf, there's no use dwelling on what's past. Please believe me, honey. I know more about these things than you do.'

He drew her arm through his and started, in a leisurely way, down the road again.

'Don't you worry about Bushrod,' he said soothingly. 'I tell you I've paid his debts, I've smoothed over his departure from Richmond, I've seen to it that he'll get a good start in New York. Of course, the next move is up to him. But let's wait and see if he doesn't make the grade before we pay him any more mind. And above all, don't give him away to your mother. I won't tell her any lies. I've never done that. But I won't tell her the whole truth. I hope you won't think any the less of me when I admit I haven't always done that, either. I don't want her troubled just now and I'm sure you don't. She isn't as well as I'd like to see her. I'll just tell her Bushrod's made a change for the better, which he has. Don't you agree with me that's the thing to do?'

Reluctantly, Cary did agree, and she did not again bring up Bushrod's name, on her own initiative, or betray her feelings about him when Lucy told her, very happily, that she had received a letter, saying he was engaged to be married and that he hoped they would all come to the wedding, which was to take place in the near future. That should be very convenient for them, he thought, because they could attend it and do their final shopping for Cary's trousseau at the same time. Bushrod was writing to Savoie also, asking him to be one of the groomsmen, provided he could tear himself away from the plantation long enough.

Upon receipt of this letter, Savoie renewed his mutterings about the delay in his own marriage; if Mabel Stoddard could get ready for a wedding in such short order, he failed to see why Cary could not. But he accepted the invitation, and they all had a very exciting trip to New York, though, as Lucy mildly expressed it, 'the Stoddards were not exactly what they had expected'. They were strict Baptists, with very rigid ideas about amusements and entertainment. Mabel had never played cards or danced or been to the theatre and neither had any of her intimate friends; no alcoholic beverage of any description was ever served at the Stoddards' table or accepted if it were offered them elsewhere. Mabel herself was another source of astonishment; she was heavy and plain and she had no grace of manner or sprightliness of speech to make up for her lack of other attractions. After returning from their first formal call at the Stoddards' huge, gloomy Fifth Avenue house, which was swathed in dark draperies and overhung with immense, mediocre oil paintings in heavy gilt frames, Cary spoke her mind to Clyde on the subject of the match.

'If Mother thinks I'm not in love with Savoie, I wonder what she thinks about Bushrod! I'll admit he's putting on a pretty good imitation of the tender passion – he always was a smooth one – and that Mabel's fallen for him, hook, bait and sinker. But no man could possibly be in love with that girl! Girl! I'll wager she's forty if she's a day. And I'll wager she never had a beau in her life before, either!'

'No takers, Cary. On the other hand, she's an only child and her father's a widower, pretty well along in years. Don't overlook that when you're talking about Mabel.'

'I don't know what you mean. I don't like her father, either. I think he's a hard, grim, horrid old man.'

'Yes, honey. But he's also a multi-millionaire and Mabel, presumably, is his only heir.'

'So you think Bushrod's marrying her just for her money?'

'Well, what do you think?'

It was hard for them to think anything else, so Lucy and Savoie, who did not know as much about Bushrod's financial situation as Clyde and Cary, were greatly puzzled, for Bushrod had never been unappreciative of pretty young girls with merry ways. Lucy was troubled besides; without knowing the nature of Bushrod's ulterior motive, and in spite of his impeccable behaviour, she was sure he must have one. But she kept her troubles to herself, not even speaking of them to Clyde, and everyone with whom she came in contact, even Mr. Stoddard, who was indeed a hard, grim old man, felt the irresistible influence of her gentleness and her charm, as he had already felt the insidious power of Bushrod's plausibility and persuasiveness. The magnate was also aware that the group from Louisiana gave a cachet to his daughter's nuptials which they would otherwise have lacked and which he did not fail to evaluate. Mabel had insisted on having a church wedding, with all possible ostentatious correlatives. She wanted everyone she knew to see the prize she had captured and Bushrod, to do him justice, looked his handsome best. He had the face and the figure, as well as the manner, to set off fine London tailoring, and Mabel's heart swelled with pride and triumph as she went down the aisle on his arm, conscious of envious glances on every side. But unfortunately, the groom's undeniable attractions did not suffice to offset the bride's lack of these. Her heavy lace veil, her stiff satin dress, her enormous round bouquet, far from giving an illusion of youth and beauty, accentuated her stocky figure and rather flat face. Her bridesmaids, of approximately her own age, were either short and stout, like herself, or tall and scrawny; and their fluffy pink dresses were wholly unsuited to their years. Only Cary, as maid of honour, was a vision of loveliness in the wedding procession; and at the stolid reception which followed the ceremony, only Cary, her mother, stepfather and fiancé, gave a slight sparkle and a certain degree of ease to the assembly. When the bride and groom had left, Mr. Stoddard, who had suddenly become a rather lost and lonely figure, urged his new connections by marriage to remain for dinner with him; and, from kindness of heart, Lucy accepted the invitation on behalf of herself and the others.

The decision was unfortunate. Savoie and Cary were both bored and restive at table and, though Mr. Stoddard did not notice this, because of his preoccupation with other matters, Lucy was quickly conscious of their attitude and troubled by it. Clyde, generally so sensitive to anything which threatened her peace of mind, was less attune than usual to her feelings of the moment, because Mr. Stoddard had almost immediately put him on the defensive regarding the status of steamboats, and he was afraid the conversation would take a turn which might cause her anxiety. In his attempts to change its trend, he overlooked not only the uneasiness of his stepdaughter and her fiancé, but the distress of his wife.

'This steamboating of yours must be a pretty expensive hobby, these days,' Mr. Stoddard had remarked, quite without preamble. The indicated comments on the marriage ceremony, the wedding reception and the display of presents had run their natural course and had even been slightly prolonged by some tactful compliments from Lucy on these general subjects. But after that there had been moments of strained silence which even her savoir-faire had not eased, and it was at this stage of the proceedings that their host had made his sudden pronouncement. 'To tell the truth, I was surprised to learn you hadn't got out from under, while there was still time, and gone in for something more profitable. Now I suppose all you can do is to grin and bear your losses.'

'Apparently your sources of information aren't very reliable,' Clyde retorted quickly. 'I'm happy to say that I've made a good deal of money out of steamboating. My first packet, the *Lucy Batchelor*, paid for herself in one year; my second, the *Cary Page*, earned four times her cost in two years.'

'All right, all right! But that was a long time ago, wasn't it? What have they earned since? And what about the third steamboat and the fourth—I take it there were a third and a fourth.'

'I'll try to answer your questions one at a time, Mr. Stoddard. Of course the *Lucy Batchelor* and the *Cary Page* haven't gone on showing the enormous profits they did at first. But they're both still on the river and they're both still carrying plenty of passengers and freight to suit my purposes. I never built or owned a fourth boat of the floating palace type. The third one, the *Sophia Peyton*, didn't do quite as well as the first two, but she did clear an average of twenty thousand for five years.'

'Well, I know that's about the average life of a steamboat. I suppose at the end of that time she struck a snag or blew up. So, if she cost you better than two hundred thousand, as I presume she must have, then you lost at least a hundred thousand on her.'

'Excuse me. She didn't strike a snag, she didn't blow up, and I didn't lose a hundred thousand on her. But a drunken pilot did run her up a cut-off as high water was dropping and put her aground just below Helena. That was in the spring of Seventy-nine and there she had to stay until the January rise of Eighty, with a part crew aboard. What it cost to overhaul her, from the oakum calking the river shrimp had eaten to the machinery parts that had to be replaced, would near have paid for a new boat. And she never was the same again. Lucy and I talked the situation over with my mother-in-law, because we didn't want to do anything that would hurt her feelings, and she was very sensible about it. She herself asked if the *Sophia Peyton* couldn't be remodelled for some other sort of service, instead of being all redecorated. And that's just what was done. She was put into use as a towboat for the C & L Navigation Company which, as you probably know, I own and operate.'

'And in a minute you'll be telling me that's been a profitable venture, too . . . Eh, what?'

Mr. Stoddard had interrupted himself to answer the butler who bent over him, whispering in his ear. 'Oh, all right! . . . Seems we're having coffee in the parlour, instead of at the table,' he said, turning back to Clyde. 'I know that's the style, but I've never liked it, and I meant to tell the servants that now Mabel was married and I could do things my own way again, I'd go back to having it in the dining-room, right with the main course, too. But I've had so many other things on my mind today. . . . Well, shall we move along? Perhaps you'll pour the coffee for me, Mrs. Batchelor?'

Lucy said she would be glad to do so and, sitting down on a low bench, busied herself with the silver service which the butler put before her. It was chilly in the vast gloomy room, and involuntarily she glanced in the direction of the fireplace, thinking perhaps she might suggest that a cheerful blaze would seem pleasant to all of them. But the hearth, like the mantel above it, was banked with a profusion of white roses, now somewhat past their first freshness; she did not like to intimate that their removal would be an improvement. Cary and Savoie retreated to a sofa in a dimly lighted corner; and Clyde, having selected a chair which seemed to offer at least a modicum of comfort, withdrew a cigar from the case Lucy had worked for him, snipped off the end with a gold-mounted cutter and struck a light on the sole of his shoe. It was not until he had looked about in vain for some sort of receptacle in which he might place the charred remains of his match that he realized smoking was not customary in this sanctuary, though one look at his host, who had meanwhile tugged at a brocaded bell pull, would have quickly disclosed his mistake. Mr. Stoddard's expression had hitherto revealed only a satisfied sense of superiority; now it was disapproving; and the tone in which he addressed the butler, who had departed after setting down the coffee service and now reappeared, was very close to sanctimonious.

'An ashtray for Mr. Batchelor, Griffin.'

'An ashtray, did you say, sir?'

'Yes. An ashtray. As you see, Mr. Batchelor wishes to smoke.'

Clyde was ready to admit the possibility of a mistake, but he thought he detected a slight arch in the butler's eyebrows which had not previously been there. At all events, Griffin's tone, like Mr. Stoddard's, was almost sanctimonious as he answered.

'I'm very sorry, sir. I don't think we have an ashtray in the house.'

'We must have something that would serve as a repository for ashes. Please bring it.'

'Very good, sir.'

The butler departed, to return with a small saucer of the same pattern as those which companioned the coffee cups. Clyde, without indicating in any way that he attached the slightest significance to the absence of ashtrays, resumed the thread of conversation where it had been broken off when they left the dining-room. He was determined that the subject under discussion should not be dropped until he was sure he had quieted any fears which Stoddard might have roused in Lucy.

'You spoke of steamboating a few minutes ago as if it were a hobby, Mr. Stoddard,' he said pleasantly. 'I therefore take it you think it's dead, as a business. I'd like to assure you that it isn't. It's only changing, as it has been for some time already. That's why I went in for towboats and barges.'

'All right. If it suits you better, we'll say it's only changing. But you'll have to admit it's the railroads that are doing the changing.' Mr. Stoddard leaned back in his Gothic chair with a look of righteous triumph, at the same time putting the tips of his spread fingers and thumbs into precise contact with each other. Clyde's answer was still good humoured.

'They're changing, too, if you come right down to it, aren't they?' he asked. 'And, if I'm not mistaken, they'll have to change a lot more — for the better — if they're to stay in business. Wasn't it the railroads' rebates to favourites and other such capers that helped put Grover Cleveland back into the White House?'

'That's a very one-sided view, sir.' The spread fingers had begun to tap against each other as if in irritation. 'You talk like a Populist. Sound finance demands——'

'Perhaps we'd better not get off on the subject of politics, Mr. Stoddard,' Clyde interrupted. 'Especially since "sound finance" came so close to scraping me down to the bare bones two summers ago that I still get cold chills whenever I think of it.' He was suddenly conscious of Lucy's startled gaze. Hang it all, he had said the wrong thing after all! But there was no help for it. Now he had started, he would have to go on. 'A good friend of mine, Valois Dupré, who's an enormously successful contractor, tolled me into the cotton market for a flyer that was going to put us in the class with Gould, Morgan and all the rest. He——'

'Speculation!' muttered Stoddard, making a small clicking sound of disapproval. 'Speculation is like any other form of reckless gambling. It's as different from sound finance, or good investment as one pole is from the other. Tch-tch-tch!'

'Well, it was "sound finance" that put sand in my gearbox,' Clyde chuckled. 'This was back in Ninety-two, and cotton had dropped to six cents a pound, because everybody figured that if Cleveland was elected, the Democrats would shoot the tariff full of holes. But old man Dupré, who is very sharp about such things, said, "No! Cleveland is a conservative at heart, and as soon as the country finds that out, prices are bound to start up. What's more, they'll be even surer to bounce back up if Harrison is re-elected!"'

'It would have been a fine thing if he had been. Even those wild-eyed shouters for free silver out West would admit it now,' said Stoddard.

'Well, the point is that Dupré had already bought I don't know how many cotton contracts at six cents, the price was by then up to eight, and his reasoning sure seemed to be tight at the seams. So I had my broker take ten thousand bales for my account.'

'At eight cents? You mean you engaged to pay out nearly half a million dollars on some man's guess at the future?' Stoddard asked incredulously.

'I wouldn't have had to pay it unless I actually took the cotton, you know,' Clyde protested, 'and I hadn't the first idea of doing that. Anyway, Cleveland did make it plain he wasn't going to let anybody tinker with the tariff, so the price of cotton started up immediately, and every rise meant money in my pocket – or would have meant it if it hadn't been for the sound financiers back East.'

'What did they have to do with cotton, pray tell me?'

'It wasn't cotton the sound financiers were playing with, but the thing you've just been pinning all those medals on. Railroads. Most especially the Reading Railroad which went busted like a smashed tumbler.'

'They had over-extended themselves, buying what were supposed to be coal lands,' Stoddard interjected hastily.

'Probably so. But they did start a general panic, and by the time half the railroads – not the steamboats, mind you, but the railroads – were in the hands of receivers, cotton was back down to six cents. I didn't wait for it to go any lower, and sold mine for whatever I could get.'

'Why that was . . .' The fingertips tapped against one another more urgently. 'Let me see, that represented a loss of . . .'

'Of a lot of hard cash,' Clyde interrupted ruefully. 'More than I cared to part with, I do assure you. But I had good luck in other ways that year. I got the highest price ever for my tobacco on an export market, and we had a high yield of cane, so I managed to pay off the banks, and salt away something of real value to boot. Especially a lesson. I learned not to back another man's game, deciding that from then on I'd stick to what I knew about. Like planting. And steamboating.'

'But that is what I've been trying to say!' Mr. Stoddard exclaimed, the disapproval in his voice less marked than it had been at any stage of the conversation. 'You pocketed your loss on cotton in order to escape further losses still on what was plainly an unprofitable venture. Why will you not do the same thing with steamboating, which is even more certain to be unprofitable?'

'That's where I don't agree with you,' Clyde replied stubbornly. But he had decided not to argue any further. How could he make this old bigot, immured in his gloomy house, understand what the wide and sunlit river meant to a man who had travelled it from his youth? How could a Croesus, measuring everything in dollars and cents, visualize the triumph of an adventurer who had flown his own flag from the three finest packets afloat between Minneapolis and New Orleans, to say nothing of the great fleet of towboats and barges which had supplemented these? It was futile and pointless, and it had been from the beginning; he should never have allowed himself to be drawn into such a discussion. He glanced toward Lucy and she rose at once; obviously she had been waiting for a chance to give the signal for departure. She bade their host good night and thanked him for his courtesy with her usual graciousness. But there was a pinched look to her face, as if she were cold as well as tired; and when she and Clyde were seated side by side, in the hack that was taking them back to the Murray Hill Hotel, he could feel her shivering. No wonder, he said to himself savagely; that baronial hall where they had wasted so much time had been as cold as a tomb. He must get her to bed at once, and see to it that she drank a hot lemonade, well laced with spirits. But Cary, who did not seem to realize the extent of her mother's exhaustion, complained that she and Savoie had thought that they would all go to the Hoffman House for a champagne supper, to make up for the sickly fruit punch which was all they had had to drink so far.

'Can't Savoie and I go by ourselves if Mother's too tired to go with us and you want to stay with her, Father? I see lots of girls in New York having tête-à-tête midnight suppers with their beaux.'

Lucy and Clyde exchanged glances. 'Why, yes, I think you might, this one time,' Lucy said, after a moment's hesitation. 'That is, if you really feel the evening wouldn't seem complete to you without a champagne supper.'

'Well, that's the way I do feel.'

There was no doubt that she meant it; champagne suppers at midnight, along with their various other extravagances had become almost a necessity to Cary. It was the prodigality of their own programme which made their stay in New York exciting, and not anything connected with Bushrod's marriage, which remained a mystery to Savoie, an annoyance to Cary, and a source of worry, though for different reasons, to both Lucy and Clyde. From the time of his own wedding trip, Clyde had insisted that 'New York was a place where you went to spend money; otherwise, it did not have much meaning'. He had always acted accordingly, reserving one of the most luxurious suites in the hotel favoured by fashion at the moment, buying the best seats for current theatrical attractions, and insisting that the lavish purchases he made for his wife and stepdaughter must be supplemented by purchases even more lavish on the part of Lucy herself and – as soon as she was old enough – Cary, too. But he had never even approached his present extravagance, partly because he had never had quite so much incentive to do so, and partly because, while Lucy had always acted as a restraining influence, on account of her quiet tastes, Cary was now urging him on to more and more reckless expenditure. She did not actually cuddle up to him, showering him with kisses and whispering, 'Pretty please!' as she had in her childhood. But though her methods were different, their meaning had changed very little and the results were also much the same.

None of this was distasteful to Clyde. He had thoroughly agreed with Cary that they must not give Mr. Stoddard the idea that there was any lack of money in the family; the Batchelors' entertainments, prior to the wedding, had been as profuse as the restrictions imposed by the Stoddards would permit, and their gifts to the bride and groom numerous and costly. Then, after Bushrod and Mabel had departed on their wedding trip, Cary's outfits and Cary's amusements became her stepfather's first concern. He wanted her to have a handsomer trousseau than any of her friends who had previously married, handsomer even than Mabel Stoddard's, if she had seen enough of that to judge what it was like. (Cary had and did.) He wanted her to enjoy herself, to see every worthwhile play in New York, to dine and sup at every fashionable restaurant, to dance with Savoie to her heart's content.

It was Lucy's continued exhaustion, still unconfessed but now all too obvious, which finally took them back to Louisiana. The new house had come along well during their absence, better than they had expected, and Cary was delighted with it; in every way, it carried out her ideas and fulfilled her expectations. The Steamboat Gothic influence was still evident in its general style, but this had been modified and simplified. The central staircase, leading from the ground level to the main floor, did not divide into two separate flights of steps, though its width and grace gave it importance; fluted columns framed the front door, but they did not surround the entire structure, which was long and low, with wings stretching out on either side of the main part; and the ornamental railings which adorned the short gallery and screened the dormers were chaste of design. Within, there was a library on one side of the front door and a drawing-room on the other, as at Cindy Lou; but both were of the same moderate proportions and of rectangular shape. The dining-room stretched across the width of both and of the entrance hall, in back; and a pantry connected this with the kitchen, at the extreme rear. Each of the wings leading from the front hall contained a good-sized, square bedroom, with its own boudoir and bath. Cary and Savoie were to occupy one wing; it was tacitly understood that, though now designated for guests, the other would be the future nursery. There was plenty of room for company in the dormer rooms, which were larger than they appeared from the outside; and a third bath had already been installed in the upper story, with the convenience of visitors in view. In fact, the construction was so far advanced that it would soon be possible for Cary to move in some of the furniture which she had selected in New York and which was being held until an order was given for its shipment. The prospect of this delighted her. She wanted to have everything in place before she went to Europe, so that her new home would be ready for immediate occupancy on her return, and she was sure, if she did not see to arrangements herself, that they would not suit her. She was soon very busy about these, and with all the preparations for her wedding, which was now near at hand. As she had predicted, her grandmother, who had steadfastly refused to go to New York for Bushrod's 'marriage to a Yankee', had consented to come to Louisiana for hers to a 'Southern gentleman'. The old lady had brought the rich ivory-tinted wedding dress of the Thirties with her and supervised the alterations which made it possible for her granddaughter to get into it. She also did what was expected of her by renewing ties of relationship with the Conrads, and she duly impressed the Vincents, besides fitting into the pattern of life at Cindy Lou—all without effort to herself or strain on anyone else. She was soon Cousin Sophie to most of the surrounding gentry and—what was even more significant—she was Miss Sophie to her son-in-law and to all the household staff. Her imperturbability, her dignity, the elegance which she never failed to achieve despite her lack of modishness, the measured tones in which she spoke, the stateliness of her bearing and the way she held her handsome head, all had a marked effect on everyone with whom she came in contact, and added immeasurably to the general regard in which the Batchelors were held, besides contributing an important element to the family circle. It was not until Bushrod arrived with his bride that the effort and the strain began.

The effort was definitely not on Mabel's part. Though she obviously doted on her husband, whose manner toward her remained impeccable, she had come to Louisiana in a mood of condescension, if not actually one of disparagement; nothing roused her admiration, nothing was even quite satisfactory to her or convenient for her. It offended her sense of modesty to use a bowl and pitcher, not to mention other articles with which the bedroom commode was supplied, in her husband's presence or to have him do so in hers; she had supposed that, of course, a private bathroom would be available and probably a dressing-room as well. She pronounced the habits of taking early morning coffee in bed and after-dinner naps as 'slothful, if not downright sinful'. She did not like Ivy, the quadroon maid who had been assigned to her; in her opinion, the girl was lazy, inexpert and disrespectful. Mabel was also affronted by the constant drinking and nightly dancing at Cindy Lou; she was not content with turning her wine-glass upside down at table and sitting tight-lipped while all the others sipped juleps and chatted merrily, or with 'retiring' when dancing began, audibly expressing her belief in the old proverb that early to bed and early to rise makes a man healthy, wealthy and wise. She made pointed remarks about the evils of intemperance and the stimulation of the waltz, reminding her hosts that even such a roué as Lord Byron had not hesitated to condemn this form of 'the Terpsichorean Art' as 'lascivious'. When she finally hinted that Ivy was probably closely related to some male member of the family or of the neighbours', Clyde could no longer restrain the mounting exasperation which, up to that point, he had managed to keep in check. He summoned Bushrod to the office adjoining the gaming-room at a time when he had been able to make sure they would not be interrupted or overheard, and announced that, while he regretted Mabel's lack of contentment, they were all doing the best they could for her at Cindy Lou, and that, if she could not adapt herself to plantation life, it would perhaps be better to take her to a hotel in the city.

'She's making your mother unhappy and I don't need to tell you I've never allowed anyone to do that,' Clyde concluded. 'Not that I've known anyone who wanted to, before. She's also upsetting Cary, who's entitled to all the pleasure she can have, just now. You'll have to tell Mabel she's either got to put up or shut up.'

'I don't propose to have you give orders to my wife, through me.'

'All right. Then I'll give them to her direct.'

'I wouldn't advise you to do that, either.'

'Why not? After all, this is my house and she's abusing my hospitality.'

'She doesn't care much for your brand of hospitality. When it comes to that, I don't care much for it myself.'

'Then, as I suggested before, we might all be happier if you and Mabel would leave Cindy Lou.'

'Do you want to create a scandal, just before Cary's wedding?'

'It won't create a scandal if you merely say Mabel's never been to Louisiana before and that she thought she'd like to see something of New Orleans. Some people may be slightly astonished at your choice of the St. Charles Hotel rather than Cindy Lou, but they'll put it down to peculiar Yankee tastes.'

'I don't care to have my wife accused of peculiar Yankee tastes. I'm quite capable of creating a scandal myself, on rather different grounds.'

'I don't doubt it for a minute. In fact, as I recall it, you did, not so long ago, in Richmond.'

'I wasn't referring to my own conduct. I was referring to yours.'

'There's nothing scandalous about my conduct. You know as well as

I do that the hints Mabel's been giving are groundless as well as insulting.'

'I wasn't talking about Ivy, either – or about anything you've done lately, for that matter. I was referring to your – earlier career. If Cary took my Richmond peccadilloes as seriously as you claim she did, how do you think she'd feel about your prolonged – and highly successful – pre-war activities on the Mississippi steamboats?'

'If you say anything to Cary that will shatter her faith in me, I'll kill you! And you'd better believe that, because I mean it!'

Clyde had sprung up, the suppressed hatred of years suddenly unleashed. Bushrod remained quietly seated and his recoil, if any, from the threat of physical violence was so momentary as to be imperceptible. He looked up at his furious antagonist with a slight smile.

'Which would, of course, create no scandal at all,' he remarked sarcastically. But he did not raise his voice, and when he went on he did so almost agreeably. 'I must hand it to you, there's been remarkably little so far. I don't know what you told Mother before you married her, or what she suspected, but my guess is mighty little. I think your aristocratic Creole neighbours may have been slightly more suspicious, judging from their cautiousness in admitting any of us to their inner circle. But they haven't known for sure, either. And Cary's never had the slightest inkling. It would be unfortunate if anything should leak out, after so many years of successful silence, just before her wedding to the scion of an old, respected family.'

Clyde was still facing his stepson with fury, but he was now almost as angry with himself as he was with Bushrod. Never, since the day he had left Sorrento without seeing Lucy, had he felt so defeated; his own failure to act quickly and efficiently in an emergency infuriated him; and it infuriated him still more that Bushrod should remain so calm in the face of his own towering rage. It had always been a matter of pride with him that he was slow to anger and that he could control his expression and conceal his emotions whenever he chose to do so. Now, he had not only been driven to fury, but he had betrayed the fact. Reluctantly, he recognized that, quite aside from the advantage which Bushrod's youth and physical fitness gave him, he was the son of a man who had four times voluntarily returned to the battle front after being seriously wounded, and that his grandfather and all his uncles had been killed in the vanguard of a valiant army. This young scapegrace did not belong to a breed which flinched from danger, and his attitude toward an assailant whom he considered his inferior was very like that of a duellist who declines to cross swords with anyone he despised. Bushrod might be a cheat and a blackmailer, but he was no coward and nothing could alter the fact that, by birth, he was a gentleman and that no less than his mother, he had been schooled to self-control.

'Of course, I've known for years,' Bushrod went on, as Clyde continued to rage inwardly. 'As a matter of fact, I think I guessed when you first began to show me and the other youngsters card tricks — you see, you're responsible for my first interest in gaming, and I should think you'd be proud that I proved to be a pretty apt pupil. I've always meant to tell you, some day, that I knew. But I've waited for a really opportune time. I'd made up my mind, when I had that little run-in with my fellow bluebloods in Richmond, that, if you didn't help me out, I'd mention the matter then. However, my letter to Cary brought you post-haste to Virginia, as I thought it would, so I waited for another crucial moment. I'm mighty glad now that I did.'

'What'll you take to get out of here, today, and not come back until the night of the wedding?' Clyde asked, violently.

'And then, just for the wedding? I follow you. And I think I might be receptive to inducement. My father-in-law's turned out to be a terrible tightwad. He's glad enough to have Mabel and me live with him, in his great mausoleum of a house, because otherwise he'd be completely alone; but he has the strange idea that a man ought to support his wife, even when the man's a pauper and the girl's father a modern Midas. I could use a little ready cash, very easily. And it wouldn't trouble my conscience to accept it. After all, if I'm not mistaken, you promised my mother, when you married her, that Cary and I were to share and share alike. You've squandered a fortune on Cary, just to gratify her whims. And you've never done anything for me, except to send me to school, so you could get me out of the way, and settle my trifling debts in Richmond, so that there wouldn't be a scandal. Well, to get me out of the way again and to avert a much greater scandal — that ought to be worth quite a little to you. I'd say twenty thousand was a very modest figure.'

'I'll give it to you the day after Cary sails for Europe, if you've behaved yourself and kept your damned mouth shut in the meanwhile.'

'Oh no, you won't! You'll give it to me now — in cash. And then you'll pay for that suite at the St. Charles you're so insistent Mabel and I should take. After all, I didn't suggest we should leave Cindy Lou. That was your idea. And of course you'll meet any little incidental expenses we might incur in New Orleans.'

The insolence of this demand was enhanced by the fact that Bushrod had remained quietly in his seat and that the slight smile had never left his lips. But, by this time, Clyde had ceased to care about his stepson's manner and cold rage had taken the place of tumultuous anger.

'Very well,' he said evenly. 'I will pay you off — now — on condition that you and your wife leave Cindy Lou immediately and do not return until just before Cary's wedding; also, that when you take your departure afterward, it will be for good. You will get the twenty thousand, but not another cent. And that means you had better not run up any bills in New Orleans with the mistaken notion I'll pay them as little incidentals.'

He had walked to the safe while he was speaking. Its heavy outer door was open and, after swinging this back as far as it would go, Clyde unlocked the inner door with a small key that hung from the end of his watch chain. One of the compartments thus revealed contained a jewel case. From another, he withdrew a japanned dispatch box and, taking from it several flat packets of banknotes, he checked the markings on the narrow brown paper tabs which bound them, tapped them against the edge of the desk to bring them into alignment, and pushed the sheaf across the table toward Bushrod.

'Ten thousand dollars,' he said curtly.

'Twenty thousand was the figure,' retorted Bushrod. Then, as he saw Clyde draw pen and inkwell to him, he added hastily, 'No cheques. Cash.'

'Of course there will be no cheques,' Clyde replied, looking at his stepson with frank contempt. 'Cheques are returned by the bank when they are cancelled. Do you think I'd care to risk having such a one fall into your mother's hands by some chance? At the same time, there isn't more than ten thousand in the house, and you already have that. I am about to write out an order on the C & L Navigation Company to deliver another ten thousand cash to bearer. And that will be all. No further cash, no incidental expenses, no future payments.'

'Suppose I don't choose to accept the case under those conditions?' Bushrod inquired. But he had risen at last. 'Aren't you forgetting who has the whip hand?'

'No. I'm not forgetting. Because I'm not sure who has it and you can't forget something you don't know. I'm surprised you feel so certain about the matter yourself.'

He was as calm as his stepson now. Neither of them spoke again, and, when Bushrod turned and left the office, Clyde continued to stand by his desk before the open safe.

With the departure of Mabel and Bushrod, the strain at Cindy Lou slackened, and its atmosphere again became one of basic harmony with pleasurable overtones of excitement. It was not until the day before the wedding that anything further happened to cause even a ripple of disturbance. Then Cary came to her stepfather, betraying a degree of agitation which bore no relation to the hectic activities which she had so greatly enjoyed.

'Father, the fans have all disappeared.'

'The fans? What fans?'

'The peacock-feather fans, of course. We were going to have the dress rehearsal for the rainbow minuet tonight. So I told Zack to go and get the box that had the fans in it and bring it up to the ballroom. It's been in the big storeroom, next to the wine closet. He came back and told me it wasn't there any more.'

'Well, somebody must have moved it then, to make way for all those packages that your wedding presents are coming in, after the presents have been taken out of them. There shouldn't be much trouble in locating it.'

'But there *is*! That's the point. I've looked everywhere myself and I've made all the servants look. And they just keep shaking their heads and saying, 'It's one of those mysteries', the way they do if we leave Cindy Lou when the fig trees are ready for the first big pick of the year, just right for preserving, and come back, two or three days later, to find every last ripe fig gone.'

Clyde, who had been working on his ledgers, laid down his pen and carefully closed the book in which he had been making entries. 'I'll find your fans for you,' he said, 'or rather, I'll see that they're found for you, in short order. Go tell Zack I want to see him here at once.'

After Cary had left to follow Clyde's directions, he opened the ledger again, and was apparently still absorbed in it when the troubled Negro came shuffling into his presence. Then he slammed the two sides of the book together and stood up.

'Miss Cary tells me that a box containing presents for her friends has disappeared,' he said curtly. 'If it isn't found within an hour and brought to me here, you'll be out of a job. That's all.'

He sat down again, reopening the ledger. It was only a matter of minutes before Zack returned to the office, his face betraying his misery, his hands fumbling at his battered hat. 'Us doesn't want all Miss Cary's nice lady friends to get conjured,' he said wretchedly. 'Peacock feathers am unlucky – everybody knows dat. Us ain' never liked dem birds, struttin' 'round. But long as de feathers am on de birds, or on de chimney-piece, us reckoned dey couldn' do much harm. Ain' never, neither. But fans, what ladies carries in dey hands, an' touches dey cheek with——'

'Miss Cary wants those fans used at the dance after her wedding. You bring them back here this instant. You know where they are and I know that you know. Miss Cary isn't interested in your damn superstitions and neither am I.'

'You done listen and Miss Cary, too, when Ah talks to you 'bout de buried treasure. An' seems like Ah done hear you believes it be bad luck to have a white horse 'board a steamboat, lessen a red dog comes a'runnin' down to de landin', barkin'.'

It was almost uncanny, the devious ways in which the Negroes on the place possessed themselves of information which their masters would have preferred to keep from them. Zack was right in believing that Clyde himself was not unmoved by certain old superstitions still current on the river: besides subscribing vaguely to the one Zack had mentioned, he did not relish a five-handed game, and he had never willingly taken great risks at cards on a boat with a name which began with the letter M. Determined not to betray his annoyance at the butler's perceptive powers, he regarded his servant with a blank stare and answered coldly.

'That'll do. You know I don't take any backtalk, Zack. Bring me that box of fans.'

Zack had brought back the fans, looking more miserable than ever; but there had been no further 'backtalk', nor did any other incident arise to mar the pleasurable preparations for the wedding. Cousin Stan had arrived, as usual emanating good cheer and laden with casks of Judge Carteret's finest; Mr. Stoddard had come down from New York in his private car, which had been switched off on the plantation spur at the Victoria sugar house; then he had made the *beau geste* of putting it at the disposal of the bride and groom — secretly except in as far as their parents were concerned — so that they might be spared the practical jokes to which they would have been subjected if they had taken the same train by which many of the visitors would go home. He did not suppose it would do him any harm, he said, in an expansively jocular manner which was rare for him, to travel in an ordinary drawing-room, himself, for once. When Mabel and Bushrod returned from New Orleans, they betrayed no resentment at this generous gesture and both appeared not only willing, but eager to make themselves helpful during the last-minute rush; and the great day dawned cool and clear, with just enough crispness in the air to stimulate such activities. The camellias were at the height of their bloom, and when the bride and her attendants were dressed, it was Lucy herself who put on the crowns and handed them the bouquets she had made for them, then fastened the loose flowers lightly into place on veil and ruffles. Finally, she sent the other girls to 'let Grandmother see how lovely they looked before they went downstairs', and, left alone with Cary, put her hands on her daughter's shoulders and looked fondly into her eyes.

'Don't hold it against me any longer that I questioned whether you were really in love with Savoie,' she said. 'I couldn't stand it if you went away from me, bearing a grudge. Some day you'll understand that I only said what I did because I wanted you to be as happy in your marriage as I've been in mine.'

'I do understand, Mother. I didn't at first, but I do now,' Cary told her; and for a moment they clung to each other, their eyes wet. Then they kissed and parted. And Cary did not need to ask to which of her marriages her mother had referred.

The late moon had already set when the last guests left, for dancing had lasted until all hours. The rainbow minuet had raised a storm of applause; it was pronounced the most charming and original feature at any remembered wedding. The girls who had wielded their fans in time to the music carried them lightheartedly away, as, aided by their willing escorts, they climbed into waiting gigs, cabriolets and surreys which were to carry them to the station and up and down the river road.

Lucy stood in the doorway, smiling and waving her handkerchief, until the last guest was out of sight; but Clyde, who was standing beside her, smiling and waving, too, had not failed to notice her growing pallor and other telltale signs of exhaustion. He put his arm around her and, drawing her gently toward him, kissed her cheek.

'There, that's the end at last. I'm ready for a good rest and I know you are. What about letting me carry you upstairs?'

'What nonsense! I would, if I were ill. But I'm perfectly well—just a little tired, that's all.'

'That's plenty. Come on now, no more fooling.'

Before she could protest again, he picked her up and, when he put her down, triumphantly, it was on their bed. Her own maid, Delphie, was waiting respectfully beside it. He waved the quadroon away.

'That'll be all for tonight, Delphie—this morning, rather—until Mrs. Batchelor rings for coffee. No—wait a minute. Make a *tisane* and put it in the *veilleuse* Mrs. Surget gave her last Christmas. A hot drink would do her good right now.'

Delphie nodded her understanding and took her departure. The order did not surprise her. It not infrequently happened that the Boss Man waited on his lady himself and that he recommended a *tisane* as a sleeping potion for her. When the maid returned, her mistress was already settled among the pillows and, after the door had been silently closed behind the turbaned figure for the last time, Clyde poured the contents of the little painted pot, shaped like a nun, into a cup and handed it to Lucy with a look of loving solicitude.

'Try to drink all of this, if you can, darling. I know you need it.'

To please him, she managed to swallow it, sip by sip, though it went against her to do so; and, though she lay down, docilely enough, when he finally took the empty cup from her, and composed herself to slumber, in her customary way, with her cheek pillowed on her arm, it was a long time before Clyde was satisfied, from her quiet breathing, that she was really asleep at last. He spoke to her softly several times, calling her by name; when she neither stirred nor answered, he was partially reassured. Then he bent over and kissed her on the forehead; she gave him no caress in return, as she always did even when she was only half awake. He could safely leave her now.

Taking off his shoes and carrying them in his hand, he tiptoed from the chamber and down the stairs, through the hall — still strewn with scattered rice and fading flowers — and into the dining-room, where the magnums stood empty and the fallen remains of the towering wedding cake were crumpled over the wrinkled white cloth and the tapers were guttering in the sockets of the silver candelabra. None of the servants was up yet; no attempt had been made to straighten out this repulsive disorder. But the Negroes had all done well; there had been no complaints about the hard work, no more whispering about 'conjures', either. The tired men and women were entitled to their tardy rest. Clyde had no desire to disturb them.

He put on his shoes again, went out into the kitchen and made himself some coffee. Then, carrying the pot with him, he continued on his way to the office, entered it and, having mended the dying fire, unlocked his desk. When he had taken his ledgers from this, he sat staring at them, his coffee untasted.

He was a ruined man. He had never been able to deny Cary anything she wanted and she had never questioned his ability to supply it. Well, she still had not questioned it, up to the time she left him. It had not occurred to her that the Big House was already mortgaged and that he would have to mortgage the coming crops in order to build and furnish her house and buy her trousseau — in fact, he doubted whether she had listened when he was telling Stoddard about his flyer in cotton. That was natural enough — she had been restless and resentful that evening; she and Savoie had sat, billing and cooing on a sofa, apart from the others, while he himself had been drawn into that cursed argument. He was glad that no shadow of suspicion, concerning the state of his finances, had ever crossed her mind. And now she was amply provided for. But there was still her mother to think of — Lucy, who asked for so little, but who also trusted him implicitly, and whom he had just left peacefully sleeping, unaware that trust and peace were both so gravely jeopardized.

Of course Cary's extravagance and the luxury with which he had insisted upon surrounding Lucy were not alone responsible for his plight. Although the largest single cargo of cotton — more than nine thousand bales — ever shipped on the Mississippi was carried by his *Cindy Lou*, he had invested too heavily — and too late — in the fleet which flew the C & L flag. From time to time he had considered the possibility of selling his barges and towboats and chartering others as these might be needed. Indeed, he had already reduced the number of such vessels in his fleet; by chartering additional ones for seasonal shipping peaks, he had even managed to pay actual operating costs out of current revenues. But he had never been able to make up his mind to abandon packet ownership altogether; neither had he consented to remodel either the *Lucy Batchelor* or the *Cary Page* for towboat service, as he had the *Sophia Peyton*. Quite aside from the natural sentiment he felt for them because of their sponsors, and all that this sponsorship had represented in the early days of his marriage, he was inordinately proud of the fact that they were the oldest passenger steamboats on the river. They had not only escaped all the usual disasters caused by snags, collisions, fires and explosions; they had given the lie to those scoffers who prated about the flimsiness of steamboat construction. Essentially, they were as sound, more than a quarter of a century after they were built, as when they had slid off the ways. And now . . .

Clyde took a telegram from his coat pocket and sat staring at the envelope. It was the only one that had come addressed to him the day before, and it was merely a stroke of luck that he had happened to notice it and extract it from the sheaf of congratulatory messages for Savoie and Cary. Even so, he had not read it immediately. It was almost time for the ceremony to begin and he had thrust it, still unopened, in beside his handkerchief. It was not until he had occasion to use this, some time later, that, inadvertently, he had pulled out the two at once. Then he had ripped open the envelope and the words inside had suddenly leaped out at him:

CARY PAGE AMONG TWENTY STEAMERS CAUGHT IN ICE GORGE AT SAINT LOUIS TODAY STOP TOTAL LOSS STOP LETTER WITH DETAILS FOLLOWS

He did not need the letter to tell him what had happened. There had been a similar catastrophe at St. Louis once before and he had been there at the time. During a bitter cold winter, ice had formed to the depth of two or three feet in that part of the Mississippi and, after a sudden rise of water, this ice had begun to move. Some of the steamboats in the port had been shoved ashore; others had been torn from their moorings and pushed toward the lower dike. As the ice drifted faster, it broke up and began to gorge; piles of it, rising to the height of twenty or thirty feet, fell on the steamboats and buried them. He had been a young man at the time of this disaster and he had tried to forget it, exactly as he had tried to forget other dreadful sights. Now he seemed to hear again the grinding and crashing of that murderous ice.

Clyde sprang up, tearing the telegram into tiny bits and flinging them into the fire. If he let himself go like this, he would soon be envisioning all the horrors he had ever seen. He tried to think collectedly, but his thoughts brought him no comfort, for they conjured up a picture of the *Lucy Batchelor* sinking, shattered, beneath the river's swirling brown surface, or burning to the water's edge. No doubt word of some such disaster was already on its way to him, and then there would be a third piece of evil news — as Zack had so shrewdly guessed, he had never rid himself of the old steamboating superstitions and none was more credulously accepted than the saying that all bad luck went in triplets. Even if this did not hold true, it would be years before he could mend his fortunes with bumper crops and record prices for sugar and perique. His cash resources had been stretched to the very limit and Bushrod's cupidity had stripped him of nearly his last money reserve. The ten thousand he had given his stepson for hush money represented almost the last of his ready cash; the little he still had would be more than swallowed up before the bills for the wedding had been paid.

At the moment, he could think of only one way which could save Lucy from want. Sitting there alone, with the open ledger before him and the untasted coffee beside him, Clyde knew that, if he could find no other, he would again take that way, hoping against hope that his devious path might still be undiscovered.

Chapter Seven
1895—1896

EVENTUALLY, from sheer exhaustion, Clyde fell asleep, still sitting in his swivel chair. When the telltale figures on the thumbed sheets before him began to blur, he stretched his hands over the desk, the better to shut out those symbols of disaster. Then, by slow degrees, his head dropped lower and lower until it rested on his arms. By that time his thoughts were no clearer than his vision. He was beset by vague but horrible nightmares and, though he struggled to free himself from these, he did not know whether they were dreams or realities. Finally he ceased to struggle and oblivion engulfed him.

With the first stirrings of returning consciousness, he shifted uneasily in his seat, aware of strangeness, but as yet unable to grasp where he was or what had brought him there. After moving his head restlessly about, he raised it from his arms and, beginning to blink, still almost unseeingly, he sensed rather than saw that sunlight was streaming into the room. Then he realized that Lucy was standing on the further side of the desk, looking down at him with loving and compassionate eyes.

He sprang up, with an exclamation that was both bewildered and apologetic. At the same time, almost instinctively, he drew the scattered sheets together and thrust them into the ledger, closing it over them.

'I—I must have fallen asleep,' he stammered.

'Yes,' Lucy replied. 'I hope you had a good rest. I know you needed it. I've brought you some coffee. I thought perhaps you'd rather have it here, now, than wait until you come upstairs.'

Apparently, she did not feel there was anything peculiar about his presence before the disordered desk in the office at such an hour, or the fact that he was still wearing the clothes which he had worn at Cary's wedding. She began to pour coffee from a pot which she took off a tray that had been set on a small nearby table and handed him a steaming cup.

'It'll taste mighty good,' he said, accepting it gratefully. 'But you shouldn't have bothered, darling. You were worn out yourself.'

'I'm not, any more. You made me so comfortable that I couldn't help having a good sleep. I slept for hours. But I've been up quite a while, too. When you come upstairs, you'll see that everything is in pretty good order already.'

'You don't mean to say you've been overtaxing your strength, getting that mess cleaned up!'

'No, dear. I haven't overtaxed my strength at all. I've merely supervised some very willing and efficient workers. Though, as a matter of fact, I'd have welcomed a little exercise. I've been growing lazier and lazier, you've pampered me so. But I've been meaning for quite a while to ask you if you'd mind having me lead a more active life again. Now that Cary's married, I think this might be a good time to make the change.'

She seated herself in a chair between the little table and his desk and poured herself some coffee. Now she leaned over to refill his cup. He had emptied his quickly, still standing and looking at her with mingled bewilderment and concern. But, as he began his second serving, he, too, sat down and, between slower sips, continued to regard her in a troubled and questioning way.

'I'm not quite sure what you mean, Lucy,' he said at last. 'Of course I want you to do whatever's most pleasing to you. But you know you're not very strong and——'

'I know my strength is limited. But I've been wondering whether we need to continue, indefinitely, to keep house on such a lavish scale. I mean, I thought we'd been doing it largely for Cary's sake. We didn't do it when we first came here, before she was old enough to want so much company and so many diversions. As a matter of fact, one of the reasons I was afraid she wasn't in love with Savoie was because she seemed to get more pleasure out of all the general excitement connected with her engagement than she did in being alone with him. A girl who's really in love doesn't think of her fiancé primarily in connection with presents and parties and pretty clothes.'

It was very seldom that Lucy spoke at such length. Nevertheless, after a brief pause to permit a comment from Clyde, if he wished to make one, she went on again.

'Perhaps that is somewhat beyond the point which I was trying to make. I started to say, that unless you'd find it dull, I should enjoy a period of quiet while Cary is abroad. Of course, we'd welcome any friends who chose to come here and we'd do local visiting, occasionally, ourselves. But we wouldn't give big parties, or take long trips. We could explain that I wasn't well enough. I'm not. That is, I'm not well enough to do things like that and other things I'm interested in, too.'

'Such as what, darling?'

'Well, I'd like to do some gardening myself, if you wouldn't mind, instead of just telling a gardener what I wanted done. I used to do a great deal, when I was a girl; I've had a hankering, lately, to take it up again.'

Clyde nodded. 'Anything else?'

'Well, yes. I thought I might even do a little riding again. You know I stopped in the first place because we both felt I shouldn't take risks, as long as there was any chance . . . And of course there isn't, any more. And then later, Dr. Bringier suggested I didn't have the strength to ride and do so many other things, too. But, as I just said, if I wasn't doing so many other things . . . I could ride with you around the plantation, the way Cary used to. I wouldn't interfere with anything. But of course I always rode with my father and my brothers, at Amalfi, when I was growing up. I'd enjoy doing it with you at Cindy Lou.'

'And I'd enjoy having you. Don't ever imagine, for a moment, that I'd find it dull with no one but you for company. If there's any better company than you are, I haven't discovered it.' He was smiling and he realized, with astonishment, that the smile was unforced, though it was only a few hours since he had believed he would never be able to smile, naturally, again. 'Of course, we'll have to find just the right horse for you,' he went on. 'And you must promise me that you won't overdo, that if you find you're getting tired, you'll tell me right away. I'm afraid you'll be awfully stiff at first. But that'll pass.'

'Stiff and sore, too!' Lucy looked across at him and laughed. Then she lifted the lid of the coffee pot and peered inside. 'We seem to have emptied this, between us,' she said. 'Don't you think perhaps it would be a good plan to go upstairs now? I'm sure you want a bath, and I have clean clothes all laid out for you. Now I must get Belle her supplies, or we may not have anything to eat today. I certainly don't want that to happen. Especially as I thought it would be pleasant to have a cosy noon meal in the library. I've got the gate-legged table drawn up in front of the fire there, set for two.'

That day marked the beginning of an era; from then on the library became the chosen centre of their daily life. The other rooms on the main floor were indeed already in perfect order when they reached this; the scattered rice, the faded flowers, the guttering candles, the crumpled linen had all disappeared while Clyde had been agonizing over his ledgers and fighting his way through dim nightmares. There was no reason why he and Lucy should not have been formally served an elaborate midday repast in the dining-room or partaken of a copious tea later on in the drawing-room. But, somehow, it seemed natural to follow Lucy's suggestion, and soon the experiment had become a habit. With its establishment, the house acquired an air of added warmth and intimacy. Moreover, the quiet conversations beside the open fire — talks which seemed to follow spontaneously after the cosy meals — were conducive to the discussion of many subjects which there had seemed no logical reason to bring up before. And eventually, Lucy broached one which, startling as it seemed at first, marked another fortunate turning point in their married life.

'I still seem to have a good deal of spare time on my hands,' she remarked one evening. She had begun her gardening in good earnest, with special attention to the camellias, which were now at the height of their bloom; and as there had been no trouble in 'finding just the right horse' for her, she was riding regularly with Clyde around the plantation, revealing an interest in its products and an understanding of its problems of which he would not have supposed her capable. 'You see what a difference it makes, not having the house crowded all the time,' she went on.

'I certainly do. And I'm certainly enjoying it the way it is now.'

'So am I. But I have too much leisure, especially as I don't have to rest as much as I used to.'

It was quite true that Lucy seemed to be stronger than she had in years. Clyde waited, without apprehension, for her to tell him how she would like to employ her superabundant leisure.

'So I have been wondering if I couldn't be of some help to you with your accounts. My own don't take me any time at all. My father taught me something about accounting and I used to work with him on his ledgers when I was a girl. Later, after he and my brothers were killed, I kept all the accounts, at Sorrento and in Richmond both. Mother can do it if she has to, and of course she has had to, since you and I were married. But she never liked doing it, the way I did.'

'Thanks for thinking of it, Lucy. But I'd rather keep the ledgers myself. That's a man's work.'

He had not meant to speak brusquely, but she had taken him entirely by surprise and had come closer to causing him displeasure than she had ever done before. Had she been any other kind of a woman, he would have thought she was adroitly seeking a pretext for discovering more about matters beyond her province than he had ever seen fit to tell her; and though everything about Lucy's character precluded such a suspicion, this still did not make her suggestion a welcome one. She did not answer and, almost immediately, he regretted his words, especially the closing ones; she had told him she helped her father with the plantation ledgers and he, Clyde, had told her that accounting was not a woman's work. She might well feel he was implying she had been unwomanly to attempt it, or that her father, whom she had greatly loved, had been lacking in manliness to require it of her. Either implication would be unfair and might presumably hurt her feelings. He strove to make amends.

'I'd forgotten, if I ever knew, that women did that kind of work on Virginia plantations, Lucy,' he said. 'But I can see now it might have been necessary, during the War. And that very possibly a father might have thought it was good mental training for his daughter, even when it wasn't necessary. The situation's different in Louisiana and between husband and wife. But I didn't mean that what you did at Sorrento wasn't suitable.'

'I know you didn't, Clyde.'

She picked up the embroidery frame that she had laid aside and resumed her fine stitching. Lucy was an accomplished needlewoman, and Clyde had always admired her handiwork very much. It had never occurred to him before that she did not really care greatly for embroidery, that she did immense quantities of it only for lack of anything better with which to occupy her time. But it occurred to him now. It even occurred to him that she might actually prefer accounting to embroidery. Besides, though as he had said to Cary, he had not always told Lucy the whole truth, he had never lied to her, either; and he had come uncomfortably close to doing so in saying that the reason he did not want her to help with the ledgers was because accounting was a man's work.

'The fact is,' he finally blurted out, 'my ledgers are in pretty bad shape. I wouldn't be particularly proud to show them to you, if you're a good accountant. I'm not.'

'I was afraid they might be rather disorganized, from the glimpse I had of them the morning after Cary's wedding' Lucy replied. 'That's why I thought I might be of some help to you in straightening them out. And then of course the loss of the *Cary Page* must have meant another complication, besides being such a terrible shock. But it was just a suggestion. . . . I think it's about time we had a letter from Cary, don't you? I mean, a letter posted from abroad. If she wrote one on shipboard and posted it as soon as she landed——'

'Lucy, I didn't mean to tell you, I didn't want to, but perhaps I'd better, after all. My accounts aren't in bad shape because I'm not capable of keeping them. I've kept them all right. But they have a good many entries on the wrong side of the ledger. In fact, at this moment, there's so much red ink in evidence that the books look as if they were dripping blood.'

'Well, almost everyone's do, at one time or another, don't they? But that isn't too serious, is it, when a man has plenty of resources and his credit's good?'

'No. But I haven't plenty of resources and my credit isn't much good, either — at least, it won't be, as soon as my creditors find out I can't meet my current obligations. And that'll be any day now.'

For the second time, Lucy laid down her embroidery frame. Then she drew her chair closer to her husband's and took his hand.

'You said you didn't mean to tell me this and, of course, I don't want you to tell me anything you'd rather not,' she said. 'I've always told you that and I've always meant it. But now that you've told me this much, couldn't you tell me a little more?'

'I suppose so. As far as that goes, I can say almost everything there is to say in one sentence. I'm head over heels in debt.'

'Well then, of course those debts must be paid.'

Her expression, though serious, had lost none of its serenity. He began to feel that he had not made the gravity of the situation clear to her, after all.

'Didn't you understand what I was saying?' he asked sharply. 'I can't pay my debts. I haven't anything left to pay them *with*. The house is already mortgaged. There's even a mortgage against this season's crops. I'm ruined. There's nowhere I can turn.'

'You know you could always turn to Cousin Stan, that he'd be glad to help you.'

'I seem to remember that he didn't give much help to you and your mother when you needed it badly.'

'Clyde, he didn't know we needed it badly. We didn't tell him.'

'Because you were too proud to let him know! Well, don't you think I have any pride?'

'Of course you have. A great deal. Perhaps too much — as we did. Please be just, Clyde. What I said is true. Cousin Stan could give you help and he'd be glad to. But I'm very thankful that, if you don't want to tell him your need, at least you've told me. Because perhaps *I* can help, perhaps you'll let *me*. Have you forgotten about my money?'

'Your money? What money?'

'The money you settled on me when we were married. You said that was mine.'

'Of course it was yours. But that was just pin money.'

'Then you must have expected me to buy a great many pins, darling, all set with precious stones.'

'Lucy, I've never known you to joke about a serious matter before. When I told you I was ruined, I was in deadly earnest.'

'I know you were and I'm not joking. I'm in deadly earnest, too. I could have dressed Cary and myself and run the house, too, on what you gave me. That's what I thought, at first, you expected me to do. Then I found out you had no idea of letting me carry the household expenses. And you insisted on buying so many clothes for both Cary and me, yourself, that there wasn't anything left for me to get – that is, anything except an extra party dress for Cary, once in a while, as a special present, and a corset or some other under-garment that you didn't think of for myself. I've sent money to Mother occasionally – sometimes because I thought a gift would please her and sometimes because I knew she really needed funds. She hesitated, at first, to accept anything from me, but I finally overcame her. Of course, I've made presents to friends from time to time and I've given regularly to certain charities. But I've never spent more than a thousand dollars any one year – usually not quite that much.'

'You've never spent . . . Good God, Lucy, I settled fifty thousand on you! That means you've had an income of more than two thousand a year for twenty-five years! If you haven't been spending it, what in heaven's name have you been doing with it?'

'I've been saving it and investing it. Or rather, Mr. Vincent's been doing that for me. You said you didn't ever want to hear of it again. So I never talked to you about it any more, after that first time. But I thought it would be all right to talk to Mr. Vincent about it, because he would know how to handle it so much better than I would. Part of it's in government bonds and homestead shares, part of it's in railroad stock – Mr. Stoddard's railroad. And some of it's in a savings bank – I mean, two or three different savings banks. Mr. Vincent seemed to feel that would be safer.'

Clyde's mouth had been gradually growing drier and drier; by now, he could hardly swallow, much less speak. He sat staring at Lucy, still unable to believe what she was saying to him.

'If we took money from the savings bank – some from each one – right away – say fifteen thousand dollars altogether – that would help satisfy some of your creditors for the moment, wouldn't it?' she inquired, as if the withdrawal of such a sum were the most natural thing in the world. 'Then, as soon as you've gone over your accounts again, you could decide how much more you'd need and whether we'd better meet it by borrowing money, using securities as collateral, or in some other way. Because of course we can meet it somehow. So there's nothing to worry about. Don't you agree with me?'

He found his voice at last.

'Lucy — I — I——' he began. But he did not finish after all. He could not say he would not allow her to pay the debts which were due to his stubborn refusal to admit that the great days of steamboating were over, to his unbridled indulgence of Cary's every whim, to his insistence that Lucy must have luxuries she did not even want and to his own love of ostentation. He knew she did not think of the present emergency in that light. She had simply foreseen, from the beginning, that the time might come when he would need her help to save their home, his and hers, and she had prepared for this, not only with prudence and understanding, but with unwavering love. He could not insult that love. He could only take her in his arms and fold her to his heart, saying nothing and thanking God there was nothing he needed to say.

Now she would never have to know how he had been led into temptation, that terrible morning after Cary's wedding, how nearly he had succumbed to it in the course of the weeks that followed and how miraculous seemed his deliverance from evil.

Of course there was no question, after that, as to whether she should help him with the ledgers. She joined him in the office every morning, having set the household machinery in motion for the day while he was taking his first ride around the plantation. They did accounts together until dinner time. Then Lucy took a short rest and, later in the afternoon, worked in her garden or accompanied Clyde on his second daily round before they went back to the office for further work on the ledgers. Grinding was over now; the machinery had been cleaned and the sugarhouse was quiet and empty. But the perique seedlings were now sprouting in the long beds where the minute grains, mixed with wood ashes, had been sown during the week preceding Cary's wedding; and, in the course of a ride about the plantation, Clyde and Lucy halted their horses beside one of these beds just as the women workers were lifting the palmetto leaves that had covered them through the night.

'This warm sunlight we're having will bring those seedlings along in a hurry,' Clyde observed. 'Barring a late freeze, we ought to have a fine lot to set out very soon now.'

'Yes,' Lucy agreed. But she continued to look down at the seedlings as if she were not wholly satisfied; and presently she said, rather hesitantly, 'Of course you know a lot more than I do about all these things. But I can't help feeling that these palmetto-leaf coverings are terribly primitive. I know they've always been used. But it seems to me that cold frames would protect the small plants much better than they do, and cold frames could be used over and over again. That would save a lot of work, too. I realize field labour doesn't seem to cost much, but just the same, it adds up. If you'd look at the ledgers with me——'

'Stop right there, Mrs. Moneybags,' Clyde interrupted. 'What you say makes so much sense that I could kick myself from here to Burnside for not having thought of it of my own accord, long ago. While you're resting this afternoon, I'll draw up a schedule of the lumber, nails, window lights and so on that I think we'll need, and if it meets with your approval, we'll drive to Gramercy tomorrow and buy them all.'

'But we won't need them until next winter,' Lucy protested. 'Why should we put out the money now?'

'Well, I'll tell you why I think we should. I've been studying about a replant bed, to have ready in case something happens to part of our seedlings; a sort of growth-insurance policy. And, instead of having palmetto leaves for protection, those seedlings will be put in the new cold frames. Check, partner?'

'And double check, darling.'

A few months later, as Clyde was finishing a detailed letter to a St. Louis factor about the favourable prospects for the season's perique crop, Lucy glanced up, with a sigh of satisfaction, from the ledgers on which she had meanwhile been working. She did not speak until Clyde had folded the bulky sheets into a heavy buff envelope and carefully sealed this. Then, when he, too, glanced up, she smiled at him in triumph.

'I thought you might like to know that, for the first time, we were completely out of the red,' she said. 'Look at that page! Every single entry in black! Aren't you excited?'

'I'm pleased — and I'm grateful. If it hadn't been for you, the pages in that book would have kept getting redder and redder, instead of blacker and blacker. But breaking even isn't making a profit. We won't do that until I stop being a wilful sentimentalist. I'm stopping right now.'

'I don't know what you mean, darling. Besides, I like to have you sentimental. I wouldn't want you to stop.'

'I'm not going to stop being sentimental about you. But neither am I going to cling any longer to steamboating — just because I can't make up my mind to surrender the memory of the river's heyday to the reality of its decline. It's going to take every first, last and in-between jitney we can make on cane and tobacco to keep the C & L Navigation Company a going concern. We shouldn't go on doing it.'

'But Clyde, we can't — we mustn't——'

'Yes, we can. Yes, we must. Hold on, honey, let me have my say out. First, we sell all the boats — every barge, every tug, every steamer that floats long enough to carry our flag. We still stay in business, but only when it pays us to do so, like during cotton-shipping time; and we *charter* boats to handle that. We won't have any trouble disposing of the fleet. There's no end of smaller rivers — the Arkansas, the Ouachita, the Yazoo — that the railroads haven't reached yet, where boats are still needed. So, we sell ours and that gives us some ready capital to use for equipment here on the plantation — like jack-screws for pressing out the perique during the curing process, for instance. The beams, weighed down with rocks, that we're still using, as just as 'primitive' as the palmetto leaves we gave up. Don't you see? And, of course, that's just one example. We'll be able to modernize all our facilities.'

'We'd be able to reduce the port establishment in New Orleans, too, wouldn't we?' Lucy asked thoughtfully. 'I mean, those clerks and purchasing stewards and freight agents.'

'Reduce? We could get rid of them all. Desk room in some office on Levee Street and one bookkeeper would be as much of a staff as we'd need. No constant repair and upkeep costs. . . . I tell you it would be the making of us as a going concern! We would cut out the unprofitable part of the operation, keep only the money-making end of it, and instead of working ourselves near to pieces for cane and tobacco profits to take up the C & L deficit, we'd have a third profit to add to the others, with a fine bonus of fresh capital right now when we need it.'

'Darling, I'd never in the world have suggested it, even though I know you're as right as can be. But will you do me one favour?'

'Only one?'

'Yes — a big one, though! Will you promise me *not* to sell the *Lucy Batchelor* — on my account?'

'Promise you to . . .' He rose, strode to her side of the table, took her hand and pulled her to her feet so that he could clasp her closely in his arms. 'You think you're pulling the wool over the old man's eyes, don't you?' he asked fondly. 'But you're not. You realized I'd rather lose a leg than that boat, didn't you? And you wanted to spare my feelings, knowing I'd never make the suggestion myself; so you put it that this would be a favour to you. Well, you can bet your sweet life, I will never sell the *Lucy Batchelor* — never in this world, honey! We'll bring her up here from New Orleans with a full crew of the oldest employees in our service, and we'll serve a banquet in the saloon for all our friends hereabouts, with every chandelier blazing and the orchestra playing. Then we'll tie her up across from Cindy Lou, where she'll be out of the main channel, and as often as need be, we'll overhaul her. We'll keep her in condition, so that if, at any time, we need to use her again, or want to use her again — and it's within our means — we can. Meanwhile, she'll remain afloat, with the C & L flag flying, as long as there's a you or a me, or a Cindy Lou where our children and grandchildren, or their children and grandchildren, live.'

So the fleet of barges and towboats was sold and the *Lucy Batchelor* was brought to Cindy Lou, where as Clyde and Lucy agreed, she belonged — it was all very well for a gay young girl to go jaunting up and down the river, but an old lady ought to stay at home, except for an occasional brief pleasure trip! And these the *Lucy Batchelor* continued to make, going to nearby towns and throwing her lights on the pavilions where dancing was taking place on shore, or carrying groups on holiday excursions. She did not seem like an abandoned boat; rather one which was resting on her many laurels. Sometimes, after the 'heat and burden of the day' were over, Clyde and Lucy rowed out to her and had their supper aboard; occasionally, they even stayed overnight there. As a matter of general practice, they went alone; but every now and then, they invited friends to accompany them — not for a big banquet, but for a quiet meal and a quiet evening. And, whether they went or not, Zack kindled anchor lights at dusk each evening and returned every morning to extinguish them and to convince himself that all was well aboard. And, just before they went to bed, Clyde and Lucy stepped out on the gallery and looked at the reassuring lights.

Meanwhile, Clyde's amazement at Lucy's sagacity in regard to his business interests and the work on the plantation continued to increase as time went on; but he was even more astonished at the reduced cost of their living expenses, now that she had taken charge of these. As far as he could see, the table she set was no less lavish than it ever had been; the daily dinners which were put before him were as carefully planned, as perfectly prepared, as beautifully served as heretofore. But almost everything they ate came from the plantation now; and though the wines they drank were sound, they were not vintage, and champagne had ceased to be among them. There were no more big parties and very few small ones; the Batchelors continued to return the hospitality of their neighbours and to extend it to other friends who had long taken a welcome at Cindy Lou for granted; but they issued almost no invitation on their own initiative, and eventually two of the younger servants, to whom Cary's continuous party-giving had been a source of pleasurable excitement, rather than one of burdensome toil, began to show signs of restiveness. When this happened, Lucy suggested that Mrs. Vincent, who had always preferred to spend more time in the city than on the plantation, might find them useful in New Orleans. The results of the suggestion were highly pleasing to all concerned; and this first break in the ranks of the household staff seemed to lead logically to a second one.

'Of course, Belle and Zack and Delphie would never be happy if they were separated from us, and we'd never be happy, either,' Lucy said to Clyde one evening, as she finished making the entry of the servants' wages in the ledger. 'But I think the others would be perfectly delighted to move over to Cary's new house, just before she comes home. And I think she'd be perfectly delighted to find them there. She'd have friendly, familiar faces around her from the very beginning, and she wouldn't have to waste any time or use up any energy getting strange servants accustomed to her ways. How does the idea strike you, Clyde?'

Although she had taken over practically all the household management, Lucy still never made any radical change in it without consulting his wishes. Her question was not merely a matter of form; she was genuinely eager for his approval.

'Why, it strikes me as a fairly good one,' he answered. 'I suppose we could get along all right here with three servants, living the way we do now, or if we couldn't, Ivy'd probably be glad to stay, too, though she's younger and less of a fixture than Belle and Zack and Delphie. I should think Cary'd be tickled to death to have the others, as you say. I don't believe they'd mind the change much, either. After all, they'd be less than a mile away. As a matter of fact, they'd probably be proud as Punch to find you thought they were capable of doing the job and besides, nothing seems to please these darkies more than to feel they're "in" on a love affair.'

'Then I'll speak to Mrs. Vincent the next time I see her and make sure she approves of the idea, too. She might have been planning to send someone from Victoria.'

'She might, but you know as well as I do it's unlikely. She hasn't the knack of handling servants that you have, Lucy. I doubt if she has any to spare. She certainly was glad when you offered her Patsy and Amos.'

'Yes, but she needed them in New Orleans. She might feel differently about the plantation. However, I think you're right; I don't believe she will. But it would certainly be more courteous to ask her. Then, if she agrees, I'll speak to the servants about the plan."

'You didn't think of consulting Cary, too?'

'I thought of it, naturally. But I don't know that it would be much use.'

Lucy looked away, and though Clyde did not hear her sigh, he knew that the feeling which made mothers sigh over their daughters was in her heart. Cary had proved a very poor correspondent. Not only had she failed to write the letter on shipboard, to which Lucy had so eagerly looked forward, but she had written very few since then, and they had not contained much actual news. For the most part, they had been brief and exclamatory. Everything was heavenly, everybody was wonderful, Cary was crazy about France. Eventually it developed that this 'craze' had caused her and Savoie to change their plans about going to any other country, at least for the present. They lingered a long time on the Riviera, because the sunshine was so marvellous and the life so gay. According to Cary, half the crowned heads of Europe were vacationing there, not to mention various Russian grand dukes and high-ranking members of the British nobility. All entertaining was on a prodigal scale, really superb; and as for the opera at Monte Carlo! Well, no one would ever think the French Opera House in New Orleans was worth a second glance after seeing that. There were any number of yachts in the harbour at Nice, and Cary and Savoie had been invited out on several of them. The Southern Yacht Club would not seem like much, either, any more. And so on and so on.

In spite of all these attractions, the bridal couple finally reached Paris for the spring season, and though no further references were made to sunshine, life was apparently even gayer than it had been on the Azure Coast. When they left the French capital, after Bastille Day, it was to begin their round of visits among friends of the Vincents who owned châteaux. Postcards depicting these fluttered in from the Norman countryside and the Loire Valley. But it was not until Cary and Savoie reached Monteregard, the de Chanets' estate in Charente-Maritime, that anything like a real letter came in.

'Dearest Father and Mother,' Cary had written then –
'This is the most wonderful place of all. You approach the château through a beautiful forest of ivy-wreathed oaks and there's something actually magical about the effect of the sun shining through their greenery. Finally, you come to a great stone portal which leads to a paved courtyard, and you drive through that toward a tower which surmounts a wide gateway – a lot like the famous clock towers in medieval cities. That brings you to a second courtyard, larger than the first, which has dependencies facing the tower and a raised triangular garden facing the château proper, on the fourth side.

'You go into an imposing stone hallway with a curving staircase, and on one side of that are the library, with more books in it than I've seen in any other French house, and the old kitchen, which is now the dining-room, and which is all hung with shining copper. Both these rooms have beamed ceilings, gorgeously painted, and you think there couldn't possibly be anything more beautiful anywhere. But that's because you haven't yet seen the Louis XVI drawing-room and the Louis XV study and the Louis XIV bathroom on the other side of the hallway. I must tell you right off, before you get the wrong impression, that the Louis XIV bathroom isn't used for bathing any more—there are plenty of modern bathrooms upstairs—and, to tell you the truth, I don't see how it would ever have been very practical for that purpose. To be sure, there is a tub in it—covered over now with a heavy, hinged oak lid—but it's in a recessed archway which is decorated with a series of rather harrowing paintings of religious character, separated from each other by golden bands. All four walls of the room are decorated in a similar way, and so is the ceiling, except that on the ceiling the paintings are circular and the gilding much more elaborate; and over the mantel, there's a wonderful portrait of some early de Chanet who looks quite delightfully worldly and wicked, as if he'd enjoy peeking at some lovely lady who imagined she was bathing in private. The room's octagonal in shape and three times the size of our library, with long windows looking out on the inner courtyard at one side and on the other toward the great sunken garden that stretches out to the reflecting pool and the fountains beyond it. (I'll simply have to leave the description of that to some other time, or I'll never finish this letter.) We could hardly tear ourselves away from the view to go upstairs, but when we did, we found ourselves in a Louis XIII bedroom and that was just the beginning of what we saw! Really, I learned more about French history and medieval architecture and period decoration in that one afternoon than I ever did in all the years I went to school.

'We had to hurry and wash up and go downstairs, because the de Chanets were awaiting us in the drawing-room, with refreshments—not with a copious tea, as you would have done, but with delicious little dry cakes and a bottled drink called Pineau, of which we'd never heard before. Of course, Charente-Maritime is cognac country, and Pineau is a mixture of cognac and fresh grape juices—very good, indeed. As for the de Chanets themselves, words fail me. The old marquis—he isn't really old, but I have to call him that to distinguish him from Pierre—is the most courtly gentleman I ever met. Such manners and such a *manner*! The marquise must be as old as Mother, I suppose, but you'd never believe it. There isn't a white hair on her head or a line on her face and what a *figure*! Of course, Mother's is awfully good, for her age, but the marquise's is extraordinary. She's very vivacious, always saying amusing things, laughing herself and making everybody else laugh, too. No one could ever have a dull moment in her company. Her son is a lot like her, I mean he's also very good looking and very good company. It turns out he's only twenty-five, but you'd never guess it—these Continentals seem *adult* so much earlier than boys at home and are so much more *sophisticated*. He's a wonderful horseman and I've

190

had great fun riding with him. You know I've always been a little disappointed that Savoie doesn't care for horses, but then of course you can't have everything in one man and aside from that, he's *perfect*, just as I knew he would be. He thinks of nothing but my pleasure and happiness, so he's delighted that I've found someone to go with me on those long rides that I adore and that are just a torment to him, and he and the old marquis – who isn't really old at all, as I said – have a great time puttering around the place while Pierre and I are off in the woods.

'You never saw such woods. As I said before, there's a look of magic about them and they stretch in all directions. You can ride through them almost endlessly, without taking the same road. Or, if you'd rather, you can tether your horse to one of the ancient stone seats surrounding a little grassy plot, so well hidden that it seems as if it were meant to be secret, and walk down a narrow, winding path that's bordered on one side by the river, thickly fringed with underbrush, and on the other by a series of prehistoric caves, which keep getting bigger and bigger the farther along you go. The largest one of all is called the Cathedral, because it has a lofty vaulted top and long, narrow passages lead out of it in several directions. Pierre said I mustn't ever venture into one of these passages, because I might get lost or something. I asked him if anyone ever had, and he wouldn't tell me. But he did tell me the legend of the Blue Pool which the river widens to form at the foot of the caves. According to this legend, a de Chanet lady who lost her lover flung herself into this pool several hundred years ago; and ever since then, a spring has bubbled up from the place where she was drowned. Of course, that's just silly superstition, but all the same, I think the story's quite fascinating, don't you? I'm sure there's also one connected with those passages, and I mean to find out what this is, some day, too.

'Anyone who wants to is allowed to come and picnic in these caves and we saw piled sticks left over from old fires, neatly gathered together and laid with fresh wood, all ready for new fires – no untidy messes of paper boxes and broken bottles, the way it would have been at home. Pierre says that, besides the peasant picnickers, who come just for the day, gipsies used to come there in large numbers, and that a few of them still do, once in a while. He said they never presumed or pilfered and that they made a lovely sight, at night, gathered around their campfires, which they watched carefully. He said it was great fun to share the suppers they cooked in open kettles and join in their dances and their singing. It sounded as if he'd enjoyed being with them very much, so I asked him if he really made friends with them, when he was a boy, and he laughed and said yes indeed, that was putting it mildly – he lost his innocence because of a gipsy girl. I wasn't quite sure what he meant by that, so I asked Savoie after I got back to the château and he and I were alone in the Louis XIII bedroom. Savoie was quite annoyed. He said it undoubtedly meant that Pierre had lured some poor defenceless young gipsy who caught his fancy into one of the more remote caves and seduced her. Then we almost quarrelled because, from the way Pierre told the story, I gathered it was the girl who had done the luring. Anyway, whatever happened, it was a long time ago, and probably no worse than lots of people do — certainly not worth a quarrel now. Besides, Savoie is so sweet, I don't want to quarrel with him.

'Pierre says the hunting here is something I simply mustn't miss, all the picturesque medieval customs in connection with it are still kept up, so I believe we'll come back here for that — if we actually get away in the meantime! But we just seem to put off our departure from day to day, though I really ought to get back to Paris to buy some clothes, everything in my trousseau is so *old-fashioned* already. Of course, I found it really wasn't up-to-date, by French standards, as soon as I got here and now it looks *positively provincial*. To begin with, my underclothes are all wrong. Corsets are cut and boned to give a "straight front" effect, and the least little bulge over the stomach betrays the fact that you don't have on the right kind. Of course that's had a great effect on tight lacing, because it doesn't do any good to pull in your waist if that simply makes you stick out somewhere else. Sleeves are *much* bigger and skirts have more gores in them, daytime clothes very plain, maybe just a little black braid on blue serge, waists lighter material — lighter weight and lighter colour, both — than the skirts and jackets, evening clothes very elaborate, stiff satins, lots of pearl embroidery, that sort of thing. The marquise has given me the names of several "little" dressmakers who she says will do very well for me, and she also suggests that I try one or two of the "important" ones who are beginning to take away some of Worth's clientele — Redfern and Doucet, for instance, though she hardly ever goes to anyone but Worth herself and Savoie says there's no reason why I should, either. But I do want to get enough pretty things to last a long time, since I suppose there's no telling when we'll get back to France. Savoie says he'll *try* to arrange for a trip every other year, which, as you know, is the custom in lots of Creole families. But he hasn't definitely *promised*, so I'm going to be on the safe side, and I'm afraid if I bought a dozen dozens of everything from Worth's, that would seem to him like too much of a good thing, even if he is the most generous, devoted husband that any girl was ever lucky enough to get.

'Well, you can't complain that I haven't written you a long letter this time, not that you actually have complained, but somehow I've had the feeling you thought I might write oftener. I don't believe you wrote many letters though, when you were on your honeymoon, so there! And unless you'd been to France yourselves, you honestly couldn't realize how impossible it is to get a quiet moment for anything like letter writing. Not much like good old sleepy Cindy Lou, where nothing exciting happens from one year's end to another.

'Loads and loads of love to you both. Your own

'CARY.

'P.S. The marquise would like to be most cordially remembered to Father, whom she recalls most pleasantly. I think she was a little piqued when I told her he didn't seem to remember her very well, so I was sorry afterward I didn't tell a lavender lie about that. She also wants me to say she hopes to have the pleasure of meeting Mother in the not too distant future. If the old marquis finds he can leave the estate, the de Chanets *may* come to Louisiana next year, to return our visit. Wouldn't that be wonderful?'

This letter had been received several weeks before the discussion about the servants and there had been no word from Cary since. Presumably, she and Savoie were still visiting the de Chanets, unless they had returned to Paris for the purpose of replenishing Cary's outmoded wardrobe; and, in any case, it was evident that they would be at the château for the hunting season. At this rate, they would hardly be home for Christmas, and Clyde and Lucy had both counted confidently on having them back by early autumn. Besides, the letter had been disquieting in more ways than one, and Lucy and Clyde both worried about it, without confiding to each other their worries, which were not the same. Accustomed as they were to mutual confidences, they found that, this time, they could not share their troubled thoughts.

When Lucy's idea about staffing the new house was submitted to Mrs. Vincent, the latter pronounced this excellent. It would take a load off her mind, she said, to know that Lucy had provided so effectively for the comfort of Cary and Savoie. Personally, she wanted to spend more and more time in New Orleans; she felt she owed it to Armande. It had been not only natural, but fitting, that Armande should grieve a long, long time for her lost fiancé; but after all, it was perhaps a mistake for anyone so young to bury her heart in the grave. Mrs. Vincent had begun to feel that, if Armande went out more, she might again meet someone who would appeal to her and who would be worthy of her. As long as Cindy Lou had been such a centre of gaiety, Mrs. Vincent had felt that any effort to provide further diversion for Armande would be wasted effort. However, now that the Batchelors were living so much more quietly — and she could well understand their preference for doing so—and that Cary and Savoie would be preoccupied with each other on their return—if they ever did return—Mrs. Vincent thought that really . . .

Lucy agreed wholeheartedly with her friend. Up to the time of Cary's wedding, she herself had viewed Armande as inconsolable; but about then she, too, had begun to think that, possibly, the days of the girl's insusceptibility to solace might be numbered. True, Armande had turned a deaf ear to numerous suitors; but that was when her grief was fresher and also—though perhaps this had nothing to do with the case—when she was younger and suitors more numerous. She was still very lovely looking, with the same soft dark hair, large brown eyes and clear pale skin that characterized her brother; but she was now nearly twenty-eight years old, and beauty of this character was apt to fade early, if marriage and motherhood did not bring it into flower. The very fact that she was less surrounded than a few years earlier might indicate that she was already beginning to lose some of her allure for the opposite sex, and perhaps she was conscious of her lessening charm; if she were, like any normal woman, she would regret this. It was conceivable that the marriage of Cary—her only remaining class-mate who, up to that time, was still unwed—had left her not only singularly isolated, but singularly thoughtful. Her face did not have the mobility which made Cary's seem to sparkle and she was not given to sprightly talk like Cary, either; but her serenity and her silence suggested an intensified pensiveness, rather than the lack of reflective powers. Was it really worth while to make a cult of the dead? Was virginity, while undeniably a virtue, dependable as an attraction after a certain age? Was not normal human companionship, between a man and a woman, better than lifelong loneliness, even if it were not permeated with romance? As far as that went, why should any girl suppose that, once having achieved the married state, she could not still inspire and return passion, even if this had seemed impossible beforehand? And was any woman complete until she had borne a child?

Such were the questions which Lucy thought Armande might very well be asking herself. And since, at the moment, there seemed to be a scarcity of suitable young men among the neighbouring families, New Orleans was probably the logical answer. Lucy assured Mrs. Vincent that she understood perfectly and that she would, indeed, do everything possible to provide for the comfort of the bride and groom, whose return, she felt sure, would not be much longer postponed. When her plan for installing some of the servants at the new house was explained to them, they received the news with the pleasurable excitement which Clyde had foreseen; and from then on, Lucy was more frequently there, stocking the place with supplies and adding to its ornamentation.

Since Cary, while she enjoyed having flowers both for her personal adornment and for the decoration of the rooms she inhabited, freely admitted that she really was not 'a gardening sort of a girl', Lucy planned and planted another garden; and she revealed so much skill and taste in the process, that Clyde asked himself, more than a quarter of a century late, whether he would not have been wise to let her develop the original design at Cindy Lou. There were no exotic trees and shrubs in the new garden, no terraces, and only two small fountains, one in the centre of each *parterre* before the house. But the whole effect was happily harmonious.

Lucy wrote to Cary, telling her of the progress that had been made, with the hope that this might rouse her daughter's interest to a degree that would make her want to see it for herself. Cary's tardy reply, obviously dashed off at top speed, gave no such indication. Of course she was pleased at the report about the grounds; but she wondered if Father had stressed the fact that she especially wanted a summer-house, like the gazebo at Sorrento. There was no mention of it in the letter, though she had talked with him about it when the question of the new house first arose and several times after that. She wanted one more than ever now, because it would help to remind her of the beautiful pavilion at Monteregard. Not that there would be any real resemblance, naturally. But, incidentally, she had decided to name her own house Monteregard, instead of Tunica, as Father had suggested. She did not think there was really anything very romantic about an Indian name, even if it were associated with the locality; and the name Monteregard would always recall to her the happiest days of her life.

Lucy replied with reassurance as to the gazebo; she had not mentioned it before, she said, because she supposed that Cary would take it for granted her wishes in this respect would be carried out by Pierre Chauvin. He had faithfully reproduced the Sorrento gazebo; the new one was at the further end of the garden, and its location would make it an ideal objective for short strolls, beside providing the most effective setting for it. Lucy was sure Cary would be delighted with it. As for the name, of course Cary had a right to choose any she wanted for her new home. Lucy did not refer to the fact that Clyde was a little disappointed at the abandonment of Tunica, which really 'belonged', for Monteregard, which did not belong at all. . . .

Christmas brought with it a cable of holiday greetings from the wanderers, and just before New Year's Lucy and Clyde sent them a cable in return, extending all good wishes on the occasion of their first anniversary. However, since the Christmas dispatch had made no mention of homecoming, it seemed better that the one destined to arrive on New Year's should not do so, either. But when the Vincents and the Batchelors met, according to their custom, to see the New Year in together, Mr. Vincent made a pronouncement.

'I hope neither of you will feel that I am in any way niggardly,' he said, looking first at Clyde and then at Lucy. 'But I've written Savoie, telling him I don't intend to supply him with any further funds for European travel – at the moment, I mean. Of course, he and Cary may want to go abroad again some time, and if they should, I'll do my best to make it possible for them. But they've been gone a year already, and I think that's quite long enough for Savoie to be out of touch with what's happening on the plantation, quite aside from what he's spend-ing – in fact, I think it's too long. I rather took it for granted that he'd be home for grinding, if not before, and I believe you did, though, as far as I know, nothing definite was said to that effect. And the boy's been pretty extravagant. I wouldn't be so astonished at what he's spent if he and Cary had travelled extensively on the Continent, as we thought they would do; but they haven't even been out of France, and a large part of the time they've been visiting. Of course I expected them to stay at first-class hotels, of course I expected Savoie to buy any little thing for Cary that caught her fancy, of course I wanted them to have a good time. But – well, I'll be frank with you. Savoie exhausted his first letter of credit before they'd been gone six months. He asked me to arrange for a second one and I did. Now that he's asked for a third one, I've told him to come home.'

'It isn't as if Savoie were an only child,' Mrs. Vincent added hastily. 'Armande wants to go to New Orleans in time for the Twelfth Night Revels and to stay through Mardi Gras. I want to have her. It's a long while since we've spent the entire Carnival Season in town. She and I are planning to leave Victoria day after tomorrow, and Lamartine will join us as soon as grinding's over. Of course, we'll be delighted to have Savoie and Cary come and stay with us for any or all of the balls that they'd especially enjoy. But since his father's going to be away, it does seem doubly important that Savoie should be on the plantation most of the time. And though we both hate to keep bring-ing it up, there *is* the matter of expense. We want to do quite a little entertaining for Armande in New Orleans, and then there'll be her clothes. And of course there may still be the question of a dowry and a trousseau and a wedding some day. We have to provide for that.'

The Batchelors assured their guests that they understood perfectly and that they felt the Vincents were not only completely right, but completely reasonable in the stand they had taken; in fact, that they themselves were in entire accord with this. Now all four must get together and plan for a house-warming. . . .

Later, when they were alone, Clyde and Lucy spoke more candidly to each other. He blamed himself, Clyde said; if he had not always indulged Cary so, if he had not actually encouraged her to be extravagant, this would never have happened. They must make her understand that his own financial excesses had very nearly brought about his ruin, they must prevent her from leading her husband into similar folly. It would be hard for them to tell her all this and hard for her to listen; but it must be done. Yes, and that was not all, Lucy replied. It was kind of Mrs. Vincent to say that Cary and Savoie could come to New Orleans as often as they chose, for the Carnival balls. But there was no doubt that Savoie's place was really on the plantation, that he should stay there steadily while his father was gone; and naturally Cary should stay there with him. She should not continue to feel that her life must be a round of gaiety, in order to be pleasant. She was old enough now to settle down. It was too bad that, apparently, there was still no prospect of a baby. That would have solved so many problems. . . .

They went on talking to each other like this for hours. But still neither of them voiced the dread each of them most deeply felt.

It was early February when Savoie and Cary finally reached home. Savoie had written his father a rather aggrieved letter, saying it had not been possible to get immediate reservations, but he had finally succeeded in booking passage on the *Xenia*, from Bordeaux direct to New Orleans. They would greatly have preferred, Savoie added, to take *La Touraine*, the newest and fastest steamer of the French Line, from Le Havre to New York, and to spend a few days there before coming on to New Orleans by train; but this would have involved additional expense, which he realized would be either resented or begrudged. He did not mean to be disrespectful to his father, but, like Clyde, he found it impossible to deny Cary anything she wanted to have or do; and, unlike Clyde, he had not yet had time to discover that such a course of action could prove extremely unwise. He went on to insist that it was quite natural that Cary should wish to remain in New Orleans for Mardi Gras; and after they reached his parents' house, he dwelt with pride on the number of call-outs she received at every ball she attended without, apparently, stopping to think that Armande might well feel chagrined by the fact that her sister-in-law's popularity was so much greater and more conspicuous than her own.

For Cary was really creating a sensation. She had always been stylish as well as pretty; but now there was a soignée look about her that she had lacked before. She was wearing her hair in a new way, piled on top of her head, instead of coiled just above the nape of her neck, and brushed back from her forehead in a high pompadour, instead of curling it in soft little ringlets; this ultra-fashionable coiffure, still quite a novelty in New Orleans, made her stand out in any group of girls, however pretty, who were less strikingly individual. So did her smart Paris clothes, representing styles which had heretofore not reached New Orleans, except by hearsay and through the pages of fashion magazines, and which showed her fine figure and set off her dazzling colour to the greatest possible advantage. She wore a different ball gown every evening, and each dress was more becoming, more elaborate, and more sumptuous than the one in which she had previously appeared. She also wore very handsome jewelry, and the amount and variety of this increased as the season progressed. There was murmuring, here and there, to the effect that some of the favours Cary Vincent was receiving were more costly than it was customary or suitable for a young married woman to accept; but none of these murmurs was voiced in Savoie's hearing and, for the most part, they were quickly hushed. Savoie himself belonged to several Krewes; so did his father and so did his various cousins. What could be more natural than for a man to shower his bride with gifts and for his kinsfolk to vie with each other in giving her a royal welcome home?

Cary herself revealed no unseemly degree of satisfaction over the furore she was causing; indeed, she seemed almost indifferent to it, as far as any special participant in it was concerned, eagerly as she craved constant excitement. Opinion was divided as to her attitude. Her detractors said that she now accepted admiration as such a matter of course that she had become blasé; she took it for granted that every man who met her would fall a victim to her charms. Her defenders insisted of course she was still so much in love with her husband that she was hardly aware of anyone else's attentions. Savoie's parents, who had always been kindly disposed toward her, now vied with each other, in self-control, as far as she was concerned. They did not admit in the family circle, much less outside of it, that they were disappointed in their only son's wife, and that this disappointment was rapidly becoming tinged with displeasure, as the balls which were to have provided such advantageous opportunities for Armande proved to be instead merely a series of *mises-en-scène* for Cary. Clyde and Lucy, who had come to New Orleans to meet the bridal couple, and who had been persuaded to prolong their visit at the Vincents' spacious establishment on Elysian Fields, were quite as gravely concerned, though for different reasons. They could not help feeling a certain amount of pride in their daughter's success. But Lucy, especially, was troubled over Cary's restlessness, and both she and her husband were secretly hurt because the girl insisted on prolonging her stay in New Orleans, instead of hastening to the new home which they had made ready for her with such loving care. Every time this was suggested to her, however, she found some new reason for continuing her ceaseless round of gaiety.

'Why, Mother, you know you wouldn't want me to miss the Proteus parade! There's a rumour that one of the floats is going to represent peacocks and naturally . . .'

'I've no doubt it'll be very beautiful and very original. But it's a long time, Cary, since you've seen our own peacocks.'

'They've been there still longer, haven't they? I suppose it's safe to assume they won't all have flown away when I do get there.'

'Of course they won't all fly away. But now that you've been to the Atlanteans and Momus——'

'*And* the Elves of Oberon *and* the first Nereus! Still, you wouldn't expect me to leave before Proteus and Comus, would you? Or the Rex parade? You know perfectly well, Mother, that unless you're in New Orleans for Mardi Gras, you might just as well not have come to Carnival at all.'

'Then you'll start for home on Ash Wednesday?'

'Well, of course Savoie always wants to go to church on Ash Wednesday. And then that rich bachelor from Washington, Wallace Ashby, makes a habit of giving an enormous luncheon at Antoine's on Ash Wednesday, and he's invited us this year, for the first time. I think it's quite subtle of him, don't you? I mean, to have a luncheon at all on Ash Wednesday. Because it's sort of a dare. Everyone's crazy to go, he's such a wonderful host, and just the same, on a solemn fast day . . . It puts all the devout Catholics to a terrible test and some devout Episcopalians, too.'

'I shouldn't have thought Mr. and Mrs. Vincent would approve of your accepting an invitation to a luncheon on Ash Wednesday, Cary.'

'I don't believe they did. In fact, I'm quite sure they didn't. Armande didn't, either—but then, she didn't get an invitation! And, after all, Savoie and I have got to live our own lives, haven't we? Besides, we have to eat somewhere and there's no boat on Wednesday. The *Stella Wilds* doesn't leave until Friday.'

'You could come by train.'

'Yes, we could, but you know we'd much rather travel by boat, just as you and Father would.'

'Then you'll come Friday?'

'Well, of course, if you insist . . .'

Lucy turned away without saying anything, much less insisting, but Savoie and Cary took the Friday boat anyway. It was soon evident, however, that this was less on account of any impatience to reach home than because New Orleans was 'dead as a doornail, now that Carnival is over', as Cary put it. Evidently, she hoped to find more of an outlet for her restless energy in the country than she had in the city. She expressed herself as being delighted with everything at the new Monteregard; but she did not take the prideful joy in getting settled there that Lucy and Clyde had hopefully expected. Instead, leaving her trunks still packed and her household still unorganized, she spent most of her time on horseback, not riding the crops, as she had formerly done, but galloping, with apparent aimlessness, up and down the river road. She did not even go to the warehouse to see the more modern appliances with which perique was now handled, or to the quarters to renew her friendship with Milly Sue and the 'little folkses', Aunt Vicey and her magical brews, and all the others. She spoke impatiently to poor old Moppy, who was now so infirm that she could hardly hobble and, far from making much of the new pinky brown piccaninnies, she merely remarked that the supply of woods babies was apparently more abundant than ever, and that Ma'y Lou would soon be hard pressed to make enough sugar tits. When this happened, Clyde felt sure something was seriously wrong; but, instead of asking her point-blank what it was, he decided to lead up to the cause of the trouble by indirect means. Giging the impression that he was meeting her quite by chance, he joined her one evening on the road, above Burnside; and, after begging her to change her canter to a jog 'out of respect for the infirmities of her poor old father's advanced age', inquired casually whether she still played catch and toss with the notion that they might have buried treasure on their land.

'Why, I don't know,' she said, looking at him without much show of interest. 'I haven't even thought of it lately. Of course, I'm old enough now to see that we couldn't go digging at random through a mass of gravel. But Murrell really did exist, didn't he? And probably he really did bury part of his surplus treasure, just as the darkies claim. I suppose some day we might run across an old map or a set of directions or something. . . . Why?'

'Because I think maybe we have got a treasure trove, but that we don't need to dig for it, after all. Valois Dupré — I don't mean that old beau of yours, I mean his father — has an idea it's right on top of the ground and that we've been overlooking it, all these years.'

Cary shrugged her shoulders. 'Valois Dupré never really qualified as a beau of mine and you know it,' she said. 'I wish you wouldn't refer to him that way. And what would a city politician like his father know about land in the country? I don't see how he happened to find out about the Cindy Lou treasure in the first place.'

'Easy there! I keep telling you I'm an old, old man and bruise easier than I used to. Valois Dupré, Junior, isn't in Savoie's class, I'll admit that; but he's a nice fellow just the same and a mighty promising young lawyer. As for Valois Dupré, Senior, he's no beer-bellied ward boss, even if politics do interest him enough so that he wants to play the game both for fun and for keeps. And I mentioned the Cindy Lou treasure to him myself.'

'But whatever for?'

'Money and the need for the same. I'd lost some at Metairie that afternoon – no, it was the other track, the one beyond Esplanade. I remember now. Young Valois had ridden in the Gentlemen Jockey Race and won it, so his father invited several of us home to celebrate. After dinner, we played cards.'

'And did you lose then, too?'

'I'm very much afraid you're right. That's just what I did.'

'It seems to me you nearly always lose nowadays. But you certainly are still lucky in love.'

'I am that. Anyway, having lost at the track and then again at the card table, I made some remark about what happens to a country mouse like myself when the town mice get him into their clutches. And in the same joking way, I said I might have to make a real pass at digging up my buried treasure, gravel or no gravel. Then I noticed that Valois – the older one, I mean, was pricking up his ears like a terrier. I thought it was the reference to the treasure that had interested him, so I made an excuse to linger after the other guests had gone and told him how Murrell was supposed to have used the streams and swamps at the upper end of Lake Maurepas for a hiding place – Blood River, Blind River, the Petite Amite and our own Bayou Boisblanc. I said every one of our darkies would take a conjured oath that at least one shipload of Murrell's treasure is still buried somewhere along our Bayou Boisblanc frontage. I also said there was no way of disproving this, since that part of Cindy Lou is one big gravel bed which nobody could dig up—it would cost more to go through it than any one shipload of treasure would come to. And Dupré called me a damn fool for looking under the ground when the treasure was on top of it.'

'How silly of him,' Cary said disdainfully, 'If it had been on top, we couldn't have missed seeing it, all these years.' She was speaking in the same tone she had used when dismissing the subject of her recent Carnival triumphs, when this was beginning to bore her. Clyde recognized the inflection with apprehension; Cary was getting tired of his talk and of their slow pace. Presently, she would be cantering off, on some pretext of haste, and he would have lost his chance to lead up to the question he wanted to ask.

'Maybe we didn't recognize the treasure when we saw it,' he said hurriedly. 'It seems gravel is worth a lot of money, especially if it's anywhere near New Orleans. Most of the craft that come there now are steamships, and they don't need the same sort of ballast sailing ships do – their machinery is heavy itself, and it's easy to pump water into the ballast tanks or out of them. That's why New Orleans doesn't get loads of granite blocks any more and has to look elsewhere for cobbles or use bricks to put on the streets; you can't leave city roadways a mass of mud any more, with stepping stones at the crossings. So people are putting clam shells down, or gravel, if they can get it. Washed gravel is a much better capper – a chunk of gravel doesn't have one side all hollowed out, the way a clam shell does.'

'Dupré meant the gravel itself was the treasure then?' Cary asked, indifferently.

'Yes. For here's gravel, lashings and lashings of it, right where it can be washed and loaded on to schooners and brought straight to New Orleans through the old Carondelet Canal or the New Basin. So the long and short of it was, Dupré paid your mother and me a visit while you and Savoie were in Europe and, after looking over the ground, he offered me a very tidy sum for the rear section of Cindy Lou – that Bayou Boisblanc piece, I mean : the only part of the place we've thought of as worthless, right along, because nobody can grow the first thing on gravel. I should have said worthless aside from your treasure.'

'And you didn't take him up?'

'Of course not. He called me every description of simpleton he could think of, but he also said his offer stood, any time I'd care to take him up, because cities would be needing more and more gravel, and after that, the turnpikes would need it and so forth and so forth. I expect he thought I was just holding out for a higher price and I didn't tell him different.'

'There *was* another reason? You kept that Bayou Boisblanc piece, when you were offered a good price for it, just because you thought I still believed I'd have the luck to find buried treasure there?'

'Well, partly – just partly, of course. More because Cindy Lou means so much to me – to all of us – that I'd almost as soon think of selling one of the family as any of the land that's part and parcel of the family, too. . . . You do still believe in the treasure, don't you, Cary?'

'More or less. But I'm not so sure I'll be the one to find it. I'm feeling rather out of luck, these days. . . . Do you mind very much if I leave you here, Father? I seem to be almost home and I do want one good canter before I get there. Sorry you don't feel like having one with me any more.'

She must have given her horse a quick cut with her riding crop, for he reared suddenly and then plunged forward at breakneck speed. Clyde made no attempt to catch up with her; he was completely baffled and he was more hurt than he would have been willing to admit. How could a girl whose mere expression of a wish had always been enough to assure its fulfilment say, even in jest, that she was out of luck? And Cary had not spoken jestingly – she had spoken bitterly. She had everything in the world to make her happy – loving parents, a devoted husband, countless friends, a beautiful home, the assurance of plenty – and she was young, lovely and in perfect health. But she was not happy and she was not pleased and touched because he had saved the land for her; she did not feel any longer about the land as he did. . . . Yes, certainly something was seriously wrong. He would not beat about the bush any more. He would ask her point-blank what the trouble was, after all . . .

When he did so, she did not come and nestle in his lap, as she would have before she was married; neither did she bury her head on his shoulder and pour out her little troubles, confident that he could smooth them all away for her, as she would have done then. Instead, she stood in front of him, twisting a dainty, lace-trimmed handkerchief around her fingers. Somehow, the gesture seemed out of harmony with her fine carriage and beautiful clothes and the new way she was doing her hair, all of which made her seem so much more sophisticated than she used to be. It was a childish gesture. Then Clyde saw that the handkerchief was wet as well as rumpled and knew that she must have been crying, which was very unlike her. She was not crying any longer; the eyes which met his were not tearful but defiant. Yet he felt surer than ever that she must be very unhappy, so he spoke to her gently and with increasing persuasiveness.

'Tell me what the matter is, honey. You know I've always told you that you could talk to me about anything, anything in the world, and that I'd understand.'

Cary rolled the handkerchief into a hard little ball and tossed it on the table between them. 'All right,' she said; and her voice was hard, too. 'I suppose I'd have to tell you some time. Perhaps it might just as well be now.'

'I think it had much better be now. Because the sooner I know what's troubling you, the sooner I can do something about it.'

'There's nothing you can do about this.'

'Of course there is. But not until I know what to do.'

'You can't help it, can you, if I didn't want to leave France?'

Clyde laughed indulgently. 'Why of course you didn't want to leave France! You were having a glorious time and you were on your honeymoon. Every girl wants to prolong her honeymoon, if she can. And I certainly don't see why you can't. From the look of Savoie, I think he'll go on acting like a bridegroom for a long, long while! You've had your fine trip and now that you and he are in your own home, the house that's exactly what you wanted, it'll seem so good to you, presently, to be there that you'll wonder how you possibly could have stayed away so long.'

'No, I won't. I'll keep wishing and wishing I could have stayed away longer. I'm not glad to be home.'

'Why, Cary?'

'I've told you. Because I didn't want to leave France.'

She came a step closer to him, and he saw that her face was hard now, too, indeed that it had become so hard as to obscure all its fresh and glowing beauty. 'I didn't mean to tell you until I'd found out whether there was something *I* could do about it,' she said. 'And I haven't yet. But you've bullied me into talking. The reason I didn't want to leave France is because I'm in love with Pierre de Chanet.'

Chapter Eight

1896

IF she had suddenly doubled up her small hand and struck him between the eyes he could not have been more shocked and stunned. But he managed to speak almost instantly and his words revealed that the first effect of her outburst had been to arouse concern for Lucy rather than sympathy for herself.

'Don't you dare let your mother guess this! If she did, it would kill her.'

'I don't want her to guess it. I didn't want to tell you, but you made me. Just the same, I don't think it would kill her if she did find out. She fell in love with you, didn't she, while she was still married to my father?'

'Don't you dare make a comparison like that, either, Cary! You married Savoie of your own free will, when you were twenty-seven years old and when he'd been your patient suitor for ten! No one urged you to do it. In fact, your mother warned you that you couldn't really be in love, that you wouldn't have kept him waiting so long if you had been. She tried to dissuade you from the marriage on that account — not that she had anything against Savoie, Lord knows! She herself was married, under pressure, when she was only sixteen. Her bridegroom left her, a week after their wedding, to join the army, and he never was at home again, except on sick leave, until his last illness. When I first saw your mother, he was a hopeless invalid. She'd never led a happy, normal married life. Nevertheless, I didn't speak a word of love to her until her husband had been dead a year and a half. I wouldn't have insulted her by making love to her while he was still alive, and she wouldn't have listened to me if I had. My God, I never even *saw* her alone! And here you are, trying to justify your outrageous confession, by pretending there's some similarity between your mother's case and your own!'

The angry words poured from him in a torrent. Cary answered with comparative calm.

'All I said was that she fell in love with you while she was still married to my father. You may remember that she told me so herself, in your presence, when I decided to get engaged to Savoie. I didn't say the details were all alike. I think that's beyond the point. Anyway, there's no use in making long speeches on the subject.'

She turned, as if to leave the room. Clyde stepped over to her and put his hand on her shoulder, not roughly, but with sufficient firmness to halt her.

'There may not be any use in making long speeches, but you and I are going to thrash this thing out right here and now. Sit down, Cary. You said, a few minutes ago, that you hadn't meant to tell me about — about this mess until you'd found out whether there was anything you could do about it. That means you must have been trying to do something. I'd like to know what.'

'I've been doing some reading,' she replied, disregarding his order to be seated and still standing as if bent on escape at the earliest opportunity. 'And I've made a few inquiries. But very discreetly.'

'What *kind* of reading? Inquiries from *whom*?'

'I've been reading everything I could find about divorce——'

'About *divorce*!'

'Yes. Not that I've found much. I thought there'd be something in those old law books of Grandfather Peyton's, but there wasn't. So I wrote to Grandmother.'

'You wrote to your *grandmother*!'

'Oh, I did it very guardedly. I just told you my inquiries had been discreet. I said I'd got interested in Grandfather's library, just as Mother always has been, but I wondered if there weren't some volumes missing, that we were supposed to have, because so many legal subjects weren't even mentioned in Mayo's *Guide*. Grandmother wrote back that the *Guide* was issued primarily for the convenience of justices of the peace and didn't contain information about anything over which they didn't have jurisdiction.'

'Even if it had, that wouldn't have done you any good. You don't need to struggle through any more law books. In the first place, you're not a resident of Virginia, you're a resident of Louisiana — where the laws are different. But, even if they weren't, I can tell you right now there isn't a court anywhere that would give you a divorce from Savoie. He hasn't been unfaithful to you. He hasn't abused you. He isn't a drunkard. He hasn't committed any sort of an infamous crime. He's passionately in love with you and he has been for years. He never looks at another woman. What's more, as far as I know, there isn't a single serious flaw in his character. I've met a good many men in the course of my life, Cary, and I can tell you he's one in a thousand. But, even if you could find grounds for a divorce, and could get one somewhere, you'd be a pariah the rest of your life as a divorced woman. There's never been a divorce in your family or in any family you know.'

'There you go, making another long, useless speech. I didn't say I had anything against Savoie. I'll admit all his perfections. But I think they're tiresome. If he were a little more daring and devilish, he wouldn't be so dull. I didn't suppose I could divorce him. But I thought, perhaps, in time, I might persuade him to divorce me.'

Again the sensation that she had struck him was so strong that Clyde found it difficult to combat. Unconsciously, he tightened his grip on her shoulder, forcing her down into a chair. It was only when she gave a little cry that he realized how rough he had been.

'I didn't mean to hurt you, Cary,' he said; but his voice was as harsh as his action had been. 'Just the same, I do intend to thrash this thing out with you. I can't believe you're really trying to tell me that Savoie has grounds for divorce.'

Cary did not answer.

'Has he?' persisted Clyde inexorably.

'No-o-o. Not — not exactly.'

'You mean that this — this Frenchman told you he was in love with you and that you listened, but that's all?'

'Not quite.'

'Then what do you mean?'

'Well, we flirted a little. He kissed me once or twice — maybe more than that. I didn't exactly slap him in the face. I guess I must have kissed back. And when we were riding in the woods . . . Well, it isn't hard for a man to put his arm around a girl, if their horses are close together. You know that. Then, there are those famous grottoes at Monteregard. We — we dismounted once or twice to explore them. And of course we danced a lot. Dancing can be just as impersonal or just as personal as you want to make it. You must know that, too. Some gipsies came and camped in the woods and they invited us to join in their merrymaking. That was one of the times when dancing became — fairly personal.'

Something very like disgust was welling up within Clyde now, mingling with his fears. It was sickening as well as unbelievable to learn that this beloved foster daughter of his, the child of a great tradition, whose rearing had been gentle, whose surroundings had been sheltered, and whose mother was the embodiment of both steadfastness and refinement, had so far cheapened herself. But though Cary was telling him all this with reluctance, she was doing it without any show of shame or repentance. Indeed, she was actually hoping that her contemptible folly might furnish her with freedom.

'If anyone else had told me this about you, Cary, I couldn't have believed it,' Clyde said. His voice was still stern, but there was real sorrow in it, too. 'I'd have given him the lie. And I was right in the first place, when I said that if your mother knew this, it would kill her. You must be completely blinded by this — this infatuation of yours. If you weren't, you'd be the first to recognize your own conduct for what it is and condemn it. And you'd realize that the only kind of a man who could be jointly responsible for it was a despicable cad.'

'I won't let you say that about Pierre! He isn't a cad! He's a witty, charming, cultured gentleman.'

'I'll take your word for it that he looks that way to you. I don't believe he looks that way to anyone else who knows him well, except perhaps his — his mother.' Clyde found that the last statement had been extremely hard to make; but he went on with less difficulty. 'Was it your idea that if you could succeed in getting Savoie to divorce you, Pierre de Chanet would marry you?' he asked sarcastically.

'Why, of course! He's crazy about me! He's told me so over and over again!'

'I don't doubt it. But has he told you that if you were free, or could get free, he would want you for his wife?'

'Not in so many words. But——'

'Not in so many words! Of course he hasn't! And of course he never will. Doubtless, he'd like very much to have you in his collection of mistresses; considering how "adult" and "sophisticated" he is — to quote from one of your letters — he's probably had several since he "lost his innocence". And he's doubtless very much surprised and slightly chagrined because you didn't succumb to his charm as rapidly and as completely as most of the women he's wanted. But he'd never marry a woman who'd been divorced by her husband, naming him as co-respondent. He wouldn't forgive her for making a scandal out of a secret liaison. You'd better believe me, Cary. I know what I'm talking about.'

'I'm sure you think you do. And I'm sure all your advice is very well meant. But I've had about as much as I can stand of it just now. Would you mind very much letting me leave?'

She rose, facing him defiantly again. He walked quickly to the door and stood with his back against it.

'I'll let you leave if you'll give me your word of honour you won't say anything about this to your mother or Savoie or anyone else.'

'That's easy. I've kept telling you that I didn't want to talk with anyone about it, and that I wouldn't have done it now if you hadn't made me.'

'Very well. But I want you to promise me more than that. I want you to promise me you'll stop acting as if something were the matter.

You'd already roused my suspicions. Presently, you'll rouse your mother's and your husband's. Then they'll start asking you questions, just as I did, and they'll find a way of making you answer, just as I did. After that, there really would be trouble.'

'All right. I'll do my best to act like a dutiful daughter and a rapturous bride. Will that satisfy you?

'I suppose it will have to.'

He stepped aside and opened the door for her. It was the first time they had ever parted without either a farewell caress or a loving glance, and he watched her leave with a heavy heart, knowing that such glances and caresses were now a thing of the past between them, and that a glowing and precious element of his existence was gone forever because this was so. But he was not prepared for the final bolt which Cary shot when she had reached the hallway.

'After all, I won't have to pretend very long. I had a letter from Pierre this morning, saying that he and his mother had decided not to postpone their visit to the United States until next fall. The old marquis doesn't feel that he can leave the estate, but they're coming anyway. They must be on the water already. If they are, they'll arrive in New York next week and in New Orleans the week after. Of course they're planning to come to Victoria, too. Then Pierre can tell you himself what his intentions are. He may be more convincing to you than I've been.'

Cary had shown no enthusiasm for an immediate housewarming; instead she had insisted she would rather give her first big party a little later on, when she was more thoroughly settled. In the light of her outburst to her stepfather, he had no difficulty in guessing that, being interpreted, this meant she intended to have it after the arrival of the de Chanets and to make it as sumptuous as its setting would permit. The idea sharpened his sense of harassment. He was unable to dismiss the scene with Cary from his troubled thoughts for more than a few consecutive moments; and he began to feel that he should have received her horrifying disclosure very differently: instead of upbraiding her and denouncing Pierre de Chanet, he should have shown sympathy with her plight and understanding of it. Without condoning her actions or the marquis's, he could have told her that he knew, all too well, how unbalancing a sudden infatuation could prove; and then he could have persuasively assured her that, fortunately, such seizures were almost invariably of brief duration, and that when their victims had recovered, they were generally the first to realize that their aberrations, however violent, had no relation to true love or even to genuine passion. If such statements proved unconvincing, as they well might have, he could have gone a step further, and confessed to her that he was only too keenly aware how nearly fatal such infatuations might be. . . .

The more he thought all this over, the more firmly convinced Clyde became that he must talk with Cary again, along different lines; but the opportunity to do this eluded him. It had been understood, when the bridal couple returned, that they would come to Cindy Lou every other day for either tea or dinner, and he had felt sure that he could get Cary away from the others, on one pretext or another. But he neither saw her nor heard from her for three days after their stormy interview. As casually as he could, he asked Lucy if she supposed anything were wrong at Monteregard; her reply was unhesitating and untroubled.

'If there were, we'd have heard of it immediately, either through Savoie or through one of the Negroes. I think perhaps we've been a little too insistent, Clyde, about seeing Cary. Of course we've missed her terribly, and it's natural for us to try to make up for lost time. On the other hand, it's equally natural for her to want to be alone with her husband. I certainly wouldn't have promised to see anyone else, as often as every other day, just after you and I were married.'

'Well, perhaps you're right. And thanks for the compliment, my dear. I appreciate it.'

The conversation switched to other subjects, but Clyde was still unable to put Cary out of his mind and, the following morning, while Lucy was busy with household matters, he stopped at Monteregard in the course of his ride around the plantation. Savoie was at home and greeted his father-in-law cordially, though the young husband also appeared rather troubled.

'Cary doesn't seem to be very well. She's been completely prostrated, these last few days, by a terrible headache. I thought I ought to let you and Mother Batchelor know; but Cary's kept insisting her migraine would pass, pretty soon, and that, meanwhile, she didn't want to bother her mother.'

'Have you sent for Dr. Bringier?'

'No, Cary didn't want me to do that, either. She maintains that she's just nervous and tired and that she wants to be left alone.' Savoie's troubled expression became more marked. 'She doesn't want to see you or her mother. She doesn't even want to see me. She just lies with her eyes shut, even though she's got all the shutters closed, to keep out the light. She won't eat anything, and I can't tell, when I go to her bedside, whether she's really asleep or whether she's just pretending to be, because she doesn't want to talk.'

'It seems to me you ought to get hold of Dr. Bringier whether Cary's willing or not. But I'll ask her mother what she thinks, and let you know.'

A fresh concern was now added to the many which Clyde already felt. At first, he was inclined to believe that Cary's indisposition was merely a form of anger, and that she was pretending a degree of malaise which she did not really feel, in order to avoid seeing him. But he quickly dismissed this theory as unconvincing. Cary was too restless to spend days on end closeted in the dark unless she were really ill. He charged Savoie to keep him informed and hastened back to Cindy Lou.

To his surprise, Lucy took the news quite calmly. When Clyde broke it to her, she was sitting in the library, reading a letter and, after putting it aside, in order to give him her attention, she resumed her perusal of it, merely saying she did not believe anything serious was the matter with Cary and that Clyde should not worry too much. He waited, hoping that when she had finished her letter, she would discuss Cary's symptoms more fully with him, but, when she looked up from it a second time, she plainly revealed that her thoughts were still on its contents, rather than on her daughter.

'I'll go over to see Cary this afternoon, if you'd like to have me,' she said. 'That is, I'll go over to Monteregard. I don't think I'd better disturb her if she's asleep, or even if she's pretending to be asleep. Probably it's not exactly a pretence. More likely, it's a feeling of drowsiness that gives a certain amount of relief from the discomfort she'd otherwise be feeling, so that naturally she doesn't want to be roused. But I'll look over the situation. Meanwhile, I'd like to talk with you about this letter I've just had from Bushrod, if you can spare the time.'

'Of course I can spare the time,' he replied, sitting down beside her, and trying to repress the feeling of mounting antagonism that the mere mention of his stepson's name never failed to rouse. 'Is Bushrod ill, too?'

'No, apparently he's well and — strangely enough — in very good spirits.'

'Why do you say "strangely enough"? Bushrod's usually in fairly good spirits, isn't he?'

'Yes. But it's hard for me to understand how he can be now, Clyde. This letter tells me that he and Mabel have separated.'

'Separated!'

'Yes. Of course that comes as — as a good deal of a shock to me.'

Lucy was still holding her letter and, though Clyde purposely avoided looking at her too closely, he could tell from the slight rustling sound of the sheets that her hands were trembling. Her voice was trembling, too.

'Apparently the main reason there is no question of a divorce is because that is contrary to Mabel's principles,' she went on, trying in vain to speak steadily. 'Personally, I can't help believing the poor woman's still deeply in love with him. But, from what Bushrod says, she seems to think he has behaved very badly.'

'Do you know in what way, darling? Or would you rather not talk about it? Don't tell me anything you don't want to.'

'I want to tell you everything — that is, everything I understand. It isn't very clear to me. Perhaps you'd better read the letter yourself.' She handed him the sheets bearing the letterhead of the Hoffman House and folded her hands in her lap. Then she bent her head and sat motionless while he read.

'Dear Mother:

'I am dashing off these lines to you on the eve of sailing for France. It's only fair that if Cary can have a year abroad, I should have one, too, don't you think so? I rather hope to get to all the cities she went to, and perhaps others besides, though, unfortunately, my itinerary won't include visits at historic châteaux, as I'm not as well provided with letters of introduction to members of the French nobility as she was. My trip will be different from hers in another respect also, for there'll be nothing of the honeymoon character about it. On the contrary, I'm going alone.

'The fact is, Mabel and I haven't been hitting it off so well, and after a number of arguments that have got us nowhere, we've agreed to disagree. Of course, I've never seen eye to eye with her father about anything, and the bigoted old tightwad has kept denouncing me, in Mabel's hearing, for every little diversion I've managed to wedge in, and every trifling sum I've managed to spend, by hook or crook, without his approval and permission. The first result of this was that she took to giving me curtain lectures on the same subjects after he finally left us alone, and I got fed up with them. So finally, I told her to shut up. That sent her sobbing back to Father and presently he convinced her she ought to get rid of me. I moved over to the Hoffman House with his entire approval, which suited me all right, too, for a time; but there doesn't seem to be anything special to keep me in New York indefinitely, and I suggested that I'd like to go to Europe. At first, Mr. Stoddard felt this might be quite a strain on him, financially; but eventually I convinced him that it wouldn't cost him any more, in the long run, than to have me hanging around here. He consulted some stodgy old lawyer on the subject, in his interests and Mabel's, but I handled matters for myself; and I think it speaks pretty well for my legal training at the good old University that I got the better of him on all counts, except that the separation isn't official, as I'd have liked it to be. As a matter of fact, I can't blame the stodgy old lawyer for that. Apparently he pointed out that there were certain advantages to such an arrangement. But they didn't go down with the pillar of the church.

'I'm heading first to Paris, but I don't know just how long I'll stay there, and though I think Monte Carlo will be my next way station, I'm not sure of that, either, so I suggest that when you write, you address me in care of Baring Brothers until further notice.

'Your last few letters haven't been very detailed, but I take it you're still living high, wide and handsome at Cindy Lou and I wish you joy of it.

'Your loving son,
'BUSHROD PAGE.'

'It's terrible,' Lucy said in a low voice. 'But I'm trying hard to tell myself that it might have been a great deal worse. There might have been children involved. There might have been an open break. There might even have been a divorce. I think that would have killed me.'

'Please try not to feel so badly, darling. It's clear there isn't going to be an open break, much less a divorce,' Clyde said, hoping that he was speaking the truth. He was still holding Bushrod's letter in his hand, but he was thinking of Cary and what he had said to her about her mother.

'Of course Mabel wasn't just the type I'd have chosen for Bushrod, but she did think the world of him and I suppose every woman feels as I do about the girl her only son marries,' Lucy went on. 'Very often she feels that way about the man her only daughter marries, too. I'm trying hard to tell myself we ought to be thankful that Savoie's everything we could possibly wish. But that doesn't seem to help as much as it should, either. Cary seems so restless and discontented.'

'She'll settle down after a while, you'll see,' Clyde said, again hoping that he was telling the truth. 'I think perhaps it would have been better if she hadn't gone abroad at all,' he added. That much, at least, he could say with complete conviction. 'If she'd gone straight to Monteregard—which wouldn't have been Monteregard in that case, but Tunica—she wouldn't have had so much trouble getting adjusted. She's been unsettled by all these foreign ways she's seen.'

'Yes, I think she has. I think you're right—it would have been better if she hadn't gone to France. I can't help feeling it would be better if Bushrod didn't go, either. And I'm very much confused. Quite aside from—from the disgrace of this separation, it seems to me most unwise for him to leave New York when he's hardly begun to build up his practice. Won't he lose all his clients? And what will he live on while he's in Europe? If Cary and Savoie spent so much money that Mr. Vincent had to intervene, I don't see how Bushrod——'

'Lucy, this won't be pleasant for you to hear and believe me, it isn't easy for me to say. But, if I'm not mistaken, Mr. Stoddard's paid Bushrod to get rid of him.'

'*Paid him!*'

'Yes. In other words, Bushrod's become a sort of – well, a sort of remittance man. As long as he stays in Europe – or somewhere else at a comfortable distance from New York – Mr. Stoddard will make him a regular allowance. But, if he goes back there, if he tries to – to resume his marital status, the money will stop. And Bushrod would rather have money than Mabel. Of course, I'm just guessing. But I think that's the way things are.'

'But he didn't have to take money! He could have come home! He could have lived with us and practised law in Louisiana.'

'Yes, he could have,' Clyde answered, suppressing the impulse to say, 'Thank God, he didn't!' He tried to choose his words carefully. 'But he would have had to study the Napoleonic Code and that's quite a change from the English Common Law and after that, it would have taken him even more time to build up a practice here than it did in New York. Meanwhile, I'm afraid he wouldn't have been contented. It would have meant a confession of failure and no man likes that. The last time he was here, he came in a private car, with a millionaire for a father-in-law and an heiress for a bride. It would have been a good deal of a come-down to arrive alone – and to tell the neighbours why. Besides, you and I aren't living high, wide and handsome just now. We're trying to live as economically as we can, and Bushrod likes luxury. I doubt if he'd have been satisfied with our present simple form of existence at Cindy Lou.'

'I suppose it is doubtful,' Lucy conceded. 'And we couldn't have changed our way of living, just to please him. Because, as it is——'

'As it is, we're keeping our heads above water,' Clyde said. 'Barely. There's no leeway yet – you know that as well as I do, honey. But thanks to you, I don't think we'll go under. I'll never be able to tell you, Lucy, what it's meant to have you stand by me the way you have. But there's something else I can tell you : this last year at Cindy Lou has been about the happiest one of my life, in spite of all the worries. Because you and I have been closer together than we ever were before, and that's saying a good deal. I can't help being glad that there's been no third person – no matter who – to claim part of your time and attention any more.'

'It's been the happiest year of my life, too. I think we *have* been closer together than ever before. But that's not just because there hasn't been anyone except you to claim part of my time and attention, Clyde; it's partly because you've let me share your adversity as well as your prosperity. You know you never have before, though you agreed to, when we got married. Don't you remember? We took each other for richer or *poorer*, for better or *worse*.'

'But you'd been so poor before we were married, darling. You'd been through so many hardships. I didn't want you to have any more poverty or any more misery.'

'I know. I've always understood. And I've always loved having you feel that way. Just the same——'

'Yes?'

'Well, of course it doesn't seem to me as if we'd been poor this last year. *Really* poor, I mean. And I've been glad the money we did have came from the land, our own land, and not from — anywhere else.'

He gave her a searching look, without making any immediate answer. Then he blurted out, 'Just what do you mean by that, Lucy?'

'Well, I was brought up on a plantation, you know. I have a special feeling for crops and timber lots and gardens and so on. Nearly all Virginians are great land-lovers.'

'So I've heard. But I don't think that's *all* you meant, Lucy.'

'No, it isn't, quite. Perhaps I said more than I should have. I didn't intend to ask you an indirect question or to force your confidence — truly I didn't, Clyde. I spoke almost without thinking. But what I did say came straight from my heart. Because, of course, I haven't been able to help wondering where the rest of the money came from and I thought, perhaps, now that we are so much closer together than we ever were before, now that we have started to share everything, good as well as bad, I could share my thoughts with you, too.'

'You're right. You can. You should. I want you to. I've waited and waited for the right moment and now it's come.' He stood in front of her, looking down at her fixedly, his arms folded across his chest. 'I got my start on the sidewalks where I could shoot craps better than anyone else in my gang,' he said abruptly. 'I did pretty well in dives, too, as soon as I was old enough to stay inside them, without getting kicked out. And then I realized that a shanty boat could be a gold mine, too, though Lord knows none of them looked much like one.'

Suddenly, the words came tumbling out of themselves, so fast that he was almost incoherent. He was telling her about his 'understandings' with the captains under whom he had worked; about the bartenders who 'co-operated' with him; about devices for stripping and stacking cards; about the games where thousands of dollars had been lost and won in the course of a single night; about the investment of winnings in ways that had been almost unbelievably successful; about the various disguises he had worn so effectively and changed so frequently that he had delayed or prevented detection. He did not tell her, as indeed he might have, that much of his phenomenal success was due to his extraordinary expertness in all games of chance and not to any predilection for crooked practices. He did not remind her that gambling was, in itself, regarded as no cardinal sin, or claim that, by and large, the gamesters on the river steamers could stand up well under comparison with almost any of the other 'gentlemen' aboard. He glossed nothing over, he pleaded no extenuating circumstances. The story was saved from sordidness only by its essential drama and by the impetuous sincerity with which it was told. Lucy sat very quietly, her hands folded in her lap; but she did not bend her head, as if to keep him from seeing a stricken look. Her face was raised and her gaze was on her husband. However, she did not speak, even when he finally paused for breath.

'And then, along came the gunboats,' he went on. 'Next — well, I don't know whether you can stand this part, Lucy — about what I did during the war and immediately after it. I've told you now about what I did on the river, but I don't know whether I can tell you why it was better we shouldn't live in Virginia.'

'You don't need to. I think I know. At least, I've guessed. I'd guessed part of the other, too. And part of it I've been told. When Cousin Mildred brought the children down, after we were married — well, you know how a lot of women get to talking together, when they haven't anything else to do, and of course all day long, in the ladies' cabin on a river boat . . . Cousin Mildred wouldn't have told what she'd heard, if she believed it. She likes you too much for that. She put it all down to idle gossip. She was very indignant about it.'

'So you've known — all these years?'

'I haven't *known*. I said I'd *guessed*.'

'And you loved me in spite of what you guessed?'

'I couldn't help loving you — from the very beginning. You know that.'

She rose and put her arms around his neck, her clear gaze still meeting his eyes.

'Just the same, I'm glad that money's gone. And I'm glad you've told me all this yourself. Aren't you, Clyde? It won't weigh you down any more, now that it isn't a secret. And I'm afraid it has before. All these years when you've been trying so hard to do right and succeeded so well. But since you've made a clean breast of everything——'

She left the sentence unfinished, because it did not seem to need finishing. She took it for granted that her statement was conclusive, that he had made a clean breast of everything and that his heart would be lighter from then on. Only Clyde knew that his heart would never be really light, that there was one secret he could not share with her.

For Lucy still did not know about Dorothée and he prayed that she never would.

At all events, his partial confession had diverted her thoughts from Bushrod and for this Clyde was duly thankful. But, as the day wore on, it was increasingly clear to him that she kept reverting mentally to the distressing letter she had received, and dwelling on the disgrace that it revealed, with more intensity than she thought of anything he had told her about his life on the river and with more concern than she thought of anything he had said about Cary, whose illness was a source of much anxiety to him. Late in the afternoon, he reminded her that she had promised to go to Monteregard; when she pleaded fatigue, for the first time in months, he knew that she was emotionally exhausted and, far from insisting she should go out, he urged her to rest. He made sure she was comfortably settled, and then set out for Monteregard himself.

He was met on the gallery by Savoie, whose troubled expression had given way to one of beaming pride. Yes, Dr. Bringier had been there, he said. No, there was nothing to worry about, nothing at all. Cary was awake now, and she would like to see her father. She wanted to tell him herself. . . .

Clyde went quickly down the hall and knocked on the door of the boudoir leading to the large bedroom in the left wing which Cary had chosen for her chamber. As he entered in response to her bidding, he saw that its shutters were no longer closed and he was conscious of the elegance of its furnishings and the luxury of all its appointments. At the same time, he was far more forcibly struck by its state of disorder. The toilet table was littered with gewgaws, the chaise-longue was strewn with soiled clothes and, though Cary had been home for several weeks now, trunks and hatboxes, partially disgorging their contents, covered every available foot of floor space. The bed did not look as if it had been properly made in several days, and Cary herself was wearing a rumpled pink satin robe, which left her neck and arms bare, and her hair was tumbling in an uncombed mass over her shoulders. In all the years of his marriage, Clyde had never entered the room which he and Lucy shared, without finding it in perfect order. As for Lucy, her hair was always neatly parted and braided in two long plaits before she retired, and her frilled, feather-stitched night-gowns, which fastened closely around her neck and wrists, were permeated with the fragrance of lavender, mingling with the fresh scent of fine cambric which had been laundered with meticulous care. Cary had been brought up to take similar standards for granted and Clyde was appalled to see how far she had departed from them. But he was even more appalled by the manner of her greeting. She sat up among her pillows, and faced him with the same angry defiance she had shown, a few days earlier, in the gaming-room.

'Well, I hope you're satisfied now!' she exclaimed furiously.

'I'm glad to see you're feeling better, Cary,' Clyde answered noncommittally.

'*Glad I'm feeling better!* I'm not feeling better! I'm not going to, either—that is, not for a long while. But I'm awake, if that's what you mean. The miserable old doctor woke me up, all right.'

'I'm sorry he disturbed you. I suppose he felt it was necessary.'

'It wasn't necessary at all. If you hadn't insisted, Savoie wouldn't have sent for him. I could have had at least a few more days of peace. And now Savoie's acting as if he were never so pleased about anything in his life.'

'Cary, you know Savoie was distressed because you weren't feeling well. That's why he sent for Dr. Bringier. He didn't do it to annoy you. If he's pleased, its because you're really better, because the doctor's reassured him.'

'He's pleased because the doctor's told him *I'm going to have a baby*! He doesn't care how much discomfort I have now, how much suffering I'll have later on. He's kept telling me, month after month, ever since we were married, that he hoped pretty soon . . . And then acting disappointed when he found it hadn't done him any good to hope! Well, he's got his wish at last! I'll probably go on feeling the way I do now, if I don't feel even worse, for weeks and weeks, according to Dr. Bringier. I won't be able to ride, or dance, or do any of the things I really enjoy. I won't be able to give any parties or go to any. I may not even be able to stand the sight of food or walk across the floor without feeling dizzy. And then I'll begin to get heavy and presently, I'll be hideously misshapen. Well, you were right! Pierre de Chanet won't want to marry me. He won't even want to see me, and I won't blame him!'

Chapter Nine

1896

CARY'S angry prediction about the manifold discomforts in store for her proved well-founded. Like many another girl, conspicuous for glowing health, she speedily developed almost every unfavourable symptom peculiar to pregnancy. The severity of the prostrating headaches, which, from the beginning, had seemed to her almost unendurable, increased to such a degree that she was almost frantic with pain; and her aversion to food soon took the form of morning sickness and, shortly thereafter, showed signs of developing into pernicious vomiting. If maternity had been an experience she had long and ardently desired, she would probably have borne these trials with patience and fortitude, feeling that the much-wanted child would more than compensate for all her sufferings; and, in that case, her mental attitude might have had beneficent results; but her furious resentment naturally affected her physical condition adversely. Her physician, like her husband and her parents, found it impossible to relieve or help her, and he voiced this feeling to Savoie as he was leaving after one of his frequent visits.

'I'll admit it's never easy for a young woman when things go this way, but it doesn't need to be as difficult as Cary's making it. . . . I suppose it isn't necessary to tell you she shouldn't be left alone.'

'We're only too glad to take turns staying with her. But she doesn't seem to want us to.'

'Well . . . Whether she wants you to or not, I think that's what you'd better do. And by "you" I mean some member of the family, Savoie — or possibly Mrs. Surget, if she'd come. I know your servants were with the Batchelors a long time, that they're capable and devoted and that you trust them. But I wouldn't trust them too far, just now.'

'You — you haven't said this to Cary's mother, have you?'

'Not yet. But after seeing your wife today, I think I'd better.' In the doctor's own opinion, there was no excuse whatsoever for Cary's outrageous attitude; but noticing Savoie's stricken look, he did his best to pretend that there were extenuating circumstances. 'Of course, when a girl's as sick as she is, she doesn't think clearly,' he said. 'She can't. But be patient a little while, Savoie. And try not to blame her any more than you can help. Tell yourself she isn't responsible.'

'I don't blame her,' Savoie said dully. 'I blame myself.'

'Good Lord, why should you?'

'I knew she didn't want to have a baby. And I did.'

'Well, she was twenty seven years old when she married you,' the doctor remarked drily, unconsciously repeating Clyde's words. 'It isn't as if she'd been sixteen. She certainly must have realized——'

'I suppose she did, in a general way. But she hoped this wouldn't happen quite so soon. In fact, not for several years yet. Even a few months would have made a difference. You see, some French friends of ours, who were very kind and cordial to us, are arriving any day now to return a visit we made them. Cary'd counted on giving them a good time — on having a good time with them herself. As a matter of fact, I had, too. But somehow the prospect of a son means so much more to me than any company could——'

'Quite natural, too. These French friends of yours — they're not the de Chanets by any chance, are they?'

'Why, yes! Do you know them?'

'I knew the noble marquise when she was Dorothée Labouisse,' the doctor replied, the dryness of his tone becoming more marked. 'And I understand she did very well for herself after she sold Cindy Lou to your father-in-law. Went back to France a rich woman and started cutting quite a wide swathe. Eventually married into the *petite noblesse* — or was it the *grande noblesse*? Either way, she must have got a lot of satisfaction out of it. I've always understood her own family was nothing much to brag about and that she didn't have a cent to her name when she caught the fancy of poor old Labouisse. Well, she had some pretty arid years after he died. I suppose we shouldn't blame her for making hay when the sun began to shine again.'

'She's a very charming woman and her second husband's a distant relative of mine,' Savoie said a little stiffly. 'He's a very distinguished gentleman and, incidentally, *grande noblesse* is correct.'

'Yes? Sorry I forgot about the relationship. But, after all, it is distant. The name's a curious coincidence, isn't it? I mean, that there should be a Pierre de Chanet in France right now — or rather, actually on his way over here from France. History does repeat itself. Excuse the cliché. . . . Well, I think I'd better be on my way to see your mother-in-law and tell her that her daughter'll bear watching. Don't forget that I've told you the same thing.'

The doctor nodded and took his departure, leaving Savoie even more uneasy than he had hitherto been. He went into Cary's room and sat down by her bed, gazing at her with pity and self-reproach. If she realized he was there, she gave no indication of it. But when Titine, Ivy's sister, who had been put in charge of the chamber work, tiptoed in an hour later and began to move about, almost noiselessly, in an attempt to restore some degree of order, Cary sat up suddenly and sharply rebuked her.

'Haven't I told you to leave things alone? I'm nervous enough anyway, without having you set my teeth on edge by rustling around like that!'

'Ah doesn't want to harm you' pretty teeth, no, Miss Cary, but de las' time Miss Lucy were here, she done say Ah was a pure disgrace, me, to her teachin', leavin' you' nice things strewed around. Ah 'specks she comin' back again, soon-soon, her, an' Ah doesn't want her tellin' me dat no mo', no. She liable to take me out de house an' send me to de fields.'

'*I'll* send you to the fields if you don't obey my orders. This is my house and you're working for me now.'

'Yassum, Miss Cary,' Titine conceded doubtfully. 'But Miss Lucy done tell me, her, it don't make no mind iffen you is *comme ci, comme ça*, Ah got to readen things up, me.'

'And I told you to get out of here!'

Cary picked up a Book of Devotions, somewhat incongruously repos-
ing on her bedside table and, before Savoie could take it from her,
hurled it at Titine. It missed its mark, but it had the desired effect.
Titine scuttled from the room, dropping an armful of clothes in her
flight, and did not return, even to summon Savoie to dinner. It was
Lucy who brought her back, some hours later.

'Go and get something to eat, Savoie,' she said, putting her hand
lightly on his shoulder for a moment. 'I had my dinner and a good rest
before I left Cindy Lou. Why don't you take a nap yourself? I know
you must have been awake most of the night. I'll stay with Cary this
evening and every evening until she's better.'

Savoie rose, looking a little doubtfully at Cary; but, as she still
paid no attention to him, he managed, in a rather half-hearted manner, to return his mother-in-law's encouraging smile and walked
away, taking care to make as little noise as possible while crossing the
floor.

'Now, Titine, let me see how quickly you can put this room to rights,'
Lucy went on, when the door closed behind him. 'Meanwhile, if you'll
pass me her brush and comb, I'll get the snarls out of Miss Cary's hair.
Then I'll sponge her off and, after that, you can help me to get her
into a clean nightgown and change her bed.'

'I don't want Titine clattering around and making a lot of noise,'
Cary cried angrily. 'I've told her so already. I'd rather you didn't interfere with my servants, Mother. And I don't want you to touch me,
either. I want to be let alone.'

'I shan't interfere with your servants when you're in a condition
to direct them yourself. Until you are, someone else will have to do it
for you and I seem to be the logical person. I'm sorry if that isn't
pleasing to you, Cary. And I'm also sorry that you don't want me to
take care of you. But I'm acting under the doctor's orders now. He
feels we've let you have your way too long already for your own good.
That's why we don't intend to do so any longer.'

Titine had already handed Lucy the brush and comb. Without saying anything further, the latter leaned over the bed, turned Cary on
her side, and began to separate the tangled strands of hair.

'Hereafter we can do all this when we see you're practically asleep,'
she said. 'Then it won't disturb you so much. And we'll try to do most
of it on alternate days — you'll find there's a sort of ebb and flow to your
worst discomfort. I don't know why there should be, and as far as
I've ever heard, doctors don't know, either. But it helps, when you're
having an especially hard day, to keep thinking that the next one
won't be quite so bad. . . . Oh, I'm sorry! That *was* a bad snarl! We
won't let your head get in this state again. . . . Do you know, Cary,

I think you have the most beautiful hair I've ever seen? It has every-thing—colour and natural wave and softness and yet it's long enough for you to sit on. I don't think I've ever known anyone else whose hair had all those qualities. Mine certainly hasn't. It never was as golden as yours, even when I was very young, and it never curled around my face, the way yours does.'

She went on serenely, undeterred by Cary's stubborn silence and intermittent retching, until the golden hair lay in two long smooth plaits over the rumpled nightgown. Then she handed the brush and comb back to Titine, who had already succeeded in picking up most of the scattered clothes and had begun to dust.

'Now if you'll bring me a big bowl of warm water and a washcloth and some soft towels . . . There must be some cologne water on Miss Cary's dressing table, too, Titine—yes, that's the bottle I mean. If I pour some of it in the water, it'll smell sweet and be refreshing and it will prevent her from catching cold, too—don't forget that, in case she should want you to bathe her some time. While you're about it, you'd better give me a fresh nightgown for her, one with sleeves—aren't there some in that further armoire? You know where the clean sheets are, of course. We'll put those on the bed as soon as I've finished giving Miss Cary her bath.' Lucy turned from the maid to her daughter. 'You've forgotten, haven't you, darling, that I used to bathe you like this when you were a little girl and had fever? Of course, you didn't have it very often, because you were a very healthy child. And now you're a very healthy young woman, I know just how unpleasant this awful nausea is, but it only lasts a few weeks or at the most a few months and presently you'll forget all about it. I know, because I did, under the same circumstances. It wasn't until your father came and told me how badly you were feeling that I remembered—back to the time I first knew I was going to have a baby. But I remembered, too, how pleased and proud I was and how much that helped.'

'Well, I'm not pleased and proud. I'm disgusted,' Cary muttered, speaking for the first time.

'Nonsense! You're disappointed because you'd looked forward to having a good time with your French friends. And you may yet. Probably they'll stay for a few weeks in New Orleans, since the Vin-cents are still there, before they come on to Victoria. And by that time you may be feeling much better. I just told you that sometimes this nausea only lasts for a few weeks—almost never beyond the quicken-ing. Now . . . Let's not try to talk any more. You see it didn't take long, after all, to get you all fixed up. I'll just sit here beside you, and watch you, and when I can see you're almost asleep, I'll moisten your lips with a little water. You won't even know I'm doing it and presently you'll pass your tongue over them and swallow almost un-

221

consciously. Perhaps by tomorrow night I can give you a little broth, the same way.'

It was longer than that before Cary was able to take the broth, but she did not again try to keep her husband and her mother and her maid from her room. Clyde was the only person she steadfastly refused to see and, after two or three futile attempts at persuasion, Lucy and Savoie ceased to insist that she should do so. Clyde himself, while hurt at Cary's attitude, divined that she was still nursing the anger he had roused when she confessed to her infatuation for Pierre de Chanet, and that she was trying to even the score with her stepfather for his uncompromising stand, by the only means within her power. His own concern, as always, was primarily for Lucy.

'I'm a good deal more worried about your health than I am about Cary's,' he told her bluntly. 'Dr. Bringier says he's seen any number of women, as sick as she is now, who made up for lost time by eating enormous meals later on and were able to nurse big bouncing babies for months. But he thinks, and I agree with him, that it's too much of a strain on you to spend every afternoon at Cary's bedside.'

'It seems to me he was the first to suggest that Cary shouldn't be left alone. Savoie takes care of her at night. He sleeps, or rather he stretches out, on the day bed at the foot of the four-poster. He never leaves the room from the time I come home until Mrs. Surget gets to the house, about nine the next morning. And *she* stays until I get there. I don't think either of them can stand any longer hours.'

'It won't hurt Savoie to be short of sleep for a while. And there must be some other reliable woman, with nursing experience, who could relieve you one day and Mrs. Surget the next.'

'Dr. Bringier doesn't know of any in the neighbourhood. And he admits it wouldn't be wise to introduce a total stranger on the scene just now. I'm all right, Clyde, really I am. Remember this isn't the first time I've gone through a siege of nursing and been none the worse for it afterward.'

'You were younger then,' he muttered. It was very seldom that she referred, even indirectly, to her first marriage; but he still felt a twinge of jealousy on the rare occasions when she did do so. 'You're neglecting your garden,' he grumbled. 'That biggest Alba Plena should be pruned, and not one of the camellias has been mulched with oak leaves and bagasse, in spite of the fact that hot weather's just around the corner. Last year, all the work was all done by this time; I ought to know. . . . You made me turn over two of my best field hands to you smack in the very middle of chopping time. Remember, though, when you showed me the flowers last December and asked me if that sight wasn't worth the time of a couple of hoe-hands? It was, too. I had to give you right, honey. But none of it's being done this year, and what about next winter's buds? You've spoiled me so, I hate to think of what we'll be missing.'

'Isn't it more important that I should take care of my daughter than of my camellias?'

'I suppose so. But you're neglecting me, too.'

'You know you don't really feel that way about it, Clyde.'

'No, of course I don't,' he said quickly. 'But I don't see why Mrs. Vincent or Armande shouldn't return to Victoria for at least a few days and spell you.'

'Why, have you forgotten? The de Chanets arrived in New Orleans last week. Mrs. Vincent and Armande both have their hands full.'

Clyde had by no means forgotten about the arrival of the de Chanets, which had been well heralded, both in letters from the Vincents and in the public prints, which had made much of it. The Vincents were delighted with their distinguished guests, whom they found charming in every respect. It was a shame that Savoie and Cary—and of course Mr. and Mrs. Batchelor—could not have been on hand to welcome them and to be present at the entertainments given in their honour. Mrs. Vincent had decided that it would be well to begin with a reception, so that the de Chanets could make the greatest number of desirable acquaintances in the least possible time. This function had already taken place and the de Chanets had, of course, been deluged with invitations to the opera, to the races, and so on. The Vincents were now planning a series of dinners; the first one was to take place the following Tuesday, a company of eighteen; everyone who had been asked had accepted with alacrity. Portrait sketches of the marquise and her son, taken in the Vincents' drawing-room, had been reproduced in the social columns of the *Daily Item* and the *Bee*; and the de Chanets had also given out interviews to representatives of the press, in which they had paid the Crescent City and its leading citizens all the compliments which were taken for granted on the part of visiting celebrities, and made none of the tactless remarks which would have caused widespread resentment. All in all, it was obvious that the Vincents were fairly basking in reflected glory; and though of course they were very, very sorry that poor dear Cary should be so miserable, at such an inopportune moment, this regret was obviously not weighing them down too heavily. It was Clyde's private opinion that they might quite properly have taken time out to come to Victoria, leaving their guests behind them, now that the latter were so well introduced and so adequately provided for; and it was this feeling that he had voiced. Since Lucy apparently did not share it, he murmured something unintelligible and would have changed the subject, if she had not pursued it.

'As a matter of fact, I'd much rather they didn't come to Victoria right now. I think the quieter Cary keeps, the better.'

'On general principles, I agree with you. But I don't see why it should upset her just to see her mother-in-law.'

'I don't think Cary feels very close to Mrs. Vincent, Clyde. I don't think she ever has.'

'Well, she and Armande are certainly bosom friends.'

'Yes, but Armande isn't in the proper frame of mind to make a good nurse right now. She's definitely restless herself.'

'I suppose you mean that she's husband hunting.'

'I wouldn't have put it quite that way. But—yes, that's what I do mean. Not that she'd marry anyone who asked her, just for the sake of being married. But if the right man *did* happen to come along, I don't believe she'd keep him waiting very long while she thought over his proposal.'

'In other words, you think it's more likely she'd interrupt him to say yes? Well, perhaps the next time you hear from the Vincents, you'll also hear that there's been an answer to the maiden's prayer. Let's hope so, for Armande's sake.'

He spoke lightly, but not sarcastically. He had always liked Armande well enough, though he had never been really attached to her, as he was to Savoie. When Lucy told him a few days later that she had heard from Mrs. Vincent again, and that the latter had written to say the hopes he had expressed for Armande were fulfilled, he took the letter from his wife without either undue interest or undue curiosity. As far as he had any feeling about it at all, this was one of relief at the prospect of finding in it less news about the de Chanets than had filled the last few communications from the same source.

'So she's got a man at last! Well, I'm glad to hear it.'

Lucy did not answer. He gave her a quick look and plunged into the letter.

'Dearest Lucy:

'I feel I must call you that, after all these years when we have addressed each other with formality, because I am now writing you with the same joy in my heart that I should experience if I were sharing glad tidings with a beloved sister. You will understand my emotion, for you, too, know what it is to rejoice in the happiness of an adored child. Yes, those are indeed my tidings. With the glad consent of my husband and myself, and with the full approval of his mother, who expresses herself as more than ready to take Armande to her heart, my darling daughter has become the betrothed of the Marquis Pierre de Chanet. . . .'

'Oh my God!' Clyde exclaimed. Then, instantly fearing that his vehemence might have betrayed that the news was more of a shock to him than seemed logical, he added hastily, 'Why, they've hardly more than met! The man hasn't been in New Orleans a fortnight yet! She can't really know him, in that length of time.'

'It doesn't necessarily take long for two persons to fall in love,' Lucy answered, with a calmness that seemed to bear no relation to her customary serenity. 'You and I both realize that. Go on reading the letter, Clyde.'

'It was a case of love at first sight on both sides' – Mrs. Vincent continued – 'in fact, both Armande and Pierre insist that they knew, with the first glance they exchanged, that they had met their fate. However, with due respect to *les convenances*, Pierre waited a week before asking my husband for Armande's hand. Naturally, Lamartine could offer no reasonable objections. The alliance is, in every respect, suitable. Pierre is the scion of one of the oldest and most illustrious families in France; he is the sole heir to a substantial fortune and a magnificent estate; he is himself cultured, charming and witty . . .'

And the last time I heard him described like that, Clyde said to himself, groaning inwardly, *it was Cary talking to me. Now he's going to marry Cary's best friend. The poor girl isn't even going to have the consolation of believing that the reason he didn't want her any more was because she was sick and disfigured. He didn't even wait to see her before he succumbed to Armande. There won't be that much salve to her hurt pride.*

' . . . and of course, completely *comme il faut* in every respect,' the letter continued. 'After speaking to Lamartine, Pierre cabled his own father – all this before formally addressing Armande. But his eyes had already told her of his love, even though his lips had not, and she waited without impatience for him to declare himself.'

'My God!' Clyde exclaimed again; and this time he felt no compulsion to qualify his outburst. 'She actually waited ten days or so! Why, that girl's patience is nothing short of miraculous, is it, Lucy?'

'It has been,' Lucy answered, in the same strangely calm way she had spoken before. 'She's been patient a long while, Clyde, waiting for something like this to happen. Now that it has, you can't blame her because she acted – rather precipitately. You talked the other day, jokingly, about the answer to a maiden's prayer. Well, every girl prays for a Prince Charming, whether she admits it or not. But she doesn't dare expect that her prayer will be answered as literally as all this. Armande's not only getting a "cultured, charming and witty" man for a husband; she's getting a title, a fortune, a storied château, a *forêt de legende*.'

'And, incidentally, she may be getting a damn scoundrel.'

H

'I think we'll have to dismiss that possibility. I don't think we're in any position to discuss it. Do you?'

She met his eyes steadily. *So she guessed*, he said to himself. *She guessed from Cary's letters. I didn't, but she did. The only thing I thought of, when I read them, was that Dorothée, who was just a light of love, had feathered her nest with money she got from me, and that Lucy, whom I worship, had been bowed down with cares she shouldn't have had. Besides, Cary's letters frightened me. They made me afraid that, if Dorothée came here, she'd say something or do something that would give me away, so that Lucy would find out, after all these years. That's what those letters meant to me. And I'm not free from fear yet. I shan't be, until Dorothée's gone back to France. Perhaps I never shall be again. There may be some aftermath of her visit. . . . Well, Lucy hasn't guessed about Dorothée and me yet, thank God. But she did guess about Cary and Pierre. I knew she was worrying over those letters, but I didn't know why. Now that I do know, I can't tell her that her fears were well grounded. I can't betray Cary's confidence by telling Lucy her daughter confessed to me that she'd been false to her heritage and her upbringing, I can't say she cheapened herself by letting this Frenchman fondle her, I can't say she was actually willing to go through the scandal of a divorce if it would take her into his bed. And Lucy's right, we can't tell the Vincents Pierre's a scoundrel. If we did, they'd naturally want to know why we thought so and we'd have to tell them that, too. We'd have to say that Cary wanted to get rid of their son and go to Pierre. So we've got to let this marriage of Armande's go through. We've got to let her find out for herself about Pierre. Well, probably she'd rather do that than not get married at all, since she's so eager to do so. We can ease our consciences by trying to think that anyway. Perhaps the title and the fortune and the château will make up to her for the misery she'll go through, every time her husband's unfaithful to her. Partly anyhow. And whether it will or not, there's nothing we can say, nothing we can do, because of Cary. . . .*

He was aware that Lucy was speaking to him. 'You haven't finished reading the letter, Clyde,' she reminded him. He picked it up again.

'The old marquis sent his blessing' – the letter went on – 'and said of course he would come over for the wedding. He hadn't felt he ought to leave the estate, at this season, merely for a *visite de politesse*. But, naturally, a wedding is something quite different. So we are planning to have it in the late spring, at the Cathedral. What a shame that Cary cannot be in the cortège, which we want to make as impressive as possible! Armande has always counted on having Cary act as her matron of honour, but under the circumstances . . .'

Well, she'll be spared that humiliation anyway. She won't have to go

226

to the wedding and chatter and laugh and pretend. She'll be glad, after all, of the refuge her darkened room gives her, she'll be glad she can't leave her white bed, she may even be glad at last that a child is coming, because that will take her thoughts away from Pierre de Chanet and what he's done to her.

'. . . under the circumstances that is, of course, impossible. However, we are writing by this same mail both to her and to Savoie, saying we hope she will release Savoie from her bedside in order that he may come to New Orleans to salute his sister and congratulate his future brother-in-law, with whom he is, of course, already on terms of warm friendship. Indeed, as Pierre and the marquise have both pointed out, the fact that Cary and Savoie spent so much time at Monteregard — I mean the *real* Monteregard — makes the de Chanets feel that their connection with our family is almost a *fait accompli* already. We are very happy that these are their sentiments and we feel sure you will join with us in urging upon Savoie the propriety of a prompt visit to New Orleans since, with all the preparations for a large wedding in the near future, we can see no immediate prospect of coming to Victoria.

'Farewell for the time being, dearest Lucy. I shall write you again very soon to let you know the progress of all the exciting events here. Meanwhile, I shall await with eagerness your answer to my letter, for I know that in it I shall find an echo of the rejoicing which rings through mine.

'As ever, devotedly your friend,
'AURELINE VINCENT.'

'So they've written to Savoie and Cary by this same mail,' Lucy said, taking the letter from Clyde and putting it back in its envelope. Her fingers did not tremble as they had when she heard from Bushrod. They were steady, as her eyes had been, and as her voice was now.

'Yes. When you see Cary this afternoon——' he had almost said, 'you'll find out how's she taking it.' He had checked himself just in time.

'When I see her this afternoon, I'll tell her that, of course Savoie must go to New Orleans immediately,' Lucy said. 'Naturally, I can't leave Cary. But I think you should go with him.'

'I'll be damned if I will!'

'It's one of those things that has to be done, Clyde. Isn't it?'

'No. I'm sorry, Lucy, but this is one of the few times——'

'Then I'll go, after all. I'll have to leave Cary with Mrs. Surget. Or trust her to one of the servants, in spite of Dr. Bringier's feeling about that. I think, as a matter of fact, that it will be quite safe to do so now. I'll make all the necessary arrangements when I go to Monteregard — the *mock* Monteregard — later in the day. Meanwhile, I'd better begin my preparations to leave for New Orleans with Savoie.'

She rose and moved away from him, without haste and without any evidence of inner turmoil. He strode after her and laid his hand on her arm.

'Lucy, if — if you feel this way about it, of course I'll go, so that you can stay with Cary. But it's the hardest thing you've ever asked of me.'

'Yes,' she said, slowly. 'It is.'

And he knew she meant, not as he had, that the doing would be hard for him, but that the asking had been hard for her.

She went up to their room with him to help him with his packing. She was taking clean shirts from the armoire and handing them to him, so that he could put them in his valise, when Delphie came to the door and passed him a note. It was written in pencil on a small piece of folded paper and it contained only one sentence.

'Dear Father —

'Will you please come to see me?

'Cary.'

He left Lucy to finish the packing without his help and hurried to Monteregard. Titine, who opened the door for him, said that Mr. Savoie was sleeping and that Miss Amy was with Miss Cary. He went through the hall and his old friend met him just outside the threshold.

'I really think Cary's better,' she whispered happily. 'She's hardly looked at the mail, since she's been sick, until today; but she's read two letters that came in this morning over and over again. Then she said she wanted a piece of paper, so she could write you a little note, asking you to come and see her. I know it's been one of her sick fancies that she hasn't wanted to see you until now. So I believe the change is a good sign, don't you?'

'I hope so. I can tell you better after I've talked to her.'

He nodded and went into the room, closing the door carefully behind him. Cary was sitting up in bed. Her face was almost as white as her pillows and there were dark circles under her eyes. He would not have believed that a few weeks of illness could so completely change a being who had fairly radiated vitality, and his heart smote him at the sight of her. But, in spite of the tragic transformation, the pale girl who stretched out her slim hands toward him was the Cary whom he thought he had lost for ever and who was now miraculously restored to him. As he put his arms around her, she buried her head on his shoulder, and her tears came freely, in a cleansing flood.

'Savoie hasn't guessed and we mustn't let him — ever,' she whispered brokenly. 'I think Mother may have, but I can't risk telling her, in case

228

she hasn't — not when she's almost heartbroken already about Bushrod. But you *know*. You *understand*. Oh, Father, I need you so much. You won't fail me, will you?'

Chapter Ten
1896

AS it turned out, Savoie did not get off immediately, and when he took his reluctant departure for New Orleans, he went alone after all. Lucy did not continue to insist that Clyde should accompany him, after she realized what her husband's presence meant to Cary; and, on second thought, she decided to postpone her own trip a few days more, meanwhile sending by Savoie pleasant letters and appropriate gifts. In a note to Mrs. Vincent — whom she addressed as Aureline for the first time, taking her cue from the latter's note to her — she said she would come to New Orleans to present her compliments to the marquise and offer her good wishes to Armande, in person, just as soon as Cary's health would permit and that she really believed this had already taken a turn for the better. Meanwhile, she sent the marquise and Armande the same assurances, and did not fail to add how greatly she was looking forward to meeting the former, and how delighted she was that a real Prince Charming had at last made his way to Armande through a forest which so many other suitors had found impenetrable.

The cordial and charming tenor of these notes was doubly convincing because they were accompanied by a large box of variegated camellias, beautifully packed and artistically wrapped, and by a heart-shaped diamond brooch, which not only had considerable intrinsic value, but an exceptionally romantic history : it had been presented to an ancestress of Lucy on the occasion of the lady's betrothal to a favoured courtier, by King Charles the First himself, at the same time that the courtier received a land grant in Virginia. In every way, the brooch was a gift which a prospective marquise could not possibly fail to feel was well worthy of her future position, and which was received with genuine enthusiasm by Armande, and viewed with great approbation by everyone around her.

'It is really too sweet of your mother-in-law to give it to me,' Armande told Savoie, after opening, with an exclamation of pleasure, the small well-worn velvet box which contained the brooch. 'Especially as she has a daughter of her own and may have a granddaughter – or several of them, for that matter! I do think she's very generous.'

'Well, I agree with you,' Savoie concurred. 'As far as that goes, I think Cary was, too – Mrs. Batchelor consulted her, of course. And Cary said she would be glad to have her mother give it to you.'

'Cary is an angel,' Armande said, putting on the brooch. Then she added, turning to her fiancé, who was standing attentively beside her, 'Of course you found that out, while she was visiting at Monteregard. I'm so glad she was married already – otherwise, I know I wouldn't have had a chance!'

'I grant you that your sister-in-law is very charming,' Pierre answered unhesitatingly. 'But *you* are the angel, *cœur de mon cœur*! The angel I always hoped I might find on earth, while never quite believing I should encounter her before I reached heaven. However, even this hope, even this half-belief, sufficed to make me persevere in looking for her. And of course I shall thank the *bon Dieu* to my dying day that I did! No, believe me, *chérie*, no one could have diverted me from the search which has been fulfilled by you!'

He bent over her and, undeterred both by Savoie's presence and by the fact that their betrothal was not supposed to become official until the arrival of the old marquis, imprinted a long and loving kiss on her ready lips. Savoie turned away and left the room. He thought the caress in very poor taste and he was feeling generally out of sorts. His sister's acceptance and return of such open and premature displays of passion, his mother's gushing exuberance over the match, and his father's un-concealed satisfaction in it, were all displeasing to him; even the mar-quise, whom he had admired very much at the château, now seemed to him unduly arrogant, as if she were trying to impress Orleaneans in general and the Vincents in particular with her superior importance. He found the endless discussions concerning wedding plans trivial and boring; and, in the absence of the ladies, his future brother-in-law made certain suggestions about nocturnal 'sightseeing' which were definitely shocking to him, though Savoie was no prude. He tried to tell himself that anxiety about Cary, whom he had been most loath to leave in any case, was largely responsible for his frame of mind; but two reassuring letters, one from Dr. Bringier and one from Clyde, made him all the more eager to go home. Now that Cary was improving, he longed to be with her, quite as much, though in a different way, as when she had been so ill. She was still in bed, she was still very weak, and the ad-verse symptoms still persisted; but the latter were lessening in severity and she was able to retain a little nourishment, if it were given to her when she was already drowsy. Her stepfather had stroked her arm one evening, merely as a gesture of affection, and the touch had proved unexpectedly soothing. Now he was doing the same thing more or less systematically, to induce the helpful drowsiness. Moreover, there were brief intervals when Cary was actually quite free from the hateful discomfort, though wide-awake; and during these intervals she listened, with pleasure, while her stepfather read aloud to her, or inspected, with interest, the carefully kept ancestral baby clothes which her mother brought to show her, and discussed the garments which they must soon start making in order to supplement these. Savoie thought it would be very pleasant to sit beside Cary's bed and stroke her arm and read aloud to her himself, though hitherto he would have considered such a caress very tame and normally he was not much of a reader. He also thought he would enjoy seeing Cary, who was almost as expert a needlewoman as her mother, though she did not so often engage in such work, sewing on baby clothes. There was something very feminine and appealing about the sight of a pretty young woman so engaged. . . .

It had been agreed, before he left home, that he should remain in New Orleans until Lucy could join him at his parents' house on Elysian Fields, or he would have found some excuse for returning to his wife, in spite of the good reports which were reaching him. As it was, he fretted and fumed until word arrived of his mother-in-law's imminent appearance on the scene, and he was overjoyed at the general contents of this note. Cary continued to improve, Mrs. Batchelor said, and they were all hopeful that the time was not far distant when she could move from her bed to her chaise-longue for a little while each day. After that, the next step would naturally be to get her out on the gallery, where she could have the benefit of sunshine and fresh air; and then they must begin to think about the proper nourishment and the proper exercise to build up her strength. Naturally, as her mother, Lucy felt she should be close at hand to supervise this gradual progress; and she was therefore sure that the Vincents and the de Chanets would understand why she felt she must limit her visit to three days. She still enjoyed river travel more than any other form of transportation; so, if convenient for the Vincents, she would arrive the following Monday on the *Stella Wilds* and leave Friday on the same boat.

Savoie met her at the levee and plied her with questions, all of which she was able to answer most satisfactorily, though her replies still further whetted his desire to get home. Once arrived at the Vincents', however, Lucy talked very little about Cary; instead, she listened, with every appearance of attentive interest, to the endless discussions concerning Armande's trousseau, the marriage ceremony and the wedding reception, which Savoie found so tedious. Though she made no suggestions except when asked for them, she hesitatingly advanced certain ideas which proved very helpful, and in many other little ways revealed her real desire to be of assistance. Pierre pronounced her the most charming woman *d'une certaine age* — except of course his future mother-in-law and his own mother — whom he had ever met. Mrs. Vincent received the implied compliment to her mature attractions with genuine pleasure, for she herself really admired Lucy; the marquise, in one of the rare intervals when she was alone with her son, voiced more tempered enthusiasm of his verdict.

'I know you feel you must be polite to these people, *mon cher*,' she told him. 'Just the same, you do not need to perjure yourself. I admit Madame Batchelor is all very well in her way. But she has no chic. I could swear the dresses she is wearing are at least two years old, even allowing for the time it takes French fashions to reach New York. And her hands are those of a working woman. I understand that she does a great deal of gardening. But if she really cared for her appearance, she would wear gloves while she was grubbing in the earth.'

'Perhaps she doesn't really care for her appearance. Perhaps she thinks other things are more important.'

'What could be more important to any woman — that is to say, any woman possessed of normal vanity and natural feminine instincts?'

'I don't pretend to know. But I have understood there are such women.'

'And she wears almost no jewellery,' the marquise continued. 'Just a few mediocre ornaments that look as if they were heirlooms, valuable only for the sake of sentiment. I distinctly remember hearing Cary say, while she was visiting us, that her stepfather had loaded her mother down with jewellery. I wonder what she has done with it all?'

'Perhaps she keeps it in a safe. I understand some women do that, too.'

'The proper places for jewels are at a woman's throat, and on her breast, and in her ears. And of course on her hands.' As she spoke, the marquise twisted the rings on her beautiful white fingers, so that the diamonds in the settings caught the light, and then raised her hands to touch her glittering earrings, almost caressingly. 'They are no good in a safe. Are they, Pierre?'

'Again I would answer that I do not pretend to know, but that I understand some women think so.'

'Well . . . All I can say is that those are very dull thoughts. I did not have the impressions that Cary entertained similar ones. Indeed, I thought, when she visited us, that her jewellery was very creditable — not astonishing, but adequate.'

'There I agree with you. Savoie gave her a handsome parure for a wedding present. And I understood that her mother turned over to her all the jewellery that came from the family of her father — I mean her own father, the Confederate colonel, not Mr. Batchelor. Apparently, the amount of this was, as you say, "adequate" even if it was not "astonishing".'

'As a matter of fact, I was somewhat surprised that there was so much, and all in such good taste. I remember Cary told us that she had most of the old gems reset, at Cartier's, after she reached Paris – she thought her mother's feelings would be hurt less, if the work were done abroad, after her own marriage, than if it were done at Tiffany's, when the two were shopping in New York together. Just the same, I imagine that Mrs. Batchelor's feelings were hurt. She is the sort who puts sentiment above taste, as you can see by those ornaments she wears herself, which I mentioned a moment ago. . . . Well, I am glad Cary shows more sense. And I am hopeful that Armande will, too.'

'If you are thinking of good sense in terms of a taste for jewellery, I am quite sure she will not disappoint you. Her mother has already given me to understand that Armande will expect a parure for a wedding present, at least as handsome as the one Savoie gave Cary, and preferably handsomer. Of course, she did her hinting very delicately. But her meaning was unmistakable.'

'Your father will probably begrudge such an expenditure – now if she had insisted on some indicated renovations at the château, he would not have said a word. But I am pleased rather than otherwise. Armande's attitude does show sense – sense and spirit. I should not care at all for a dull, sentimental daughter-in-law.'

'You have not found Armande dull so far, have you?'

'No, not exactly – so far. But she does not seem to have a great deal to say for herself. Now Cary is much more sprightly – or rather, she was. How tiresome that she should have got herself in such a fix, just at this time! When I planned this trip, I was rather looking forward to more of her lively chatter – as I believe you were, too.'

' "*Homme propose*——" ' began Pierre. His mother interrupted before he could finish the quotation.

'At the risk of making a bad pun, I am going to confess that I did not think the man about whom I was talking came to the United States for the purpose of proposing to Cary's best friend. I thought his original intentions were somewhat less honourable – and infinitely more exciting. And I doubt whether God had much to do with disposing of poor Cary by causing her to become *enceinte*. I think for that we must blame Savoie who, Lord knows, is very dull indeed. Fortunately, however, he is neither suspicious nor perceptive by nature. Well . . . No doubt everything is turning out for the best. Armande has an excellent background and a suitable dowry. She is lovely to look at and she is grateful to you for having looked at her. She will make a very tractable and a very presentable wife. She will not plague you by talking about the tedium of life in the country, as I have sometimes plagued your poor father. She will adorn the château and her presence there will make it possible for me to spend more time in Paris. She will probably have as many children as you wish, quite uncomplainingly – it is my recollection that Creole women are very prolific. And she will not begrudge you your little diversions while she is *hors de combat* — she will take those for granted, too. I think Savoie is probably the first male of his family who has not had his little establishment on Rampart Street and, believe me, Armande knows all about such things. Her mother will leave to you the privilege of initiating your bride into many mysteries, but will not have failed to tell her daughter that a husband's peccadilloes must be overlooked — as long as he does not commit them too openly, *bien entendu*. Since it was high time you thought of marriage, it is perhaps just as well, after all, that it is Cary who is *hors de combat*. Yes, as I just said, I am sure everything is turning out for the best in our present venture.'

As a matter of fact, the marquise was not feeling quite as complacent as she tried to sound, or rather, as she tried to give the impression that she was trying to sound; and her son, who understood her very thoroughly, was well aware of this. She had enjoyed the experience of creating a sensation in the society which had once turned a rather cold shoulder on her; and she foresaw, in her only son's marriage to a wealthy and doting girl, certain distinct advantages to herself as well as to him. But she missed the excitement she had anticipated. She had taken it for granted that most of her time in Louisiana would be spent at Victoria, close to the mock Monteregard and to Cindy Lou. She had visualized a resumption of her son's flirtation with Cary and of all sorts of delightful but hazardous possibilities in consequence. Savoie could not remain blind for ever; sooner or later, he might challenge Pierre to a duel, and Pierre was one of the best swordsmen in Paris. Clyde and his dull, virtuous wife would not be blind indefinitely, either, and they would shudder at the very idea that the fair name of their cherished daughter might be jeopardized by a *crime passionel*. The marquise would have taken no slight satisfaction in striking at them through Cary. She really rather liked the girl; but this liking was not sufficiently strong to outweigh her long nourished sense of injury because Clyde had remained essentially true to his betrothed, in spite of his brief deviation from complete loyalty. She had never forgiven him for this faithfulness and she had never ceased to resent the other woman's hold over him. Now that she had seen Lucy, she was disposed to be less forgiving and more resentful than ever. It was nothing short of ridiculous that a man who could have had his choice between Dorothée Labouisse and Lucy Page should have selected the latter, and not only selected her, but given her unswerving devotion for a quarter of a century. Certainly there was a score to even there.

Moreover, she could visualize the possibility that this score might be evened, not only indirectly, through Cary, but directly, through Clyde.

After all, he was not immune to temptation—no one was in a better position to realize this than she was. Probably very few temptations had offered themselves in the course of the humdrum life he had so inexplicably chosen. But she was not yet ready to admit she was past the point where she could offer distraction or rekindle dormant embers. She and her elderly husband had long since ceased to stimulate each other and, with reluctant wisdom, she recognized the fact that the days when she could hope to stir any man's senses were now numbered. But they had not ended, even though they would in the near future. She had wanted and intended to improve the present. And she had had no opportunity.

As long as Cary was immured in her dark bedroom, Clyde would remain at Cindy Lou and the Vincents would continue to say that there was no sense in going to Victoria. And presently, the marquis would arrive from France, and the wedding would take place, and Armande and Pierre would be off on a honeymoon. Her husband's presence would be a handicap to the marquise, perhaps not an insurmountable one, but still one which would present complications. Besides, he would wish to make his sojourn in the States as brief as possible; he was never content for long away from his château and his forest, his meadows and his marshes, and she would have no excuse for prolonging her own visit past the point of his departure. Pierre would be beyond Cary's reach, too; it was doubtful whether he and his bride would return to Louisiana at all after their wedding journey, especially as Armande had expressed such impatience and eagerness to see the real Monteregard. Even if they did return, Cary would be unsightly by that time. No duels would be fought over her; nothing would shake her husband's complacent faith in her or shatter her parents' pride. And Clyde and Lucy would go on and on, contentedly leading their Darby and Joan existence.

The consciousness of that placid, uneventful domesticity was what rankled most. If once—just once—she could have troubled its tranquillity, the marquise would not have asked for more: that would have been enough to shatter Lucy's security, to test Clyde's susceptibility, and to prove her own diminishing, but still dangerous powers. She rose from the armchair where she had been sitting while talking to her son and while brooding over her disappointment, and, walking over to the great cheval glass, which stood in a corner of the room where the light was excellent, she regarded herself long and critically. The results of this survey were not only reassuring; they were encouraging. Given the one opportunity which was all she asked, she felt sure she could still provoke passion and gratify desire.

Granted that the passion would be as ephemeral as it was intense, the desire solely one of the flesh; that was the way it had been before;

and yet, after all these years, the memory of it stabbed at her vitals, the yearning for its renewal was still unappeased. She still seemed to feel Clyde's fingers digging into the small of her back, she could still evoke the delicious sensation of compliance with which she had yielded to his embrace. So powerful had been his domination, so instantaneous her response to it, that there had been no need of words to express their mutual understanding and their mutual craving.

She remembered that in the brief interlude between his kisses when he had given her a chance to speak she had managed to murmur, 'But I have not shown you the whole house yet. Perhaps when you have seen the second story, you will feel it is inadequate.' But vivid as all the rest was, she did not remember what he had said in reply, or indeed, if he had said anything; only that they had gone up the stairs together, and that his arm had been tight around her all the time, pressing her close to him; that then they had been in her room and that presently, when his hands encircled her waist again, he had laughed exultantly at finding it even smaller without the stays than with them; and finally, that her pliancy in the garden had been mere acquiescence compared to her eventual state of complete self-abandonment. . . .

Hours later, Clyde had roused himself from his slumber of satiation and muttered that he must get back to the hotel. Then, belatedly, as he stood fully dressed before her in the first glimmer of the dim light that presaged the dawn, he had asked her whether any of the servants slept in the house, whether someone might have been aware of his presence and might now be aware of his departure. She had been able to reassure him : Belle was the only servant she had left, and Belle went back to her own man and her own dusky brood in the otherwise empty quarters by mid-afternoon. Indeed, she usually went as soon as the midday meal was over; she had remained to serve coffee the day before very grudgingly; her mistress did not pay her enough to exact favours from her. There were not any dogs on the place, either; no inopportune barking would betray the departing visitor. Sometimes the neighbours had remonstrated, saying that no woman should remain by herself at night in that great lonely house; there was no telling what might happen. But Dorothée had never been afraid; indeed, she had rather vaunted her valour. And now she was thankful for it. If she had been a timid woman, scared of her own shadow, she would never have had the joy of experiencing such a rich reward for her courage. . . .

Clyde's response to this rapturous declaration was far less impassioned than his previous behaviour would have led his hostess to expect. He left her almost abruptly, with no warm assurance of an early return and no farewell embrace. In fact, he seemed eager to be gone. But that might well have been on account of impending dawn. Dorothée lay quietly in bed, listening as he went down the stairs and out of the front door, which he did almost noiselessly. Then she heard the click of the garden gate and that was all.

She was drifting off to sleep again when she remembered what he had said before she swooned into his arms: that, as a proof of good faith, he would give her forthwith five thousand dollars to bind their bargain for the sale of the property. He had not spoken of money or of Cindy Lou since then. What a ghastly trick of fate it would be if he had changed his mind, if he would now want to keep her on the plantation, if she could not go back to France after all! Shivering with dismay, she sprang up and opened the shutters, letting daylight flood the dim room. Then she looked wildly about her. But she did not have to search long. Propped up against the mirror of her dressing table was one of the envelopes which she kept in her nearby desk. Clyde must have taken it from there while she was still half asleep. It was sealed and it had her name scribbled on it. She tore it open feverishly, counted the thousand dollar bills which it contained, and then re-counted them, thinking that she had made a mistake—or that he had. There were not five, but six. And, after a moment, she understood. . . .

For the next three or four days, she waited and watched in vain for his return. When he finally came, he was not on foot and alone, but in a smart gig, accompanied by a certain Gilbert Ledoux, who was one of the best known notaries in the parish. His call was as formal as if they had been meeting for the first time, and as if her sale and his purchase of Cindy Lou were the only matter of mutual interest. He was pleased to say that investigation of the title had shown it to be completely clear; he was now ready to pass papers, if Madame Labouisse were also prepared to do so. He believed that fifty thousand dollars was the sum on which they had agreed as the purchase price and he had already paid five to bind the bargain. So, according to his reckoning, he still owed her forty-five thousand, which he was ready to pay now. He spread the money out before her and the notary began to rattle documents. Her signature would be required here and here and here . . .

It was all over so quickly that she could hardly believe it had happened. It was she who asked the only questions which caused a slight delay in the final arrangements.

'I shall need a little time to pack my personal belongings. Would a week seem too long?'

'Of course not. I do not wish to inconvenience you in any way. You must not overtax your strength.'

'I appreciate your consideration. Shall we say ten days then?'

'That will be quite satisfactory. Indeed, I shall be glad of the opportunity to familiarize myself somewhat with local conditions, before coming here to live.'

'Did you wish to have the house closed when I leave it? Or would you care to have my servant, Belle, stay on as caretaker? She is lazy and shiftless, like all the Negroes hereabouts, but she has never stolen anything, to my knowledge, and that is more than I can say for most of them. And she is familiar with the place. She might prove useful.'

'I agree with you. And I wish the place to be in the best possible order. It is my intention to bring my bride here in the autumn. Perhaps I did not mention to you before that I am engaged to be married.'

'No, you did not.' The words came so quickly that Dorothée instantly feared her answer might have betrayed the fact that his announcement had come not only as a surprise but as a shock. She pressed her lips together, forcing herself to say no more, and looked away, lest the expression of her face might also be one of betrayal.

'It must have slipped my mind,' Clyde said evenly. She did not dare glance at him, but it occurred to her, she did not know why, that if she had, she would have beheld that same blankness which had caught her attention on the occasion of his previous visit. How was it Americans described it? Oh yes – 'poker-faced'. She was sure his expression was poker-faced as he went on.

'I have asked Monsieur Ledoux if he could tell me of some lady in the neighbourhood who might be willing to supervise the preparation of the house for Mrs. Batchelor. He suggested the widow of a physician, a Mrs. Surget, whom I am sure you know, as she lives not far from here. Since I had the pleasure of seeing you before, I have called on this lady and I am happy to say that she has consented to help me. I shall leave the matter of hiring suitable servants in her hands. But I think there is no doubt that she will wish to keep Belle who, as you say, is honest and familiar with the place. I gather that she has done cooking for you, as well as other work. In your opinion, if she had no other work to do and received some expert instruction, could she become a really first-class cook? I feel it is very important that we should have one. My fiancée tells me that if there is a good cook at the helm, the rest of the household staff can be dealt with very easily.'

'I must remind you, monsieur, that I am a Frenchwoman and that to the French cooking is a fine art. When I told you that there were no longer any royal dinners at Cindy Lou, I also told you that this was because I had not the heart for them, after the death of my poor husband. But I can assure you that what little I have eaten has still represented a cuisine that was soignée. It will not be necessary for Mrs. Surget or anyone else to give Belle "expert instruction". I myself have given her that.'

Her voice was trembling with rage now; she could not control it and she did not care. So that colourless relict of a country doctor, that cold pillar of righteousness, Amy Surget, had been selected as possessing the high qualifications requisite to prepare properly for a chaste bride! The offer had probably come just in time to save La Surget from starvation, for her impractical husband had never tried to collect his bills and there was little or no land connected with their house; he had chosen to ply his profession in the country because he preferred this to the city—as if that in itself were not enough to show what manner of man he had been! He had left his widow practically penniless not because, like Marchand Labouisse, he had spent money elegantly and prodigally, but because he had never cared for it or any of the goodly things it could provide. And now Amy Surget would be creeping around Cindy Lou, snooping in every corner where dirt might be lurking, probably scrubbing floors and woodwork herself because she would not trust the darkies to get them clean enough without her good example! Worse than this: she would be spreading the word around that she had found the house filthy, that it was cluttered with trash of all kinds, that much of its seediness was due to neglect and that a little prudence and a little industry would have prevented these telltale signs of deterioration!

Well, Dorothée would not give her that satisfaction at least! She would not need more than a few hours to pack her clothes—she had not many left and most of the shabby old trunks she would take with her on her departure would be practically empty. She would spend those ten days which she had at her disposal in giving the house such a cleaning as it had never had before, even though this might mean that she, and not Amy Surget, would be the one to go down on her knees and scrub! And before she left it, she would give a dinner which would prove to this *parvenu*, this *nouveau riche*, this coarse creature who had treated her like so much trash, that she was a *grande dame*, after all, one with red blood in her veins, to be sure, but a *grande dame* just the same and not a *cocotte*. He could not refuse to dine with her—not if she invited the notary and the doctor's relict and the Vincents to dine on the same night! And they could not refuse, either, though they had shown her little enough friendliness throughout the desolate years. Now that she was off to France, a rich, beautiful, independent woman, they would view her differently. And she would find a way, even with all these superfluous guests, of taking aside the one guest who mattered, of proudly returning to him that extra thousand dollars, of telling him that a woman like her might, under certain very exceptional circumstances, grant favours, but that she never sold them. . . .

These were the thoughts which had raced through her volatile mind while Clyde was civilly assuring her that he regretted his mistake in so much as questioning Belle's complete capability as a cook; it was only that he wanted to be certain. His fiancée was a Virginian, and Virginians also set great store by a cuisine which was soignée. Dorothée countered, by extending, then and there, her invitation to a farewell dinner the exact date of which should be determined by the convenience of Mrs. Surget and the Vincents. Both men, taken by surprise, which Monsieur Ledoux betrayed and Clyde did not, accepted it and took their leave of her; and having thus easily secured their assent, Dorothée dispatched beautifully written little notes to Mrs. Vincent and Mrs. Surget. Their acceptances were also unhesitating, as Dorothée had foreseen. Fired by such enthusiasm for her project that she remembered to be angry only at intervals, she set to work on the house.

Belle proved unexpectedly co-operative. She not only worked herself, with a zeal which belied the reputation her mistress had given her for laziness, and which was all the more astonishing in view of her unwieldy proportions; she also found ready helpers among her cronies and progeny, who had learned by the grapevine that there were prospects of remunerative employment at Cindy Lou, and who were eager to prove that they were qualified for it. Before a week was up, the house was clean as it had never been before, the woodwork sweet smelling from soap and water, the windows shining, the brass and silver glittering. Every cupboard, every armoire, every drawer had been opened, aired and washed; even the dark store closets had lost their cobwebs and their mustiness. And still Dorothée had time to spare. As she sank back surveying her handiwork with weary satisfaction, another idea occurred to her.

Why should she not improve the days which would still intervene before her farewell party by going to New Orleans and buying herself a completely new outfit? She had heard that, even during the war, a few beautiful French clothes had somehow been smuggled into the Crescent City, through the roundabout route of Texas via Mexico, or more directly through the blockade. She had never put these rumours to the proof because she lacked the money to do so; but there had been no reason to doubt their truth and the war had been over four years now; so opportunities for adornment must certainly be more favourable by this time. And certainly, she did not lack money. She would not start off on her travels or give her farewell dinner wearing her old, rusty, outmoded black; it was falling to pieces anyway. And, after all, her husband had been dead eight years now. She had never intended to wear crêpe all her life, like these lugubrious Creoles who made such a cult of mourning, because they had nothing better to do; and even they would make allowances for her, as a Frenchwoman; she could safely experiment with soft greys, pale lavenders and pure whites . . .

But when she reached the dressmaking establishment that had been recommended to her, it was not the soft greys and the pale lavenders and the pure whites which caught her covetous eye and held her fascinated gaze. It was a gorgeous outfit, imported on purpose for a popular actress to wear in a current play, where she was to have portrayed a wealthy woman of fashion. The actress had died, suddenly, just as the play was about to open, and the wardrobe had been left, intact, on the dressmaker's hands.

It contained 'walking' dresses and 'carriage' dresses and ball dresses and a dress purporting to grace a royal garden party; also calling costumes and *robes d'intérieur* – among the latter some which might logically be worn for informal dinners and some which suggested the intimacy of the boudoir – the play was a daring one. The actress had been a slender, striking brunette, and every item in the collection had been designed to show off her figure and her complexion to the best possible advantage on the stage. There were no colours or styles suggestive of half-mourning. Brilliant reds and greens predominated, and the lines and cut were as provocative as custom would permit. Dorothée tried on all the splendid creations, not hurrying over the process, but in the same leisurely, gratified way in which she might have savoured some sweet, heady wine; they fitted her and became her as if they had been made on purpose for her. Finally she stood before the couturière clothed in crimson satin made with an off-the-shoulder neckline, a long, tight basque, and a trained skirt whose fullness was drawn back over the hips and finished with cascades of fluted ruffles.

'How much will you take for the lot?' Dorothée inquired without further preamble.

The couturière gasped and, recovering, named an astronomical figure. Both women enjoyed to the full the subsequent bargaining. The couturière pointed out that the wardrobe consisted wholly of exclusive models from a world-famous Parisian house, that the materials and workmanship were of the finest, that the styles were those of day after tomorrow, that such a complete collection had never been seen in New Orleans before and probably never would be again. Dorothée pointed out that there were very few women in the Deep South – if, indeed, there were any, besides herself – who had any present use for such an extensive wardrobe, that if she did not take the collection it would have to be sold piecemeal and that this would take a long while to do – by the end of which time the styles would no longer be those of day after tomorrow, but of year before last. She further called attention to the conservative taste of the Creoles, the amplitude which their figures were apt to attain when they had passed their first youth and – last but not least – their straitened financial circumstances since the war. How many customers did the couturière suppose would come to her carrying reticules bulging with banknotes?

As she asked this question, Dorothée unclasped her handbag to extract a wispy handkerchief; then she snapped it to again, but not before the couturière had seen the yellowbacks which it contained. Quickly, she suggested a compromise price. Dorothée shook her head and began unhooking the crimson basque. The couturière gave a little cry, indicative of the ruin which was staring her in the face; then, sobbing that she had no choice but to give pleasure to such a charming customer, she capitulated. Dorothée reopened the reticule.

'Very well. You may send the collection to my apartment at the Hotel St. Louis, just as it is, today, except for this one dress, which I shall expect tomorrow. Meanwhile, I wish you to make two slight alterations in it.'

'But the fit, like madame's figure, is already perfect!'

'I appreciate the compliment. Nevertheless, I wish you to make it an inch and a half smaller round the waist and that much lower at the neckline.'

'Then madame would never be able to get into it! And she would never be able to wear it in public!'

'That is my concern, isn't it, not yours?'

Her mood was exultant as she left the dressmaker's and continued her shopping. She bought a huge Saratoga trunk and a smaller one, designed especially to hold headgear, underwear and accessories. Besides a divided tray for hats, the latter contained a special compartment for gloves, another for hosiery, another for shoes, and still another for an umbrella. Dorothée bought everything she would need to fill these separate compartments; and finally, she bought new stays.

It was a thousand pities that madame could not give her time to make these to measure, the corsetiere told her; no ready-made stays would do her figure full credit. Dorothée agreed with her, but said that, unfortunately, she must return to the country the next day. She asked the corsetiere to measure her waist before she took off the old stays and then she stood, clad only in her fine chemise and her silk stockings and her high-heeled shoes, and waited for the new ones to be adjusted. When they were in place, she asked to have her waist measured again.

'It is half an inch smaller now!' the corsetiere told her with satisfaction.

'That is not enough. Draw in the lacings until it is an inch smaller still.'

The corsetiere cried out in protest, much as the couturière had done, though for a different reason. But she obeyed, and no cry came from Dorothée as the lacings did their cruel work, and the two sides of the stiff stays came closer and closer together until at last they met. The corsetiere seized her measure and cried out again, this time in triumph.

'Madame is very brave and behold her reward!' The corsetiere marked the measure and handed it to Dorothée. 'So few of my customers know the truth of the saying, "Il faut souffrir pour être belle!" It is not more than madame can bear, the pain of such compression?'

'Of course not,' Dorothée answered proudly. It was true that she was suffering, but she would not let the corsetiere loosen the new stays, much less remove them. It seemed to her that the pain they gave her was somehow akin to the other, still deeper and sharper, which gnawed at her vitals, and that only with the assuagement of that should come release from anything that was part of her purpose.

The conviction of this still sustained her when she welcomed her guests on the night of her farewell dinner. She was wearing the red satin dress, and she was aware that all eyes were resting on it, as she had intended they should. It mattered to her not one whit that those of Mrs. Vincent and Mrs. Surget were so soon averted. She expected — at least she hoped — that she need never see Amy Surget again; and since she had already secured from Mrs. Vincent a letter presenting her to the de Chanet kinfolk in France, that lady's usefulness to her, for the time being, was past; if they did not meet again, she could trust to Mrs. Vincent's natural tolerance and short memory — with both of which she had had some experience — as far as the dress was concerned. A doting mother, a devoted wife, the Creole lady's interests were bounded by her own family, and she neither greatly heeded nor long remembered anything which did not concern them. Mr. Vincent was a man of the world, not easily shocked, except when it came to a question of his own womenkind; he would have spoken sternly to his wife, if he had seen her in such a dress, and sent her back to her dressing-table for more veiling, before going out with her; but he would think none the less of his hostess for her bared bosom, so white against the crimson of that basque, which tapered almost to nothing from the full breast to the tiny waistline, only to expand as suddenly again below it. Gilbert Ledoux was nothing but a local notary, a provincial; his opinion, good or bad, did not count, though, as a matter of fact, there was unconcealed admiration as well as unconcealed astonishment in his gaze. It was only Clyde who counted. And Dorothée could see that Clyde was in a fever of restlessness. He looked at her and then looked away, only to look again.

She put him opposite her at table, which was only natural, since hereafter that would be his place, as the host of Cindy Lou. But though she was duly attentive, first to Mr. Vincent, at her right, and then to Gilbert Ledoux, at her left, in tactful rotation, she caught Clyde's avid look upon her and, tossing her head ever so slightly, neglected to return it. The dinner was perfect and he complimented her on it, as the others did. But though he drank freely, he neglected his food, as he did the ladies on either side of him; Dorothée wondered whether his straying, sensual thoughts were as obvious to them as they were to her and, in deciding that they were not, also decided that she would not have cared, even if they had been.

The avid look followed her as she gave the signal for the ladies to retire to the drawing-room, leaving the gentlemen to their cigars, their port, and the stories customarily exchanged on such an occasion, which were reputed to be offensive in character to delicate feminine sensibilities. Dorothée recognized the resemblance of this gaze to the one Clyde had directed toward her on the occasion of his first visit; but it was more intense now and more purposeful. The cigars, the port, and the stories consumed far less than the usual amount of time; but Dorothée's astonishment at the reappearance of her male guests was well feigned. Perhaps it would be pleasant to play a few hands of cards after they had finished their coffee, she suggested; it was too bad there was no game in which six persons could all engage at the same time – except poker, with which, of course, none of the ladies was familiar. But they could play whist at one table and bezique or cribbage at another and change partners frequently; perhaps such changes would actually add to the atmosphere of festivity, by making their friendly little gathering seem more like a large party.

Her suggestion was accepted, and so was the further one that, at the beginning, Mrs. Surget and Mr. Batchelor should play cribbage together, and that the others should make up the foursome of whist. It was very late before the logical rotation brought her and Clyde at the small table together. As he held out her chair for her, he adroitly slipped a tiny piece of paper into her hand. He must have scribbled it very swiftly, some time while places were being changed, for though she thought she had kept him under close observation and had, indeed, noticed how steadily he was winning, she had not seen him do any writing. But she already realized that his movements were some times almost uncannily quick.

It was ridiculously easy for her to dispose of the note in the bosom of her dress, at the same time that she reached for the handkerchief which, though apparently so fragile, served so many useful purposes. But she had no immediate chance to look at her *billet-doux*, for she did not trust any aptitude she herself might have for legerdemain. Her guests had all gone, praising her party and wishing her a pleasant journey, before she dared look at the note. It contained only four words :
'*You win, damn you!*'

She went about the main floor in a leisurely way, extinguishing all the lights except for one lamp in the hall and that she dimmed, until it shed only a faint radiance. She assured herself that the dining-room and kitchen were not only orderly, but empty. Belle and her cohorts had done their work well, but there was no question that now they were gone. Lastly, Dorothée tried the front door, not to make sure it was locked, but to be certain it was still on the latch. Then she went to her own room and undressed. She had bathed just before dinner, but now

244

she sponged herself off again, with perfumed water, and lay down on her Empire bed to wait.

She did not have to wait long. She was sure that Clyde would not have left the hotel, where Gilbert Ledoux would have dropped him off on the way home, until everyone else in the building was asleep. Still, she did not see how he could have got back there, in Ledoux's gig, and then come down the river road on foot so quickly. But from the way he mounted the stairs and burst into her room, the swiftness with which he could move was again borne in upon her.

'You she-devil!' he said, and seized her.

His precipitance failed to frighten her, his assault gave her no feeling of outrage. As long as he had come back, after all, as long as her will had prevailed against his, this was all that mattered. In a way, his very violence bespoke the futility of his rebellion against her. Now that he recognized its futility, he meant to make her pay for it instead of paying for it himself and she accepted this as a tribute. It was not until at last they spoke together that she was conscious of hurt.

'This time,' she murmured, clinging to him, 'this time, you'll stay.'

'Stay!' he echoed sharply. 'What do you mean, stay?'

'I mean, of course, that we were destined for each other. I knew it from the first. It took you longer to find this out. But you must know it now, too.'

'I know I'm leaving Louisiana tomorrow morning — this morning, rather. Before you have a chance to make me play the fool again. What happened before was just an explosion. I'm not blaming you for that, or myself, too much, either. But you planned and plotted for this. You laid a trap for me. I saw it and I walked into it just the same.'

'If I hadn't thought you really loved me, at least you would——'

He laughed, harshly. 'You didn't think anything of the kind. You're not in love. You're in heat. And God! What a beast I've been myself!'

He was gone almost as precipitately as he had come. She had tried to keep him, throwing her arms around his neck, and telling him that she was ready to give up everything for him, even her return to France, that she would not ask for marriage, for any kind of public recognition, if only they could be together in secret. To the same degree that she had flaunted her flesh to tempt him, she now grovelled before him. He released himself and left her, without another word.

She had never forgiven him for treating her like a wanton. It did not occur to her that she had behaved like one.

Now, twenty-seven years later, the Marquise de Chanet stood before her cheval glass, in the home of the girl whom her son was about to marry, again 'planning and plotting'. Nothing that had happened since she left Cindy Lou had served to erase the memory of that passionate interlude or quench her desire for revenge. To all appearances, her life had been not only a pleasant one but a highly successful one. She had left Louisiana and reached France without any untoward incident and, upon her arrival in Paris, had installed herself at the Hotel Bristol; then she had presented her impeccable letters of introduction without delay and with gratifying results. The Marquis de Chanet, whom she met almost immediately, had, like Marchand Labouisse, fallen in love with her at first sight. Before the Franco-Prussian War had cast a blight over her second blooming, she had already remarried and was installed as the châtelaine of Monteregard, far out of harm's way. In due course of time, she had given the marquis the requisite heir to the title and the estates and he was properly grateful. Nothing else had ever been asked of her. She had been the recipient of benefits, not the bestower of them, for a long, long time. Nothing had marred the serenity of her existence or jeopardized the security of her position. And still she had not been content. There remained that ancient grudge to pay off.

And when at last she thought the time was ripe to do so, she had been thwarted. She was stuck in this dull New Orleans house, every bit as dull as Monteregard. She was forced to smirk and smile at countless ladies' luncheons, at countless pink teas, at countless stiff soirées. She had been in Louisiana for weeks and she was no nearer accomplishing the purpose for which she had come than when she landed there. Or so it seemed. . . .

And then, out of a clear sky, came a letter from Cary herself, only a few days after her mother and her husband had gone home. She was much better, not well enough yet to travel, of course, but sufficiently improved to be up on the chaise-longue for a few hours each day. Since she could not come to New Orleans, she hoped very much that the Vincents and the de Chanets would come, as soon as possible, to Victoria. Savoie joined her in expressing this hope and in sending fond greetings.

Chapter Eleven

1896

THE Vincents and their guests reached Victoria to find Lucy's unfailing thoughtfulness made manifest in many ways. She was not there when they arrived, but this was obviously a sign of delicacy rather than neglect; she had brought flowers from her garden, admittedly far superior to the one at Victoria, and the fresh vegetables in which Cindy Lou also excelled. A ham, cured at Sorrento and cooked by her favourite method, freshly caught fish, and one of her famous Spanish Creams were all ready to grace the supper table; and in the most charming of notes, she wrote expressing her pleasure at having her neighbours home again, and said that she would call the next day to make plans.

She came late in the morning, on horseback, cool and slim in her linen habit, a grey veil floating from the small hat neatly set on her netted braids. She dismounted with the grace of an accomplished horse-woman and, patting her horse affectionately as she surrendered it to a waiting groom, looped up her long skirt and ascended smilingly to the gallery. Mrs. Vincent had settled herself there with her needlework – a garment she was making for the expected baby – directly after break-fast, and had taken it for granted that the Marquise de Chanet would keep her company there though she had seen that, as usual, the French-woman's restless hands were idle. The gentlemen were out on the plantation somewhere, Mrs. Vincent told the visitor, a little vaguely. Her husband had found a great deal that required his attention after his long absence and had needed Savoie with him. Pierre, who was see-ing cane and tobacco fields for the first time, had been interested in join-ing his hosts; so of course Armande had been interested in joining Pierre!

She could well understand all this, Lucy rejoined; and she was sure that Aureline and the marquise would understand that Clyde was busy about the plantation, too, and that this was why she had come alone. She had, however, stopped by to see Cary on her way to Victoria, and was glad to report that her daughter continued to show improvement, and was hoping very much that her mother-in-law, the marquise and Armande, would take tea with her late that afternoon. Dr. Bringier had advised her not to try to see many persons at the same time to begin with; but she hoped very much to receive the gentlemen as well, in a day or two.

Again, there were expressions of mutual understanding; but the mar-quise could not bring herself to put much enthusiasm into her accept-ance of Cary's invitation. Tea had never seemed to her a very stimu-lating beverage; and the prospect of drinking it with four other women, one of them half-sick and another sighing for her absent fiancé, was far from satisfactory. Neither did the only other suggestion which Lucy made hold out much promise.

'I do hope it will not be painful to you to see your old home in our possession, madame,' she said solicitously. 'I know I never could have gone into our Richmond house again, after it passed into alien hands! I thought that perhaps a *fête champêtre* . . . Since the war prevented you from developing the garden, which must have been a great cross to you, I believe you might actually enjoy seeing how faithfully the original plans were carried out, as soon as it was possible to do so. Later, I could not resist the temptation of introducing a motif which would remind me of Sorrento, my mother's plantation on the James; so I added a herb garden and a sun dial surrounded with roses. Later still, I became greatly interested in the cultivation of camellias, as I told you in New Orleans, and now a good deal of space is given over to them. But none of these additions has interfered with the harmony of the first design. A least, I hope and believe they have not.'

'Indeed, they have improved it,' Mrs. Vincent hastened to say. 'Everyone who has seen it concedes that, thanks to you, the garden at Cindy Lou is the most beautiful one at any plantation hereabouts. I think your idea of a *fête champêtre* is delightful, Lucy, and very practical, too. Like our first reception in New Orleans for the de Chanets, it will serve to present a far greater number of our friends to them, at one and the same time, than would be possible at a dinner party. And of course the dinner parties will come later. You agree with me, I am sure, madame, that dear Lucy has made an excellent suggestion?'

The marquise had no choice save to agree, but again, real enthusiasm was lacking in her acceptance, and she added that Mrs. Batchelor must not suppose, for a moment, that it would cause her any pain to see the interior of the house. On the contrary, she was most eager to do so. She understood that the former gaming-room was now the library and that the gaming-room had been moved to the ground floor. Since she herself had actually been the one to suggest, the first time Mr. Batchelor came to see her, that this change would be an improvement, she was naturally curious to see how it had worked out. And then the ballroom . . . That, like the garden, had been in an unfinished state when she left Louisiana. As Mrs. Batchelor said, the terrible war had imposed so many hardships! But she had heard glowing tales of the magnificence the ballroom had eventually attained and of the splendid functions that had taken place there.

'Yes, Cary was very fond of dancing and of course we tried to give her every possible pleasure,' Lucy said, gathering up the white chamois gloves which she had laid aside when the inevitable 'small blacks' made their appearance. 'But of course she cannot dance now, and I am afraid it would be a quite natural grievance to her if we gave a ball she could not attend. We are all making her our first consideration at present. I am sure you will understand that, too. Not that this will interfere with your seeing as much of the house as you would like, now that I know of your interest – indeed, our little fête need not take place wholly outside. I was simply thinking of what would give you the most pleasure. . . . Well then, I will tell Cary that she may expect you this afternoon?

Around five? And I shall look forward to seeing you myself again then, too.'

Her mount was brought around and she sprang into the saddle so swiftly that she hardly seemed to touch the horse block or the groom's outstretched palm. Then she was gone, with a final wave of her white-gloved hand, her grey veil floating out behind her. Mrs. Vincent, gazing after her with affectionate admiration, was amazed, on turning, to catch a look that was half-sullen and half-hostile on the face of her remaining guest. Mentally, she groped for the possible cause of this and, when she thought she had found it, tried tactfully to remove it.

'Lucy Batchelor is one of the sweetest women I have ever known in my life,' she said, 'and one of the most hospitable, too. But, as she told you, her first concern just now is for Cary and I am afraid the poor girl has really been very ill. I'm afraid, too, that the Batchelors have found it necessary to curtail their expenditures somewhat; they have been living very quietly ever since Cary was married, and have given no lavish parties. My husband knows more about their private affairs than I do, because he has often given them financial advice, upon request; but of course he has regarded everything he has been told as confidential. However, it is common knowledge that a great deal of Mr. Batchelor's fortune was tied up in steamboats, and the days of their prosperity, like the days of their glory, are gone, alas! for ever. If he has been obliged to retrench, Lucy is the sort of wife who would help her husband in every possible way.'

The marquise made a reasonably adequate rejoinder, saying she was sure she would enjoy the tea with Cary and the *fête champêtre* very much; also, that she was sorry Cary was not as much better as she had somehow expected from the girl's letter, and that it was indeed unfortunate if the Batchelors had lost the greater part of their fortune. Then she changed the subject by talking about various characteristics of the Paris social season, which would soon be in full swing. Mrs. Vincent, whose parents had been among the wealthy Creoles that visited France every other year — a habit which the Vincent family had never acquired — began sighing for the delights of which her marriage had so early deprived her and which the marquise all too vividly recalled. She was glad Savoie and Cary had been able to enjoy these the previous year, she said, a little enviously, especially as, with the turn things had taken, it was doubtful whether they would be able to go abroad again very soon; and she was gladder still that Armande would be able to have these pleasures right away. But she herself was going to miss her daughter terribly. She could not bear to think of the parting which was now so close at hand.

'You will come to visit her. You will persuade your husband that he should make these biennial trips.'

'I shall try. Yes, now that Armande will be in France, I believe he will permit himself to be persuaded. There never were a father and daughter more devoted to each other. In fact, our whole family is singularly united. As I said before, the parting will be hard indeed.'

This was a new tack, even less to the taste of the marquise than Mrs. Vincent's previous outspoken satisfaction over Armande's engagement and impending marriage, which hitherto had included no dolorous references to separation. The titled guest found a pretext for retiring to her own room to rest briefly before dinner, and later, while the others were resting, she managed to have a few words with her son, to whom she confessed she feared the visit in the country was going to prove disappointing. He shrugged his shoulders.

'When we were in New Orleans, you kept saying you wanted to visit Victoria. *Eh bien*, now we are at Victoria and that does not suit you either.'

'Of course I thought, from Cary's letter, that she was up and about at last; I did not picture her as still lounging around, nor did I suppose she had so much false modesty that she would decline to receive gentlemen *en negligée*.'

'As I understood the situation, it was not "false modesty" which caused Cary to limit the number of her guests, but her physician's advice. I think undoubtedly she will ask the rest of us within a few days. Evidently, you and I did not interpret her letter in quite the same way. I thought she was making a real effort to sound cordial at the earliest opportunity, not that she was prepared to go in for immediate entertaining on a lavish scale. As for the "dimmed glories" of Cindy Lou, I had suspected something of the sort, partly from chance remarks of Armande's and partly from Mrs. Batchelor's lack of jewellery, taken in connexion with those remarks. She is exactly the sort of woman who would strip herself of every form of luxury, if she thought she could help her husband by so doing.'

'Are you actually taking sides with these people against your own mother?'

Pierre, who had been sitting in a relaxed attitude, smoking a cigarette, extinguished the cigarette and rose. 'This is the second time you have referred to "those people" in an extremely disparaging way,' he remarked coolly. 'Yet they are exactly the same people whom you were so determined to visit, and you declared yourself delighted at my proposal to Armande. It seems to me it is your attitude which has changed, *ma mère*, and for no very sound reason. As for taking sides, I'm not conscious of doing that, either for or against anyone. But I'm ready to repeat what I said once before: that I think Mrs. Batchelor is one of the most charming women I ever met in my life. However, the more I see of her, the more I am persuaded that the word "charming" is inadequate to describe her. She has charm, certainly. But she also has character. She commands my utmost admiration and respect.'

To the best of his mother's recollection, Pierre had never spoken to her in this vein before, and she found it anything but pleasing. It was particularly distasteful to hear Lucy Batchelor's charm extolled by her son, immediately after listening to Mrs. Vincent's fulsome praise her sweetness; and the marquise did not care a fig about the character of this paragon. She was already in a bad humour when the ladies set out, that afternoon, for the mock Monteregard in Mrs. Vincent's phaeton; and the tame visit which she had foreseen did nothing to improve her mood.

The day was warm and pleasant, and Cary received her guests on the gallery, where she lay on a glorified hammock, clad in a negligée of shell-pink chiffon and cream-coloured lace, which was extremely becoming to her. Her mother poured tea for her, using an ancestral silver service which, along with the heirloom jewellery, she had turned over to Cary on the occasion of the girl's marriage; and an impeccable maid passed beaten biscuits stuffed with ham, toasted English muffins spread with butter and marmalade, and dark rich fruit cake. Cary drank her tea à la Russe, with lemon in it, and said she had learned to like it that way — in fact, she highly recommended it to the others; and if she ate less than they did, she did this inconspicuously. When they had finished, she said she had thought the marquise might be amused by the gazebo, which was something of an anachronism in Louisiana; she was sorry that her garden was nothing much to see as yet, but the marquise would find that the one at Cindy Lou would more than make up for any disappointment at the new Monteregard; and she was really rather proud of her house, which she realized neither Mrs. Vincent nor Armande had seen since her return from France. She was sure they would want to inspect the improvements she had made in it, now that she was settled there, and she hoped the marquise would also enjoy going through it. Her mother would conduct them, if they were perfectly sure they did not care for any more tea. . . .

The marquise was bound to admit that the interior of the house, no less than the exterior, was extremely pleasing. The furnishings throughout were extremely tasteful, many of them old English pieces, which, like the heirloom jewelry and the fine old silver, had obviously come to Louisiana via Virginia; but these had been supplemented with comfortable modern upholstery, bright rugs and soft hangings, which mitigated their austerity. All in all, greatly to her disappointment, the marquise could find nothing which did not bespeak taste, culture and tradition. She had no choice, when the ladies returned to Cary's hammock after their tour of inspection, but to echo the Vincents' enthusiastic approbation of everything they had seen, even though she did so rather half-heartedly. However, she could not resist the temptation of adding she was sorry Pierre had not been with them.

'But of course you will come again,' Cary said cordially. 'I shall be able to assure Dr. Bringier that your visit has not tired me in the least, that, on the contrary, it has given me the greatest pleasure. So I am sure he will let me make the next one more of an occasion, even if he is a regular old dragon. He is spacing his calls farther apart, now that I am so much better; but he will be looking in tomorrow morning, all ready to rebuke and warn, as usual! When he finds nothing to rebuke me for or warn me about, he will leave defeated. And then I shall send you a little note, asking you all to hasten over. Meanwhile, please give my regards to Pierre, and say that I am looking forward to seeing him.'

She rose, and walked to the top of the steps with them, looking even more lovely, while she moved, than while she was lying in her hammock. 'I'm so glad you like the house,' she said, glancing proudly around her. 'However, I have just been telling Father that I thought I'd like to have a supplementary flight of steps built at the rear of the wing back of the drawing-room. It would be so convenient for taking the baby straight from the nursery through the garden to the gazebo for his outings without bringing him into the front of the house, when there was company, or when there was any special reason for saving time. Since Father built the house for us, and I told him it was perfect just as it was, I didn't like to make even a slight change in the design without consulting him. But he agreed with me that it's an excellent idea. What do you all think?'

Though there were different degrees in the shade of interest that was expressed, everyone agreed that the idea was a good one. As Cary was saying good-bye, Savoie rode up, shouting a welcome, and Cary persuaded them to wait until he could join them on the gallery. He hastened to do so, embraced his wife warmly and his mother and sister affectionately, and then laughingly asked the marquise if she would permit a similar salute. He apologized briefly, and without any show of real concern, for his appearance, saying that he had been in the saddle practically all day and that it was very warm in the fields already; he thought Cary was extremely tolerant to say nothing about the disastrous effect his dirty riding clothes might have on her elegant laces, and put his arm around her again as he spoke, gazing at her with loving pride. Really, he had never seen her in anything more becoming than that negligée – he would be sorry himself to have it ruined. And wasn't it wonderful that she was so well on the road to recovery? He put the question generally, apparently without expecting any special answer or caring much whether he had one or not. His complete and rapturous satisfaction with his wife was transparently evident. Contemptuously, the marquise set him down as uxorious; she doubted whether anyone could shake the faith of such a fond fool.

Savoie himself brought the promised invitation from Cary the following day. Dr. Bringier had been obliged to admit that she was getting better and better. She was going to sit up for supper with Savoie that very evening, for the first time in nearly two months. She was still not too sure of herself, the earlier part of the day, or she would suggest midday dinner on Sunday, so if they would all come Saturday night instead. . . . It would be just a very informal evening meal. But she would look forward to it. . . .

'Which is more than I shall do,' the marquise told her son. 'But at least I am thankful we will not be obliged to sit through one of those deadly Sunday dinners after Mass, which have not a single redeeming feature, unless they have changed very much. And I doubt it. This whole region seems to be in the same state of desuetude as when I left it.'

'Well, if you want to go back to New Orleans, you have only to say so. It is my impression that Mrs. Vincent does not care any more about the country than you do.'

'No. . . . But her husband keeps harping on the need for his supervision, and there is another couple to whom separation never seems to occur! Then there is that silly *fête champêtre* — I suppose we would be considered insufferably rude, if we left before it took place. We have not heard anything more about it, but no doubt all sorts of elaborate preparations are being made to serve fruit punch and lady fingers to large numbers of the local gentry.'

'You say "another couple". Were you mentally comparing the Vincents to the Batchelors?'

'Yes. Have you any reason to consider the mental comparison inept?'

'I have not had the pleasure of meeting Mr. Batchelor yet. And after all, Mrs. Batchelor did leave, not only her husband, but her sick daughter, in order to bid you welcome in New Orleans. As for the *fête champêtre*, I do not believe the refreshments for that will be as insipid as you are indicating, either. But, even if they are, the gardens, by all accounts, are well worth seeing. And, as I have said before, I find Mrs. Batchelor's company delightful in itself.'

Decidedly, these tête-à-têtes with Pierre were getting her nowhere and neither was anything else. Savoie had explained his father-in-law's failure to call immediately by the exigencies of work on the plantation, to which Lucy had previously referred, and by the fact that Cary was still so dependent on Clyde's company that he spent every moment he could spare with her; no one seemed to cheer her as much as her father, Savoie said, quite without any note of jealousy, but rather as if he were gratified at such filial appreciation. These explanations seemed to the marquise mere pretexts. She was sure that Clyde was deliberately avoiding her, and had begun to tell herself that he did not intend to come at all, that he was actually afraid to face her, when she saw him from her window, walking across the lawn, toward the house, deep in conversation with Mr. Vincent.

She would have recognized him instantly, anywhere. He was a little heavier than when she had last seen him, but not much, and his added weight was becoming. It gave him an air of stability well suited to a substantial citizen, and he carried it off well; if such had been the current fashion, he could still have worn a gold watch chain dangling across the white expanse of a figured waistcoat. He was dressed country style now, which of course was suitable; he no longer affected urbanity, but preferred to be included among the local gentry to whom she had referred so scornfully. The sun was shining on his bare head, and she could see that his reddish blond hair was as abundant as ever; probably there was a good deal of white in it, but, if so, it did not show at this distance, and doubtless would not show at close range, any more than his wife's did. His colour was ruddy, his step brisk; all in all, he looked a good ten or fifteen years younger than his slender, stooped companion. Every now and then the two men stopped, and while Mr. Vincent fumbled with a handkerchief, Clyde Batchelor slapped his leg with his riding crop or drew patterns with it on the grass. The marquise could see that his hands, like his face, bore no telltale signs of age; evidently, if the rumours about his fallen fortunes were true, he had found some compensations for his lost wealth, since everything about him bespoke contentment and well-being. When he and his host had almost reached the house, they stopped for the third or fourth time and their colloquy became more animated; then they suddenly turned and hurried off in the opposite direction. Just then, the marquise heard a knock at her door.

'Missis done send me to tell you de phaeton waitin',' announced the servant who entered in response to an impatient order.

'The phaeton?'

'Yassum. Missis done ask me if you clean forgot you'all gwine take coffee with Miss' Surget dis ebenin'.'

Yes, of course, that would have to be the day they were going, by appointment, to visit Amy Surget, whom the marquise had so ardently hoped she would never have to see again, but who had called, promptly and correctly and—also promptly and correctly—invited them to her house! If the marquise pleaded a sudden headache, and said she could not go, after all, then she would have to remain in her chamber all the rest of the evening; if she went out with Mrs. Vincent, Clyde would undoubtedly have left the premises before they returned. Either way, she would miss him. She snatched up her parasol and left the room, slamming the door after her.

On her return, her son greeted her with smooth speeches. Mr. Batchelor had been to call, but had not come immediately to the drawing-room, because Mr. Vincent had persuaded him to go to the warehouse first. The last of the previous year's perique crop did not appear to be curing properly, and it seemed wise to talk over the matter on the scene of the trouble, the better to get at the cause of it. Mr. Batchelor regretted that he had missed the ladies, but he would look forward to seeing them at his daughter's house on Saturday evening and at his wife's *fête champêtre* the following Tuesday. Meanwhile, Pierre had greatly enjoyed meeting him. The deserted males had drunk juleps, made by a recipe of Mrs. Batchelor's, and these had been excellent. Also, Mr. Batchelor had proved a very interesting conversationalist — in fact, the most interesting Pierre had met since coming to the United States. His viewpoint was far more cosmopolitan than that of most Louisianians, possibly because he had travelled a great deal more than most.

The marquise flounced away from her son and went back to her room, slamming the door again. Then she decided to have the headache after all. It proved so severe that she did not recover sufficiently to leave her room until it was time to start for Cary's supper party. Meanwhile, she received a letter from her husband, which had been delayed by the necessity of forwarding. He had secured passage on the s.s. *Nicholai II* from Bordeaux and expected to be in New Orleans within a fortnight of the day he had written. This meant he would be arriving there the latter part of the following week.

Decidedly, she did not have much time to lose.

The Batchelors had arrived at Monteregard a little before the Vincents and the de Chanets, and were already in the pleasant drawing-room, drinking vermouth. This time, Cary was fully dressed, and was wearing one of the most attractive models she had purchased in Paris — a white grosgrain silk trimmed with coquettish little black velvet bows. Both her mother-in-law and the marquise were quick to observe that her figure had not altered in the least, that indeed her dress fitted her a little too loosely; but this, they both decided with equal swiftness, was to be expected — it was too soon for any real change in her form and she had lost weight during her illness. But she looked bewitchingly pretty, and the black velvet bow which quivered above her pompadour gave the finishing touch of chic to her costume. She and Savoie welcomed his parents and sister affectionately and their guests with appropriate cordiality; then Lucy and Clyde came forward and, quite as naturally, Lucy kissed dear Aureline on both cheeks, as the latter expected of her, pressed the lovely hand of the marquise, and extended her own for Mr.

Vincent and Pierre to kiss in turn. Clyde had never followed French fashions in hand kissing, and no one who knew him expected it of him any more; after all, he had never been to France, he was not a Creole, and he had married a Virginian. It therefore seemed perfectly logical to everyone but the marquise that he should shake hands heartily with both men, bow, somewhat formally, to the older ladies, and give Armande the brief, affectionate hug of a privileged friend. Savoie poured out more vermouth, as he broached the subject of his hunting dogs, which had not yet been brought over from Victoria; Clyde began to talk with Mr. Vincent about getting out more lumber from the swamp, for the 'improvements' Cary wanted; while Lucy outlined the developing plans for the *fête champêtre*. The men then drifted into a political discussion about Senator McKinley and the sugar tariff, while the ladies, led by Mrs. Vincent, reverted to her favourite subject of the wedding. It was typically provincial, the marquise thought, again contemptuously, that the sexes should separate in this way at a social gathering. She would have supposed that Mrs. Batchelor, with her much-vaunted tact, Mrs. Vincent with her pretentious urbanity, or Cary, with her admittedly greater sophistication, would have prevented such a division. As for Clyde, he was either deliberately avoiding her, or else he was stupidly following the custom of the countryside. . . .

The same impeccable maid who had served tea a few days earlier announced that supper was ready. In spite of Cary's deprecatory statement that it would be 'just an informal evening meal', the marquise was again obliged to admit to herself that she could find no fault. The supper was bounteous and imaginative and it was perfectly served, while the delicate porcelain, the heavy silver and the well-rubbed mahogany all showed to great advantage in the soft candlelight. The table was circular, and around it conversation became more general than it had been in the drawing-room; but it was still impersonal until Mrs. Vincent once more steered it to the wedding. It was also she who announced that the marquis was already on his way to the United States, and that, therefore, the visit to Victoria must be curtailed. Of course they would all stay until after the *fête champêtre*, which dear Lucy had so thoughtfully arranged; but as soon as possible after that, they must be on their way to New Orleans. They hoped the others would join them shortly thereafter; so many pleasant prenuptial parties had been planned in Armande's honour by her friends.

'My love, I must remind you that Savoie and I should not both be absent from the plantation, for any length of time, at this season. . . . I tell my wife this every year,' Mr. Vincent remarked, turning from her to the company at large. 'I have been doing so for at least a decade — ever since Savoie was old enough to share with me the responsibility of supervising the crop. And still it makes no impression.'

256

He spoke with proper playfulness, so that the observation would not seem like a public rebuke; still it was quite evident that he was in earnest. Clyde instantly followed up his statement with a similar one.

'Since I haven't a son to whom I can relegate authority, I'm in even a worse fix than you are, Lamartine. I'm looking forward to the day when my grandson will take over for me, but unfortunately that's a long way off. I'll get down to the wedding, of course, but it'll be a case of going to town one day and coming back the next. Lucy and Cary are planning to stay a little longer, but that's so Cary can rest up before and after the great event. We can't have this girl giving out on us again, now that we've had such a struggle to get her on her feet and have been successful at last.'

He reached for his stepdaughter's hand and pressed it affectionately, his smile bespeaking the same solicitous fondness as his gesture. Really, he was as doting in his way, as her husband in another, the marquise told herself impatiently. Releasing Cary's hand with a final pressure, Clyde made another unwelcome announcement.

'By the way, Mrs. Vincent, it's more than kind of you to urge us to stay with you, but you'll have your house, as well as your hands, full with this wedding. Lord knows, I'll never forget the upheaval we were in when Cary got married! And Lucy says you'll need to set aside at least two rooms, just for the wedding presents – which I can well believe, when you're marrying off such a popular daughter!' This time he reached for Armande's hand and, though the gesture revealed none of the tenderness which had been so apparent when he took Cary's it bespoke sincere friendliness and goodwill. 'So I've written the St. Charles for rooms. . . . Yes, Lucy said you'd protest; just the same, she agreed with me it was best I should do so.'

Mrs. Vincent was, indeed, protesting and calling upon everyone else to do the same. While the clamour was at its height, the marquise sat silent, reflecting that she was the only woman at the table to whom Clyde had not spoken directly and warmly. As if he had read her thoughts, he looked straight across the table toward her, meeting her eyes squarely. *So you think I'm afraid of you*, the look seemed to say. *Well, you're wrong. I thought, before you came, that I was going to be. But I'm not, after all. I've found out that you're not a menace to my happiness any longer. There's nothing you can do to hurt me, no matter how hard you try. What's more, you're not a temptation; you're not even an attraction. You're a vindictive, venomous, vain, middle-aged woman whose evil thoughts show in her face, who dyes her hair to hide the white in it, and puts on too much rouge, and starves herself to keep slender without realizing that hunger makes her haggard. The reason I haven't talked to you is because there's nothing I want to say to you or to have you say to me. The reason I haven't looked at you is because I hate the sight of you. It's as simple as that. I told you twenty-*

I

seven years ago that I was through with you and you wouldn't believe me. But you'll have to believe me now. Aloud, he said, 'I should think you ladies would like to hear something about weddings in France. None of you've ever seen one. I'm sure the marquise could give you all kinds of fascinating details. I'd enjoy hearing about them myself. What about you, Lamartine?'

When Mrs. Vincent gave the signal for departure, the marquise was still trying to fight down her futile rage, at least to the point where it would not betray her; but she was seething within. She had only one crumb of consolation, and this was in the reflection that at the *fête champêtre* Clyde could not possibly elude her; she would ask him to show her the gardens and, as her host, he would not be able to decline. But again she was outdone. She had hardly arrived at Cindy Lou when she made the contemplated suggestion; but it was still so early that no other guests had arrived and Lucy was not preoccupied with her duties as a hostess; Clyde seemed to take it for granted she would accompany them. He had never learned the names of half the things his wife had planted, he said; Lucy would have to tell these to her visitor herself. It was too bad the camellias had gone by; they were really the greatest glory the garden had, except the roses, which were fortunately in full bloom. No doubt she had a rose garden at Monteregard? Cary had not said much about the gardens; would the marquise herself tell them what species of plants she had found most successful?

'I suppose Cary had more to say about our so-called *forêt de legende*,' the marquise observed. 'That seemed to intrigue her more than the gardens — that and our famous grottoes. Before she finally left, she had explored all those quite thoroughly. Of course, Pierre was delighted to act as her guide.'

'Yes, she did tell us about those. They must be remarkable. No wonder she was fascinated — and of course your son was a most ubiquitous host. No one could doubt that he would be, even after meeting him casually. . . . Ah, Lucy! You forestalled me! I was just thinking that perhaps the marquise would condescend to wear one of your tea roses. Is that Amy just driving up? I believe it is, but I cannot see who is with her. I suppose we must think of getting ready to receive.'

So the stroll had come to an end because of that wretched woman, who was certainly always in the wrong place at the wrong time, and afterward there was no chance for another ramble. Clyde received with his wife, and quickly revealed that he had considerable *savoir faire* as a host. Though he singled out no one for special attention, he gave every guest a sense of personal welcome. And, like Cary's supper party, the *fête champêtre* as a whole left nothing to be desired from the viewpoint of acceptability. The marquise found that the beauty of the

258

garden had not been overpraised, and that her slurring remark as to the probable character of the refreshments had been quite undeserved : the punch was made with champagne and Bourbon was also provided in great abundance. There were a dozen different kinds of cake and as many sorts of sandwiches, besides chicken salad, cold ham, daube glacée, shrimp aspic, jellies and creams, and, indeed, everything that could make a cold buffet complete and attractive. A Negro orchestra, stationed on the small, second-story balcony at the rear of the house, played and sang picturesquely and melodiously; and as the brief twilight faded, candles were lit in the hundreds of Japanese lanterns strung among the trees. The evening was a perfect one, and the guests lingered on and on; but the marquise was all too well aware that this was due to a sense of general enjoyment, rather than as a special compliment to her; and when Mrs. Vincent, for the second time, gave an inopportune signal for departure, the marquise voiced a complaint.

'Mrs. Batchelor promised me that I should see the interior of the house. Naturally, I'm interested in doing so. After all, it was my home for nearly ten years! And I have not been inside the door !'

'Lucy is still in the receiving line — really, it is a great compliment, the way her guests are lingering! But I do not feel it would be proper for us to outstay everyone else and, in any case, she will be exhausted after the fête is over. I'm sure Clyde will insist that she should go to bed immediately. He takes the greatest care of her — it is certainly very touching! And, as you see, he makes a practice of receiving with her. . . . But perhaps Cary would take you through the house — I will ask her if she feels able to do so. Of course, I would not consider it delicate to suggest that I should do the honours.'

Cary would be glad to show the marquise the house, she said unhesitatingly, when the question was put to her. She had come to the *fête champêtre* rather late, and she had neither stood in the receiving line nor done much walking about; but she had managed to give the effect of the helpful daughter of the house by shepherding small groups to pleasant places under the trees, where wicker furniture was cosily arranged, and by having refreshments brought to guests there. The friends who surrounded her when Mrs. Vincent came up were laughing heartily over some sally which they protested they could not repeat for her benefit because it was much too modern in tone. Nevertheless, they welcomed the older lady warmly to their midst, and she agreed to stay with them while Cary was gone.

'Since we're on ground level now, would you like to begin with that floor and work your way up, or would you rather do it the other way around?' Cary inquired. As she spoke, she picked up the scarlet parasol which had been unfurled to an immense size as long as the sun was out, but which was now lying beside her on the settee. She was in white again, a lingerie dress this time, its scalloped flounces and eyelet embroidery scarlet-edged, a wide scarlet sash around her secretive waist. To the marquise, there was something arrogant about her appearance; she seemed almost to be flaunting her unimpaired figure and her ready resumption of the gaiety upon which her illness was said to have had so sobering an effect.

'By all means let us begin with the ground floor. I'm especially eager to see the gaming-room. Perhaps your father has told you that I suggested its present location,' the marquise replied, assuming something of the arrogance which she was imputing to Cary.

'Father didn't. He hardly ever talks about the dim, distant past. But Mother said you mentioned it yourself, the first day she called. Well, here it is. I hope you will think the results were worthy of your idea.'

Cary opened the door and drew back, so that the marquise might precede her. Dorothée sauntered in and glanced around her. Then she shrugged her shoulders. 'I see that it's changed in more ways than in location,' she observed. Her tone was not actually aggrieved; at the same time, it suggested that she did not consider the changes an improvement. 'The original furnishings seem to have been rather relegated to the background – not that the new centre table isn't handsome in itself. But it rather crowds the room, don't you think so?'

'I never thought it did. But perhaps that's just because I've been used to seeing it here so many years. And then, I've an affection for it because Father designed it himself, and because we've all had such good time playing games around it.'

The marquise shrugged slightly again. 'Those river prints are rather crude, aren't they?' she remarked, moving closer to the wall and inspecting them critically. 'Hardly worthy of that magnificent armoire which, I am glad to see, is unaltered. And that portrait of your mother – is it the work of some local painter?'

'No. As a matter of fact, it's a Sargent. He made a special trip to Louisiana in order to do it. Father and I like that very much, too. But of course there are lots of people who don't admire Sargent's special technique. . . . Would you care to see the wine closet and the storerooms? I'll send for the keys if you would. Father used to pride himself on having all the best vintages, but that was mostly for the benefit of my wine-bibbing friends. He and Mother are both naturally abstemious, so I don't know whether they've bothered to restock since my wedding, and I do know we cleaned the place out pretty well then. However, Mother's sure to have rows and rows of preserves – figs and kumquats and everything else you could think of.'

'Thank you. I should not like to put you to the trouble of sending for the keys.'

'It's no trouble. But of course I realize that, compared to the *caves* at

Monteregard, our wine cellar wouldn't look like much, even at its best; and I can imagine that jams and jellies wouldn't be exactly in your line. Shall we go on to the library? Perhaps that will interest you more than the gaming-room — after all, when you suggested the location for one, you more or less automatically suggested the location for the other one, didn't you?'

The marquise agreed that they might logically visit the library next, and this time expressed herself as delighted with what she saw there: the great globes were especially noteworthy; but everything about the room had *cachet*.

'I think so, too,' Cary answered. 'Of course, the library's primarily Mother's creation — as you know, there was none when she came here, so this room was practically bare after the furniture for the gaming-room was moved. Father and Aunt Amy did the best they could, getting the house ready for her, but they knew she'd rather take charge of this herself. It reflects her personality, doesn't it? Of course, she's got no end of *cachet*.'

Cary walked over to the window and looked down into the garden. She was holding her scarlet parasol, and it was conceivable that she was using it as a means of support while she walked. But it did not have this effect.

'She and Father are really a wonderful couple, aren't they?' she inquired. 'Just look at them, madame! Don't they make a picture standing there, with the big dark tree behind them and the bright flowers blooming all around them and the light from the lanterns shining down from overhead? I don't wonder no one wants to go home! Everybody loves them. And perhaps it sounds like a silly thing to say, but everyone *respects* them. They've stood for so much in the community. . . . Well, I didn't mean to get sentimental, but somehow, seeing them as they stood there. . . . Shall we go on to the drawing-room?'

'I understand that and the dining-room have hardly been changed at all. Suppose we leave those for later inspection, if there is time. I'm really more interested in seeing what has been done upstairs.'

'Just as you like. Of course, there are only four upstairs chambers — strange in such a large house, isn't it? Why, as you've seen, I have as many in my little one! Do you care which room we visit first?'

'Yes. I should especially like to see the one on the right at the rear.'

'Just as you like,' Cary said again. 'That's always been the guest room. The other rear room's normally Bushrod's — my brother's. But he never was here much, even before he married, and he hasn't been back at all since my wedding. So that room's virtually another guest chamber. As far as that goes, mine is too now. But I'll go on thinking of it as mine, and I know Father and Mother will, too; I'm sure they'll always keep it just as I left it and call it "Cary's room" and not put guests in it unless there are so many they can't be accommodated elsewhere. I'll show it to you afterward, and the view you get of the river from there, in case you've forgotten how beautiful it is. I love the river, just as Father does. . . . But this is where you wanted to go first, isn't it?'

Again Cary threw open a closed door. There were subdued lights in the room and pale flowers – evidently it had been readied for the possible convenience of some guest at the *fête champêtre* who might wish to retire briefly in order to 'fancy up'. But it had the telltale look of a room that is seldom used and never really lived in. The house was in shining order throughout, but elsewhere it lacked the sterile immaculacy of this one. The marquise drew back with a little cry.

'But this is entirely changed! My beautiful Empire furniture is not here! Where was it put?'

Cary shook her head. 'Why, I don't know! Those convent beds have been in it ever since I can remember. I'm sure I'm not mistaken, I've heard so many persons comment on them. I don't need to tell you that most typical Louisiana beds are immense, that generally, only nuns slept in narrow ones, and that when a convent was dismantled, and the beds were bought by other people, they were regarded as a curiosity. . . . Well, of course sometimes "youth beds" were narrow, too – my own was, for that matter. It was just as pretty as it could be. I've kept it and I'm glad I have – I'll enjoy seeing it in use again. But it's years since I've slept in it myself. I have a spool bed in my room now.'

'A spool bed! You mean that cottage type Jenny Lind is supposed to have favoured?'

'Yes. I happen to favour it, too. Perhaps it's an odd taste, but I do.'

'And that magnificent Empire furniture – it simply disappeared?'

Cary shook her head again. 'I'm sorry, I don't know. It certainly isn't here. The storerooms are cleaned religiously every year, and I've seen my "youth bed" put in the sun, along with the other pieces that aren't in use, and then put carefully back in storage again. There isn't any Empire furniture among them. And, as you'll see for yourself, Bushrod's bedroom set is quite good Mallard and Father and Mother have a superb Seignouret.'

'Then I shall inquire from your father what has become of my valuable possessions, and ask to have them returned, since he so misprized them.'

All the frustration of the past weeks suddenly burst its bounds. Standing on the threshold of that room which had been the scene of her most voluptuous delights, and which was now as cold and conventual in its austerity, the marquise was beside herself with rage and beyond watching her words. Cary answered her quite coolly.

'Are you quite sure you want to do that? I mean, Father bought everything from you outright, didn't he – the plantation with all its equipment and the house with all its furnishings? If there were some things he didn't care for or couldn't use, there was no reason why he shouldn't dispose of them, was there?'

'There was every reason why he should not make kindling wood of the furniture in my chamber and put the beds of nuns in its place! It is a personal insult! I shall tell him I found it so, no matter how hard you try to stop me.'

'I shan't try to stop you. I shouldn't think you'd want to, that's all.'

'That's all! That's all! Let me assure you, my fine young lady, that is not all! You have been bragging about your mother's "*cachet*", you have told me how greatly "respected" your father is in this community. Well, your mother did not have enough *cachet* to keep her fiancé faithful, and your father would not be so much respected if I told all I know about him. This mutual show of conjugal devotion is very touching, I admit! But I could pull the props from under it in one minute. There would be no forgiving and forgetting then in your mother's case, I promise you. And as for your father, he would be glad to slink away in shame!'

She paused, breathlessly, and glared at Cary as if defying the girl to put an end to her torrent of speech or to prevent her from dashing down the stairs and denouncing her host in his own garden. The fact that Cary continued to look at her coolly and speak to her calmly increased her fury to the point of frenzy.

'I'm not sure I follow everything you're trying to tell me,' the girl said quietly. 'It's hard for me to believe you want to proclaim that something shameful happened in this room, while you were living here, which involved my father. Because that would involve you, too, wouldn't it? I shouldn't think any woman who's passed, more or less, for a lady, would want to destroy the illusion by announcing that she's not. As I've said, Father's never talked much about the dim and distant past, and anyway, he isn't the kind that would ever kiss and tell. But I suppose various kinds of women were mixed up in his early life — there are in most men's early lives, aren't there? Even so, they know the difference between the various kinds, don't they? I mean usually. Perhaps Father was mistaken about thinking you were a lady, at first. But he never, never would have made a mistake like that about Mother.'

'If you think I'm going to stand here and let you insult me——'

'I'm not trying to insult you. And I've told you already, I'm not trying to stop you from doing anything you want. But I believe it's a kindness to try to make you understand that Father thinks the sun rises and sets on Mother's head. He always has; he always will. That doesn't mean he mightn't do things he was ashamed of afterward — especially if he had a lot of provocation. But he wouldn't ever slink away in shame any more than he would kiss and tell. If you really do want to go out in the garden and shout to everyone who will listen that he made kindling wood out of your bedroom furniture, why don't you do it?'

As if she were actually encouraging the marquise to take such vehement action, Cary closed the door of the guest room and moved in a leisurely way toward the stairs. There was no question, now, that she was leaning on the scarlet parasol and that she was glad of its support. But for all that, her words continued to come easily and quietly.

'There's one thing you're right about though,' she said. 'That's the part about forgiving and forgetting. Of course Mother wouldn't *forgive* Father for something that happened more than twenty-five years ago. You don't forgive people you love. You just love them. And you don't have to force yourself to forget something that doesn't matter anyway. Besides, if you think this announcement you want to make would come as a surprise or a shock to Mother, perhaps I ought to warn you that I believe you're wrong. Naturally, she's never mentioned the matter to me, but if I'm not terribly mistaken, she's known all about it for years. I didn't know it until a few weeks ago, when I overheard Belle talking about you to her daughter, Titine, who's my maid now. They thought I was asleep and they didn't notice that my bedroom door was open, either. Probably something accidental like that happened in this house, too. I know Belle wouldn't purposely do anything she thought would make Mother unhappy. But Negroes have a sort of sixth sense about love affairs, especially illicit love affairs—what they don't know, they guess, and they're awfully good at guessing, particularly when they combine it with a little eavesdropping. And they do gossip among themselves about what they've guessed, or overheard, or seen, when no one knew they were looking. And sooner or later, someone overhears *them*. . . . Well, shall we go downstairs? Evidently, there's nothing more you want to see here.'

The marquise gripped the newel post. 'So your mother is sacrosanct,' she sneered. 'But what about you? Is it conceivable that, in your case, a man might have some difficulty in deciding what kind of a woman you were?'

'Why yes,' Cary answered unhesitatingly. 'Yes, it's quite conceivable. Only, in my case, he'd find out that, even if I gave a wrong impression at first, I really was a lady after all. Because you see, that's what I decided I wanted to keep on being. Of course I was born one, and that's an advantage to start with. For a while I thought maybe such an advantage wasn't important. But fortunately I found out my mistake before it was too late. And who do you suppose helped me to do it when no one else could have? Father! He was quite insistent on the point. So that——' Cary concluded, her foot already on the first step, 'will give you some idea of what he thinks of strumpets.'

Chapter Twelve

1896

THE hope which the marquise had expressed to her son of an early return to New Orleans, after the *fête champêtre*, had been repeated, without overmuch finesse, to her hostess, in whom she found a ready listener. Yes, the sooner they were off, the better, Mrs. Vincent agreed heartily; it was all very well for Lamartine to keep harping on the necessity of overseeing the crops at this season; men never realized how much was involved in preparing for an important wedding. Besides, Savoie and Mr. Batchelor were quite capable of looking after the land, between them; now that Victoria and Cindy Lou were, to all intents and purposes, one and the same plantation, the situation was entirely different from that which had prevailed before the two families were allied by marriage; and if Lamartine did not agree with this reasonable viewpoint, he could stay by himself at Victoria, where the servants dear Lucy had trained so well were quite capable of taking care of him. For that matter, he could stay with Savoie and Cary at the new Monteregard; after all, the *lune de miel* was now long since over, the household well organized; the *jeune ménage* should not object to a visitor. . . .

With the two ladies in such complete accord, plans had been made for them to take their departure the day following the *fête champêtre*. Armande and Pierre were to accompany them; and Mr. Vincent had raised no objection to the prospect of a period of comparative solitude at Victoria—in fact, his wife had somewhat indignantly gathered that he would enjoy it. Cary had also inferred that Savoie was far from displeased at the arrangement; although he had not actually said so, she had guessed, without too much trouble, that the more he saw of the de Chanets the less he liked them, and that his devotion to his mother and sister was suffering from the strain of listening to the interminable discussion of nuptial preparations. She had never seen him in better spirits than when he took his customary affectionate leave of her before going out to ride the crops, the morning after the garden party; and his good humour was enhanced by the consciousness that Cary seemed more like herself, in every way, than she had in a long while. Her malaise had apparently disappeared completely; her colour was good and so was her appetite; she rose soon after her husband, joined him in a substantial breakfast, and chatted with great sprightliness about the success of the *fête champêtre* over their hominy grits, cakes, *cuite* and coffee. Savoie was whistling as he went down the steps of the gallery, and he turned back twice to wave a gay farewell to Cary, before he finally cantered out of sight.

When he had gone, Cary found time hanging rather heavily on her hands. It was only a matter of minutes for her to set her well-oiled household machinery in motion; after that, there was absolutely nothing of urgent nature for her to do. Though she was now feeling so well again, she was debarred from riding, and she had also been warned to undertake no other strenuous exercise of any kind for the present. Nearly all the flowers in her garden had been sent to Cindy Lou, the day before, to supplement her mother's in the scheme of decoration; it did not take her half an hour to gather and arrange those which were left. Her mother would be resting, she knew, at her father's insistence, and Clyde himself would be out with Savoie. Her mother-in-law and Armande and their guests would be in the last throes of packing; she had said good-bye to them all the evening before, in order to make sure she would not be a hindrance rather than a help at the last moment. There were no other neighbours near enough to make mere morning visiting feasible and Savoie would be expecting to have her with him by dinner time. Suppressing a slight sigh, which came from boredom rather than actual discontent, she took her sewing basket and went out to the gazebo.

Thanks to Lucy's teaching, she was an expert needlewoman; but fine sewing had never held the attraction for her that it had for the women of her mother's generation. She stitched away rather intermittently, laying down her handiwork every few minutes to look at the satisfactory, but unstimulating scene before her, and trying to refrain from day-dreaming because such dreams seemed so persistently to take her in a direction from which she was resolutely trying to withdraw. At the same time, she could not help wishing that some unexpected diversion would present itself, though if she had been able to guess the form this diversion would take, she would have tried to suppress the wish with the same perseverance that she was trying to suppress the day-dreams. While she was growing increasingly restless because of unbroken monotony, she was conscious of approaching footsteps, and looked up from her sewing to see Pierre coming toward her down the garden walk.

She sprang up, her genuine surprise mingling with an unwelcome sense of shock and a still more unwelcome pang of pleasure. Swiftly and involuntarily, as she had so often done before, she compared his air of sophistication and accomplished ease to Savoie's more ingenuous and less urbane manner. At the same instant, she thought for the first time, with gratification, that Pierre looked far more like his father than like his mother. To be sure, he had her fine high colouring; but the two men had the same graceful though wiry build, the same proud carriage and the same inescapable charm. The smile with which Pierre now greeted Cary, in response to her startled and stammered welcome, was dazzling in its effect. She tried to tell herself that this was merely the result of extraordinarily white teeth beneath a closely clipped, but very black moustache.

'Why, Pierre! I thought you had gone back to New Orleans!' she exclaimed inadequately. In her sudden rise, she had dropped her work basket, scattering its contents in every direction. Before replying, he stooped over, retrieving the strawberry-shaped emery, the tomato-shaped pin cushion, the scissors simulating tiny birds with long beaks, the jewel-topped gold thimble, the various packets of small needles and the many spools of fine thread. Having restored all these objects to their proper places, he handed her the basket with a sweeping bow; she did not notice until afterward that he had not replaced her handiwork.

'I had expected to go,' he answered imperturbably. If he had noticed her confusion, as she was sure he must have, he gave no sign of this; and he did not make even an indirect reference to the fact that he had gathered up the small belongings which had been strewn over the floor of the gazebo because of her precipitate movement. 'However, this morning my mother sent out word, through the maid who took in her tray, that she was completely prostrated by migraine,' he went on. 'It was quite out of the question that she should travel, it was even impossible for her to drink black coffee. This sudden indisposition was, of course, somewhat upsetting to the general programme.'

'Has Dr. Bringier been called in?' Cary inquired, again quite inadequately.

'No. My poor mother declined to consult a physician. I went in to see her, after her message had been delivered, and gathered that she was suffering from a *crise de nerfs* as much as from anything else. She not infrequently has those, sometimes on very slight provocation, if I may say so. This time it appears that the sight of her old home was too much for her delicate nervous system to support without injury. Personally, I do not see why it should have upset her. I have never heard her express the slightest affection for Cindy Lou, or any regret because she had sold it—indeed, I had always gathered that your father's purchase of it was more or less providential. And certainly, he and Mrs. Batchelor have maintained it beautifully. I was charmed with it, myself.'

Cary, who, by this time, had begun to recover her composure, made no immediate reply, and nothing in her face revealed either sympathy or surprise. Indeed, her expression had suddenly become singularly non-committal.

'As a matter of fact, I am charmed by everything connected with this region,' Pierre continued. Cary had not asked him to sit down, but

267

he seemed to take it for granted that she would be glad to have him do so, and had seated himself beside her; it was then that she noticed, for the first time, the piece of fine cambric which he was still holding in his hand. 'So I am very glad of the pretext, which my poor mother's indisposition gives me, for lingering in the vicinity a little longer.'

'But I thought Armande had made an appointment with her dressmaker for tomorrow.'

'She had. She left on the morning train. Since obviously she could not go alone and since her mother, without showing herself remiss as a hostess, could not leave mine, Mr. Vincent most reluctantly accompanied his daughter.'

'Surely Armande must have taken it for granted that you would accompany her, too!'

'By no means. A man who reveals himself neglectful, as a son, is a very poor prospect as a husband on whose sympathetic devotion a wife can unfailingly count. Armande required practically no argument to convince her of this. She understood my position almost before I had explained it to her : I could not leave my mother unassuaged in her suffering; my duty to remain with her was very clear.'

'I don't see why. You've said that she didn't want a doctor, and that quite often she has slight nervous upsets which, obviously, you don't take very seriously.'

'Ah! I should have been more careful not to sound contradictory. But somehow, I thought that while Armande required very few explanations of my attitude, you would require none at all.'

'I'm afraid I'm not as subtle as you give me credit for being. I still don't see the slightest reason why you shouldn't have gone on to New Orleans with Armande today. From what you've said, I should think your mother would probably be well enough to follow tomorrow or the day after. In the meanwhile, if she doesn't even feel like drinking coffee, no doubt all she wants is to lie still in a dark room with a handkerchief wrung out in cologne water on her forehead.'

'But I have told you quite candidly that I was charmed with this region, that I welcomed a pretext to linger longer in it.'

'Yes. But of course you're even more charmed with Armande than you are with this region. What's more, you're engaged to her.'

'Your second statement is correct. Your first leaves something to be desired in the way of complete accuracy. I have never thought you were subtle; indeed, I have always found your naïveté one of your most appealing attributes, Cary. But surely you're not such an ingenue that you require an explanation as to the real reason that I was glad to stay over a day at Victoria, without the pleasant, but somewhat handicapping presence of my fiancée and her father.'

Pierre looked at her with a smile that was even more engaging than the one with which he had greeted her. But this time Cary did not think of it merely as dazzling; she also thought of it as dangerous. She had seen that look on his face before, when they were riding together in the enchanted forest, toward the gipsy camps and the wooded slopes leading to the grottoes which fringed the river that widened into the Blue Pool, where a girl who had lost her lover had drowned herself, long, long ago. . . .

'I don't believe I'm altogether an ingenue,' she replied, with a calmness she was very far from feeling. 'I don't believe your mother thinks so, either — in fact, I'm very much afraid that her *crise de nerfs* may be partly due to some remarks which I made yesterday. Since you're a devoted son, I doubt whether your regard for me would stand up under the knowledge of just what those remarks were. In the light of them, and of your mother's illness, I don't think it's fair for me to detain you here. I think it would be far better for you to go back to Victoria and see if there isn't something you can do — what was the expression you used? — to assuage her sufferings.'

As she spoke, Cary made a movement as if to rise and bring their interview to an end. Pierre leaned forward and, still holding the piece of cambric in one fine, flexible hand, laid the other over both of hers.

'Cary, I need assuagement myself. I need your assurance that you understand.'

'Of course I understand,' she retorted, withdrawing her hands from his reach. 'A girl doesn't have to be a complete nitwit, even if she is an ingenue. And I've just told you I'm sure I'm not even that.'

'You're by no means a nitwit and, if you prefer, I will concede that you're not an ingenue, either,' he replied, with surprising quiet. He did not try to take her hands again. However, something about the very fact that he refrained from doing so made his speech more compelling. 'But I am more and more convinced that you do not understand — at least, not what I want you to.'

'Very well. Then I will listen while you explain. But I would like to go on with my sewing while you do so. Will you please give my work back to me? I'm afraid I didn't thank you properly for picking up the other things. Perhaps that's why you've kept on holding the cambric — to remind me of my manners.'

'Not at all. I have been holding it because it was yours, something with which you were intimately connected and — as such — precious to me.' He spread the cambric over his knees, scrutinizing it for the first time. 'I've been holding it all crumpled up,' he remarked apologetically, smoothing it out as he spoke. 'I did not realize what it was — I thought probably a chemise for yourself. Now I see that it is a baby's dress. Is that why you want it back, Cary? So that you will be reminded, while I am talking to you, that you are going to have a baby?'

'No. I'd rather keep busy, that's all. I don't need any reminder that I'm going to have a baby – or that I'm married to one of the best men in the world.'

'But you are reproaching yourself because you feel that sometimes you forgot about your married state and your husband's great qualities, while you were visiting at the château?'

'Yes. I reproach myself very much for that. I always shall. But at least I don't intend to have any more reason for self-reproach on that score.'

'I don't intend that you shall, either. But neither do I intend to leave you without convincing you, if I can, that what happened between you and me last year was important to me, that I didn't regard it like one of many pleasant amorous episodes and nothing else – nothing more.'

'It isn't in the least essential that I should know how you regarded it, Pierre.'

'Indeed it is. It is very essential to me, as I shall try to explain, if you will give me a chance. And I believe it is essential to you also. I believe you will be much happier in the future if you know that I never thought of you as a light of love – not even potentially. I thought of you, and still think of you, not only as one of the most desirable, but as one of the most companionable, one of the blithest, one of the loveliest women I have ever met in my life – a woman whom I should have been proud to have for my wife, if she had been free. I'm speaking in deadly earnest now, Cary. Don't you believe me?'

She turned her head away, without answering. Again he leaned forward and took her hands and, this time, she did not withdraw them.

'Please look at me, Cary. Please answer me. I asked you if you didn't believe me.'

'You make me believe you – almost,' she whispered, still without looking at him.

'That isn't enough. I want to make you believe me – not almost, but wholly. Because I swear that what I'm telling you is true. If I swear it, won't you believe me?'

'Ye-e-s, I think so.'

'And won't you admit that if you do believe me, you'll be happier than you've been in a long while? Happier than since you knew you were going to have a baby? Happier than since you learned Armande and I were engaged? Happier than you've been at all since you knew there wasn't any escape for you and since you began to think that I'd held you cheap?'

'Yes,' she said again. But this time, though she still did not turn to look at him, it was not because of hesitancy and doubt, but because there were tears in her eyes which she did not want him to see, even if he knew they were there.

'Then I can be very candid with you, which is what I hoped. I did not look on you as a light of love, I would have asked you to marry me if you had been free. But since you were not, I did think that, in time, I might persuade you to become my mistress. I do not mean one of many loose women with whom I had transient affairs; I mean what used to be called in the days of royalty, a *maîtresse en titre,* a great lady who was completely loyal to her lover, whose station and standing were understood and, strange as it may seem to you, respected. There are still many such women in France, even if that special designation is gone. Indeed, there is hardly a Frenchman of any standing who has not had, or does not have, such a woman in his life. It is more or less taken for granted that he should. And it does not create a scandal, as I now understand it would — and does — when such an arrangement is made in the United States.'

'And do you mean to tell me that the mistresses of these prominent men are still respected, too?'

'Yes, in a way.'

'It must be a very strange way. . . . What about their husbands?'

'Well, of course the husbands . . .' For the first time, Pierre himself hesitated. 'Perhaps we had better not try to go into the husbands' side, in such cases,' he went on a trifle hurriedly. 'After all, I was only trying to interpret the lovers' side — the *real* lovers, not the incorrigible libertines. So I will repeat that, when I came to Louisiana, it was with the hope that I could persuade you to become my mistress — my dearly beloved, highly regarded mistress. And I had hardly landed when I was told you were *enceinte.*'

Again he smoothed the baby's dress across his knee. 'It was a blow, I admit,' he said, 'a very great blow. Not only to my love, but to my pride. I had thought of you as waiting to welcome me, of counting the days until we could meet again.'

'I was,' Cary said in a low voice. 'I shouldn't have been, but I was. I was even poring through old law books, trying to find out whether I couldn't discover something in them that would prove Savoie had cause for divorce.'

Pierre released her hands, and though he did not actually draw farther away from her, somehow he gave the effect of doing so. 'Ah, divorce,' he said in a changed voice. 'There I must differ with you, Cary. If you had been free when I met you, as I have just told you, nothing would have made me happier than to have you for my wife. But marriage with a divorcée — especially with a woman whose husband had divorced her for cause — that would have been quite impossible for me.'

'So my father said. He said that was the way you'd feel about it,' Cary remarked scornfully.

'You discussed the matter with your stepfather? I'm rather sorry you did that, Cary. Inevitably, he must have formed a very low opinion of me. And from the way you spoke just now, I gather that he was fairly successful in turning you against me. I was conscious, of course, that you were avoiding me, but I thought that was because – well, because of Armande. Let me finish what I started to say. I was counting the days until we could meet again, and I was confident that when we did I could persuade you to become my mistress. I thought we would arrange to see each other, very discreetly of course, but constantly and – intimately. Then I thought you would persuade your husband to bring you back to France, in the near future, for another long visit, and that thus we could resume our liaison. I thought this delightful arrangement could go on and on. It never entered my head that you would already be with child – Savoie's child. Of course it should have. I can see now that the wonder is you weren't *enceinte* much sooner, that you did not either have a baby while you were still in France, or hasten your return so that you might have your *accouchement* at home. This present pregnancy of yours might well have been your second. It is evident that you are destined for the rôle of *mère de famille*, not of *grande amoureuse*. I was very blind not to realize that in the first place. And when my eyes were opened, I confess that I was very angry – unreasonably, with you; logically, with myself. And it was quite natural that when I was in such a frame of mind, I should succumb very easily and quickly to the charms of a girl like Armande.'

'I see,' Cary said, still scornfully.

'There is no reason why I should not say that she fell in love with me at first sight, since she and her mother have both said the same thing themselves,' Pierre went on, disregarding the scorn this time. 'And of course, that was not only very flattering to me, since she is such a beautiful and accomplished girl, but very soothing to my hurt pride. I responded instinctively to her affection.'

'Just the same, I don't suppose you tried to seduce her.'

'Certainly not. A gentleman does not make improper advances to his fiancée, when she is a *jeune fille bien elevée*. It would be offensive to his principles. Besides, what would be the point? She will soon be his bride in any case. Why should he deliberately lessen the triumphant joys of his wedding night by anticipating them?'

'I don't know any reason why he should. But then I don't know, either, why a gentleman should deliberately set out to make another man's wife disloyal to her husband. And I don't believe, Pierre, there is anything you can say that will make me understand, or that there's anything to be gained by continuing this conversation any longer. I hope you won't try to see me again, either, no matter how long your mother's illness detains you. In fact, I shall tell the servants to say I'm not at home if you call. Now, if you'll please give me back my baby's dress . . .'

She rose and stretched out her hand. As Pierre surrendered the piece of cambric, he pressed her fingers, but he found he could not continue to hold them unless he did so forcibly. He looked at her reproachfully and shook his head.

'It grieves me very much to part from you like this,' he said reproachfully.

'It grieves me, too,' she answered. But her voice was not reproachful. It was still scornful. 'However, we are not saying good-bye to each other for good,' she added. 'I shall be seeing you again at your wedding.'

It was universally and enthusiastically agreed in New Orleans that the wedding of Pierre de Chanet and Armande Vincent was the outstanding social event of the spring season.

For the occasion, golden ornaments from the cathedral treasure had been brought forth and set on the high altar, where they glittered in the radiant candlelight. The archbishop, always a majestic figure, seemed to have achieved added stature and dignity as he stood at the entrance of the sanctuary, clad in full pontificals, awaiting the arrival of the bridal procession, which advanced toward him to the strains of Meyerbeer's 'Prophète'. First, clad in their multi-coloured medieval costumes, marched the two huge Swiss Guards, who acted in their official capacity only at the most important ceremonies. Then came the twelve ushers, in formal evening dress, their glacé gloves and stiff shirt-fronts in complete harmony with the waxen tone of their white boutonnières: They were followed by the twelve bridesmaids, in white mousseline de soie, their 'half-veils' confined with wreaths of white roses and garlands of roses linking them together in couples. Next came two little flower girls, also wearing 'half-veils' and wreaths of roses, but dressed in sheer mull instead of mousseline de soie, as being more suited to their tender age, and scattering petals from gilded and beribboned baskets, instead of carrying garlands. They in turn were followed by the bride, on her father's arm, a coronet of diamonds encircling the rose-point lace which fell in creamy cascades over her shoulders and flowed out behind her to the full length of her court train; and last of all, in accordance with time-honoured custom, the groom's mother, escorted by the groom, and the bride's mother, escorted by the groom's father.

Though the stir which the de Chanets had at first created had begun to subside somewhat by the time the wedding took place, the appearance, in juxtaposition, of the old marquis and the young one gave rise to whispered remarks that both were certainly looking their polished best. The ushers had all appeared correctly attired to the last detail, until Pierre came up the aisle; now, by comparison, not one of them seemed perfectly turned out. As for the marquise, her costume left nothing to be desired in the way of chic. But the great surprise, the really startling sight in the cathedral, had been the appearance of Cary Page Vincent.

Naturally, the news that she was *enceinte*, at last, had spread, and there had been much murmuring — some of it sympathetic, some of it satisfied — because, in consequence of her condition, she would not be in the cortège and this created a vacancy for a 'real Louisianian'. It had also been vaguely assumed that if she did come to the wedding at all, she would be wearing some sort of a loose wrap, no matter what the weather, and that she would be seated inconspicuously. The ladies who had been busily ticking off time on their fingers had somehow over-looked the fact that she could not yet be far enough along to have a noticeably altered figure. The more general assumption had been that she would not put in an appearance at all. According to rumour, she had made a great deal of fuss about her morning sickness — as if nine out of every ten women did not have it and some of them practically every year, during the early stages of their married life! But then, everyone knew that Cary Page had always been an *enfant gatée*. . . .

She entered the cathedral on her husband's arm. The organist was already playing the chords which presaged the beginning of the special music for the cortège and everyone was on the alert for its arrival; therefore, all eyes were on the centre aisle and the older and more hide-bound contingent among the guests gave an audible gasp. Instead of some nondescript dark-hued sacque, Cary was wearing a dress which was almost exactly the colour of her hair. This, in itself, was a drastic departure from custom. Baby blue was traditionally the favoured colour for blondes; they might, occasionally, switch to a very pale pink or a very delicate green, for the sake of change; but yellow was something that they never, never wore! Yet, here was Cary wearing it, one might almost say flaunting it, in the face of the public; and strangely enough, the effect, if it had not been so startling, would have been distinctly pleasing. The dress was made with enormous sleeves, and below them, Cary's wrists and arms were encircled with glittering bracelets. The bodice was cut surplice fashion, with a V-shaped neck just low enough to set off a heavy gold necklace to great advantage; and the folds of the satin were so arranged as to display the shape of the breast in the most effective possible manner. If Cary's figure could have been said to possess a fault, heretofore, this was because it had lacked the allure of full-blown femininity; now the curves of her bosom were beautiful. Moreover, she had achieved a 'straight front' unparalleled in New Orleans for its perfection, and her many-gored skirt flared out from her trim waist, catching every variation of light as she moved. Two small yellow wings, evidently the plumage of some bright bird, fastened together at their base with a bow of yellow ribbon, constituted her headdress; the feathers were poised delicately over her hair, creating the illusion not only of added height but of swift and effortless motion. They made the laden hats worn by other women look top-heavy and grotesque. She was carrying a large bouquet of yellow roses, from which streamers of golden gauze fluttered; and, as she progressed, she glanced brightly from side to side, smiling and bowing to acquaintances. When she finally reached the front pew, she slipped her arm easily from Savoie's, releasing him so that he might hasten to the rear of the church and join the cortège; then she sank gracefully to her knees, after laying her bouquet on the seat beside her. Her bracelets tinkled pleasantly as she crossed herself. She knelt for some moments, and this position afforded an excellent view of her flawless profile and equally flawless figure. Finally she rose and, picking up her flowers again, turned in the direction of the aisle, just as the archbishop emerged from the sacristy and the organist began the march from 'Le Prophète'.

'What an entrance!' A cousin of the Vincents, who was seated slightly to the rear, whispered to his wife. 'If you ask me, Savoie's wife has stolen the show.'

'I didn't ask you,' she answered in an annoyed undertone. 'If you ask *me*, I think all that was in the worst possible taste—making herself so conspicuous at another girl's wedding! Even if it hadn't been for her condition——'

'No one would have known about her condition if a lot of old wives didn't seem to think it necessary to shout it from the housetops. As for being conspicuous, a girl with looks like that can't help it. She'd stand out in any crowd. I don't wonder she's been such a belle, ever since she let down her skirts and put up her hair.'

He was not able to say any more, at the moment, because the cortège was already half-way up the aisle; his wife was nudging him and various other women were casting venomous glances in his direction. For the most part, they had not been able to hear his words distinctly; but they had experienced no difficulty in getting the drift of his remarks and they resented it, just as his wife did. *The jealous old harpies*, he said to himself, resolving to seek Cary out at the reception and feast his eyes on her when she would not be gliding past him so rapidly that he could hardly get a good look at her. But he found it more difficult than he had foreseen to carry out his resolution. A number of other gentlemen had apparently been inspired by the same idea, as they watched her progress up the aisle, and he found her already surrounded, the centre of a convivial group which was sipping champagne, and nibbling at *petits pâtés aux huitres* and squares of *massepain*. Cary had a champagne glass in her hand, and every other moment or so was raising it to acknowledge a toast; whenever she did so, she made some witty little remark or one that gave the effect of being witty because of the arch, amusing way in which she said it. The Vincents' cousin tried hard to catch her eye and succeeded — all too briefly; Cary smiled at him and raised her glass and made one of her droll little speeches. The newcomer felt very much encouraged; but almost immediately there was another claimant for her attention, and presently he decided it was no use, this was the way things were going to be as long as the reception lasted. . . .

As he turned away, he was rewarded by a tidbit of gossip which he had not previously heard, and which temporarily did something to compensate for his disappointment, as far as Cary was concerned. It had leaked out that in spite of all its glittering appearances, the wedding had not been a complete success from the viewpoint of either the groom or his father. The old marquis had hoped very much that his daughter would let bygones be bygones and attend her brother's wedding with her husband and their two girls. His *daughter*! But surely Pierre was an only child! Yes, the only child of a second marriage. But it seemed the old marquis had been married before, to the Princess Asceline de Herbemont, who had died when her baby girl, whose name was also Asceline, was only a few weeks old. So, as the widower did not feel equal to rearing an infant of such tender age, the dead wife's parents had taken charge of the poor little thing and she had remained with them at their château in northern Indre. They had regarded their son-in-law's second marriage as a mésalliance, and had never forgiven him for contracting it. On the other hand, his delight over the birth of Pierre had been so great that he had made no immediate effort to regain possession of his daughter; and the present marquise had said quite frankly that she did not want to be saddled with a half-grown stepdaughter, or to be snubbed by some decadent old aristocrats who imagined themselves to be better than she was. So matters had drifted along: little Asceline had never gone back to Monteregard as a child or a young girl; and, eventually, she herself had married, a certain Etienne d'Ambly, who also possessed a very fine château. After her marriage, she had been respectful to her father, agreeable to her half-brother and civil to her stepmother when they met by chance in the same social circles; but she had never invited them to her own fine establishment in Morbihan. Doubtless she had so often heard them disparaged that she had ended by believing it would be better if the estrangement, already of such duration, should be prolonged indefinitely. Tardily, the old marquis had tried to bring about a rapprochement; now that it was too late, he realized how much he wanted the companionship of his daughter and how greatly his granddaughters might have contributed to the happiness of his declining years. Moreover, Pierre was very proud of his sister's aristocratic connections and superb property. He had done everything he could to persuade her that their father needed her; and he had moved heaven and earth to convince her that she and her family should come to his wedding. However, all his efforts had been in vain; the princess had sent Armande a correct note and a handsome gift; but she had remained quite unmoved by the pleas that her attendance would add prestige to the marriage ceremony.

The Vincents' cousin, like the friends who related all this, relished the flavoursome gossip to the full; but it did not prevent him from hankering for a chat with Cary, and he lingered in her vicinity, hoping for better luck than he had had before. However, he seemed doomed to disappointment, for eventually Savoie came up and said that Armande was ready to cut the cake and wanted Cary to be there when this was done. She linked her arm through his and went off with him, calling something back over her shoulder which the Vincents' cousin did not quite catch, but which he gathered was very gay, like everything else she had said, and perhaps the least bit risqué, too, from the way it was received by those who did hear it. He also wanted to see the cake cut, so he wedged his way into the dining-room; but it was very crowded, and he could not get anywhere near the table himself, though he could catch a glimpse of Cary, for her yellow satin dress and the wings in her hair made her outstanding among all the girls in white mousseline de soie, with wreaths of white roses on their heads. Some of the 'half-veils' were torn now, and some of the wreaths were askew, and the general effect was not as ethereal as it had been in the cathedral; even the bride, upon closer inspection, was not such a dazzling figure as he had previously thought. Of course, since he was a Vincent, he had a feeling of pride in her rose-point—no other New Orleans family owned so much of it; and as he happened to be something of a lapidary, in an amateur way, he could appreciate the value of the diamond parure—it was seldom indeed that the groom's present to the bride included a tiara as well as a necklace, a brooch, earrings and bracelets. But the truth was that the rose-point in such immense quantities lost its light, lacy look, and that a seven-piece parure was also too much of a good thing. The radiance which Cary seemed to emanate had remained quite undimmed, however. It gave lustre to all its surroundings.

And then suddenly the lustre was gone, for Cary had disappeared. . . .

It was Savoie who persuaded her to slip away unobtrusively and to go back to the St. Charles, without waiting for the bride and groom to take their departure. Neither her mother nor her stepfather made any effort to hasten her, though when she complied, pleasantly, with Savoie's anxious advice, Lucy returned to the hotel with her and helped her undress. The bodice of the yellow satin, which fastened down the back with large hooks and eyes, was lined with stiff taffeta, rigidly ribbed with whalebones inside, and was kept in place, over the binding of the separate skirt, by a two-inch waistband of strong webbing, which fitted very snugly and which was also secured by hooks and eyes. As Lucy managed, with an effort, to undo the last of these fastenings, she peeled the bodice away from the corset cover which concealed the 'straight front' corset and tossed it on the nearest chair.

'It won't be but a minute now, darling. Start undoing your corset cover yourself.'

Obediently, Cary untied the pink bow of the baby ribbon run through the eyelet embroidery which formed the border of the corset cover and started on the buttons which went from the bow at her bosom to the waitsline. Meanwhile, Lucy had unhooked the skirt of the yellow satin, and Cary stepped out of it, so that her mother could lay it over the back of the chair where the bodice had already been tossed. After that, there were the strings to four starched petticoats to untie. But at last Cary stood clad only in chemise, corset and ruffled drawers.

'I'll cut the lacing, darling. It'll be quicker.'

'No, don't. I'll take my drawers off, too, if you don't mind. Then I can unclasp the corset all right.'

The drawers fastened with a string, too. This was tied in a hard knot and it took their combined efforts to loosen it. But finally the frilled drawers dropped to the floor. Never, since she was a little girl, except during her recent period of invalidism, when Lucy had been obliged to bathe her, had Cary's mother seen her daughter as nearly nude as she was now, and to both of them, the exposure of her thighs resulted in self-consciousness. To lessen this, they simultaneously endeavoured to unclasp the corset. Just as they succeeded in doing so, Cary fell to the floor in a dead faint.

'Naturally, the corset was much too tight for her,' Lucy told Clyde, when he came back to the hotel, several hours later. In accordance with the wishes which both Cary and Lucy had expressed, he had remained at the wedding reception until after Pierre and Armande had taken their gay departure, in a shower of rice and confetti. 'That webbing belt, too. . . . If dresses could only be made in one piece! Perhaps they will be, some day.'

'Yes, perhaps they will,' Clyde answered abruptly. He crossed the floor and opened the door which separated his room and Lucy's from the one which Savoie and Cary were occupying. He knew that Cary would be alone, for Savoie was still at the reception, discussing with his parents the great success of the wedding and sipping one last glass of champagne, when he, Clyde, had left it. Clyde thought that, possibly, Cary might still be awake, that he might have a chance to talk with her. But she had sunk into the profound sleep of complete exhaustion and lay, with her head cradled on her arm, and her golden hair bright against her pillows. He closed the door noiselessly and turned back to Lucy.

'She won't have to wear those tight, stiff clothes again until after her baby's born, will she?' he asked. Then, without waiting for an answer, he added, 'But I tell you, Lucy, it was one of the proudest moments of my life, when I saw her come sailing up the aisle of the cathedral in that gold satin dress.'

'I know it was,' Lucy replied. And neither of them suggested that the tight corset might not have been the only reason for Cary's fainting fit.

Chapter Thirteen

Autumn, 1896—Spring, 1897

THE latter part of Cary's pregnancy proved as painless and pleasant as the first part had proved troublesome and trying. True to her mother's prediction, none of its distressing symptoms lasted beyond the quickening, and most of them had ceased to cause her much discomfort before then. She carried her child well, with almost no real disfigurement until she was near her time; up to then she merely appeared heavier than before and the added weight was not unbecoming. Her colour was good, her expression cheerful and the charm of her manner had never been so marked; if it lacked a little of its former sprightliness, it had also gained in gentleness and grace; and if her step was less light and rapid, her carriage had more dignity. Clyde, watching her with loving pride, told himself that she was growing more like her mother every day; and though Lucy, when he said the same thing to her, answered a little sorrowfully that she had never qualified for the comparison, he retorted that he was talking about mental and spiritual attributes, not physical ones.

Meanwhile, however, Savoie's adoration was permeated with anxiety. He kept meeting men whose wives' *accouchements* had been accompanied by horrors which they described in great detail, or who had actually died in childbirth; the thought that Cary might suffer such anguish and that he would be responsible for it, the fear that he might altogether lose her, haunted his days and nights. When her pains began, Dr. Bringier's assurances that everything was proceeding satisfactorily, and that a rather slow labour was often really preferable, in the case of a first child, to one that was more rapid, only served to infuriate the tormented husband.

'Why don't you *do* something for her? Once in three hours you come out here, rubbing your hands as if you were immensely pleased about something and say, "Everything is perfectly normal and I think that in about three hours more . . ." I sit here with my eyes glued to the clock, and when the three hours are up, you come out here and say the same thing over again! Don't talk to me about a *first* child! I tell you this is going to be an *only* child! I wouldn't have Cary go through this again for anything in the world!'

The doctor turned away with a slight smile, but refrained from making the answer which, twenty years earlier, had been his stock reply under such circumstances. He glanced toward Clyde, expecting that the older man would return his look in kind; but Clyde, though he refrained from expostulation, was obviously quite as wretched as Savoie.

'He's telling himself, for the first time, he's glad his wife never had a child by him,' the doctor thought sagely. 'Nothing will ever convince him that there's no hell she wouldn't have willingly have gone through if she could have given him a son.' His train of thought was interrupted by a muffled cry which, though quickly smothered, reached the room where they were sitting. Savoie bounded from his seat.

'Can't you give her chloroform? Can't you put an end to that torture by taking the baby with instruments?'

'Yes, of course I can give her chloroform, and I will, by and by — in whiffs, when she's further along and really needs it. But I'm not going to until she does — it would simply slow things up. And of course I could use instruments. But I'm not going to risk tearing her to pieces and injuring the child unless and until I'm sure she can't get her baby into the world herself. And I think she can. I've told you half a dozen times already that she's coming along finely.'

He left the room abruptly, slamming the door after him. A few minutes later, it was reopened by Lucy, who regarded the two miserable men seated there with compassionate understanding.

'Dr. Bringier tells me he doesn't seem able to convince you that everything's going just as well as possible,' he said. 'He thought if I told you I wasn't at all worried, it might help to reassure you. And I'm not. Of course, Cary's suffering. She has to, you know. But she's taking it all splendidly, doing just what the doctor tells her to and helping herself along. I think it would be a relief to her, though, if she could scream once in a while without being afraid you'd hear her. Why don't you go out in the gazebo for an hour or two?'

'*An hour or two!*' Savoie echoed. 'An hour or two *more*?'

'I should think it would be at least that long,' Lucy said calmly. 'She wasn't in her second stage when I came in here and until she is——'

'What do you mean, her second stage?'

'I think perhaps I'd better let Dr. Bringier explain to you, later on, if you don't know. You may go in and see her for a minute, if you want to, but I really believe——'

'Of course I want to go in and see her. I'll probably never see her alive again.'

Savoie rushed out of the room, slamming the door even harder than the doctor. Lucy put her arm around her husband's shoulder.

'Do get him outside. I don't suppose you could persuade him to play cribbage, or chess, or do anything except worry and rage, but if you could it would be the best thing in the world for him.'

'I don't see how I could do anything like that myself, but I'll try, if you think I ought to.'

'I do think so. Thank you, darling.'

She lingered a moment or so longer, laying her cheek affectionately against his. Then she left, not hastily and noisily, as the others had done, but in her usual serene way. Clyde, making a determined effort, pulled himself together and, after a little rummaging, found a crib and some cards, a chessboard and some chessmen, and carried them out to the gazebo, where he laid them down on one of the seats while he returned for a table. Next, he went to the kitchen, where he found the entire household staff gathered together in a state of idle but gloating expectancy, the enjoyment of which was enhanced, rather than lessened, by the consciousness of Cary's prolonged travail. Somewhat curtly, he ordered drinks and sandwiches brought to the gazebo, adding that Dr. Bringier and Mrs. Batchelor might be calling for coffee at any time, and that he hoped it was not necessary to say there should be broth on the stove and custard in the cooler. Then he went back to the gazebo. When Savoie rejoined him, mopping his brow and cursing, Clyde had the table set up, the chessmen in place and the drinks already poured.

'Here you are,' he said, handing his son-in-law a glass whose alcoholic content was practically undiluted. 'When you've swallowed that, see if you can't beat me, for once in your life. Want to bet on it? And want to bet that Lucy'll be bringing us good news before we've finished the game?'

Savoie did not want to bet, he did not want to play either chess or cribbage, he did not even want to drink; in fact, his hand shook so that he could hardly hold the glass. But somehow, Clyde managed to prevail. When Lucy finally came to them, they did not hear her light step until she was half-way across the garden. But as they leaped to their feet, upsetting the table and spilling and scattering everything on it in their haste, she called out to them in a glad voice.

'A beautiful big boy! And Cary's as right as rain! She'll want to show her baby to you herself or I'd have brought him with me.'

Lucy had not exaggerated in her joy; the baby was undoubtedly a fine specimen and Cary a radiant mother; instead of being exhausted by the ordeal through which she had so triumphantly passed, she seemed exhilarated. To be sure, once she had proudly displayed the new-born child, lying in the curve of her arm, to her husband and father, she had fallen into a deep, profound slumber, which lasted so long that Savoie, hovering entranced near her bedside, became impatient for her awakening. He felt he could not wait to tell her that he adored her and that she had made him the happiest of men. It did not matter that he had told her this countless times already; that was before she had made his happiness complete, for he worshipped her now as the mother of his son. Words would be lacking to express all this, yet he yearned to try; when she finally opened her beautiful eyes, smiling up at him, he could only stammer out his rapture.

He had supposed she would seem very fragile to him for a long time, he had feared that he would hardly dare touch her, and that even if he did dare, he should not, because she would still be very weak and very resentful, since he had been the cause of all her suffering. He thought he must be very gentle and very patient. But as she lay in bed, with her golden hair spread out over her white pillows and the baby at her full, beautiful breast, she seemed to him more vital, as well as more desirable, than ever before; there was nothing about her to suggest frailty. It took him days to grasp the fact that childbirth had done her no harm, that, instead, it had given her physical fulfilment, and that far from resenting maternity, she was glorying in it. He felt that some miracle had come to pass when he found that she shared his sense of ecstatic thanksgiving.

'Why do you keep telling me how much you owe me?' she asked him one evening, jestingly. She had made such a rapid recovery that she had dispensed with the monthly nurse ahead of time and begun to train Titine's sister, Tudie, to help her with the baby; and although Dr. Bringier was extremely conservative in such matters, he had not tried to confine her to her room as long as he did most of his patients. He had, however, wrung a promise from her that she would breakfast in bed, rest every afternoon, and retire immediately after supper, threatening her with the greatly dreaded 'loss of milk' if she did not compromise with custom at least to this extent. She had consented, on the condition that Savoie would sit beside her and chat with her after supper 'until a normal bedtime' — a condition she need hardly have imposed, since he never willingly left her side. 'Don't I owe you just as much as you owe me?' she went on laughingly, stretching out her hand to him.

'I don't know what you mean, darling,' he answered, pressing the extended hand fondly.

'Well, Larry's wasn't a virgin birth, you know. You had something to do with it, too.'

They had agreed to let Clyde name the baby, since he had never had a son of his own, and Clyde, of course, had asked Lucy to make the choice. After some hesitation, she had suggested Lawrence. It did not sound like a Louisiana name, she knew, and she would understand perfectly if, on reflection, Cary and Savoie would rather have one that did. But it had been a name of frequent and important occurrence among the Peytons and the Carys, as it had among the Washingtons. Her favourite brother, the one who had been killed leading a cavalry charge at Manassas, had been the last Lawrence Cary, and he had never had a son of his own, either. There had been a Lawrence Peyton in the Revolution and a Lawrence Cary who was a colonial governor. In fact, the first Cary to come to Virginia — the one whose bride had been given the diamond brooch by the King of England — was named Lawrence, too. She had hoped that she herself . . .

Everyone had instantly agreed that Lawrence Cary Vincent would be a perfect name for the new baby and he was baptized, with due pomp and ceremony, in the parish church of St. Michael's at Convent. The religious ceremony was followed by a large reception at the new Monteregard, during the course of which the baby, clad in robes of ancestral lace, was shown off to a host of admiring beholders. All the guests agreed that this christening was a most auspicious occasion on which to gather friends and relatives together for the first time in the newly established home. No one regretted any longer that the proposed housewarming had never taken place. Besides, the present function served a dual purpose: it was not only a christening party, it was a bon voyage party. Mrs. Vincent had prevailed at last, and she and her husband were off to France to pay Pierre and Armande a long visit — and, incidentally, they might even visit the Princess d'Ambly, for Armande, with her never-failing tact, had actually succeeded in bringing about the long desired rapprochement between the two branches of the family, when everyone else had failed. It was really wonderful, nothing short of miraculous. What was more, Armande was 'expecting' already, which, Mrs. Vincent kept archly telling everyone who would listen to her, was just what she herself had expected! She hoped that, once she got her husband away, he would consent to remain abroad for a good long time — not only long enough to visit the d'Amblys as well as the de Chanets, but also long enough to attend a *French* christening. Of course, nothing could be nicer than the one they were celebrating now. Still, with a magnificent private chapel in a historic château for a setting — well, the next one in the family would be exceptionally thrilling!

Everyone agreed with her and, by the time the christening party at the new Monteregard was over, the same persons who had said that

Lawrence Cary Vincent was a perfect name for the new baby were also agreeing, over their champagne, that they must find a nickname for him. With comparable unanimity, it was decided what this should be; so, by the time Cary was jesting with Savoie about his share in producing such a wonderful infant, 'Larry' came readily to her lips. She said she had always despised parents who referred to their offspring as 'it', and that parents who merely said 'Baby this, Baby that' were almost as bad; she was very glad the whole question had been taken out of her hands.

'I never thought of it that way before,' Savoie told her, in a wondering voice.

'That I ought to be grateful? Or that the baby's been called by a sensible name from the beginning?'

'That you ought to be grateful to me, of course. I don't think you should – I don't see how you can be. You had all the pain and I had all the pleasure.'

'Oh, Savoie! It's beneath you, conversationally and mentally both, to use that old cliché! Besides, from what Mother's told me, you didn't enjoy the day Larry was born very much yourself.'

'No, but——'

'That's what you meant when you talked about the pain, isn't it? As to the pleasure——'

She stopped, looking up at him with sparkling eyes.

'I was terribly slow about making up my mind to get married, wasn't I?' she asked. 'Perhaps I was a little slow about grasping all the advantages of the married state, too. I'm sorry.'

'I wasn't reproaching you, darling. I just said I knew——'

'Well, I wouldn't blame you if you did reproach me. But you won't have a chance to reproach me any more. Because I realize those advantages now. And I'm determined to make up for lost time.'

He was still holding the hand she had stretched out to him. He pressed it again and raised it to his lips.

'Don't you think you might give me a real kiss? You haven't, you know, since Larry was born.'

'Why yes I have! I've kissed you every day – several times a day.'

'Not the way I'm talking about.'

He rose and looked down at her. Never had he seen such welcome in her face and, as he bent over and kissed her, he could feel the welcome in her lips, too. He straightened up again, swiftly.

'It's – it's too soon,' he said thickly.

'Is it? Do you really think so? I should have supposed you would think it wasn't half soon enough,' she answered.

'I mean, if – if anything should happen . . . . It might be bad for you.'

But, looking at her again and seeing the way she looked at him, he forgot he had meant to be very patient and very gentle and remembered only how much he wanted her.

Well, yes, Dr. Bringier conceded drily, when, rather shamefacedly, Savoie sent for him again; it was sooner than he would have advised, if he had been consulted. But it was no sooner than he had anticipated. He had been expecting to be called in, about this time, ever since Savoie had raved and ranted about an only child; he had never known that to fail. He would have liked to see Cary nurse Larry through the following summer; but the baby was in such splendid condition that it would do him no harm to shift gradually to cow's milk. As for Cary, it was obvious that she was made for maternity. She was in a very different mood than before, wasn't she? Yes, that was what he would have thought. And he doubted whether she would have much trouble with morning sickness this time. As for her confinement, she would probably just kick off her slippers and have the baby. He would tell her so, since he might not even get there himself; but now perhaps he had better be getting in and looking her over. . . .

There was no question at all about the different mood. When Cary said she was very glad she was going to have another baby, she did so in such a way that the doctor could not possibly doubt that she meant it. Indeed, when she added, quite spontaneously, that she hoped she would have a very large family, he permitted himself the jest of saying it was too bad she had started in so late; she probably would not be able to have more than ten or twelve, unless she had twins, whereas, if she had married at sixteen, like her mother, she might have had twenty. Cary retorted that, quite likely, there would be twins, sooner or later, possibly more than one set. Then, without even mentioning faintness or morning sickness or anything else of the kind, she went on to say that she hoped, this time, she would have a girl, so that she could name it Lucy. She had already told her mother and her stepfather about her prospects and they were pleased, too. They did not think it was too soon for her to have another. Something in her tone seemed to dare the doctor to say again that he thought so and he did not accept the dare. He was really very fond of them all and he was glad they were all so happy. It was not his policy to pry into the private affairs of his patients; but, like most family physicians, he could not help learning a good deal about these. He knew, for instance, that Clyde had suffered great financial reverses after fighting his way to a fortune and that Lucy had endured many trials with great fortitude; he knew Cary had been a spoiled child and that, besides causing her parents considerable anxiety, she had given Savoie a run for his money, though Savoie was as fine a fellow as ever lived, even if he were not overburdened with brains. But Cary was settling down at last, she was proving to be a good daughter and a good wife and a good mother after all; there was not a family the doctor knew on the river road more deserving of happiness or with a better prospect of it. . . .

And then Savoie came galloping up to Dr. Bringier's house late one night, when the exhausted physician had finally sunk into bed after a long, hard day, and implored him to come post-haste to Monteregard. Larry, who had never been sick for a single hour, had suddenly been smitten with some strange and terrible illness. Mrs. Surget, who was visiting them, had said at first that it was only croup, and Tudie had agreed with her. They had fired a kettle of water on a small oil stove, under a blanket, so that the steam would envelop the baby in his crib, and had prophesied that this treatment would quickly bring relief. Instead, Larry's breathing had become more and more laboured. Then Mrs. Surget had begun to talk about membranous croup, and had admitted steam would not loosen that. Tudie had not said anything more; she had put her apron over her head and moaned and groaned. Now the poor baby seemed to be strangling. . . .

While Savoie rattled distractedly on and on, Dr. Bringier had been flinging himself into his clothes. He did not underestimate the gravity of the situation. Unless there were apparently a question of life or death, no Creole planter would have come pounding up the river road himself, to summon a doctor, instead of sending one of his servants; and even allowing for Savoie's constitutional excitability and natural anxiety, the symptoms he described were unquestionably alarming.

'Sulie's hitching up the buggy right now,' the doctor said, shrugging himself into his coat and abruptly interrupting Savoie's torrent of talk. 'I'll be at Monteregard almost as soon as you can get back there yourself. Meanwhile, the best thing you can do, my friend, is to go home and let Cary know I'm on my way. I tell you frankly I'm afraid, from what you say, your baby is bad off. But don't repeat that, you hear? Membranous croup? Bah! There is no such thing! Diphtheria, more likely. A killer. But don't repeat that, either. After all, I've nothing to go on as yet but your incoherencies. Now hurry along. You're doing no good here.'

Larry was still hooded in Mrs. Surget's improvised steam tent when the physician entered the nursery and, bending over him, curtly ordered the hissing kettle and the small oil stove removed. The baby's face was purple, his lips blue, his struggle for breath already nearly futile. Only an occasional wheezing rattle showed that he had managed to suck a bit of air into his straining lungs.

'As I thought,' Dr. Bringier announced tersely. 'Diphtheria. No use wasting time on medication. I've only one chance of saving him. That's by making a cut in his throat and inserting a tube. If I can do that quickly enough . . . If not . . .'

He did not finish the sentence. Cary buried her face against Savoie's shoulder to smother a wild surge of sobs. Beneath the damp fabric of his shirt, she could feel the trembling of his body; and suddenly she knew she could not count on him for support in this dreadful moment. Instead, she must somehow summon strength to meet it unaided.

'No time to lose,' she heard the doctor saying as she raised her head. 'First, let's get this table cleared — and be quick about it! Now, Mrs. Surget, you and Tudie go back to the kitchen and stay there until I send for you. Meanwhile, put some water on to boil.' Then, when the old family friend and the young coloured mammy had tiptoed obediently from the room, with fearful backward glances toward the crib and the baby's stricken parents, Dr. Bringier added, 'They mean well, but I couldn't risk Larry's life with either of them. I've got to have intelligent co-operation. One of you'll have to give it to me.'

While he was speaking, he dragged the marble-topped centre table nearer the mantel and speedily transferred the two lamps which stood on the dresser to the mantel shelf. 'Got to have light, too,' he grumbled. 'And I can't afford to take a chance of having either of you keel over, maybe, with a lighted lamp in your hand, at the sight of a little blood.'

Dr. Bringier had acted with almost unbelievable rapidity; now, the suffering baby's parents felt that he was not acting at all and Savoie impulsively started toward the bathroom himself, thereby blocking the path of the returning physician. He jerked his head, motioning Savoie out of his way and, lifting Larry from the crib, placed him on the table in such a manner as to bring the narrow pad beneath his shoulders and permit the small head to loll back.

'I'll prop back his chin myself, but one of you'll have to hold his arms against the table,' Dr. Bringier announced. 'I expect it'd better be you, Savoie. After all, you're a good deal stronger than Cary.'

Savoie approached the lighted table, bent forward, and placed his corded hands over the baby's soft little arms. But he was still shaking, and suddenly he released his grip, swayed backward and crumpled in a heap beside the table, while deep racking sobs came from him.

'I can't do it!' he cried. Dr. Bringier looked past him contemptuously, and saw that Cary was already close to him, placing a steadying hand on his bowed head.

'It's all right, darling,' she said soothingly. 'Don't worry. I know how you feel. But I can keep him quiet. I've done it lots of times already.' She took hold of the struggling baby's arms and pinioned them to the table. 'Go ahead, Dr. Bringier,' she said, still composedly. 'Everything will be all right. Only please hurry.'

She looked down at her child, marvelling at the strength he showed in trying to escape her. She did not see Savoie, who had somehow got to his feet and stepped out of the way. She did not see Mrs. Surget and Tudie, who had crept back as far as the dark doorway, and stood, with their hands pressed hard against their lips, staring in horrified fascination at the lamp-lit scene by the mantel. But she saw the doctor's clean, gnarled fingers, press Larry's chin up and back, and a dazzling gleam of light from a polished blade.

She saw no more, because she felt as if she were commencing to spin in a slow vortex, and she stopped looking down at Larry and pressed her eyelids together as though Larry's life depended now upon her sightlessness—as indeed she feared it did.

Then, abruptly, Larry's tortured gasps and his pitiful writhing ceased at the same instant, and someone was speaking again, saying she did not need to hold the baby any longer and someone put an arm around her. . . .

She did not instantly recognize the voice as the doctor's, because it was not harsh any more, but very, very gentle; and she did not instantly realize that it was Savoie who was embracing her, because the arm which encircled her was steady and not trembling. But she dared to look at last and, through a blur of unshed tears, she saw a glint of metal at her baby's white throat, just at the place where she had so often nuzzled it to make him gurgle with laughter. She rubbed her eyes to make sure that this and everything else she saw was not a delusion. For the baby's face had lost its deadly purplish cast and was pink and warmly alive again. His little body no longer twisted and writhed in agony; instead his small breast rose and fell in the peaceful rhythm of effortless breathing, and his eyes were closed in deep natural slumber. . . .

'You can't blame him for dropping off, either,' Dr. Bringier chuckled, shooting his cuffs over his knuckles and snapping the steel fasteners into his shirtsleeves. 'I expect he's been through more than he'll ever be called on to undergo again. At least, I hope so. But he's still going to need a great deal of attention right around the clock. And, judging by what happened here a little while ago, I'm afraid you're the only one that can give it to him, Cary. But I know now I can count on you.'

The doctor had begun to move the miscellany of bright metal from the table and stow it back into his black leather bag, item by item.

For more than a week, Cary watched over Larry night and day, ministering to his every need. Not once, during this interval, did she complain of morning sickness or dizziness, though it was obvious enough she suffered from both, nor did she refer in any way to her own condition. Then, when the silver tubes had been painlessly removed, and Larry was well on the road to complete recovery, she suddenly fainted dead away, for the only time in her life, except on the day of Pierre's wedding. Savoie carried her to bed and undressed her; and when she struggled back to consciousness and instinctively tried to rise, she realized that it was her physician and not her husband who was sitting beside her, and that the fingers on her wrist were there to feel her pulse and not to caress her.

'Lie still, Cary,' Dr. Bringier said abruptly; and, as she continued her vain effort to sit up, he added, more sternly, 'Larry's pulled through and it's thanks to your care, even more than his fine physique. But you've got to turn him over to someone else now.'

'There isn't anyone else. You've said yourself, over and over again, that Tudie was developing into a fine nurse, for a well child, but that she didn't have enough experience yet to take care of a sick one. And none of the other servants——'

'True enough. But——'

'And you've said Mrs. Surget was beginning to feel her age and show it, too, so much that you didn't——'

'That's also correct, but——'

'Well, then——'

'Will you kindly let me finish what I started to say, Cary Vincent? There's your mother. She's as good a nurse as I ever saw. She has a natural gift for it and she's had plenty of experience besides. Instead of just letting her spell you, for an hour or two at a time, as she has been doing, you'll have to let her take Larry at night, from now on.'

'You mean send him to Cindy Lou!'

'Certainly not. I'm not proposing to move him. He's out of danger and I think he'll make a rapid recovery; children go down hill fast, but they have remarkable powers of recuperation. However, though it's no longer necessary that anyone should sit up all night with him, he still requires considerable care. And you can't give it to him.'

'Yes, I can.'

'I'm telling you that you can't. You might faint again—at a very bad moment, not just for you, but for Larry. And you've got another child to think of now. You want this new baby—it means more to you than Larry did, before he was born. It would be a hard blow to you if you lost it. And I'm telling you that you very well may, if you go on as you have been doing. What's more, if you lost this one, you might never have another—don't forget what happened in your mother's case. And then what would become of that big family of yours, I'd like to know?'

The latter part of the doctor's speech sounded less severe than the first; there was even an obvious attempt to introduce a mildly jesting note. But this superficial lightness in no way obscured the underlying gravity. Cary sank back on her pillows.

'Who's with Larry now?'

'Both Savoie and Tudie. Mrs. Surget's in the house, too. She's still able to help another nurse, for a few hours at a stretch, in the daytime. But you're right; I can't give her any more night nursing.'

'Mother isn't here?'

'No. Larry's sleeping peacefully, so she went back to Cindy Lou to have dinner with your father. I told her I'd stay with you until she got back, that I wanted to talk to you like a Dutch uncle, without any interference. And I know she thinks your father needs her, too—he's got his hands pretty full with the spring crop, what with Lamartine Vincent gallivanting around France and Savoie refusing to stir out of this house. And I believe he's expecting some business visit or, due to arrive at any moment. But I'm going straight from here to Cindy Lou myself on purpose to ask your mother to come back to Monteregard, now that you're awake and I'm through talking to you—I promised her I would. I'll also tell her she must be prepared to stay overnight—over several nights. But first, I want you to promise *me* you won't get out of that bed, except to nurse Larry, until I give you permission. You'll find you won't be able to satisfy him anyhow, when he's well enough to be a little hungrier. I'm thankful we got him started on cow's milk before all this happened, because your supply will have to be materially supplemented from now on. Even if you hadn't worn yourself out, you wouldn't have had enough for him much longer. So let your mother start feeding him at night. I'm telling you the truth, Cary. It's not just a question of what's best for you; it's also a question of what's best for Larry—and for the new baby.'

He had hard work wringing the promise from her. Indeed, it was not until Savoie joined them briefly, and added both his assurances of Larry's continued and peaceful slumber to those of the doctor, that she agreed to stay where she was, at least until the baby wakened and cried for her. Before that happened, her mother arrived, and proved more successful than either of the others in coping with Cary. Lucy had never enlarged, before, on the poignancy of her disappointment in her failure to give Clyde a child; but she did this now, and in a way so infinitely moving that Cary could not keep back the tears while she lay listening to her mother; and, as she was quietly weeping, her thoughts turned more and more to those children, still unborn, who would be the outward and visible sign of her fulfilment as a woman and of her triumph as a wife. Gradually, a fierce desire to safeguard the future flooded her being and helped her to forget her anxiety of the present.

'Anyway, you and Father have had each other,' she said at last, knowing that she was speaking inadequately and believing that she was also speaking inconsequentially.

'Yes. We've had each other,' Lucy said. And, brief as the answer was, its adequacy was complete.

'Did he mind too much, having you leave?'

'Oh, no! He agreed with Dr. Bringier that I should. But he wanted to come with me. I had hard work dissuading him. However, Valois Dupré has just arrived at Cindy Lou—he has to be in Baton Rouge tomorrow, and apparently, it's very important that he and your father should have some sort of a consultation before them. Besides, there's no reason why your father's rest should be disturbed because Larry needs care—he couldn't help anyway. An aptitude for nursing is not among his many talents.' She rose. 'I think I will go to the nursery now,' she went on. 'If Larry finds me beside him when he wakes, he will be less likely to cry for you. After all, he recognizes me now and we are pretty good friends, too. If he seems contented and comfortable, I will send Savoie in to you, and keep Tudie to wait on me. Please believe me, darling, Larry will be all right.'

'I do believe you, Mother. And thanks for talking to me the way you did. It helped a lot. I promise you I won't try to get up. I'll lie still and take good care of little Lucy while you're taking care of Larry.'

They kissed and clung to each other for a moment; then Lucy left the room and, for a little while, Cary lay quietly, thinking less of the sick child, with whom she had been so wholly preoccupied during the last few days, than of the new life within her, of her husband's overwhelming love for her, and of the tardy quickening of her own response to him, which had already transfigured their marriage relationship, and which gave such rich promise of future harmony and future fecundity. How much more fortunate she was than her mother had been! It was true that Lucy and Clyde had been ideally happy together; but Cary realized now that this happiness had never been quite complete and, with thankful wonder, she told herself that hers was—or that it would be, as soon as she was sure, beyond any shadow of a doubt, that all was well with Larry.

When Savoie came back to their room from the nursery, an hour later, he was able to give her this assurance. Larry had not cried at all when he wakened; he had indeed recognized his grandmother—the precocious intelligence of that child!—and had been glad to see her; he had even drunk the milk she offered him, with apparent relish. Then he had dropped peacefully off to sleep again. Mrs. Batchelor had almost completed arrangements for the night. Tudie had brought in more milk, which had been put in the beautiful *veilleuse* Mrs. Surget had given Larry for a christening present; it would be kept at just the right temperature and he could have more whenever he was hungry.

Now Mrs. Batchelor had packed Tudie off to bed, telling her to get a good night's rest, and was herself preparing to retire. She sent her love to Cary, and promised to let her know instantly if Larry should take a turn for the worse; but she confidently expected him to keep on feeling better.

'And I think so, too,' Savoie concluded hopefully. 'So there's not a thing on earth for you to worry about, darling.'

She was beginning to feel sleepy herself. She had fought off the drowsiness natural to her condition all the time she had watched beside Larry. Now she could succumb to it. The sensation was delicious.

'Can I get you anything? Is there anything you want?'

'You can't get me anything and the only thing I want is to know you're here with me. It's bedtime for all of us, isn't it?'

'Very nearly. We can call it bedtime if you want to.'

'I do want to. For over a week——'

For over a week their every thought had been of Larry. Now at last they could think of each other again. They went to sleep in each other's arms.

In the nursery wing, on the other side of the house, Lucy remained wakeful for some time. She had spoken the truth when she said she felt there was no further cause for anxiety; still, to make assurance doubly sure, she sat beside Larry for more than an hour, listening to his breathing and occasionally feeling his forehead. His breath came softly and regularly, his forehead was faintly moist under his clustering curls. The awful periods of strangulation were over, the burning fever had completely subsided. There was no doubt now that he would sleep peacefully for hours. Besides, his cradle was drawn up close to the big bed; she would hear his slightest cry. It was needless for her to sit up any longer; in fact, it would be much better if she, too, rested as long as possible, so that she would be refreshed the next day.

She prepared for the night in her customary, calm, orderly way, hanging up her dress, folding her underwear over the back of a chair, brushing and braiding her long hair and sponging herself off, before slipping into her clean cambric nightgown. Then she knelt down to say the Lord's Prayer, adding to this her more personal petitions for those who were nearest and dearest to her; she gave thanks for Larry's recovery from mortal illness, for her daughter's growth in grace, for her husband's devotion, for everything good that had come into her life; and she did not fail to add a plea for a return to the fold by Bushrod, the black sheep. Finally she rose from her knees and, after one last look at Larry, blew out the lamp and laid down in bed. The faint glow from the *veilleuse*, formed like a madonna, shed its soft light over the slumbering child.

She did not fall asleep instantly. She had always been sensitive to her surroundings and, aside from her feeling of responsibility, she had a feeling of strangeness. She had never occupied this room before, at night, and it was a long while since she and Clyde had been separated. In the early days of their marriage, she had not always been able to accompany him when he travelled on business, because she could not leave Cary; but ever since all his interests had been concentrated at Cindy Lou, she and he had been together constantly. She thought of him, alone too, and knew that he must have the same feeling of strangeness that she did, and the same feeling of isolation.

She forced herself to lie quiet and relaxed, instead of following her impulse to toss restlessly from side to side, or to become tense under the strain of solitude. She prayed again, short, formless little prayers this time; and between them, she raised herself on her elbow and looked down at Larry, to find that he had not stirred since she last looked at him. At last, soothed by the beneficent stillness of the night, she slept. When a slight, sudden puff of wind upset the *veilleuse*, she did not hear its soft fall. The sound was muffled by the silken scarf covering the chest where it had stood and it did not tumble to the floor. But the milk from its little pot and the oil from its lamp flowed out of it together, and on top of the oil floated the tiny lighted wick. A second gust of wind sent the burning oil farther on its wicked way, setting fire to its surroundings.

Lucy never knew whether it was the sound of a banging shutter or a sudden scream from Larry which wakened her. The two came together, and she leaped from her bed into a room already ablaze, realizing with horror that there was not a second to lose. The first little licking flames from the lighted wick, rippling into larger and larger waves, had quickly reached the draperies. Escape through the dressing-room was already cut off, for the curtain which hung at the doorway was afire. Lucy snatched the screaming child from his cradle, enveloped him in a blanket, and rushed toward the door leading to the rear stairway.

By this time, the sudden wind storm had reached the proportions of a gale, and it was all she could do to battle her way across the garden. She did not dare lay Larry down on the cold ground; but once she had reached the gazebo, he would have shelter from the storm, inadequate to be sure, but enough to serve until she could summon more help. She had not paused, even to put on slippers, and, in the darkness, she could not choose her path. She kept stumbling, and once she fell; but she struggled to her feet again, unconscious of any hurt, and hurried on. Though her first dazed, waking thought had naturally been for Larry, she realized now that she must get back to the house and warn the others. Again, there was not a second to lose.

Her foot touched the step leading into the gazebo before she saw it.

Wrapping the blanket more firmly around the still screaming baby, she laid him on the floor; and, as she did so, she tried to murmur a few words of comfort. But she did not dare stay to soothe him, and his pitiful cries followed her as she turned and ran back toward the house. Darkness was no longer a handicap, for the whole nursery wing was now ablaze, and flames had already reached the rear of the building; but she could see that the great, outer stairway, leading to the main floor, was still clear. Surely she could get up it, battle her way through the hall, and reach the wing where Savoie and Cary were sleeping—if they still slept. She could only pray that the wind had wakened them, too, that they had already made their way to safety. But, even as she prayed, she feared her prayers were vain; if Savoie and Cary had come out through the hall, she would already have seen them; and there was no stairway leading directly from their quarters to the ground. Unless they leaped from a window, they could not have reached it. And such a leap, for Cary at least, would have been only one degree less dangerous than fire itself.

Lucy reached the great, outer stairway, mounted it two steps at a time, and gained the front door. Doors at Cindy Lou were never locked, but Savoie had always followed his father's custom of bolting everything at night. Desperately, Lucy threw her weight against the solid panels; then, realizing the complete futility of pitting her slender strength against such solid structure, she doubled up her fist and struck one of the glass side windows to the door with all her might. This time, her effort was successful. The blow shattered the glass, and she thrust her hand and arm through the opening and managed to reach the bolt and draw it back with her bleeding fingers. Then the knob turned easily under her hand and the door opened, releasing clouds of smoke. She stepped across the threshold and ran down the length of the hall, until the smoke stifled her and she fell.

Chapter Fourteen

Spring, 1897

IT had become second nature for Cary to stretch out her arms toward Savoie as, still deliciously drowsy, she began to nestle around in the morning. He was invariably wide awake already, for he instinctively kept the 'planter's hours' to which he had been accustomed since childhood; but he was careful to remain completely motionless, until the welcome signs of his wife's imminent awakening encouraged him to turn toward her. Then he drew her to him, first burying his head in her breast, and then kissing her shoulders, next her throat and lastly her lips. She was naturally a very lazy girl, she was apt to tell him; however, no amount of somnolence could have been proof against the persuasive powers of that culminating kiss. She had to wake up, so that she would get the full benefit of another like it. . . .

She was waking now, but it was not a kiss that had roused her and her arms encountered only a strange void as she stretched them out. When she became fully conscious of this, she also became conscious of pain, a pain which was dull rather than poignant; and there was a strangeness about the dullness, too, as if it were not really part of the pain. It was a little like the dullness that came from the chloroform she had been given when she was in the last stages of labour, merciful but stupefying. Yet, it did not seem quite like chloroform, either; and of course she was not in labour, it would be months yet before that happened again, and she had been assured that, this time, it would be much easier than before anyway. She was trying to decide what the dull pain could be, still without bothering to open her eyes and still groping aimlessly for Savoie, when someone took her hand and called her softly by name. Since that was not Savoie's way, nor his voice which she heard, she reluctantly opened her eyes at last and saw that her father was sitting at her bedside. And next, before she could ask him why he was there and why Savoie was not, she realized that she was at Cindy Lou instead of at Monteregard, and that she was lying alone in the little old spool bed that had been hers before she married.

'Cary,' Clyde was saying again. 'Cary, my darling. . . .'

It was Clyde's voice, there was no doubt of that, yet there was something strange about this, too. Everything was very strange. She did not understand at all. She had always thought with great affection of her own room at Cindy Lou and of the little old spool bed where she had slept alone; but now that she was back at Cindy Lou, in the spool bed, the strangeness troubled her. She was not happy about it because she was so puzzled. She tried to question her father, but her own voice seemed strangest of all, and the dullness of the pain did not keep it from getting worse, now that she was wide awake.

'Monteregard was – damaged by fire, during a storm at night,' Clyde was telling her. At least that was what she understood him to say. She was not quite sure, because everything still seemed so strange, and she was so bewildered and suffering so much. 'It seemed better for you to come – to come home for the present.'

'But Savoie didn't stay at Monteregard without me, did he?'

'No. He's at Cindy Lou, too. But he had to fight the fire, you see. It's hard work, fighting fires, you know that. So he's – resting now.'

'I don't see why he couldn't rest here, beside me.'

She did not understand why she should begin to cry. If she had been able to follow, accurately, what Clyde told her, there was nothing he had said which should cause her grief. Of course it was unfortunate that there had been a fire at Monteregard; but fires were not infrequent occurrences, in plantation houses, and happily they did not often amount to much. She was sure her father would soon repair any damage that had been done and then she would go back to Monteregard and she and Savoie would be together again. Meanwhile, she ought to be thankful that her old home was so close that she could return to it, in any emergency, thankful that she was in the pleasant room which had been hers for so long, thankful that Savoie was resting comfortably, after having helped to put out the fire. Probably he had been afraid of disturbing her by coming to her room when she had gone to sleep. But how could she have come from Monteregard to Cindy Lou without waking up, without knowing there was a fire?

She tried to puzzle it out, but she could not and presently, in spite of the dull pain, she went to sleep again. When she waked, the pain was worse, but she was able to think more clearly. She began to remember now : she had been sound asleep, after many nights that were wakeful, because she had been watching over Larry and . . . Suddenly, she screamed.

'Larry has died! Larry has died and you haven't told me!'

'No, darling. Larry hasn't died. He's much better – completely out of danger. But he's sound asleep, in Bushrod's room, and Tudie's there with him. She's taken wonderful care of him ever since – well, ever since we brought him here. Dr. Bringier says he couldn't be in better hands. You don't want me to wake him up, do you, when he needs sleep so much?'

'I don't believe he's all right. I shan't believe it unless I see him.'

'Cary, I swear that I'm telling you the truth. Did I ever lie to you?'

'No, but I don't understand. . . .'

She must not cry again, she would not. She bit her lips to keep them steady and tried to go on remembering. Yes, she had been sleeping very, very soundly, after her nights of vigil; and then she had been roused by Savoie, who was shaking her, so that she would wake up; and the room was full of smoke, so full that it choked him while he tried to talk to her, to tell her that the house was on fire, that she must leave it at once, by a window, and he would go through the wing into the hall and make sure that her mother had left the other wing with Larry, by the steps on the further side. He was convinced this was what would have happened, but he would go and make sure, as soon as he had seen her safely on the ground. She had tried to argue with him that she must go through the house with him, and he had told her there was no time to talk; he had picked her up and carried her to the window. . . . She tried and tried, but she could not remember anything after that. She turned again to her father, who was still sitting quietly beside her, with his head bowed, and this time she did not cry out, and she did not find it so hard to question him, either.

'Things are coming back to me, Father.'

'I knew they would, if you wouldn't try to hurry yourself, darling.'

'Mother carried Larry straight down the new staircase, didn't she?'

'Yes. That's just what she did. We can't be thankful enough you thought of having it built.'

Briefly, Cary was conscious of immense thankfulness herself. But now that she found she could, she wanted to go on asking questions.

'Then it was no trouble at all to get Larry out of the house?'

'No. Your mother took him straight to the gazebo. He was sheltered there from the storm and safe from the fire.'

'And what did Mother do next?'

'Well, naturally, after she was sure Larry was safe, she hurried back to warn you and Savoie.'

'And I suppose it was while she was hurrying back that the smoke waked Savoie and that he waked me?'

'Yes, that must have been the way it was.'

'Savoie said he would go through the house to make sure Larry and Mother were all right. Probably they met in the hall.'

'Yes, Cary, they did.'

'Then she's resting now, too?'

'Yes, Cary.'

'But what happened to me? That still isn't clear.'

'You were — hurt, falling from a window. Perhaps you were unconscious before you fell. You'd already swallowed a good deal of smoke, more than you realized. Or perhaps the fall caused your unconsciousness, and you had a slight concussion. We don't know. It doesn't matter anyway.'

'But I was unconscious when I was found?'

'Yes. I picked you up myself, I brought you over here. You never stirred until you waked up a few hours ago and asked for Savoie.'

'Was that *hours* ago?'

'Yes, Cary.'

'Has anything happened since?'

'Well, Dr. Bringier's been here to see you again.'

'*Again?*'

'Yes. Of course we sent for him right away. And he gave you something to deaden your pain right away. He's kept on giving you something. He'll continue to do so. He — we won't let you suffer any more than we can help.'

So it was medicine that was responsible for that dull feeling, some kind of medicine which was very powerful, even if it were not as powerful as chloroform. But now that she could think more clearly, Cary could not help wondering why she should still be in so much pain. The pain was there all the time – not just when she moved a little. So evidently she had not broken any bones. She did not believe that burns could be causing the pain, either. Like everyone else, she had burnt her fingers, occasionally, and though the burns had been slight, they were unforgettable. The pain she felt now was not like the pain they gave. This was like only one other that she had ever had, not exactly like it, either. But then, the effect of the powerful medicine was not exactly like the effect of chloroform. . . .

'Father, you don't mean——'

'I hoped you wouldn't guess, darling. Try not to grieve too much. Remember you've got Larry.'

'But——' It was no use. No matter how hard she bit them, she could not keep her lips from trembling now. 'But this time I was *glad*!'

'Yes, Cary, I know.'

'And Savoie was so glad, too. And Mother. Mother'll be terribly worried, Father. You see, she told me to be very careful, because if I had *one* miscarriage, then probably . . . She's been so terribly disappointed herself, Father, because she didn't give you a child.'

'She did give me a child. She gave you to me. You're my child, Cary. You always have been. But you're doubly my child now.'

There were tears on her face and they were not her own. And suddenly she understood everything.

Everything except that she herself was dying.

She was not sure how long it was before she understood that, too, because time meant nothing to her any more. Every now and then Titine or Mrs. Surget came into her room and did things which, apparently, seemed to them necessary. They gave her broth and gruel, and sponged her off with sweet-smelling water and changed her nightgown and her bed linen. She accepted their ministrations with docility, but she never craved their company and she was always secretly relieved to have them go away. Her feeling about her grandmother and her Cousin Mildred, who had come down from Virginia and were occupying the room with the convent beds, was more neutral. She did not really crave their company, either; on the other hand, she was not actually relieved when they left her. She took a certain vague pleasure in their talk of Sorrento, as it was now, and of Amalfi, as it once had been; but she had no desire to share in this conversation or to expand it. When Tudie brought Larry in to her, early every morning and again just before bedtime, she was glad to see him; but she did not resent it at all when Dr. Bringier said the baby must not stay with her too long at a time, because it would tire her. She did not feel she needed to see him long at a time to assure herself that all was well with him now. Neither did she feel that she needed to see, for long, the priest who had married her to Savoie and who had also baptized Larry, or the rector of the little Episcopal church which her mother had faithfully supported, and of which she herself had been a nominal, but rather casual member. She recognized that they were both good men and that they were both devoted to her personally, besides having her spiritual welfare at heart. She thanked them for coming, but she did not suggest that either should come a second time. They did not add to her sense of peace or her sense of happiness. It was Clyde that she wanted with her.

She and he talked to each other freely about everything again now, just as they had before she was married; and she thought it was when he told her about her mother's funeral, and her husband's, that she began to realize he would have no one to talk to in just that way, after she died. She was troubled because she was afraid he would be very lonely then; but otherwise she was not troubled at all. It did not tire her or make her sad to talk; on the contrary, it exhilarated her, because she was glad to feel she was giving her father some comfort. She knew he had hesitated to avail himself of this comfort, because he had asked Dr. Bringier if talking would do Cary any harm. He had put the question almost in a whisper, when the two had gone out into the hall; but Cary had heard it, and the doctor's answer to it.

'You're sure it wouldn't help if she could conserve her strength?'

'She hasn't any strength left to conserve. I'll keep her as comfortable as I can, with drugs. It's your job to keep her as happy as you can, in any way that you can.'

So Clyde came back into Cary's room and talked with her until the merciful drugs had done their work and she was drowsy again. He did not pretend to any false cheerfulness; instead, he paid her the tribute of sharing his sorrow with her. And when he paused, after talking to her about the past, and about her mother, she talked to him about the future, and about Larry.

'You said I was your child, Father, and I'm glad you did, because I've always felt as if I were. You said Mother gave me to you. Now Larry must be your child. I'm giving him to you.'

'I'll be an old man, Cary, long before Larry's grown up. I feel like an old man now.'

'But you're not old. Grandmother really is old — over eighty. I couldn't ask her to take Larry. I couldn't ask Cousin Mildred to do it, either. Cousin Mildred seems almost as old as Grandmother, though of course she isn't. Perhaps that's because she's never really lived. It's funny, isn't it, that spinsters always seem older than married women the same age?'

'I never thought of it before. But you're right, they nearly always do. And yet, their delicacy's never been outraged by a man's grossness, they've never been through the agony of childbirth.'

'Perhaps that's the very reason why. Men and women need each other, don't you think so, Father? Doesn't a man's grossness, as you call it, help a woman to overcome false shame? Doesn't her delicacy help him to overcome what some people call "baser passions"? Not that I like those words. And I don't like grossness. Savoie wasn't gross. You aren't, either.'

'No woman ever really knows any man, Cary.'

She sighed. 'Perhaps not. But what she does learn about them helps her a lot. And certainly, every woman needs to have a child. I can't be thankful enough that before——'

She did not say, 'before I had to die.' She left a good many sentences unfinished now, partly because it did tire her, a little, to talk, after all; partly because she did not want to cause her father pain; partly because she knew he would understand her anyway.

'Besides,' she continued, reverting to what he had said about growing old, 'it'll make you feel younger, having a baby in the house. You'll take wonderful care of him.'

'I'd do my very best for him, of course. But your grandmother may feel that wouldn't be good enough. She may feel he'd be better off at Sorrento than he would here. Even though she is so old, she's very wise and very experienced. She'd know how to supervise his care. She could give him the right background.'

'I'll tell her I don't want him to go to Sorrento. I'll tell her I want him to stay here, that I'm sure you'll take good care of him, that he'll have all the background he needs. I don't believe backgrounds mean as much as they used to. Anyway, Sorrento doesn't mean a thing to me. She doesn't mean a great deal. That is, really. Of course she's my grandmother, I respect her and all that, but it's you I love, it's Cindy Lou that's my home. She'll understand.'

Clyde swallowed hard. 'Well, perhaps she will, darling. But don't forget Larry has another grandfather – a *real* grandfather.'

'Don't say "real" that way, please, Father.'

'I won't, Cary, again. But Lamartine Vincent's going to feel he's got a claim on the boy, and rightly – his only son's only son.'

'Armande may have a son, too. We ought to be getting news from her any day now.'

They had not spoken of Armande before, since speaking of Armande meant speaking of Pierre, too; and though nearly all the barriers of speech were down between them, that one still remained. Cary had never mentioned Pierre's name to her father since the scene in the gazebo. But now, at last, she did so.

'There's something I want to tell you, Father.'

'Then you must.'

'Pierre came to see me before he went away. I mean, he came alone. It was the morning after the *fête champêtre*, when his mother wasn't well enough to go back to New Orleans. He came through the garden and found me in the gazebo. He did it deliberately.'

'If I'd known that, Cary——'

'Yes, and that was why I didn't want you to know — then. But it's also why I do want you to know — now. Because, you see, he told me he loved me.'

'He had no right to tell you that.'

'No, I suppose not. And you weren't mistaken — he wouldn't have married a divorced woman. He told me so himself. He said he came to Louisiana hoping I'd become his mistress. But he also told me that if I'd been free, when he first met me, he'd have wanted me for his wife. He never thought of me as — well, as just another woman with whom he'd enjoyed having an affair. So I'm glad he told me he loved me even if he didn't have a right to.'

'Why, Cary?' Clyde could not help asking. But he knew without being told.

'Because I loved him. I tried hard not to, honestly I did, Father. I knew I had the best husband in the world and I did all I could to be worthy of him — after I realized how close I'd come to — well, to un-utterable folly. It wasn't hard, either, except — except when I first knew Pierre was going to marry Armande. And you helped me over that bad time. Then, afterward — well, when a girl's husband loves her the way Savoie loved me, she can't let him down. She doesn't want to. And what she gives him in return isn't pretence. It's sincere — as far as it goes. But just the same . . .'

'I've been afraid this was the way it was, Cary.'

'But Savoie never knew. He never guessed. You know everything, Father, you guess everything. I'm so glad you do and that Savoie didn't.'

It was first evening when they talked together like this and later Cary fell into a quiet sleep. Clyde continued to sit beside her, and about midnight Dr. Bringier, who had been called far up the river road on an emergency case, came in to see her before finally going home. He looked at her and shook his head.

'I don't think I'll need to give her anything after this. Of course, I'll stay downstairs. But she isn't suffering now and I don't think she will.'

'No, I don't think so, either,' Clyde answered.

There was still no light breaking through the darkness when she wakened again. She felt for the hand that she knew was already stretched out to receive hers.

'Father, I want to thank you for not saying anything against Pierre.

Of course I know he couldn't hold a candle to Savoie. But somehow, if you love a man, you just love him anyway.'

'I know that, Cary. Because your mother just loved me – anyway.'

'But you never did what Pierre——'

'I never tried to win a woman away from her husband. But it so happens I never wanted to. I did other things just as bad, when I did want to. Men don't all sin in the same way.'

'I don't think of you as a sinner. I'm not going to. But since you're speaking of them . . . You've cabled Bushrod, haven't you? It's only fair he should know.'

'I realized that. So I did cable him and I've been expecting a cable in reply. Of course he couldn't get here before your mother's funeral. But he's probably on his way home now.'

'I hope . . .' Her voice trailed away into silence. Clyde wondered if she were hoping the same thing he was, that Bushrod would not get to Cindy Lou until after she died, that he and she could have these last precious hours to themselves. But she had drifted into semi-consciousness again and she never told him what it was she hoped. The next time she spoke to him, it was about something entirely different.

'We never found the treasure, did we, Father?'

'No, not the buried gold. But it didn't matter. We've had so much, without it.'

'I know we have. But I wanted the other, too. Golden treasure, buried in the ground. Not dirty gravel on top of it. I've never told you, Father . . . I'm so glad you didn't let Dupré have that land. And I'm sorry I didn't act as if I were, that day you told me about his offer.'

'Don't be sorry, Cary. I understood afterward – when you told me about Pierre.'

'Yes, but you were hurt just the same. That's what I'm sorry about. Because you've never hurt me. You're right though – it doesn't matter now about the buried treasure. I'm not disappointed because I didn't find it, truly I'm not. You know I told you, that same day I was so hateful——'

'You weren't ever hateful, darling.'

'Yes, I was. Anyway, I told you then I'd stopped believing that I'd find the treasure myself. And you're right, it doesn't matter now, because you and Larry will find it. I'm sure you will. Because of course it's there. . . . You won't forget what I said about Larry, will you, Father? That he's yours now and that no one must take him away from you.'

'No, Cary, I shan't forget.'

They continued to talk about Larry for some minutes. Cary's mind was completely clear. Though there was still no word from Bushrod, the expected message from the Vincents had come in, telling them that Armande had a son and that his name was Pierre Lamartine. Cary was sure this was going to make Clyde's guardianship of Larry far easier to safeguard and Clyde was inclined to agree with her. He could visualize, as she did, that the Vincents might be spending more and more time in France, that their most absorbing interest would be centred in Armande and her children.

Cary was calm and contented as they dwelt on this, and afterward she fell into another deep sleep. When she began to stir again, she held out her arms and Clyde thought she was groping for Savoie, as she had the first time she wakened after the fire. But he was mistaken.

'Pierre,' she said distinctly, 'Pierre!' She paused a moment and then she went on, still in a clear voice, 'It's terribly dark in this passage, isn't it? Of course I was warned that it would be, that I shouldn't go beyond the great chamber of the cave. It's a little frightening, isn't it? At least it would be, if I were alone. But since you're with me at last, dearest . . .'

She died in Clyde's arms, just before dawn. He laid her gently back on her pillows and went out of the room, closing the door very softly after him. The feeling that she must not be disturbed persisted so strongly that he continued to move as quietly as possible while going down the stairs and out into the garden. It was very still there, too. But the morning was a beautiful one, and the first rays of the sun were already gilding the grass and the flowers; and suddenly Clyde saw, with surprise, that Lucy's favourite camellias had burst into bloom, almost overnight. The garden was transfigured by their loveliness. He stopped and stripped the snowy blossoms from the laden shrubs, and when he went back to Cary's room, his arms were full.

'This time,' he murmured to himself, 'this time they can't hide my dead away from me, before I've even had a chance to say good-bye. This time they can't tell me I mustn't see her. I can strew flowers all around Cary, while she's still lying in her own bed – her mother's flowers. Then I can sit and look at her this once more. No one will come to disturb us for hours yet.'

With the tenderest care, he placed the flowers around the quiet form, laying a cluster of buds on the still breast and putting a single perfect blossom between the hands which he folded himself. Then, long and lovingly, he looked down on his daughter. Never, in her most radiant moments, had she seemed so beautiful to him. But he did not sit beside her after all. A faint cry came from the room which had been Bushrod's, where Larry was now quartered, with Tudie faithfully watching over him. Again, Clyde left Cary's side and this time he walked rapidly down the hall and rapped on the door of the improvised nursery.

'Bring the baby to me, Tudie,' he said.

'Yassuh, Massa Clyde, just as soon as Ah has him readied up.'

Clyde waited patiently until the door opened to disclose Tudie, carrying Larry, who was still crying, over her shoulder. As she wheeled around and the baby caught sight of his grandfather, his wails suddenly ceased; he grinned broadly and gurgled with infantile joy. Tudie shifted him skilfully from her arms to her master's, while Larry continued to coo with contentment.

'Ah specks you wants to take him in to see Miss Cary you'self,' Tudie said solicitously. 'Ah know she's bad off. But please, suh, don't forget dat baby's hongry.' Clyde tightened his hold on Larry's warm little body and spoke reassuringly.

'Miss Cary isn't bad off any more, Tudie,' he said. 'She's at peace. And you're right. We mustn't let him go hungry. I'll just hold him while you fetch his milk. I'm counting on you to help me see that he gets everything he needs.'

Chapter Fifteen

Spring, 1897

CLYDE'S confidence in Tudie was not misplaced. She helped him all she could; she did her very best. No haunting doubt of this was among the many which tormented him as he lay through the long sleepless nights. But, in the last analysis, Tudie, for all her faithfulness, kindness and efficiency, was only a young, unlettered coloured girl, and she would have no one but himself to direct her after Miss Sophie had left. . . .

Of course there was still the chance that, when Miss Sophie left, she might insist on taking Larry with her. Cary had never referred a second time to her intention of telling her grandmother that she earnestly desired to have Larry remain at Cindy Lou under Clyde's guardianship. He thought it was quite possible that such a conversation had never taken place, for Cary had weakened so rapidly, toward the end, that she had been almost incapable of making the agonizing effort to talk. It was also possible that, even if Cary had said she wanted to leave her baby to her stepfather, Miss Sophie might have avoided making a promise which would bind her to the fulfilment of such a wish. She might have felt it would really be her duty to keep the baby with her, at least until Mrs. Vincent's return. And if she did, perhaps it would be *his* duty to uphold her in such a course. If Larry had been older —

five or six, for instance—Clyde felt he could have put forward a more logical claim to the child. But how *could* he direct Tudie? Though he had doted on Cary, when she was a baby, he had never ministered to her physical needs or supervised anyone else in the performance of such tasks; he did not know what a baby should eat or wear or how often it should be bathed or how much fresh air was good for it. Lucy had known all that and had attended to all such matters, just as she had attended to everything connected with household management. It had never been suggested that he should assume responsibility for anything of the sort. Now—supposing that Miss Sophie did leave Larry with him—he would find himself responsible for every phase of domestic arrangement, from the proper care and feeding of an infant in arms, to the daily allotment of supplies from the storeroom, the wine cellar and the linen closet, all of which commodities he would have to keep under lock and key and distribute at the proper time to the right servant. He would also have to superintend the work in the kitchen garden, the flower garden and the pecan orchard. And all this at a time when he felt he would have gladly sold his soul for the privilege of being alone.

To be sure, from the moment of her arrival, Miss Sophie had taken over the reins, and every member of the domestic staff had unquestioningly accepted her authority and responded to it with touching willingness. Clyde knew he should be thankful for the reprieve which this gave him and, in a sense, he was. In another sense, he was almost resentful of it. Any alien presence in the shadowy house seemed intrusive to him now. It was still peopled with the dead. He needed to commune with them in peace.

Not that he thought for a moment that his mother-in-law and her elderly cousin were deliberately outwearing their welcome; he could understand the reluctance of Miss Sophie to entrust him with the sole care of her infant great-grandson; and he knew that her cousin Mildred shared her feelings, in as far as it was possible for a woman who had never borne or lost a child to experience the emotions of one who had known travail and its triumph and the grief which belongs with both. And certainly there was nothing about the bearing or behaviour of these two black-clad old women to suggest they thought he himself should try to surmount his sorrow and look hopefully toward the future; on the contrary, they made him aware that they respected and understood his loneliness and his loss, as he did theirs. But he wanted to have his home to himself while he groped his way toward a solution for the complete readjustment of his life. He longed unutterably for silence and solitude.

He had reached a point where the urgency of this need was so great that he had almost decided to confess it to his mother-in-law when she relieved him of the necessity by telling him, one afternoon when they were leaving the dining-room, that she would like very much to have a quiet talk with him, and asking him when it would suit his convenience for her to do so. He had been sitting at the head of his table, with his mother-in-law at his right and Cousin Mildred at his left, averting his eyes, as far as possible, from Lucy's empty chair opposite him, yet unable to bring himself to order its removal; and the hushed meals had been the most trying periods of all. The erstwhile cheerful servants crept noiselessly around the table, offering food which nobody wanted; and though the three who were seated at the dinner table all tried to ease the situation by sporadic attempts at conversation, there were long pauses between forced comments and equally forced replies. This was not the sort of silence for which Clyde yearned; it was even worse than clatter and chatter would have been. Yet there seemed no way to overcome it; they were all engulfed by it; they seemed to sink deeper and deeper into its abyss. The chasm between himself and the stern old lady who had opposed his marriage to her daughter had narrowed with the years; but though he had come to admire her and believed that she no longer resented him, they had never been on easy or affectionate terms with each other. He answered her now with the formal courtesy which had always characterized their association; however, the fact that she had spoken as if she were asking a favour of him was unexpectedly heart-warming.

'Any time that would suit you would be agreeable to me, of course,' he said. Then, as another empty, cheerless afternoon seemed to stretch out endlessly before him, he added, 'Would you care to talk with me right away?'

'Thank you. I should like that very much.'

She had not lowered her voice, in making her request; and now she glanced toward Cousin Mildred, who instantly murmured that she had a slight headache and would like to retire, if Cousin Sophie and Cousin Clyde would excuse her. Then she scurried off toward the stairs.

'Perhaps we might have a little fire in the library,' Miss Sophie continued. 'It is still rather cool for this time of year – or aren't you finding it so? At all events, there is something cheering about a fire.'

They had been using the drawing-room when they met for tea and when they received visits of condolence. Clyde had found both experiences appalling. He still seemed to see the beautiful painted parlour arranged for a funeral, he still seemed to smother in the heavy scent of banked flowers. On the other hand, he had not entered the library since Lucy's death; the door had not even been opened. Hardly less than the chamber they had shared for so many years, this had been essentially their personal room. When he was alone, he had sat in his office, but he could not ask his mother-in-law to go there. She was right, the library was the proper place for their talk. It would be hard to go in; but once there, it would be less oppressive than the drawing-room.

He opened the door and stood back for her to precede him. Evidently no one had remembered to close the shutters here; at all events, they were opened now and the late afternoon sunshine was pouring into the room. It was in perfect order, but its order was homelike and not artificial: Lucy's workbasket still stood on the little table beside her favourite chair, and on another table, nearby, lay the book from which he had been reading aloud to her when they had last sat there together. The place was full of her presence, but it was a presence unrelated to the closed casket and the sickening scent in the drawing-room. He was conscious of overwhelming relief, almost of thankfulness, as he bent over and touched a match to the neatly laid fire. When he straightened up again, having assured himself that it would burn, he saw that his mother-in-law was already seated; and, as soon as he had drawn up a chair, she spoke, without waiting for him to do so.

'I received three letters this morning, which I should like to discuss with you,' she said. 'One of these was from my overseer. He says I am very much needed at Sorrento. I will not burden you with the details of the situation which requires my presence, especially as I feel completely capable of coping with it, once I am on the spot. But I think the sooner I *am* there, the better.'

'Is it a situation in which I could be of any help?' Clyde inquired. He could hardly have responded otherwise. Yet the thought of leaving Cindy Lou was even more unwelcome to him than the requirement of sharing it.

'Thank you. But as I just said, I feel quite capable of coping with the situation. However, I should be much obliged if you would make the necessary travel arrangements for Mildred and me. We can be ready to leave whenever you can get suitable reservations. I should prefer not to stay at an hotel just now, if that can be avoided – in other words, if we could take a train from Convent for New Orleans that would make good connections with one going north from there——'

'I'll see about it the first thing in the morning, Miss Sophie. Not that I want you to feel hurried, you understand.'

He hoped he spoke with conviction and, in one sense, he spoke with complete sincerity. He did not want her to feel hurried – that would be inhospitable and unfair. But to have Cindy Lou to himself again! . . .

'Yes, I do understand,' she said quietly; and suddenly he knew that she did and that the understanding had in it no element of hurt feelings. 'Of course, if everything were not going well here, I would not leave,' she continued. 'But I have purposely stayed long enough to satisfy myself that it is. Your servants are capable and devoted. Tudie is developing into an excellent nurse. I do not think she will need any advice or help in her care of Larry. However, if she does, Mrs. Surget and Dr. Bringier are both close at hand. So you really do not need me — especially as Larry is a remarkably vigorous baby. I doubt if you will have any anxiety on the score of his health. But I know you will watch over him with the utmost care.'

'I would try,' Clyde answered, rather huskily. 'That is, if you really feel——'

'That he should be left with you? There would have been no question about that in my mind, even if I had not promised Cary, on her death-bed, that he would be. You have inspired me with a great deal of confidence, Clyde, through the years. I know that Lucy found complete happiness in her marriage with you and that you were a true father to her daughter. You never failed either of them in any way and you will never fail Larry. Cary was sure of that. I am sure of it, too.'

'Thank you,' Clyde said in a low voice. He would have liked to say more, to ask for details about the talk which now, for the first time, he knew had actually taken place. He would have liked to voice the doubts which still beset him about his own competence for such a responsibility as the care of Larry would entail. But he could not.

'So it is not of anything connected with Larry's immediate welfare that I wish to talk with you,' Miss Sophie went on. 'It is about his future prospects.'

'His future prospects?'

'Yes. I assume that, of course, he will be one of your heirs. But I have been wondering whether, in the interests of complete justice, I should not make him one of mine also.'

'I'm afraid I don't quite follow you, Miss Sophie. You're right, of course, in assuming that he'll be my heir. But——'

She raised her hand and something about the gesture robbed her interruption of all discourtesy. 'Let me explain. You knew, of course, that Lucy wished to have Bushrod inherit Sorrento and Amalfi. Cary was so young when she left Virginia and was there so little afterward that she never had any special feeling for my plantations — all her interests were in Louisiana. Besides, she was amply provided for, both by you and by her husband. So it was understood between Lucy and myself that Cary should not have any share in my property. But this understanding was never put into writing — at least to my knowledge. Was it, to yours?'

'No. Lucy never discussed the matter with me, beyond saying what you've just told me — that she wanted Bushrod to have Amalfi and Sorrento. That seemed to me eminently fair. As you say, Cary had no special interests in Virginia and she was provided for here.'

'And you are very sure that Lucy left no will or even any memorandum?'

'Reasonably sure. She never spoke of that, either. And I think I'd

308

have been bound to know it, if she had. She wouldn't have done a thing like that secretly — in fact, I don't think she could have. She talked with me freely, she respected my judgment. She certainly would have asked my advice and we'd have consulted a lawyer together. We — it was our habit to do things together.'

'I know,' Miss Sophie said; and again Clyde was moved by the consciousness of her understanding. 'Nevertheless, in a case like this, we must take every precaution. I assume you haven't looked through her desk — or in any other place where she might have kept papers?'

'No. I haven't touched anything that belonged to her. I — I can't.'

'Would you like me to do it for you? I realize how painful all this is for you, Clyde. It is painful for me, too, of course. But this is your first experience of the kind, and I have had to meet others like it, many times already. If it would help you — or relieve you — to have me — I will not say to put Lucy's personal belongings in order, for of course she always kept them in perfect order — but to have me go through them and decide what should be done with them — her clothes, as well as her papers——'

She paused, and Clyde knew she was thinking of those other personal belongings which she had been obliged to go through — her husband's, her four sons', probably her parents' as well. No, bereavement and tragedy were nothing new to this aged woman, who still bore herself with such calm dignity. He was shamed by her fortitude, but he was grateful for it.

'Thank you,' he said again. 'It would help me — it would relieve me very greatly.' Then, with an effort, he added, 'I suppose some of the clothes should be given away — those which we would have no special reason for keeping and which might be of use to someone else. And probably some of the papers should be carefully preserved and others destroyed. I will leave you to decide about all such things.'

'I will try to merit your confidence. . . . And now, let us go back to this question of inheritance. My will, as it stands, leaves everything to Lucy. My first thought was that, in altering it, I should leave everything to Bushrod, in accordance with Lucy's expressed wish. Now I am not so sure that it would be right. It is true that Cary did not need my plantations or care for them. But it is no longer a question of Cary — it is a question of her son. Is it conceivable to you that he might care for them, or need them?'

'I hadn't thought of Larry in connection with Sorrento and Amalfi. I'd only thought of him in connection with Cindy Lou. But now that you speak of it, I can see it's conceivable that he might care very greatly for them, that he might even need them. I'll do the best I can for him, you know that; you've been good enough to say so. I think I have enough so that he'll never lack for any essentials. But of course I can't be sure. I nearly went under once before. I would have, if Lucy hadn't been here to help me. And now, there isn't anyone. . . . Besides, I'm not a young man any more. I'm – well, I'm pretty close to being an old one, though I don't like to admit it. If I should die——'

'I have faith that you won't die, and I have faith that you'll never go under, that you'll be able to give Larry all the necessities of life, even if you can't give him all the luxuries. At the same time, I can't lightly deprive him of the heritage which might be his in Virginia. I know that, as a Virginian, I'm prejudiced. But I still feel it to be a very special heritage.'

'Yes, you're right. It is – a very special heritage.' He looked across at her and, as he did so, he felt that she herself personified much which gave that heritage a special value. 'Of course Cary entrusted Larry to me on her deathbed,' he said. 'As I said before, I've never thought of him except in connection with Cindy Lou. But if it were for his welfare——'

'That's what we must decide. We must weigh one advantage against another. Let me repeat that I would not lightly deprive Larry of his Virginia heritage. On the other hand, if Bushrod were the sole inheritor of Sorrento and Amalfi, it might simplify things for you.'

'I don't think I quite follow you.'

'I believe you promised Lucy, when you married her, that her children should both be your heirs, that they should share and share alike. Cary is dead, and what you would normally have given her, naturally goes to her son. But Bushrod is alive. He will certainly expect his share.'

Clyde rose, thrusting his hands behind him, so that his mother-in-law should not see how convulsively he had clenched them. He could still control the expression of his face – that much, at least, he owed to his career as a gambler; but at this moment his hands might very well betray him. *Bushrod's share!* As if the wastrel had not already had more than was due a scoundrel of his kind – the substantial sum which had settled his Richmond debts, the twenty thousand he had extracted from his stepfather just before Cary's wedding! Clyde realized that if he told Miss Sophie about this, she would feel that any promise he had made was already more than fulfilled. But how could he tell her that her only grandson, for whom her unshaken love was the only weak spot in her armour, had been expelled from the gentlemen's club where membership was part of that Virginia heritage in which she felt so much pride? How could he denounce Bushrod for what he was – a card cheat and a blackmailer? She had already bravely borne, in her lifetime, more than any woman should be called upon to bear. Now that life was drawing to an end and, after losing her home, her husband and her four sons in a horrible war, she had lost her only daughter and her only granddaughter in a personal disaster which was even more horrible. He could not give the blow which all too literally might be the death stroke, even to save Larry.

'Certainly Bushrod will expect his share, ma'am,' he said gently, though a little heavily. 'And certainly he shall have it. A promise is a promise.'

'Of course. I was quite sure you would feel that way about it. That is why I brought up the subject; and that is what I meant when I said I thought I might suggest something which would simplify matters all around.' Clyde was caught off guard by the directness of her gaze; the wise old eyes were wells of understanding and – could it be possible? – of sympathy. 'Before there was any question of Larry, Lucy wanted Bushrod to inherit all the Virginia properties, in which Larry now has a right to share,' Miss Sophie continued. 'I am eager to follow Lucy's wishes, but it would be manifestly unfair to Larry if, after being excluded from the Virginia heritage, he were still expected to surrender part of the Louisiana heritage as well. In a word, it should be made plain to Bushrod that, if he takes full title to both Sorrento and Amalfi, any claim he might otherwise rightly have to a share in Cindy Lou is thereby cancelled. That was what I meant when I referred to simplifying the situation for all of us.'

For a moment, Clyde stared at her dumbly. The waves of relief and of thankfulness which had swept through him while she was speaking, left him, literally, without words. With the same calmness that had characterized everything she had said in the course of the interview, his mother-in-law returned his look. At last he broke the silence.

'Miss Sophie,' he said huskily, 'I want you to know I feel it wasn't only in giving me Lucy's heart that God was very good to me. I feel He was good to me in letting me know you.'

'Thank you for telling me that,' she said. 'I knew how you felt about Lucy and, of course, there is every reason why you should. As far as I am concerned . . .' She turned away, but not so quickly that he failed to see there were tears in her eyes and that her face had suddenly softened. 'You – you are magnanimous in your estimate of me, Clyde.' She opened the volume which was lying on the table beside her, the one from which Clyde had last read to Lucy, and glanced at the passage where a bookmark indicated a stopping place. Then she laid it down again. 'About this will,' she said, 'I will take the necessary legal steps as soon as possible. Of course, in ordinary circumstances, Bushrod should be consulted. But since he will not be available immediately – and I am coming to the reasons for that presently – and since I do not feel that, at my age, I should delay any important undertaking, I shall draw it up at once – or almost at once. But it occurs to me that I may have an ally on whom you probably have not counted, and that I had better talk with her, too.'

'An ally?' Clyde inquired, sitting down again and clasping his hands lightly in front of him. He was no longer afraid to have Miss Sophie see them.

'Yes. I should not be surprised if Mabel were secretly longing for a reconciliation. We are talking with each other very candidly, Clyde; so why not admit, in confidence, that Mabel has probably not had many admirers in the course of her life? She is not—well, she is not exactly the type that commands widespread masculine attention.' This time, when Clyde's glance met his mother-in-law's, he saw there was actually a slight twinkle in her eye. 'Bushrod's courtship, when she had almost reached the age where any woman, however fascinating, is conscious that her powers of enchantment are waning, must have seemed to her like the suit of a Prince Charming,' Miss Sophie went on, imperturbably. 'And whatever his faults as a husband, I have no doubt that Bushrod showed himself very charming after marriage, too. I do not see how Mabel can help missing his—ah—companionship.'

'Perhaps she does,' Clyde admitted. Now that Miss Sophie had presented the idea to him in this way, he did not find it surprising.

'There is also another aspect of the case which might be helpful to us. Numbers of rich New Yorkers seem to be discovering Virginia, so to speak, just now. The quantity of estates they are buying, or attempting to buy, in the Old Dominion, is really amazing. I do not quite understand why they seem to fancy themselves suddenly in the rôle of country gentry, but the fact remains that they do.' Again, Clyde caught the humorous glint in the wise old eyes. 'I think Mabel would be very much gratified at the prospect of establishing herself and her husband as landed proprietors,' Miss Sophie continued. 'Especially as it could be done with comparatively little expense. If I'm not mistaken, she shares her father's aversion to loose purse strings. My suggestion to her would be that, if she and Bushrod can agree to let bygones be bygones, they should build a house on the ruins of Amalfi, following the original plan in as far as that is practical for present-day requirements. The house would be theirs. Then, after my death, they could move into mine if they preferred—or they could hold it in trust for their offspring, if any. I suppose it is still imaginable that they might have a child. Mabel may not be as old as she looks. But, even if she is, motherhood is probably not an impossibility.'

'No, I suppose not,' Clyde muttered. He had never thought of Mabel as a potential mother, and he did so now with reluctance, as the beautiful maternal images of Lucy and Cary rose before him. Moreover, if Bushrod and Mabel should have a child, there would be little or no possibility that in time the Virginia estate, or any portion of it, might come to Larry. But that, he reminded himself, would matter very little, if it were made certain that no claim against Larry's undisputed ownership of Cindy Lou should ever be raised. . . . With a start, Clyde realized he had not been listening to what his mother-in-law was telling him.

'. . . my purpose to stipulate,' he heard her say, as his attention focused on her words, 'in this will I propose to draw, that any child of Bushrod's and Mabel's, or of any marriage he might enter into in the event of her death, could inherit Amalfi and Sorrento. But if he should die without such issue, the property would naturally revert to Larry.'

'I see,' Clyde said. He did not add anything further. He did not feel anything further was needed. He gathered that Miss Sophie did not think so, either, from the way she went on.

'Now that those questions are settled, as far as they can be in the course of one conversation,' she continued, 'I think I should speak to you about the other letters which reached me this morning. I said, a few minutes ago, that I would tell you why I realized that Bushrod would not immediately be available for consultation. One of those letters was from him. It seems that he has had typhoid fever — a light case, fortunately. There is no cause for alarm. But he was slightly delirious at the time you cabled him about his mother's death, and his physician — a Dr. Norchais, who seems to be a man of good sense — felt it would be better to withhold the news from him until he was stronger. I do not know why he did not ask the doctor to cable a reply for him, when he did get it, but doubtless there was some good reason. This letter from him was written before you sent the second cable, announcing Cary's death. You probably will hear from him yourself within the next day or so.'

'Probably,' Clyde muttered. While he had been somewhat puzzled by the delay in hearing from Bushrod, he had been too preoccupied with other matters to give it much thought; and when he did think of it, he had regarded it as a reprieve. He was, therefore, inclined to regard the attack of typhoid fever as a blessing in disguise, and to regret only that it had not been more serious. However, he could not say any of this to Bushrod's grandmother, whose vision, clear as it was in most respects, was naturally obscured by love when she looked at him.

'It may be some time before he will be strong enough to undertake an ocean voyage,' Miss Sophie went on. 'And, if you approve, I shall write him, suggesting that, before coming to Cindy Lou, he stop off to see me at Sorrento. I would then lay before him immediately the arrangement on which you and I are agreed. I believe I could do so in such a way that he would grasp its advantages and the whole question would be settled without further delay.'

'That might be a good idea,' Clyde answered, still in more or less of a mutter; he would have liked to say that he had never found Bushrod slow to grasp anything that was to his advantage.

'The third letter,' Miss Sophie continued, as if she had now dismissed the subject of Bushrod for the time being, 'was from Pierre de Chanet, who wrote to express the sympathy of the entire family. But it was more than a letter of condolence. It also contained some rather bad news.'

Clyde lifted his head quickly. He had not been able to feel that the news from Bushrod was bad, as far as he was concerned, and he could not believe that any news coming from Pierre de Chanet would cause him much distress, either. But he was eager to know what it was.

'Of course everyone at Château Monteregard was deeply affected upon hearing of our terrible losses,' Miss Sophie went on. 'But poor Mr. Vincent was more crushed than any of the others, especially by the death of his only son. After all, this is natural. Mrs. Vincent is closer to Armande than she was to Savoie, and Armande has her husband and her baby to divert her thoughts from her bereavement. But Mr. Vincent could think of nothing else, and his mental condition has had a sad effect on his physical condition, as so often happens. He has had a stroke. Evidently, he has rallied, to a certain extent; but he speaks with difficulty and two of his limbs are affected. Mrs. Vincent is devoting all her time and strength to him. Of course there can be no question of moving him for a long time.'

'I am very sorry,' Clyde managed to say. But the words were perfunctory. He *was* sorry that Lamartine Vincent, who had long been a good friend of his, should have come to such a pass through grief; and fleetingly, he resolved, for the first time, to put an end to his own brooding, before it could get the better of him. But he could not feel sorry that the Vincents would not be hastening home, that he would not have to share Larry with them. His thoughts raced ahead and, in his mind's eye, he saw Mrs. Vincent, who had never cared about Victoria, relinquishing her rights in it to Larry — for a consideration, of course, but still doing it. He could see her persuading Armande to do the same. Armande was, to all intents and purposes, a Frenchwoman now. She inhabited a magnificent château, she moved in the most sophisticated Continental society, she was addressed as Madame la Marquise. She was dressed by Worth and Redfern. She could not have all these things in Louisiana and they meant much to her. Yes, some day Victoria, as well as Cindy Lou, would be Larry's. He could well afford to do without the Virginia heritage, great as this was. He would have one greater still in Louisiana. And his grandfather, Clyde Batchelor, would safeguard it for him. . . .

'I am sure you are,' Clyde heard Miss Sophie saying. He did not realize, at first, with what she was agreeing. He had been looking so far into the future that, for the first time since Lucy's death, he had been unmindful of the present. And, before he could fully collect himself, his mother-in-law had risen, saying she did not think they had anything more to discuss.

A fortnight later, she and Cousin Mildred left for Virginia. In the meantime, though no more formal conferences had taken place, she had made numerous helpful suggestions to him, all more or less casually, about the care of Larry and the management of the house; and she had seemed to take it for granted that they would go on spending their evenings together, beside a cheerful fire. Sometimes, Cousin Mildred joined them for an hour or so, and once or twice Mrs. Surget dropped in. Vaguely, Clyde was aware that their presence was becoming more and more of a comfort and less and less of an ordeal; but he still felt the need of reassurance and support, he still lay wakeful and troubled through the long nights. A great weight had indeed been lifted from his heart by Miss Sophie's decision about Larry's heritage; a great wave of triumph had surged through him when she expressed her complete confidence in him. But this was not enough. He wanted to feel more confidence in himself. It was probably irrelevant to compare his present sense of inadequacy to that which had overwhelmed him when he first met Stanard Daingerfield. But, involuntarily, he did so. Then, he had not known how he should respond to the man who embodied every quality for which he had longed in a friend, though he had known exactly how to deal with the miserable cardsharper whom he despised. Now, he did not see how, without Lucy's help, he could safeguard the child who represented all that was left from the wreckage of half a lifetime's happiness; he would have needed help from no one to cope with a lazy perique picker, a mutinous cane cutter or an impudent overseer. Perhaps, after all, there was some basis of logic in the comparison. Both situations represented a major crisis in his life. The happiness of his marriage might have hinged upon the wisdom of his action in the first instance; the welfare of an innocent and beloved child might hinge on it in the second. He felt if he could present the case in just this way to someone who would visualize it, perhaps he could find the solution of his problem; but he knew that, for all her kindliness and understanding, Miss Sophie was not that person. He doubted whether any woman would see it as he did. If he could only talk about it to some man! . . . And suddenly, as if his train of thought had led straight in that direction, he thought of Stanard Daingerfield. . . .

Stan had not been able to reach Cindy Lou in time for Lucy's funeral and, though he had come for Cary's, he had left immediately after. Obviously, he had sensed Clyde's need for solitude then; perhaps, if he could be reached, he would sense Clyde's present need for support; and this time, Clyde did not feel too proud to ask it of him. He wired Sapphire Downs, inquiring whether Stan could return to Cindy Lou in the course of his next trip south. The answer came from New Orleans. Stan had not yet gone back to Kentucky, but his manager had relayed the telegram. He would arrive at Convent on the nine forty-five the following evening. . . . Reading the message, it seemed to Clyde as if Stan had been waiting just such a summons.

Clyde met him at the station, sent Zack with his bags to his chamber and took him straight to the gaming-room. All the house servants, except Tudie, who slept beside Larry's crib, had gone back to the quarters, and Miss Sophie and Cousin Mildred had already retired for the night. The house was pleasantly warm and softly lighted, but it was blessedly quiet. A tray laden with sandwiches, cheese, fruit and cake stood on the card table and Clyde turned to the cellarette, took out a bottle of Judge Carteret's Bourbon and poured out the whisky with a lavish hand.

'As you said, when we met on the *Richmond*, I believe I prefer my Bourbon straight, if it's as good as this,' he said. And, while Stan nodded assent, they sat down opposite each other, glasses in hand. 'Do you remember, too?' Clyde went on. 'I don't mean just about the Bourbon. I mean about everything.'

'I wouldn't go quite so far as to say that. But I remember a good deal.'

'Then perhaps you'll understand why I asked you to come to Cindy Lou now.'

'Perhaps I will. I hope so. Suppose you tell me.'

Without preamble, Clyde plunged into his story. Stan did not once interrupt him, and he himself hardly paused for breath until, as clearly and concisely as he could, he had told his kinsman about Cary's dying request and her grandmother's promise to her. Then, after a brief interval, he spoke of Miss Sophie's decision in regard to her property and of the tremendous relief this had been to his mind. 'At the same time——' he added. And stopped suddenly.

'At the same time,' Stan repeated, 'you don't want anything to happen which, in the end, wouldn't be best for Larry. All this hesitation, all this uncertainty, is on his account, just as before it was on Lucy's.'

'Of course. As far as I'm concerned, keeping him here, feeling he was mine, would mean all the difference between having something to live for and—utter desolation. But I can't help feeling that, perhaps, I'm not the right person.'

'Not the right person? Why shouldn't an upright, well-to-do citizen, highly respected in the community where he lives, be able to provide the best possible kind of a home for a growing boy? Why shouldn't a man who was an admirable husband and father make just as good a guardian?'

'That isn't all I've been.'

'It's all you've been as far as Larry's concerned. You asked if I remembered our conversation on the *Richmond*. Well, I don't claim to remember every word of it, as I said before. But I do remember telling you we were meeting then for the first time. Ever since I've known you, the description of you I've just given fits. And what was it Cary said to you herself? "I don't believe background counts as much as it used to." She was right. Anyway, not her kind and mine—the kind she was talking about. Yours may.'

Clyde looked up in astonishment and Stan smiled in his disarming way.

'You fought your way up to decency,' he said. 'You didn't take comfort and culture and gracious living and high principles and everything that goes with them for granted, the way we did. So you could judge what they were worth, better than we could. You've made more of an effort to deserve them than we ever did. Yes, I know Sophie and Lucy never did anything wrong in their lives. They represent the fine flower of a certain type of American civilization—a great civilization, if you like. But one that's almost as dead as that Lost Cause we remnants of it talk so much about. And there are lots of tares and weeds in it, too. Your dear stepson, for instance. And when you get right down to it, neither Forrest Page nor I . . . Not that we couldn't be trusted with a pack of cards or a roll of money. Of course I don't mean that. But neither of us did much to protect those fine flowers I mentioned, though we claimed to worship them. You backed up your claims. Perhaps we've been overbred for too long. Perhaps there's going to be another type of American civilization, another cause that'll be won instead of lost. I don't know. But anyway . . .'

He paused in his turn and again looked up with a smile.

'Don't take offence at what I'm going to say next,' he said, 'especially as I'm only guessing now. But somehow I've had a feeling—nothing but a feeling, mind you—that Cary herself wasn't without a certain streak—well, not bad, but certainly not strong—in her make-up that might have got her into trouble, if she hadn't been able to find support, when she needed it most, from the right quarter. I think she trusted her son to you because she had an almighty good reason for it. I think she also knew this would be what her mother would have wanted her to do—would feel she was safest in doing. People see pretty clearly sometimes when they're dying—just at the moment when their vision seems to be getting dim. I think Sophie senses all this, too, even if she doesn't know it. I certainly hope she doesn't know too much. Above all, I hope she doesn't know about Bushrod. I think it would kill her if she

317

did — for sure. As long as she only suspects and drugs her suspicions. . . . *That's* the only flaw in the Southern gentlewoman's character — she can't see, or won't see a flaw in the Southern gentleman. For which the Southern gentleman is, I assure you, very, very thankful!'

Stan took a long drink and set down his glass. 'I seem to have emptied that, while I've been rambling on,' he said. 'I'll have it refilled, if you don't mind. Because I'd like to drink a toast: to Larry Vincent, the first — not the last — of his line. And to the man who's going to help him lay the foundations of a new family — in the new America!'

Two days later, after a visit which had meant a great deal to all of them, Miss Sophie, Cousin Mildred and Stanard Daingerfield took their departure. Neither Clyde nor his mother-in-law said anything about a future meeting when they took leave of each other. They both knew there would be few, if any, such meetings. But not because of ill will. After years of antagonism and resentment, they had arrived at mutual respect and mutual understanding. All this was understood between them when they said goodbye.

On returning from the railway station, he saw, as he approached the garden, that Tudie had taken Larry out in his perambulator. The baby was bare-headed and the sun, shining on his hair, which was glossy and black like his father's, gave it an added sheen. He was wearing a little blue knitted jacket which Lucy had made for him and which was exactly the colour of his eyes — Cary's eyes. He was vigorously banging a silver rattle against the strap which confined his plump little person and, as usual, he hailed his grandfather with delight. But Clyde noticed a sign of progress which had gone unobserved before.

'I didn't realize he could sit up straight, all alone,' he said admiringly. 'Why, he hardly touches those fluffy pillows behind him at all!'

'Yassuh! Nossuh!' Tudie agreed with pride. 'Won' be no time atall afore he starts to crawl. I never see no such smart baby, me, or either one feel his strength so young.'

'Could he sit up in a high chair, do you think?'

'Jes' as good as he kin in a carriage.'

'Very well. Get Miss Cary's high chair out of the storeroom and put it in the dining-room. I'll have Larry with me, at meal-times, from now on.'

He gave his grandson a hearty hug and turned away, in the direction of the little enclosure where Lucy lay. Then he halted and turned again. He could visit that sanctuary later, after the day's work was done. Meanwhile, many matters, too long neglected, demanded his attention. Larry had been left to him in trust, and it would need all the effort of which he was capable to fulfil that obligation. He could truly serve the dead only through his service to the living.

318

He walked back toward the house and entered it by the door leading to his office. Then he rolled back the top of his desk and opened his safe. The entries in the ledger were complete, through the day when he and Lucy had last worked on them together – the day of her death. As he assembled his neglected papers and carried on the figures from there, the results were so reassuring that he wondered, more logically than ever before, why he had allowed Valois Dupré to talk him into selling the narrow strip of land, at the rear of the plantation, where the gravel bed was located. He had not confessed to Cary, on her deathbed, that he had done this, because he had been greatly moved by her admission that she was sorry for what she had said to him about it, the day when they had met on the river road and he had told her of Dupré's offer. But he had promptly taken her at her word, the first time, feeling that he should do everything he could to lighten the load of indebtedness which Lucy was helping him to shoulder – and to lift. Necessarily, he had told Lucy about the sale because, after she began to help him with the ledgers, she was obliged to enter all credits and debits in their books; but she had taken the news with her usual calmness, saying – just as Clyde had said to Cary on the occasion of their last talk – that their lives had been so full of treasure in any case that they did not need to dig for more. Besides, Lucy had added – considering the question from another and more practical angle – why should they give even a passing thought to parting with a few barren acres when the sale would help them to safeguard hundreds that were giving a rich yield of sugar and tobacco?

Her wise and dispassionate attitude had been a source of such immense relief to Clyde that, to a certain degree, he had eventually come to share it. But he had never ceased to chafe over the loss of anything connected with Cary, or to regret his failure to keep intact the property he had originally acquired. Now, as he looked at his books, it occurred to him for the first time that possibly he might some day be in a position to buy back the tract of land where he had sat in the sun, watching his little daughter as she dug and dug until finally, hot and weary, she had flung down her small spade and come to nestle in his arms. . . . He could not buy that land yet, of course, but perhaps some day. . . . Evidently Dupré was really not much interested in the property after all since he had not yet started the process of washing the gravel, much less loading it and transporting it. If Clyde's mind had not been so occupied with other things, he would have asked Dupré when he intended to do so. But then, they had not seen much of each other lately. The next time they met, Clyde would ask him. . . .

Meanwhile, the longer he worked on the records and accounts which had lain untouched since Lucy's death, the more causes for reassurance he found. Over two thousand carrots of strong dark tobacco were ready for shipment and they would bring a good price, now that two families — the Guglielmos and the Roussels — were competing with each other as perique factors, whereas the Roussels had formerly controlled the entire market. The cane fields had also yielded abundantly. Fair weather had permitted the harvest to proceed almost without interruption; not one heavy frost had closed down to threaten the tall growth, even with the coming of December. Sugar was selling at three and a half cents for plantation raws; altogether, he should realize forty thousand dollars after paying the Vincent tollage for processing. From that, of course, land taxes, labour, fertilizer and other costs of cultivation would have to be deducted; but the net profits would still far exceed his expectations.

For several hours, Clyde worked steadily and intensively on his ledgers. But when Zack came to tell him that dinner was served, he smiled as he looked up.

'I believe I have a young gentleman dining with me today, Zack,' he said.

'So you does, suh, for a fac'!' Zack answered, returning the smile.

Larry was already at the table when Clyde reached it and after that, he did not dread going into the dining-room any more. He knew that the silent sombre meals were a thing of the past. What was far more important, he knew that he was already laying the foundations for the new family, and that this was to be part of the new America.